The

Caged Countess

Mercer Addison

www.merceraddison.com
or
Windtree Press
www.windtreepress.com

Publisher's Note: This is a work of fiction. Names, characters, places, and incidents are a product of the author's imagination. Locales and public names are sometimes used for atmospheric purposes. Any resemblance to actual people, living or dead, or to businesses, companies, events, institutions, or locales is completely coincidental.

Book Layout ©2013 BookDesignTemplates.com
Cover design by Gilded Heart Designs
Ordering Information: Amazon.com

The Caged Countess/Mercer Addison. 1st ed 2016. 1st Women of Valor Series.
ISBN 978-0-9891947-7-8 print book
ISBN 978-0-9891947-6-1 ebook

Dedication

In memory of my mother, Madeline Moore Carlson, who died from the ALS (Amyotrophic Lateral Sclerosis) disease. Mom fought to the end and never complained while this brutal illness robbed her of her life. She was and always will be my first woman of great valor and courage.

Also, this is for all women throughout the ages whose acts of valor have been the backbone of men.

"A horse, whether good or bad, needs a spur; a woman, whether good or bad, needs a lord and master, and sometimes a stick."

Florentine proverb from the 14th century.

1 Deirdre

Northern Scotland, 1306

Deirdre Brodie, told to remain close to Foxlair castle and its large perimeter stockade, disobeyed her father, the laird of Brodie clan. Even though sightings filtered in about the King of England's movement against Scotland, no marauding enemy had yet ventured this far north.

Barefoot, and on horseback, she rucked up the skirt of her blue gown to let her legs feel the summer breeze. On her right thigh she wore a dagger given to her by her father. The weapon came with the caution to allow no man other than a Scots to come near her person. Using her hand to shade her eyes, she glanced at the high rugged cliffs that tapered down to end at the sparkling waters of the inlet and cove. Two hawks battled one another in the cloudless sky; their piercing shrills echoing around the inlet.

She urged her roan-colored mare, Wicker, along the cove's pebbled beach. Wicker's course hair tickled the insides of her bare legs, but she wouldn't be long on the horse. Behind the beach stood her destination, a forest of tall pines and the man waiting within.

A soft whistle coming from the nearby woods creased her lips into a secretive smile as she hurried toward the beckoning sound and the cool shade. The steady drone of crickets stopped when she rode through the brush only to commence as soon as she passed. With its evergreen trees and thick underbrush the forest became its own cathedral, shutting out the sun. Birds twittered, and squirrels scampered about. The smell of warm pitch, the richness of decay, and the scent of heather wafting from the basket she carried mingled to create a heady perfume.

Bonnar Cameron, Deirdre's betrothed from Clan Cameron, stepped out from behind a tree and took the reins. Dressed as a warrior in a leather jerkin and a dark plaid kilt, his handsome body excited her.

"Deedee," he said in a voice barely above a whisper. His eyes, brown and bold, searched her face as his hand caressed up her left leg. With a look of pure devilment, he kissed her thigh. His blond head buried against her flesh, silencing words, forcing her to shut her eyes and moan at the sensations he invoked. He stopped kissing her long enough to put his hands around her waist and help her to dismount.

"I'll hobble the horses," he said. His lips brushed her ear, her mouth with kisses lazy with desire.

She nodded, reluctant to release him, but did, and went to stand next to where he'd spread a worn blanket at the base of a pine tree. In the center of the blanket set a well-used basket that held a round loaf of bread and cheese. A bladder filled with wine was near two metal goblets. This spot had become theirs, where they met daily, away from the prying eyes of her father and the rest of the clan. When she spotted Bonnar's claymore with its double-edged blade within easy reach of where they would be sitting, her secure feeling faltered.

Several hills away and advancing on Brodie land the King of England led his soldiers. Tall trees and thick brush lined the hilly ribbon of road. More like a well-used goat trail, it slowed the cumbersome army to a cursing crawl. Intent on surprise, the king's outriders had already silenced Clan Brodie's lookouts with a quick slice across their throats.

Even an overnight rain had dampened down the bumpy trail, preventing the telltale brown clouds of dust that churned into the air with advancing soldiers.

French warlord, Richard de Laci, Comte de Strasbourg, listened to the metallic swishing of chain mail hitting against the armored thighs of the soldiers behind him. He found comfort in their strength. Yet, the feeling of anticipation and dread before a battle engulfed him. Would he meet his death on foreign soil for a cause that wasn't his? Sweat rolled inside his chest armor, dampening his tunic. He removed his helmet and strapping it onto the saddle horn, tossed his head trying to dislodge strands of dark hair sticking to his forehead.

Richard glanced at Edward, the King of England, who rode beside him. The king reminded Richard of a gyrfalcon soaring on a current of air, his sharp eyes searching out his prey, his talons ready to draw blood. That prey was Robert the Bruce who now wore the crown of Scotland, and who was reported to have traveled this way most recently garnering support from the clans. England's ruler dubbed Robert the Bruce the king of summer, and predicted he wouldn't last into winter. And believing his predictions, England's king planned annihilation of any clansmen that stood with the Bruce. Using his mighty war machines, Edward squelched the Scots and their fight for freedom from the English throne.

Richard could see no good in the planned attack on yet another clan. A clan filled with innocent people who couldn't hold their own against seasoned warriors. He turned to the king. "*Votre Majesté*, this castle, Foxlair, is fortified with high battlements, *oui*?"

"Nay, Frenchman. In truth, 'tis a mere upstart of a castle that cannot withstand my assault." His majesty's mouth parted in a sly grin as he transferred his reins from one hand to another. His overtunic of purple with his crest blazoned on it concealed his armor. Yet, even covered with dust from the long journey, the king who had lived over sixty years looked regal.

"Mayhap you should consider…" Richard paused as loud shouting came from the back of the line. It stopped their progress. He twisted in his saddle to see what was happening.

A soldier galloped past the foot soldiers and reined in his mount in front of the king. The soldier tore off his helmet and bowed his head. "My Liege, an accident—hasten please!" he blurted.

They wheeled their horses about. King and warlords alike sped to the back of the column where a group of men surrounded a screaming warrior.

Richard dismounted in haste and pushed through the throng. He knelt beside the wailing man whose right leg was swallowed mid-thigh underneath the wagon.

With a quick glance, Richard took in the dire situation. The metal cleats securing the battering ram to the wooden bed had pulled loose, forcing a shift of weight and causing the wagon wheels to break. The ram tottered precariously.

"Help—help me—Milord...the pain!" Out of his mind, the soldier writhed, tears coursed through grime as his lips pulled into a grimace. Even the presence of the king didn't stop his loud screams. He clutched Richard's overtunic. Several soldiers tried without success to lift the wagon.

"You and you—come," Richard ordered while pointing at several tall and burly soldiers.

Half a dozen young men obliged. Tossing down their pikes, they put their weight and backs against the wagon. Sweat broke out on their faces, their grunts made a fierce noise as they forced the wagon upwards.

"Harder," Richard yelled at the straining men.

The King and his nobles were content to watch the events from atop their horses.

One noble, Henry Dufray, the Earl of Wrothbury, called out, "Chop the leg off, what difference does it make? Leave him—I say."

Ignoring Wrothbury's cruel remarks and the nobles ensuing laughter, Richard urged the soldiers to push. At last, the wagon creaked, groaned, and was lifted high enough to allow Richard to pull the man out. The wagon's weight had driven the man's leg armor deep into his thigh. Blood spurted out to stain the ground dark.

The injured soldier rose up on his elbows to stare at his mangled leg. His face blanched white, his eyes widened, terrified he grasped Richard's arm. "Milord—help…"

"Where's the healer?" Richard called for the king's doctor. Catching Wrothbury's approach from the corner of his eye, he glanced upwards just in time to see the earl's spiked mace plunging downward. In an instant Richard caught the weapon's chain stopping its deadly path and used it to pull himself upright. He faced Wrothbury. Richard took the earl's red overtunic within his fists and jerked him close, lifting him as he did so. "God smite you. You would kill a man under your own command?" he gritted out. "We can take his leg—perhaps save him—"

"For what? To hop into battle on one leg? His life is over. If you do not like my actions—go back to France from whence you came." The Earl, lethal as hemlock and still holding the mace, snaked his arms around Richard's middle and locked his hands behind Richard's back. The material of their tunics became one as their chest armor pressed together.

"You are most fortunate your sire didn't think the same of you," Richard ground out. His barb against Wrothbury direct and on target.

Wrothbury, born with a deformed right leg and foot, started to squeeze. "Your mouth might be your downfall, Frenchman. And like the wagon minced the man's leg, I can force thy armor through your gut."

Undaunted, Richard glared down into eyes the color of gray stone and just as cold. With a will as strong as Wrothbury's, Richard forced his arms outward, breaking the man's herculean hold. Richard thought Wrothbury a misshapen spawn of the devil whose appearance was deceiving, for the man had the strength of two.

"Cease with this," the king commanded. "Whilst you two try to best the other, my soldier bled out. He's dead." The monarch's mouth turned downward as he shot a disparaging challenge at Richard. "Careful who you prepare to fight, Frenchman. I'll need the both of you when we reach Andrew Brodie's clan."

Wrothbury, slovenly, with stringy gray-hair, stepped back and laughed. As he went to mount his steed, he continued his deep chuckle, drawing attention to his limp, a strange up and down gait. Once seated, he took on the appearance of a normal man without disfigurement.

Richard speared a look of rancor at Wrothbury who was fast becoming his adversary. Wrothbury returned his glare with one of equal hostility and slowly wrapped the chain of his mace around his saddle horn. Although Richard felt nothing but contempt for the earl who had risen in the ranks of nobility by the king's generosity, he decided to say or do nothing more. At all cost, he must protect his true reason for being here. If the king, or anyone else, discovered his secrets, Richard's life would be snuffed in an instant.

"'Tis a bloody mess, for certes," said the king, not referring to the dead soldier, but of his precious battering ram rendered useless.

"Majesté, if Foxlair Castle is without high towers, leave the siege machines behind. They slow our progress." Richard nodded in reverence.

"Thy suggestion has merit, Frenchman." He signaled for his sergeant-at-arms and gave orders to cut out enough men to stay behind and guard the equipment, but he gave no order concerning the dead soldier.

Richard spurred his horse, sliding in behind the king's nobles. They were almost within striking distance of their destination.

Deirdre sat in the center of the blanket and deftly arranged her gown across her shins. Bonnar removed his leather jerkin and tossed it aside. Dressed in his linen shirt and kilt, he knelt beside her. Smiling over at her, he took up the chalices and carefully filled each with Elderberry wine.

They touched goblets.

"To us, Deedee love. To our weddin'." He grinned, showing strong even teeth.

"Aye, Bonnar." Her eyes roamed his face, proud he would soon be her mate. She loved the lopsided grin he turned on her. And with a caressing smile of her own, she tilted her head in a saucy manner. "I'll be yer wife in two days. Are ye content with that?"

"Somewhat." He sat next to her.

His answer meant he would rather bed her right now and not wait for the ceremony. It forced Deirdre to laugh.

Wariness covered Bonnar's face as he asked, "Where is yer sire? Think he'll come lookin' fer ye?"

"Nay. Papa and Davey left for the smithy's to have Papa's horse shod. They should be gone until midday or later."

"Yer sire's fist is hard on the chin. If he's going to come rattling the bushes lookin' fer ye, 'tis for certes we can jest eat our food, and get ye back home shortly."

He ran his hand across his clean-shaven jaw where the bruises no longer showed.

Knowing what he meant, she burst out laughing. True, he'd tried to become too familiar with her when first they'd met. But her papa, Andrew Brodie, wise in the ways of a young rutting male, was quick to realize Bonnar's intent. Upon seeing just how familiar he attempted to be with Deirdre, Andrew busted Bonnar's jaw a good one then ordered him from Brodie land. However, Bonnar prevailed by asking for her hand in marriage.

Bonnar reached out to take a long lock of her hair, a bright chestnut and let it slowly fall back into place. "Ye are most beautiful."

His compliments always made her preen and she was quick to reply. "Och, ye have a honeyed tongue, aye that ye do." She gestured at him. "Hand me the basket so I can prepare our meal."

Breaking the bread into quarters, she put a piece into his outstretched hand, followed by a larger chunk of cheese that he immediately started eating. She kept a smaller piece of bread and cheese for herself and leaned back against the rough tree trunk. He settled next to her, and tilting his head drank deep of the wine.

A black beetle scurried halfway across the blanket where Bonnar flicked it away with his finger. Crows cawed from overhead branches.

She nibbled at the cheese. "Tell me again about yer sire and Mam. D'ye truly believe they'll like me?"

"O'course. My sire is sendin' five head of cattle to yer papa so I can have ye."

"And goats," she added.

"Aye, two goats. My sire's a goodly man. And my mam is most gentle. Ye'll do fine livin' with them. In time, we'll have our own dwelling."

"D'ye think 'tis safe fer us to journey to yer clan? Mayhap we should remain here. Foxlair seems a much safer place than travelin' across Scotland. I overheard Papa telling Davey that England's King Edward is in lower Scotland seeking Robert de Brus. What if the king knows the Brus was here a mere fortnight ago?"

His brows knit together in thought. "I canna think like a king, therefore I know not his intent." He shrugged. "Right now, the only thing I can think of is how much I want ye."

"Why, Bonnar Cameron, ye'll just have to wait 'til ye can call me wife."

Blithely ignoring her words, he ran his hands over her neck, pausing to push her hair out of his way, taking tiny nips at the base of her throat. He removed the chalice from her hand and set it aside before scooting away from the tree. On his knees, he grabbed her legs and pulled her down next to him, evoking giggles as her gown rode up to her thighs. He untied the strap holding her dagger in place and placed it next to the blanket. When she would protest, he silenced her with another kiss while deftly unlacing her bodice. She allowed his hand to creep inside, touching her bare breasts, his fingers caressing her nipples into peaks of desire.

"Let me have ye. Yer all I think about," he said.

"Nay, Bonnar. We must wait," her voice was shaky with passion.

His urging was a powerful aphrodisiac, his hand hot on her skin slid underneath her gown to the juncture of her legs. She tensed up slapping her thighs tightly together.

"D'ye tease me?" he said with sullen discontent.

Her body wanted him to teach her all he knew, but her mind forced her to say what she did. "Nay, I dinna tease. We will wed in two days, 'tis fer certes ye can wait."

He lay half on her and half off, one leg thrown carelessly across her hips. His tarse hard and pressing against her hip only aroused her curiosity. His hands surrounded her face as he slowly dipped forward into a kiss, slow and sensual his lips moved against hers, his mouth pressing tight, his tongue seeking and tasting of the spiced wine shared between them. She ran her hands through his long blond hair, feeling his scalp as her fingers explored his head.

"Touch me," he urged, forcing her hand under his kilt, pressing his bare flesh against her fingers. He moaned.

His flesh, soft textured yet firm, stirred under her caress, making her blush from the intimacy of feeling the most private part of a man. She finally managed to pull her hand from his firm grip and shifted out from underneath him.

"We canna do this. To do so would dishonor my papa. And fer certes ye made a pledge to Papa as well."

"He will never know. 'Twill be our secret." He started to roll back on top of her, but she pushed hard against his chest, stopping him. "Why d'ye come here then?" His displeasure showed in the firm set of his mouth.

Hurt by his words, she gasped. "How can ye say such? If this is all ye want, then mayhap ye should leave Brodie."

Like a pouting child, he turned away from her and onto his back, covering his eyes with his arm.

"Dinna be angry with me." She tried to undo the damage their unfulfilled passion always caused.

"I am not," he muttered.

It was easy to tell he lied and most upset, she sighed. "I must get back before Papa and Davey return from the smithy." Hurt more than she could admit, she jerked the laces of her bodice closed. Picking up her dagger, she tied it back in place on her thigh. She then packed up the remaining food.

Bonnar stood and put his leather jerkin back on. Without a glance her way, he picked up his claymore and wormed his head and shoulder through the holster allowing the lethal blade to dangle at his hip. He went to un-hobble the horses and led Wicker back to her.

"Come." He signaled with his hand.

"Ye are angry with me. Ye say not, but I can tell otherwise."

Not bothering to answer, he formed a stirrup with his hands, helping her to mount.

"As ye say, two days until we wed. I can wait. But dinna come here again, there's no need. Here, take this." He handed her the food basket. "Now get home. I will be right behind ye."

After seeing her to the edge of the forest, Bonnar returned to their trysting place. His flesh throbbed and he thought to go seek out Maeve. She'd slake his lust. Maeve never barred her door, or her thighs.

He knelt and started to fold the blanket when the chatter of the forest stilled, becoming quiet as death. Hearing a chinking noise, he paused, instantly alert. The sound he recognized as chain mail rubbing against armor. Glancing where Deirdre had gone, it was too late to call her back. Instead, he grabbed up the blanket, and led his horse into the thick underbrush. Pulling with all his strength, he forced his horse down on its side and placed his hand over his steed's muzzle, praying it would remain silent.

A soldier regaled in the English King's colors walked within yards of him. His heart tripped and sweat broke out on his face. More soldiers came on, moving in silence, scouting the area, their lethal spears held out before them.

A flock of crows and sparrows took flight from the forest, their loud cawing and their wings frantic flapping startled Deirdre's horse. Wicker snorted and pranced. Deirdre reached out to stroke Wicker's neck.

"There—there," she said, and urged Wicker on.

Unsettled about her argument with Bonnar, she wanted to talk with Seonaid, Davey's wife. There had to be more to marriage than the act of love. She'd only known Bonnar two months and he'd asked for her hand the first day they'd met. Her brother had cautioned her that Bonnar had a tendency to lift many a maidens' gown. Perhaps he only wanted her maidenhead, but when she asked if Bonnar had desired to take any of his former conquests as a wife, Davey had to admit he did not. Her papa, also suspicious of Bonnar's actions, had sent a message to Bonnar's clan to seek proof of his lineage. An answer had been forthwith. All was in order with Bonnar.

Yet, desiring Bonnar as she did, she was still reluctant to leave her beloved Papa and Foxlair. Having lost her mam when she was but five, Papa was the mainstay for not only her life, but Davey's as well. Even though Papa was a strong laird, how would he get along without her as chatelaine of their home, ordering meals, seeing to fresh rushes, and keeping everyone busy? Would he starve and Foxlair fall into shambles? It didn't matter that he was a handsome virile man that single women of the clan coveted. No one could take the place of her mam. Papa often said as much.

Heading inland, she skirted the fields of ripening wheat that rustled and surged like a golden sea under the warm breeze. The fields were empty of the workers that usually toiled in them until sundown. Feeling disquieted and sensing something wasn't right, she kicked her bare heels against Wicker's sides, urging her into a fast clip. In the far distance, Foxlair's watchtower peeked into view. But when she topped the knoll, she reined in Wicker so fast the mare's front legs pawed the air. Deirdre blanched, her skin prickled with dread.

She faced a line of mounted English soldiers that fanned out across her path. Behind the cavalry stood foot soldiers with tall spears pointing skyward, looking like a forest of limbless trees. The English had positioned themselves between the clan and the protection of Foxlair. The tall wooden stockade surrounding the sturdy stone keep stood like a lonely sentinel beckoning safety none of them could get to.

Her gaze flew to the center of the arc and the colorful banners proclaiming the King of England. The king wore armor, and the crown that encircled his helmet reflected the sun's rays making him resemble a great God. He was close enough that Deirdre could make out his piercing gaze and gray beard.

On the king's right was a nobleman in battledress. His long, stringy gray hair stirred in the breeze as he held his helmet nestled in the crook of his arm. He narrowed a look of speculation at her.

To the king's left sat another warrior. His banners, a field of bright blue with golden leopards pulled together by a fallen crown, were different from that of the king's. The wind furled and snapped the flags making the entwining leopards dance. As Deirdre stared at the warrior, threads of long dark hair blew across his face and he tossed his head removing the offending strands. His handsome gaze never wavered from hers. An intense stare, that was without malice.

They all watched her.

Fear seized her throat like a giant hand, slowly cutting off her ability to breathe. She scrutinized the area. Where was Papa? The clan, corralled like bleating sheep, huddled together. Their desperate gazes stole from her to the English. The elders appeared resigned, while the young men directed their anger at the English with tightened fists and darts of hatred. Husbands kept their families close. Anxious mothers hushed their children who peered fearfully from behind the cloth of their skirts.

Where was Bonnar? He should have been right behind her. But a quick glance over her shoulder showed he was nowhere in sight. She turned to stare at the line of soldiers that swept out from the king's sides. Their horses whinnied and snorted. The king's black warhorse pawed the earth and raised its head.

Soldiers carrying lances scurried past Deirdre, startling her.

One of the men knelt in front of the king. "Majesty. We swept the woods. No trace of Robert the Bruce."

The king nodded. "Guard the whore," he commanded.

Deirdre watched the soldiers hurry to form a small detail behind her.

The aging warlord next to the king pointed at Deirdre. "My Liege, yonder maiden's mine—I want her."

Deirdre's heart squeezed. Her hand stole to her thigh, her dagger, for certes, its puny presence gave no reassurance against so many.

"Ye surprise me, Wrothbury." The king smirked, his eyes still trained on her. "I thought ye wished nothing but death to all Scots. Ye boast of your hatred for anyone that reeks of Scottish lineage, women included."

"I do not hate what is nestled between her legs," the warlord affirmed.

At this remark, the king laughed. He turned to another warrior next to him and asked in a loud voice, "What say you, Comte de Strasbourg—is she not a beautiful wench to spill your seed into?"

"Oui, most beautiful."

They argued over her like she was a piece of chattel, a mere nothing to be bargained about. Suddenly the corralled people pitched forward, distracting the English. Deirdre wheeled her horse around forcing the soldiers around her to make way. She sent Wicker into a fast gallop toward the inlet. Close to the forest, she glanced over to see Bonnar melding back into the dense foliage.

"Bonnar! Help me—'tis the English. Get the boat!" She reined in Wicker and held out a hand, urging, pleading. Bonnar remained in the shelter of the trees, holding his finger across his lips, shaking his head. He withdrew even further.

Unable to grasp what had just happened, Deirdre wildly sought escape. Not knowing what else to do, she went for the water. Leaping from Wicker, she dashed to the boat. She pushed at it. The sand locked it in place. Frustrated, she hurried to the stern, tugging even harder, the wood scraped her hands making them bleed. The boat moved several feet.

"Bonnar—help me!"

She glanced to see the one called Wrothbury was almost upon her. A scream ripped from her throat.

She ran down the beach. Her foot caught on a piece of driftwood, sending her sprawling face first against the wet sand, knocking the air from her lungs. Gulping in pain and air, she shot to her feet. She lifted up her skirt and splashed into the water. Her gown heavy with water slowed her down. Her limbs turned to stone.

"Please—Bonnar help me—help me!"

The horse's heavy breathing was loud as it bore down, almost trampling her. She found herself lifted and roughly deposited like a dead deer across Wrothbury's saddle.

"Put me down. Put—me down. I am the daughter of Andrew Brodie—laird of this clan." Kicking her feet, she tried to dislodge herself from his hold.

He met her outcry with silence and whipped his horse toward the king.

"Hear that, my Liege? Like a fish from the sea, I caught Andrew Brodie's daughter." He tightened his grip around Deirdre and forced her to a sitting position in front of him. When she struggled, he said, "Hold still—'twill do you no good to fight me."

She glanced at his stern face seeing hatred in his hooded eyes.

"Your way of life is now over. You are mine." The metal from his gauntlet-encased hand bit into the soft flesh of her waist.

In defiance, she hissed, "Never will I be yours—unhand me." She thrashed about. Seeing his bare wrist, she bit down hard, tearing flesh, drawing blood.

"You Scottish bitch!" His blow against the side of her head almost knocked her from the horse, but her captor grabbed her in a bruising grip. "Heed my warning—try that again I'll spread your legs here on the ground in front of everyone."

A ruckus diverted everyone's attention as the line of soldiers parted and Deirdre's father and brother rein their horses to a stop in front of the king. Relieved to see them, Deirdre was also fearful for their lives. She glanced at the king, seeking his intent, but his face betrayed nothing.

Andrew Brodie, a giant of a man, with long graying-black hair and blue eyes the exact color of hers, took in the scene with one shrewd glance. David, almost an exact replica of their father, glared in disbelief.

"Bow yer head, David," Andrew warned showing homage to the king. After a brief moment, Andrew raised his head.

Laird and King locked eyes.

"Yer Majesty, what brings ye to Clan Brodie?" Andrew Brodie asked in a deep commanding voice.

"I seek Robert the Bruce."

"I dinna know his whereabouts."

Deirdre drew in a sharp breath. Papa spoke a half-truth, for he'd given succor to Robert the Bruce not more than a fortnight ago.

The king situated the hauberk around his face, and then slowly pulled on his mittens of mail. "I will annihilate anyone harboring the Bruce, this I promise."

"Then yer promise is not meant fer me. He is not here." Andrew Brodie matched the king's hard stare. "My signature's on the Ragman's Role submitting fealty to ye. I've done nothin' against England."

"The Ragman's Role. Ah…yes…a most noticeable sham swearing fealty to the crown of England. The ink not even dry on the document before those that signed it turned traitor and took up arms against me. I wonder, Laird Brodie, how much of your fealty truly resides with the English—and me." The king glowered. "Give me this upstart the Bruce, and I'll give up your daughter."

When Wrothbury started to protest, the king sharply raised a hand for silence.

Deirdre watched her papa's eyes narrow, his mouth a firm line.

"I canna give ye what I dinna have. The Brus isna here. I ask in all God's graciousness that ye release my daughter."

"Let me have the maiden." The French warrior next to the king spoke, surprising all who had forgotten his presence. He moved his horse out of the line and stopped in front of the king whose face betrayed his displeasure at the Frenchman's actions.

Wrothbury forced a laugh. "Ah…Count Strasbourg, perhaps you have forgotten your reason for being here with the king. Or was that a lie? Mayhap bringing a trebuchet to siege a castle is not your true reason. My Liege, I would say he now sides with your enemies."

Laird Brodie interrupted the bickering. "She is for neither of ye. My daughter's set to marry in two days. Again, I ask that ye release her."

"By the Saints, Wrothbury, this muddies your desires does it not?" Edward grinned at Wrothbury who thrust his chin out in defiance.

Wrothbury's hold tightened, his fetid breath hot against Deirdre's cheek. He spoke, "Nay, it muddies nothing for me. Perhaps the future husband will be out of sorts at losing such a prize, but I am content." He pointed and shouted at the clan. "Let this husband to be come forward and show himself."

Deirdre eyes followed his gaze.

Not a soul moved.

When no help was forthcoming, he captured her breast and squeezed. She pushed at his hand to no avail for he forced her into an unwanted kiss. His breath was stagnant, his lips chapped.

Out of the corner of her eye, Deirdre saw her papa move with lightning speed. As he rode next to her, she reached out, allowing him to snatch her away from Wrothbury. Situated behind him, Deirdre held tight to his strong waist as they galloped through the wheat field, the stalks falling under his horse's stride. Her brother was right beside them.

Two soldiers were in fast pursuit.

Whipping the reins, he called over his shoulder. "Dinna worrit—Deedee lass—I will not let them harm ye."

"Papa—I fear for us!"

An arrow whizzed within inches of her face, punching through her papa's left shoulder, burying deep. He grunted with pain as blood spurted from his wound. Deirdre screamed.

A volley of arrows skewered Andrew's horse. Bucking and snorting, neighing a death peal, the steed crashed to the ground sending them both tumbling. Deirdre skittered across the terrain. Rocks grazed her face, her palms, her legs. Dazed from the fall, she dug her fingers into the soil and managed to stagger to her feet.

Laird Brodie rose upon one knee. "David—get yer sister!"

Before David could reach her, one of the pursuing soldiers did so. As arrows fell between the soldier and David, the soldier jabbed his lance against her flesh, forcing her to give way. She tried to see how wounded Papa was, but the soldier's body blocked her view. He prodded her like an animal towards Wrothbury and the king.

Cries of warning came from the soldiers, too late. Andrew ran toward the soldier capturing Deirdre, and with one quick blow from his deadly claymore severed the man's head.

Laird Brodie mounted the dead soldier's horse.

Once again Edward signaled his archer. Another arrow pierced her father's chest. He reeled in the saddle but remained seated.

"Papa! Stay back—stay back! I'll go with the English." Tears streamed down her cheeks.

With two arrows protruding from his torso and blood turning his shirt red, the Laird, his claymore held aloft, charged them. "No filthy English scut will take my daughter."

An arrow hissed through the air, striking Andrew in the stomach. The impact knocked him from the saddle. He writhed on the ground. Deirdre's brother dismounted and hurried over to him.

"Nay!" Her limbs froze, as Papa's bloody hand grab Davey's tunic.

"Davey…go…save yerself."

"But—Papa—Deedee. Seonaid—my children—"

"It canna be helped…live to lead…go…"

His dying words carried to her, his last breath.

David stood. His face contorted with grief, he shouted, "Ye piece of dung." Snatching up a large rock he threw it with all his might. The rock slammed into the king's face, cutting his nose.

"Get him," Edward roared.

David leaped on his horse and rode headlong for the inlet.

Deirdre ran after her brother, her feet plowing through the wheat. "David." She gaped after him. Bonnar burst out of the trees after David, he'd witnessed all. "Bonnar…how could ye…" she whispered, unable to believe that he was abandoning her, that he'd refused to help her, that he could have gotten them both safely away. His cowardice ripped at her.

The soldiers gave chase. She watched Davey and Bonnar push the rowboat into the water, ducking a barrage of arrows, paddling like madmen toward the safety of the inlet.

Wrothbury brought his horse up next to her and pulled her up in front of him. Now alone with her enemy, Deirdre wished she was dead.

They put the fields to flames. Horrified, Deirdre saw the fire lick close to where her father lay.

Wrothbury unlaced her bodice. He bared her breasts and pinched her nipple. "You are most lucky I have a battle to fight, or I would be between yer legs."

She endured his groping hand, and sat in numbed silence watching the fire abate leaving charred stubble in its wake. When Wrothbury relaxed his hold, she struggled out of his grip. She landed on her feet and rushed toward her father's body.

"Papa—Papa…" Mindless of her bare feet, she ran. The charred stubs, razor sharp, pierced her skin. Her need to get to Papa blotted out the pain. She stopped amidst the acrid smell of burned wheat. Dropping to her knees, she gathered her father's lifeless torso against hers. His blood soaked into her bodice. Her tears fell onto his cheeks, making rivulets on his soiled skin. She pushed strands of long hair off his face and gently closed his eyes.

Vaguely aware that someone had dismounted and stood beside her, she steeled herself for Wrothbury's wrath. Instead, kind words floated down to where she sat.

"*La femme*, your *père* is with God. Let me help you."

Unable to do otherwise, she laid her father back down. In a daze she unsheathed his dagger and started to plunge it into her chest.

"Non!" The dagger was knocked aside.

"Mayhap ye will kill me instead."

"Mademoiselle, I wish you no harm. I'm Richard de Laci, Comte de Strasbourg." He pulled her to her feet and whispered against her ear. "Somehow, I will save you. Stay alive."

His words calmed her, shielded her, an answered prayer amidst so much danger. She allowed him to pick her up and hold her close. She clasped her hands behind his neck, and stared into eyes the color of moss. He placed her on his horse's saddle. But before the Frenchman could mount his steed, Wrothbury rode up.

"Count Strasbourg, you vex me and are becoming bothersome. Do not incur my anger, 'twill be most swift if you do." He paused long enough to give orders. "Squire, take this woman to the castle and lock her up." Wrothbury rejoined the army that moved on the clan, the chain of his mace swinging above his head in a deadly circle.

Deirdre, still on Richard de Laci's horse and led by Wrothbury's squire, glanced back to see the French count standing where she left him. He stared after her.

Frightened, Deirdre sat in the middle of her papa's bed. She lifted the torn hem of her filthy gown. Smudged with charcoal, her legs and feet bled, and large blisters had formed on both. Her arms and hands were bruised, her bodice stiff with Papa's blood. The vision of him dying and of Bonnar hiding in the trees kept going through her mind. His cowardice had closed her heart against him. How could he? If he'd helped her flee, Papa would be alive.

Oh…God, Papa…

The screams from outside died. Smoke coiled through the window slit like an eerie gray snake bringing with it the smell of death.

She glanced at the floor and the rushes that covered the trapdoor. Perhaps she could crawl and escape through the secret tunnel. But before she could move, the door to the room creaked open. Fearing that it was Wrothbury, she grabbed the thick bedpost for support and started to squirm from the bed. She stopped when the man who entered was not Wrothbury. It was the Frenchman, Richard de Laci.

He shut the door and crossed the room. Grime streaked his face, his black hair coated with gray ash, and yet his eyes were kind.

"Mademoiselle, again, I seek only to help you." He knelt in front of her and being careful lifted one of her feet. Upon seeing the blisters that covered her feet and shins, he blurted, "*Mon Dieu—bâtards—*all of them!" He appeared to be fighting for control as his eyes searched her face. "You must be in extreme pain."

"The pain in my legs canna compare to the pain in my heart." Unable to understand his concern, she asked, "Why are ye here with the English?"

"Why I'm here does not matter, oui? What matters most is getting you away from here. Is there another way out of this castle?"

Again, she placed herself in the safety of this man. She pointed to the floor's thick rushes. "That covers a secret door and tunnel that comes out behind Foxlair. From there ye have to climb the hillside. But I canna walk and 'tis too steep fer ye to carry me."

"I can and will carry you—we must hurry." Kneeling, he pushed the rushes aside and lifted the hinged door. Cool stagnant air rushed into the room. After looking down into the dark gaping hole, the warlord grabbed up a lit candle and handed it to her. He scooped her off the bed and headed toward safety.

Their eyes met.

"Mademoiselle—" he swallowed his words as the door burst open.

Deirdre screamed as King Edward and the Earl of Wrothbury entered.

Unsheathing his broadsword, Wrothbury quickly took in the scene. "It appears the Frenchman does not realize that he holds my future wife in his arms," he announced in a low growl directed at Count Strasbourg. "Put her down."

Deirdre drew in her breath. Never would she be his wife.

"All this bickering over a woman who should be dead tires me," the king interjected. A feral smile hardened his face.

The warlord continued to hold her, appearing unconcerned for his own safety. "Wrothbury despises her race, oui? Allow me to take her away from here. I can treat her burns."

Deirdre tightened her grip on his neck as a flicker of hope filled her. His intentions failed her, but his arms cradled her like she was the finest of womanhood.

But the king determined all. "I gave her to Wrothbury. Why he wants to marry her puzzles me. For certes, he does not need this pile of stone as a prize." He tapped his finger against his chin, pondering. "She is a laird's daughter after all, mayhap that will suffice. Count Strasbourg, I suggest you put her down. Wait for me in the great hall."

When Count Strasbourg didn't comply and shifted her weight in his arms, Edward called out, "Guards." Immediately, two armed soldiers entered. One slammed the trap-door shut, the other went to stand behind the count.

The King pulled his short dagger and approached. He was close enough for her to see the cruel set of his mouth which foretold his intent. He placed the tip of his blade against the base of her throat and pressed. She didn't dare breathe. Her flesh stung from the cut. Needing to blot out the vision of nobility she pressed her face against the warlord's warm neck. Her lips felt the wild jumping of his pulse. Knowing he faced defeat, she trembled against him.

"Put her down, Count Strasbourg," his majesty warned. "I'm bored with this game and crave rest on yonder bed. If I must, I'll put you in a gibbet and hang it from the wooden stockade out front. And I just might ride off without your gallant presence. People die when left alone and locked in a gibbet. They become food for the vultures. Or would you prefer I end yours and Wrothbury's squabble over this woman here and now? Your choice, as one less Scottish woman to breed is most preferable."

The blade pierced deeper into her skin sending warm blood trickling down between her breasts. A low moan escaped her.

"Non, Majesty, there's no need to harm her." Count Strasbourg backed away and went to place her on the bed.

Deirdre's hand went to her throat which was wet and stung from the cut. Despair cloaked his face, and Deirdre knew that her death would be preferable to what was about to happen.

Kneeling in front of her, the count took her hand within his. "Mademoiselle, please forgive me for failing you."

"Dinna think such," her voice trembled, "for I'll never forget that ye tried to help me." She caressed her knuckles against his rough cheek, finally letting her hand drop to her lap. He simply nodded and started to stand. Deirdre watched Wrothbury come up behind Richard de Laci and use the hilt of his sword to club the count on the back of the head. The gentle warlord crumpled at her feet with a loud thud. Blood spread into the rushes, the straw soaking it up.

Thinking him dead, a silent scream roared in her head. Never again would she allow the English to see her weak—never.

Carried back to her sleeping chamber and deposited down upon her bed, Deirdre sat as though a fog had settled about her. She tried to shut out the drone of the priest's voice marrying her to this evil man.

When she refused to speak during the ceremony, Wrothbury leaned down to where she sat on the bed and issued a warning, "Say the words or I'll beat them from you." He turned to the priest. "Now ask her if she takes me for her husband."

She whispered, "Aye."

The King strode across the room and paused by the door. "We continue our search for Robert the Bruce at first light. Be ready."

Wrothbury stood in anticipation as his squire removed his armor and clothes. "Quickly—make haste." His turgid manhood was testimony to his urgency. When his squire started to pick up the discarded items, Wrothbury pushed him toward the door. "Leave it—out—out."

As Wrothbury paraded his naked, misshapen, aging body before her, she compared how protected she'd felt in Richard de Laci's strong arms. But even those feelings were starting to blur.

Wrothbury bent to stare at the soles of her blistered feet. "Thou cannot escape me," he said without concern. And to prove such, he tore her scorched gown from her and tossed it away. "What's this?" His gaze settled on the dagger still tied to her thigh. He unsheathed the dagger and threw it to stick in the wood of the door. "Tsk tsk, madam, you will not kill yourself or me this day." He grasped his swollen manhood and pointed it like a sword. "To think, two days later and I would not have me a maiden bride." Beside her on the bed, he forced her onto her back and pushed his fingers inside her cleft. Slapping at his invading hands, she struggled against him and locked her knees tightly together.

"You will not deny me this," he said, and tried to pry her thighs apart. Seeing her chance, she kicked him hard between the legs. Yelping from the blow and grabbing himself, he twisted away.

She jumped from the bed. The blisters on her soles popped shooting agonizing pain up her legs. She grit her teeth.

Her voice trembled with grief. "Who are ye to treat me as thus? I am the daughter of Andrew Brodie—laird of this clan." Tears blinded her progress as she stumbled across the room. The awful vision of Papa's death tore at her. Her scream started deep within, a deep guttural sound that escaped and knifed the air.

Wrothbury grabbed her by the hair. Pulling her back to the bed, he unceremoniously dumped her on it. Capturing her tear-slicked face in his hand, he forced her to look at him. "The next time you kick me—you will die—do you hear me?"

"I—am—dead," she screamed and spit in his face.

...She suffered through his pillage of her body by willing herself up the hill to sit with Davey, the both of them young, and watching their papa as he made his way up to them. Papa picked her up and played his game of tossing her high into the air. He then acted like he would miss her, but he never did, he always caught her...

2 The Cage

Wrothbury Castle, Northern England
February 1307

Deirdre stood in silence on the castle's high battlement. The sun was beginning to rise over the distant land like an eye slowly opening, coming awake. A pink haze cut through the deep purple, changing the land from dark to light, and casting the stone in front of her from a cold gray to a warm rose. Try as she might, she couldn't absorb the beauty of the beginning day, and turning her back on God's splendor walked to the northern side of the castle. Again she stared outward over the treeless landscape wondering if her brother David would come this way.

Deirdre would never accept being the Countess of Wrothbury. Her title did not bring prestige, only endurance. She was a captured countess, a caged countess, living in an isolated castle with a nearby village of sullen peasants who tilled the soil and tried to make the barren land sustain life. They also lived in fear of Wrothbury.

Clan Brodie, to her had ceased to exist. She hadn't seen David since the day Wrothbury adducted her from Foxlair close to a year ago. Nor did she know if David's wife Seonaid and their three young children lived or died. Wrothbury more than relished telling her that after David

hit King Edward with the rock, he was an outlaw and the king's proclamation bore a lofty amount of coin for his head. Although the price on
David's head was high, it was not as high as the price Deirdre paid for
being born Scottish.

The sun, now a round orb above the horizon, lit the earth and allowed Deirdre to make out movement in the far distant. The patter of
shoes hurrying up the stone stairs made Deirdre smile.

Mary Clair, Deirdre's handmaiden, a slender young woman with dark
features, hopped from one foot to the other as she pointed to the soldiers that rode toward the castle. "Milady—Milady, Countess Wrothbury.
Look! Riders approach. The banners they carry are not the Earl of
Wrothbury's."

"I see them, Mary Clair. Stop yer fussin'. I know whose heraldry it is.
And I heartily welcome the man those banners pronounce." Deirdre
looked over the rough stone to see that a group of riders broke from the
main army and continued toward the castle.

"And who might that be, milady?" Mary Clair's head pivoted between
Deirdre and the approaching men. Her dark eyes wide in her pretty face.

"'Tis Robert de Brus." Deirdre's hand slipped into the sleeve of her
blue gown and wrapped around the missive from David secreted there.
He was with the Bruce's army and traveling close to Wrothbury Castle.
Deirdre could hardly contain herself.

Mary Clair's ebony brows furrowed in alarm. "Robert the Bruce?
That Scottish heathen—here? Oh—milady—tell the soldiers to protect
us from this man who rapes women and devours children!" She waved
her arms about reminding Deirdre of a chicken that had its head cut off
and not knowing the difference, continued to run around in defiance.

Deirdre caught her distraught maid by the arms. "Stop it—I say. Ye
be actin' like a blithering idiot. We have nothin' to fear from this man,
nor his company. I'm opening my gates to Robert de Brus. Go to the
kitchen and tell cook to prepare a meal fit for a king, for the Brus is declared King of Scotland." She turned and started down the spiral stair-

case with Mary Clair fast on her heels.

Deirdre approached the tall, heavy timbered gates set between the thick walls of stone and secured with a heavy crossbar. John Ward, Mary Claire's father and Wrothbury's sergeant at arms, stood in front of it with his arms crossed. Several soldiers stood behind him.

"John Ward, we have visitors. I ask that ye open the gates and let them in."

"Nay." The big man shook his shaggy gray head.

It was no secret to Deirdre that the sergeant tolerated her because she was Wrothbury's wife. But it didn't make his insolence any less abiding. The man's belligerent actions during Wrothbury's long and lengthy absences bordered on disrespect. Deirdre stood firm. "I'm mistress of this domain. I order ye to allow Robert de Brus entrance."

"Madam, we war against this man. 'Tis said the good King of England masses an army to go against this man and all Scots who side with him. Ye of all people know our King Edward proclaims himself to be ruler of Scotland and does not recognize Robert the Bruce to be king of anything."

Deirdre, trying to remain calm, curled her hands into tight fists. "Have ye forgotten I'm Scottish?" she reminded rather harshly. "Robert de Brus is my king. Now open the gates."

Mary Clair plucked at Deirdre's sleeve. "Milady, please pay heed to my father's words. No good can come of this visit."

The men behind John Ward moved closer, their hands on the hilts of their broadswords. John's face looked carved from stone, his mind as closed as the gates behind him.

"Is this yer answer then?" Deirdre asked.

"Aye."

Expecting nothing less from Wrothbury's men, Deirdre, unable to suppress her anger, lifted the hem of her gown and ran back up the stairs. She rushed to the battlement wall and peered over. A group of men waited outside the entrance. Others stood behind them at the ready.

"Robert de Brus?" she shouted down.

"Aye, that I am," he answered in a deep voice, his eyes meeting hers. He was dressed for battle, but unlike the King of England who flaunted his presence, the Bruce's helmet was bare of a crown. "Is there trouble, Deirdre Brodie?"

His use of her maiden name warmed her as she smiled at the contingent of men. One face in particular, with eyes as black as a raven, looked upward and grinned.

"Hello, Deirdre," said her brother. "Is this the way ye treat yer guests? Talk to them from behind stone?"

Deirdre couldn't help but laugh. "Then if ye be tired of doing so, what d'ye have that might smash the wood keepin' ye out?"

"Will a battering ram do?" The Bruce laughed, his teeth shone in a dust coated face. His men joined in, their deep laughter drifting up to her.

"That will do just fine," Deirdre said glancing down into the courtyard and at John Ward who belligerently stared back. "D'ye hear that, John Ward? The Brus has a battering ram. Are ye going to open the gates?"

"But…milady…" John blustered, his strong stance faltering.

"If ye fear fer yerself, then I'll take the earl's wrath. He has been gone fer months and I doubt he will be comin' here soon. Ye and I both know he is beside his king. Open the gates, John Ward, and stand aside." Pleased, she watched him nod to his men, sending two of them to lift the heavy crossbar that secured the gates.

Deirdre flew down the stairs, breathlessly coming to a stop in the courtyard as several dozen armed men rode slowly through the entrance.

"Mary Clair," Deirdre spoke to her maid, "do as told. Go to the kitchen and have cook prepare a meal for our guests."

"Aye, milady," she said curtsying. With a fearful glance at the armored men, she scooted for the safety of the kitchen.

Deirdre bowed low in front of Robert the Bruce. "I bid ye welcome,

Yer Majesty. I give my fealty to ye and the crown of Scotland." Her heart thumped so loud, the king must hear it astride his horse. Still kneeling, she caught a smile from the king. Deep furrows started beside his long nose and etched even deeper alongside his mouth. His hauberk of mail covered his hair. Even without a crown his bearing was one of royalty, and his status as a warrior king hard fought.

"I accept yer hospitality, Countess Wrothbury. Since he isna present to greet me, I assume the Earl of Wrothbury is not here. I hoped to change his mind and convince him that Scotland's side is the true side." He glanced at the small contingent of castle guards who in a flurry laid down their weapons. "I pray that my being here on yer husband's soil will not put ye in jeopardy."

Deirdre shook her head. "Nay, yer Majesty, he isna here. As always, the earl is with his English king. And even if he was as Scottish as we are, Wrothbury wouldna side with ye." No longer able to contain her excitement, she singled out David who was dismounting. In a flash, she was past the Bruce's horse and standing close to her brother.

"Ah…Deedee…" His hands clasped her upper arms, holding her at arm's length as he looked her over. "Ye are a sight to behold. It has been a long time, aye?"

Deirdre could only nod, for a lump had formed in her throat allowing no words to pass. Her mouth quivered as tears formed behind her lids, scalding as they slipped from beneath her lashes. David's hand was warm as he sought the side of her face and she sobbed for everything that had been lost. Papa, her innocence, her betrothed, the clan, her world.

Everyone waited patiently for the brother and sister who upon last seeing the other had their lives ripped apart.

At last her tears ceased and David, as he was wont to do as a young lad, knuckled the top of her head in jest. Evoking a surprised laugh from her, he grinned. "We've a lot to talk about."

"Aye, we do, Davey."

Some of the men that accompanied the Bruce inside the gate dismounted. One man in particular approached Deidre and gave her a wide grin displaying a gap between his two upper teeth. Deirdre couldn't help but smile at the gruff looking warrior whose gray eyes twinkled with friendliness.

He gave her a curt nod, his head a riot of reddish gray hair. "Countess Wrothbury, I am Macadie Gunn, friend of yer brother, and soldier to Robert de Brus." He raised thick bushy eyebrows at her, and winked.

"Yer most welcome, Macadie Gunn. Dinna call me Countess Wrothbury as I liken being Wrothbury's wife to falling on a gorse bush, or worse. Call me Deirdre Brodie, if ye would."

"Deirdre Brodie, it is. Are there guards inside the castle?"

"Nay, only a small guard outside, mostly to see that I don't escape. The earl's large army remains with the English king. What ye see gathered over there is the lot of them."

Macadie took charge and ordered their men to tie up the guards and stand watch. After doing so, they unsheathed their claymores and rested their long double-edged swords pointed against the ground. Their eyes focused on the English soldiers.

Deirdre spoke to the servants who had gathered in stunned silence as the King of Scotland stood in the courtyard before them. A sight they never thought to see. The King of England, yes, but never this man, not in the earl's home. Taking orders from Deirdre, they scurried inside to do their mistress's biding. John Ward from where he sat tied and gagged, glared at her.

Deirdre ignored him. Nothing would spoil this day for her. Taking the king's and David's offered arms, she allowed them to escort her toward the large entry.

She beamed at both men. "I canna tell ye how happy I am to have my own brother on one arm, and the King of Scotland on the other. Davey, ye are a sight to behold. Ye resemble Papa, for ye have grown in girth and height to match him." Stark pain replaced her joy. She longed for new softer memories.

Nodding, David gave her arm a gentle squeeze. She could tell from the firm set of his mouth that his thoughts were the same as hers. A heavy silence mantled the both of them.

The interior of the castle was as dull and gray as Wrothbury himself. It was as though his animosity darkened all. Only a few thick pieces of elaborately carved furniture were within view. She led them into the great hall where a trestle table held steaming platters of food and goblets of wine. Pleased, she inspected the dishes of baked fish, eels, and meat pies in a thick crusted pastry. Round loafs of bread fresh from the bake oven were stacked three to a platter. Cherry tarts and almond cakes were for dessert.

The three men divested themselves of their helmets and put them down on the rush covered floor. Next they unsheathed their claymores, careful to lean them close to where they would sit. Deirdre indicated for his majesty to take his place at the head of the table. She took the spot on his right and David sat on the Bruce's left.

Without ceremony, Robert the Bruce snatched up one of the fragrant loaves and tearing off a chunk tossed the remaining loaf to Macadie seated next to Deirdre. A servant filled the king's wooden trencher with every dish on the table. He then served the others.

The king sopped his bread with the juice from the steaming meat pie. They didn't talk, and ate using their knives, the scraping sound loud and followed with even louder belches. As they devoured the food, Deirdre wondered when last they supped. She ordered the servant to take food to the soldiers in the courtyard.

Another servant poured wine into the king's chalice, then hastened around to serve the rest.

The Bruce tipped his head and drank deep, some of the wine trickled down his chin. He used the back of his forearm to wipe it away. Clearing his throat, he placed the chalice on the table, and said, "Deirdre Brodie, I do not know if ye are aware of this, but the King of England is most ill. He was coming against me and got as far as Lanercost Priory before taken to his bed."

Dread coursed through Deirdre as she almost choked on her wine. Where was the earl? If the king were ill, certainly Wrothbury would remain by his side. "Mayhap this means that the king will no longer fight against ye?" she offered.

The Bruce's mouth pulled into a frown. "I wish that were true, Lady Deirdre. England's king has told his whelp that if he dies before I'm brought to heel, he wants his bones carried at the head of the army that comes against me. Nay, the English will not rest until all of Scotland runs red with blood."

Deirdre thought about this fearsome news. The English king would rise from his grave to slay Scots. "Yer, Majesty." She leaned forward while wiping her fingers on her napkin. "There was a French warlord with the King of England that day at Brodie land. He tried to help me. When he started to take me from Foxlair, the Earl of Wrothbury stopped him. Mayhap ye can tell me what happened to him? His name was Richard de Laci, Count of Strasbourg."

Both David and Macadie shook their heads.

Only the king answered. "Nay, I wasna aware of this man…Richard de Laci. I would remember such a name. Ye say he showed ye kindness?"

"Aye, the only one to do so." Disappointed that no one remembered the warlord who had become simply Richard in her mind, Deirdre would never forget. His handsome face, his commanding voice, his defiance of England's king, was on her mind daily. Thinking of him allowed her to replace the horrible happenings of that day with kinder memories. Considering how Wrothbury hated the Frenchman, she didn't dare mention Richard's name to him. Although the Bruce claimed he didn't know Richard de Laci, Deirdre noticed his eyes flickered for a brief moment, perhaps in recognition?

They languished over good conversation and drink, until the king asked where he might rest for a while before they took their leave. Deirdre signaled to Mary Clair, who timidly came forward, still in fear of the man who stood before her. She did a deep curtsy and grinned when he put out a hand and helped her to her feet.

"Mary Clair, would that ye take the king to Wrothbury's chambers." She ignored the returned look of surprise, and knew the maid thought her bold to allow the King of Scotland in Wrothbury's bed. "Go on, 'twill do fer his majesty to take a rest."

Macadie Gunn wiped his mouth with the back of his hand and stood. "I'll see how our men fare." A wide smile crinkled his craggy face.

When their footfalls died away, David moved to sit beside his sister. Dressed in a plain gown of blue, she wore her hair in one long braid down her back. On her head was a veil held in place by a plain circlet of gold. No longer the apple-cheeked sister of his memories, she was a beautiful woman with regal bearing. And although her face was much slimmer, her eyes had changed the most. Gone was the teasing snap she had, now replaced with eyes that appeared to hold a great sadness within their blue depths.

Unable to think of any other way to soften his words, he said, "Deirdre, I ask that ye forgive me for leavin' ye that day."

Surprise and disbelief covered her face. She grabbed his hand within hers. "Why...Davey, ye did as papa ordered. And if ye hadna left, ye would be dead and buried beside Papa. What good would yer death have brought? Mayhap satisfaction to the English king," her voice trembled.

How hard it all had been on his sister. For a brief moment, she appeared to be like the young innocent sister he'd lost.

She sighed and fingering the stem of her metal goblet, said, "There are many 'ifs' for that day, are there not? We can all take a little piece of blame, but the king was on his way to Brodie and there was no stoppin' him. I always have it in my mind, if Bonnar Cameron had not hid in the forest like a coward and helped me with the boat, Papa might still be alive. Nay, dinna blame yerself when there are others who shoulder that burden."

"But…I rowed away. Then I heard ye screamin' clear out in the middle of the water where we sat."

"Did ye get to the other clans and warn them the English were comin'?"

"Aye."

"Then ye saved lives, did ye not? After ye left, I ran across the scorched field to get to Papa. My feet and legs were burned. I'll carry those scars to my grave. Every time I undress and see myself, I think of Papa dying."

"Deirdre, dinna say anymore. I canna abide it," his voice became hoarse with emotion as pain seared through his very being. He was a warrior, a laird, and yet the image of his father's death was almost more than he could bear.

His sister reached over and touched the brooch that held his plaid over his shoulder. "Papa's brooch. The last I saw of it was—"

"Aye. I know when last ye laid eyes upon it. I have Papa's dagger, too." He groped for something else to say. "What did the king and Wrothbury do to ye?"

"After the Frenchman, Richard de Laci, tried to help me and was stopped, I was forced to marry Wrothbury. I couldna walk because of my blistered feet, or I would have tried to get away from him. I need not tell ye what he did to me. A strange thing did happen though. Sometime that eve, someone started shouting that Robert de Brus and his army approached Foxlair. Hearing this news, the English king took me from Foxlair as he searched for the Brus. I didna learn it was a falsehood until much later."

David smiled an all knowing smile. "A ruse to be sure, but it worked, aye?"

"Ye did that?"

"Aye. My hope was to take ye away to safety. But they had ye surrounded like the king himself." He grinned at her astonishment. "How is it fer ye here amongst the English and Wrothbury?"

She plucked at the napkin on the table. "At first he would beat me if I said the wrong thing or what he didna want to hear. I learned to curb my tongue and stay out of his way."

"D'ye have any bairns?" he asked.

Deirdre smirked. "Nay, fer his seed is as weak as he is filled with hatred. My failure to conceive chafes at him. He never blames himself. I think that God wouldna give such a cruel man children and has indeed struck him barren. To my relief, he is absent more than not. "

"Dinna ye ever think to escape back to Foxlair?"

Deirdre sipped the last of her wine and taking a flagon, refilled their chalices. "I couldna. At first, he took me to London. When we returned to his home here, he sequestered me away like a nun. John Ward and others constantly watch me. Mary Clair is the only one who befriends me, and being John Ward's daughter, she has to be careful."

David's brow creased and he leaned forward in his chair. "D'ye know how close ye are to Scotland's border? Well a so-called border. The English have taken so many of our lower castles, 'tis hard to keep the land straight."

"Nay, not the border. But I can stand on the battlements and look north to Scotland."

"Ye are but three days ride from Lanercost Priory where the king lays ill, due west as the crow flies. If ye went straight north from here, ye would be in Scotland within two days ride."

"I never dreamed 'twas so close."

"Deirdre, our clan thrives fer I've seen to its resettlement. I can help ye return to Foxlair."

"Brodie land is not barren?" she asked, her face filled with hope.

David was delighted with her obvious joy. "Nay, it flourishes."

"Then tell me how so." She bubbled with excitement.

"Ye need to know that me wife and children are well."

"How did…how did they escape?"

"Bonnar and I started the story that the Brus was riding toward Fox-lair. As the English scurried away, I found my Seonaid and wee bairns hiding by the water." He cleared his throat. "When it was dark we went back. I buried Papa, and we helped the clan bury the rest of the dead. My Andrew is now nine. Little Dee is six. She is a hellion that takes after her aunt."

Deirdre smiled and dabbed at her eyes. "That is well and gude. I re-member yer wee Blake toddled about. Is he…?"

"Alive, aye. Our wee Blake is a strapping lad of three. I doubt he re-members his Aunt."

"'Tis happy I am for ye, Davey that yer family is alive. Then do ye say that Foxlair wasna burnt? I thought it put to the torch when we left."

"Some of it burnt, but 'tis hard to burn stone. Seonaid refuses to live in it and no amount of encouraging or bullying will make her. Instead we have a cottage amidst the clan's village."

David enjoyed the shine in his sister's eyes and was wont to make it go away, but he had a question he'd promised to ask. "Deirdre, Bonnar Cameron is outside. He has asked that ye talk with him. He still loves ye."

Deirdre shook her head so vehemently her veil threatened to fall off. She laughed bitterly. "Bonnar Cameron is as dead to me as Papa. Nay, that part of my life is over. I would do yer bidding with anything ye ask of me, but not this." Her face became rigid.

David disliked that she scorned his friend, a man who also had a price on his head from the English. "When did ye become so bitter? Has Wrothbury taken all the sweetness and left this harsh shell of the sister I knew?" He regretted his words as soon as he spoke them, for her gasps told him he'd erred badly. Her hand shot out and slapped him hard.

"How dare ye say such to me, David Brodie—how dare ye," she hissed.

He touched his stinging cheek, no doubt he'd be wearing her

handprint the rest of the day. "Forgive my words. Ye have a right to be angry. Bonnar did wrong. But ye need to give up yer grudge fer he has suffered the same as ye. When a man is branded a coward, he either takes it to his grave, or spends his life proving it wrong. Bonnar has proved it wrong many a time over. He is no coward." He patted her hand that had just so effectively slapped him. "I dinna think it is safe to leave ye here. When Wrothbury finds out we've been inside his home and ye allowed it, I fear fer yer life. I'll see ye get to Foxlair."

"When?" And the hope that swept her face was enough reward for him.

"We ride to battle so I canna take ye with me. I'll leave a handful of men who will escort ye to Scotland and Dundee Castle where ye'll be safe until I can get ye to Foxlair. Be ready to leave before dawn. Bring only what will fit into a small saddlebag."

"May I bring Mary Clair?" Such a simple request and so like Deirdre to always think of others.

"Aye, ye may."

The Bruce entered the great hall. Though to her, she and Davey had spent little time together, the sands had emptied out of the hourglass several times. Despite his rest, the king appeared tired and Deirdre thought how hard it must be to constantly fight for the right to lead Scotland.

"Deirdre Brodie, we must take our leave. I'll never forget what the Brodie family has done for me and Scotland."

She bowed low and said, "Robert de Brus. David, I ask that ye follow me into the chapel that I might offer up a prayer for ye."

The two men followed her into the castle chapel. Deirdre walked around, lighting the candles in the small chamber. When finished, she motioned for them to take her hand. She let out a long breath, and suggested they kneel.

"I ask for God's guidance that He may make ye Robert de Brus, King of Scotland, to rule by wisdom and not force. That God in His wisdom will keep ye safe. That in His wisdom will keep my brother, David safe from harm."

When they would stand, she kissed Robert's hand. "God be with thee, My Liege," she said, and then whispered, "Please take care of my brother."

Deirdre spent a restless night with sleep coming in rare snatches. Feeling more tired than when she went to bed, she was secure to have a handful of the king's men downstairs in the great hall. Wrothbury's men were still trussed and gagged.

She turned over and was startled awake by a whisper of a noise. She stared at the open bed curtains. For sure Mary Clair had closed them upon Deirdre retiring. The oil sconce burning on the opposite wall caught her attention. She'd watched Mary Clair snuff the sconce before leaving the room. Mary Clair must have recently re-lit it. Reality of her impending journey replaced her apprehensions. Packed saddlebags were under both her and Mary Clair's beds.

Excited about finally leaving this place she so hated, Deirdre swung her legs over the side of the bed. Her feet encountering the cold stone floor made her toes curl. She took several steps then abruptly stopped. Goosebumps waved across her skin. Her hand shot to her mouth, holding back moans of despair. She groped the bedpost for support.

The earl sat in a wooden chair across the room leisurely watching her. His arm was in a bloodied sling, and a path of blood originating from a deep cut near his right eye had dried upon his withered cheek.

"You are most beautiful when you sleep."

His unexpected words made her blurt out, "Ye are wounded."

"Beautiful, until you speak, and although your voice can caress a man without a touch, it also brings forth the Scottish brogue I so hate," his voice was edged with sarcasm.

Fighting the chill that invaded the room, she slowly sank upon the bed and pulled the wool blanket across her legs. Of all the weeks, all the months gone, he chose now to return, and had encountered the soldiers below. There was no way around this. No way.

He reached down to the floor and picking up a wadded piece of material tossed it onto the bed. It was a bloodied tunic bearing Robert the Bruce's heraldry.

"A bungled Scottish attempt of escape, no doubt. Your escort will not be taking you away to Scotland as planned." He abruptly came to his feet. Age bent his once strong upper body even more, and yet he was fast, for he was beside her in two shuffling strides. His hooded eyes stared down at her.

He smelled of war.

"You Scottish bitch!" He took her by the throat and holding her in a bruising grip, squeezed. Her throat closed. Frantic, she tried to pry his fingers loose. She fought to breathe. Her head pounded. Her eyes felt to burst from their sockets. She raked at his hands.

When he released her, she grabbed at the post and managed to rasp out, "Please...stop..."

"Stop? You ask me to stop?" He pushed her back against the bed as he climbed on top of her. With his weight pinning her, he shrugged off his sling, freeing his injured arm, and quickly used the bloody rag to tie her wrists together.

No amount of struggling could break the bond.

"Did you think you could feed that upstart Robert the Bruce in my own castle and me not hear of it? Did you think that pig of a Scots dare lie upon my bed and me not hear of it? Did you think your brother could leave a handful of men inside my domain to guide you to Scotland and me not hear of it? I know all that goes on here—all! They are dead, and I'm bloodied because of it—and you." He clout an ear-deafening blow against the side of her face.

"Damn you—I curse the day I took you. I should have killed you alongside your father and been done with it. I desire and detest you at the same time. You are like a festering wound in my mind." His face, cruel with admissions of hate, was barely inches from hers.

His confession stunned her. He was going to kill her. She didn't want to die like this, not beaten to death by a man she loathed.

He straddled her. "I thought in time you would accept me, refute your heritage, and realize your life as my countess wasn't such a hardship. Certainly a preferred life over the one you led at Brodie. A simple laird's daughter."

"If that laird was still alive, aye, that would be a preferred life."

His eyes flared with her answer. "Tell me how you managed to bring Robert the Bruce through my gates."

"I dinna know he was coming," her words tumbled out. "I was forced to open the gates—they came with a battering ram—"

"Battering ram—Madam?" His face contorted with anger, his rage beyond control. "Would you like to see how one works? Shall I siege your castle? I'll show you a battering ram—you barren bitch!" He tore her flimsy nightdress down the middle. She tried covering her naked body with her tied hands, but he jerked them upwards and secured them against the head post. She tugged at the restraints that held firm.

"You can't even give me what I desire—a son…"

Her heart pounded so hard she thought it would burst open her chest. "How can I carry a child for ye, when ye as much as force me every time ye have me? My heart and body close against ye. A child of yers would be like the spawn of…" she stopped her words.

"Of…the devil?" He chuckled and lowered his mouth to her breasts.

Deirdre held her breath as her chamber door slowly opened. Her dread abated as Mary Clair peeked in.

"Mistress?" she whispered. "I've been sent by the Earl of Wrothbury to help ye get dressed." She approached and loudly gasped. "Oh…milady…what has he done to ye?" She started untying Deirdre's hands.

With Mary Clair's help, Deirdre managed to sit up. "Why does he want me dressed?"

"He takes ye away from here. His men wait in the courtyard with saddled horses."

"Are ye to come with me?" Deirdre held onto the bedpost and managed to step into her gown held by Mary Clair. Her battered body screamed with each movement.

Mary Clair shook her head and tightened the laces on the back of Deirdre's gown. "Nay, I'm to remain here. He says ye will not need a maid where ye are going."

Deirdre bitterly said, "Mayhap he will kill me. And 'tis fer certes, I'll not need help to make me bed in the cold ground, will I?"

"Do not say such, milady, for it frightens me. What is to become of me when you are gone?"

Mary Clair's words forced Deirdre to temper her tongue. She slipped her feet into her shoes and went to sit at her dressing table where Mary Clair combed and braided her hair. When finished, she covered Deirdre's hair with a white linen veil and secured it in place with a gold circlet.

Deirdre took her maid's hands and beseeched her. "If ye could get away to Dundee Castle in Scotland, ye'd be safe. Ye must tell my brother what has happened here."

"I cannot do that by myself…please…Milady, do not ask such. I'd be so afraid—"

Wrothbury entered the room. With a flick of his head, he motioned Mary Clair out before turning his attention to Deirdre. "Are you ready to travel?"

Deirdre clutched at his arm. "Let me go. Ye love me not. Let me ride out of here today and ye'll never have to look upon me again."

"Oh, I expect in good time to never look upon your face. But release you to go where you please? Nay, I think not." He pried her hand from his arm. "Careful, I am wounded, remember."

"Are ye going to kill me?" She barely got the words out.

"Not this day. But I believe soon you'll wish to have died here and now."

At his words, her breath froze in her lungs. "What are ye goin' to do with me?"

"Why…madame, since you like to consort with king's, I'm taking you to mine. I'll let Scotland's true king decide your fate." He laughed as he pushed her out of the room.

The journey to Lanercost Priory took three days, and during that time, Wrothbury treated Deirdre as if she was a specter of the night. When she would ask that he stop and allow her to rest, he forced his entourage to move at a brisker pace. Each pounding hoof beat of her horse went through her body as though someone welded a hammer against her flesh. At night when Wrothbury finally stopped, no blanket, no tree bowers, nothing was offered to soften the ground beneath her, so she sat leaning against a tree. But sleep defied her. A drink of spiced wine from a flagon and a chunk of bread was the only permitted food.

Their third day of travel Deirdre spotted a church's thick bell tower and then a large priory of gray stone came into view. Soldiers by the hundreds massed around the priory surrounded by colorful blue and white striped tents. Several soldiers rode by their party and hailed Wrothbury in recognition. Never did Deirdre fear or dread for a journey to end as she did this one. But all too soon, they entered the priory's gates. Monks in loose fitting gowns of brown with their hands hidden in bellowing sleeves conversed as they heeded the call of the bells. They scurried toward a structure with stain-glassed windows. Several grooms-men wearing the king's livery ran up to take the earl's and his retinue's horses.

They were ushered into an outer chamber, where Wrothbury left her. Under guard, Deirdre waited for the earl's return. Taking a seat on a long wooden bench, she stared at the stark interior of the priory converted from a place of men who served God, to a place that held the ailing king and his courtiers. Wall sconces burned, giving flickering light to the long corridor. At the end of the corridor armed guards faced her way and stood at the ready, lances in hand.

The wait became insufferable and her imagination soared with all sorts of possibilities. What could be the worst punishment meted out? She didn't think the king would kill her, but with Wrothbury's influence, she wasn't so sure.

At long last, the large double doors opened and a small man in a long black flowing robe hastened toward her.

"Countess Wrothbury, follow me."

She obeyed. The faster her heart beat the slower she walked. She didn't want to go through those doors. The monk's tonsured head gleamed in the many wall sconces lighting their way. He held the door for her and offered her a tight smile as she stepped within. He then shut the door with a loud clang, making her flinch.

Wrothbury stood beside the king who sat on an improvised throne. A thick blanket covered his lap and legs, a fire snapped and burned hot from the nearby fireplace. The king's hair, white as a swan's, flared out beneath his crown. Even in sickness he wore his status.

Most men would have been prostrate on the floor in front of the king, begging for forgiveness, and trying to keep their heads attached. Not Deirdre. She clasped her hands in front of her and stared at the king. To her, he appeared quite shrunken, a mere shadow of the formidable man he once was. He coughed a loud rattling sound, and a retainer was quick to his side with a goblet. The smell of warm spiced wine and medicinal herbs filled the air. Holding the cup to the royal lips, the retainer urged the king to drink.

"Kneel before your king, Countess Wrothbury," barked another attendant.

Deirdre knelt, but not toward Edward, she knelt in the direction of Scotland.

"Madam, what are you about?" Wrothbury said, the anger in his voice edging to the surface.

"I'm doing as told—I kneel to my king."

Realizing what she was doing, everyone exclaimed in dismay.

"The devil take you, madam." Wrothbury cursing under his breath jerked her around to face King Edward.

"He already has," she spat at Wrothbury. Her meaning well noted.

Wrothbury planted a booted foot in the middle of her back and forced her flat against the cold stone of the floor. "Would my Liege rid me of this woman and her insolence?" He stood like a conqueror with his arms crossed, his club foot pressed hard against her back.

Deirdre wisely said nothing.

"Ah…Countess Wrothbury. Like a worrisome fly on a horse, you have defied me. I still remember that long ago day when you rode over the hillside. Tell me, how did it feel to see your father die before your very eyes?" said the king.

Deirdre struggled to get out from under Wrothbury's boot. Her movements almost upended him, and he fought to regain his balance. She stood. When Wrothbury would grab her again, Edward flicked a warning with his hand.

"Let her be," he ruled. "Come closer, Countess."

Deirdre slowly moved directly in front of him. Up close, the ravages of age were even more noticeable. His face was a spider-web of wrinkles and deep grooves. His voice, shaky, was no longer the firm voice that had ordered England for the past thirty-five years.

He spoke, "Ah, madam, it is with reluctance that I must carry out the sentence that I've promised your husband I'll do. I ask that you swear fealty to me here and now, tell me I'm your only king, the King of England as well as Scotland."

She stared into eyes that were opaque with ill health and death. Gone was the brilliant blue, replaced with clouded watery eyes that had seen far too many disturbing things in a lifetime. Those eyes watched her with curiosity.

"I canna plead fealty to England whilst I stand before the verra man who killed my father and laughed as he did so. Ye are no' the man that Andrew Brodie was, nor will ye ever be. I curse ye for all the Scots ye have killed. Nay, Robert de Brus is my king. And if I could, I would place on his head the crown that ye wear before me."

Wrothbury swore under his breath.

The king stared at her. Only a small twitch in the corner of his mouth betrayed his anger. "On your knees—now!"

Deirdre did as told.

King Edward pointed a shaky finger at her. "You will wish you had died back at Brodie land. For, I'm putting you in a cage to rot and the vultures will pick your bones!" A guard jerked her to her feet as the king continued. "This will take place in the walled city of Falconshire, a township under your husband's control. Falconshire is so close to Scotland you will be able to smell its air. And since you like kneeling in the direction of Scotland, I will make sure your cage hangs facing it…" his words eroded into a dry hacking cough.

Deirdre was dismissed. Wrothbury took her arm and backed them out of the room.

Once outside the king's chamber, the earl steeled a glance at her. "Falconshire," he spat. "Like a yoke to oxen, you hang from my neck. Damn your accursed fealty." And with those words, he turned and left. His deformed gait made a strange dragging hiss on the floor of stone.

Soldiers ushered her away.

As foretold by the king, Falconshire was in England's far Northwest region close to the Scottish border. The land and township was part of

Wrothbury's vast holdings recently awarded to him by his majesty. Falconshire was also strategic for troop movements, and a coup for whichever country held the walled city. The township, as of this day, was under Wrothbury's strong command, but perhaps in another year, it would be taken by the Scots. Inland from the North Sea by several miles, Falconshire found itself shrouded in a prevalent morning mist until the sun broke through. The area had an unforgiving climate.

Upon Deirdre's arrival at Falconshire, they took her inside the walled city, and put her inside a dungeon. With only one guttering candle to cut the darkness, she sat in damp clothes in a filthy cell and waited. Loud hammering echoed as they built the cage that would house her. She bowed her head and prayed for the strength needed to brave what was ahead. If Jesus could endure carrying his cross to his crucifixion, for certes, she could endure imprisoned in a cage.

She'd been here for two days when four guards came for her, rattling the lock and her nerves as they swung open the wooden door. The earl was not around when she stepped out into daylight for the first time in days and began her journey to the cage. A slow drizzle of rain and heavy mist grayed the area.

Frightened, she quivered to the core of her being. How would the townspeople receive her? Her escort walked her through the center of the village which was inside the tall walls of stone. A scattering of dwellings and vendor stalls ringed the walls perimeter. A blacksmith worked his forge, and women called out to one another while cooking food in large kettles suspended over crackling fires. Deirdre's stomach growled from the aroma. She longed to stand near the fire and warm herself.

The town's citizens stopped what they were doing and formed large groups to watch her pass. Snatches of conversation carried to her. *"Here tell King Edward put Robert the Bruce's sister in a cage like this, but he rescued her."*

She glanced at their faces, old and young alike. Some returned looks of hostility, others wore compassion, and still others were simply curious. The soldiers took her outside through the thick wooden gates and toward the tall outer wall surrounding the township.

The milling people stepped aside bringing the cage into view. Stunned, she sucked in her breath. Certainly all could hear the pounding of her heart. The cage, made entirely of wood, had a solid floor and top and was bigger than she expected. It easily held a chair and a piss pot. Strong vertical bars placed close together ringed its perimeter. Her eyes traveled upward to the top of the cage and followed the chain that snaked up to the battlements and the large metal pulley mechanism that would raise and lower the cage.

So, I'm to swing on the side of the city wall like a wild animal, she thought.

Then in a flurry of excitement and murmuring the crowd parted. The earl, along with the king's retainer, and some other men she didn't recognize, came to a stop next to her.

Deirdre paused in front of Wrothbury who was dressed in his rich clothing of somber black. "Canna ye stop this?" Her eyes beseeched him.

"Are you sayin' you will be obedient? A good wife? I think not. Your waspish tongue and actions before his majesty are your undoing, madam." His mouth tightened into a thin line. She could see his face closing up as his eyes all but looked through her.

When the guards would take her arms, she jerked free of them. "Let me go! I can walk by myself." They ignored her cries and grabbed her.

The guards propelled her forward and yanked her to a stop directly in front of the cage. Desperate she glanced around. But there was no escaping this.

A tall thin man with a long face and the bearing of someone important, approached. As though this was far beneath his dignity, his dark eyes glared at her with disdain. From the cut of his clothes, it appeared he'd dressed in his best finery for just this occasion. A black feather sticking jauntily out of his red felt-hat defied the mist. Beside him stood a plump woman whose brown eyes gazed upon Deirdre with pity.

"Countess Wrothbury, I am Thomas Warren the constable of Falconshire, and your jailer. My wife, Maude, will take care of your needs."

Deirdre lifted her head high.

Thomas Warren unrolled the parchment and began to read in a high nasal voice.

"Be it declared to the populace that on this day, February 25th, the year 1307 of our Lord, that the Countess of Wrothbury is to be imprisoned in said cage that will hang from the walls of Falconshire, England, as so ordered by His Majesty, Edward Plantagenet, the King of England."

Upon completion of reading her sentence, Thomas Warren signaled, and the two guards again took her arms in a bruising grip and escorted her to the cage. They shoved her inside. She stumbled, but managed to break her fall by grabbing the bars. Her hands gripped them so tight that the newly hewn wood bit into her flesh.

They closed the door and locked it.

The constable signaled the soldiers on the top of the wall and they began ratcheting the cage upwards. As the cage swung and bounced in short squeaky jerks, she remained standing. Nothing, not even the imprisonment of her very essence for the last year by Wrothbury prepared her for this. This was even more terrifying. Defiant, she stared at Wrothbury whose face became smaller the higher she went.

When she was jerked to a stop, Wrothbury shot a steely gaze upwards and spoke in a loud voice. "Admit fealty to England and say that you will obey and love your husband, mayhap, King Edward will find forgiveness in his kind heart."

Deirdre, knowing she could never love this man, reacted to the feeling of rebellion that coursed through her. She looked downward, out over the crowd. Sticking her arm through the bars, she pointed her finger at those before her, finally stopping at Wrothbury.

"Long live King Robert de Brus," she yelled with valor.

3 I Will Serve France

Richard de Laci, Comte de Strasbourg, along with his brother Philippe, were summoned to court. Since that disastrous day against the Brodie clan, and Richard's return home, he continued to amass great power by becoming his king's defender on the Germanic border. Although Richard's domain wasn't part of France's territory, France's king had declared that it was and was set on keeping it that way. Richard spent time repelling incursions upon French soil by German poachers, and bandits who upon caught, pleaded that they acted in their Emperor's name, Albert l, and the House of Hapsburg.

Upon their arrival at Vincennes, the brothers were housed in the finest of chambers and waited until early evening before being brought into the king's private quarters.

They knelt on bended knees, side by side in homage before King Philip. The brothers greatly resembled each other, but where Richard's hair was black and his body tall and muscled, Philippe's hair was brown, his body tall and lithe. Both men were garbed in elaborately designed mid-calf tunics that flowed over tight hose. Richard's clothing was of subtle, dark rich browns. Philippe, the more outgoing of the two, wore colorful hues of red. They wore their cloaks pulled back over one shoulder to show off their fine garments and their weapon belts that held long daggers with jeweled-hilts.

Richard, still kneeling, raised his head and met the king's blue-eyed gaze that topped a long slender nose. King Philip IV, known as 'Philip the Fair' because of his fine looks, had ruled France since the age of seventeen. Now in his prime at forty, he set lofty goals, and obtained them. He was pious, self-righteous, and had the killer instinct of a hawk. The Templars who he'd long persecuted could attest to the king's killer instinct.

"I give you leave to stand, brothers de Laci," the king said in a commanding voice while situating his long purple robe covered with golden fleur-de-lis's. "Are your chambers to your liking?" He sat on a high backed chair close to the fireplace that a tall man could walk into with ease and where large burning logs threw out a roaring heat.

Richard nodded and got off his knees that felt flattened from the hard marble floor. *"Oui, Votre Majesté, most comfortable."* He wished the king would speak of the true reason he'd been summoned. But the king never acted in haste, and his relaxed body more than confirmed this.

His majesty allowed his grandiose robe to drop from his shoulders and fall on the marble floor. A young page standing behind him stepped forward to scoop up the royal wrap and was almost lost in its voluminous folds.

"Ah…" his highness sighed, rolling his neck making the bones pop. He left his chair and approached the elegant set table to gaze with appreciation at the food that filled the chamber with mouthwatering scents making hungry stomachs growl. He paused to sniff at each dish before sitting down behind the long table. *"Venez—venez."* He motioned, making his rings on each finger glint in the candlelight.

Richard glanced at his brother, Philippe who returned his amused gaze with one of his own. They took chairs deliberately placed across the table directly facing the king. Richard knew his majesty liked to study facial reactions and could gauge a man's thoughts by them. Richard did his best to keep his face passive no matter the king's spoken words. But his brother had yet to master the art of subtlety, and Philippe would give his true reactions away by loudly exclaiming.

After the servants put a sample of each dish on the men's trenchers and filled their wine goblets to overflowing, they were dismissed with the wave of a royal hand.

They ate in silence. Richard found the stuffing in a game hen most delectable and couldn't place the spice used in it.

King Philip finally spoke. "I would impart vital information that is to be kept secret until the event actually takes place." The sound of clattering spoons against the fancy metal trenchers stopped.

Richard put his spoon down and gave the king his full attention. "Oui, my liege, and that information is?"

"That my daughter Isabella is to finally wed England's King Edward." He grinned, apparently liking the surprised affect his announcement made.

Even this news made Richard struggle to maintain composure. "And when is this marriage to happen?" He admired the man for this incredible coup of joining two of the most powerful countries in Europe. He also knew rumors swirled about the courts of Europe saying the young English King was *effeminate*. Constantly compared to his late father, the word is that he couldn't have possibly came from the loins of Edward I, for the son lacked the want to hound the Scots to hell and back. But in all fairness, England's king was new to the crown and the throne.

King Philip imparted with more astounding information. "The wedding is to take place at Boulogne in the New Year. The contracts are signed, and later this week I'll meet with his highness's emissaries to go over plans for the event."

Philippe de Laci leaned slightly forward. "Majesté, will you need an escort to the ceremony?"

"Non, my plans are well laid, including my escort," the king said most pleasant. He then took a sip of wine swishing it inside his mouth.

"*Votre Majesté,*" Richard said politely, "If you don't have need of my, or Philippe's services, then I fail to see what this has to do with us. Why are we here?" Richard tore a leg from the game hen and continued to eat the juicy meat.

"France must take advantage of England's unfortunate leadership or should I say lack of it. By putting my daughter on the throne of England, I'll be indirectly ruling England. I'll know all that happens on English soil. Rumors abound that England's king is no ruler, and to the dismay of the land barons, his rumored *lover*, Gaveston, does the ruling for him. Old King Edward must be turning over in his grave." The king continued to study the food, and pointing to a dish of cooked eels, he tapped his trencher. His retainer quickly complied and dished the eels onto his majesty's trencher.

"Then do you say your daughter is willing to go to the bed of a man whose desire is not for women?" Richard heard a slight snort from his brother, and could well imagine the smile on Philippe's face.

"Oui, Isabella does and will do so. She is my daughter and knows this little inconvenience is part of ruling a country."

"*Little inconvenience* you say?" Richard's back stiffened, the king's words perplexing. "*A monumental* inconvenience if an heir is to be produced, is it not?"

The king's blue eyes danced. "Ah…my friend, you must know that a king, as well as commoners, are cuckold everyday."

"I suppose you speak the truth, but I would never cuckold or betray a man and most of all, a king. Wives are forbidden fruit to me." Richard's uncompromising thoughts on the subject surfaced.

Greatly amused, Philip tossed his royal head back in a jovial laugh. "I had forgotten how firm your beliefs are." He singled out Philippe. "Is your brother always so staid?"

"Most always. Richard takes life too serious. He thinks to carry the ill weight of all those about him. He hasn't learned to share the burden with others."

Indeed, Richard hadn't been able to share the burden. Being the eldest of three siblings and upon the death of their parents almost ten years ago, Richard had inherited the family castle, Château Falaise, and its massive holdings. But having inherited all and helped to raise his siblings, Richard was loath to turn his brothers out to seek their own fortunes. Instead, they earned their way in life by working for him. Philippe, closest to Richard in age by two years, was in charge of their large army. Valentin, two years younger than Philippe, was part of that army and patrolled the vast borders of Falaise. Richard wasn't sure what to do with his sister Pernelle who in his eyes was a hellion. Being the only girl and the youngest they spoiled and coddled her unmercifully. King Philip was intent on making a match for Pernelle, one that would further his ambitious schemes. The name of Julien Quesnel, the son of a baron whose domain was next to Luxembourg was a name mentioned more than once to Richard.

Turning his attention back to the king, Richard ignored the barbs made against him, and said in a level voice, "I still do not understand why we've been summoned."

"It is most simple. I've secretly pledged to secure the crown of Scotland on the head of Robert le Bruce. He fights not only the English, but some of his own barons to keep it there. I see in this Bruce a formidable ally, one who is willing to fight for his beliefs and those of his country. He has Scotland's interests at heart, not his own. He is a rare man whose personal ambitions do not cloud his vision of a free and independent Scotland. It's been years of fighting with England to secure my own crown. I think to help this man with an army to fight against the English."

Richard's throat, along with the bird he chewed, became quite dry. He washed his food down with some wine. The meaning of backstabbing more than shed its light. The king played a deadly game of subterfuge. His appetite gone, he rinsed his fingers in the tiny water nefs provided for that very thing, and dabbed them on the napkin. It was all so clear. He dipped his head toward his majesty.

"I'm to take an army to Scotland to fight against English tyranny. That is why I'm here. Oui?" Richard stated.

King Philip laughed. "How perceptive of you. During his long reign, England's King Edward covered Scotland with castles he built to garrison his soldiers. Also, rebellious Scottish earls that give their allegiance to England now sit most comfortably behind those fortresses. Your orders are to gather an army of mercenaries of which will be dispersed between fighting for the Scottish king and helping you siege the castles. I'll factor in some of my own soldiers and the money to finance this campaign. Do not wear or fly any standards proclaiming you to be French," he commanded.

Richard glanced at his brother whose eyes were already shinning with the impending mission. "How long do you expect us to be in Scotland?" He was remembering his own last failed attempt when sent by this very king to spy on the King of England. Richard contemplated the beautiful Scottish maiden that had almost been his undoing. Deirdre. He couldn't help but wonder how she fared. But knowing the Earl of Wrothbury, Richard would not wager that she lived past the day he'd met her. He often thought of the time when he'd held her so near to his heart and the soft heather scent of her skin had wafted around him. He became aware of the king's voice…

"…That will depend on what's achieved while there—will it not," the king countermanded. "I send you de Laci's because I know you both place France's welfare before all others."

"Then you have no qualms about sending us to fight against the very people you are marrying your daughter to rule?" Richard's brow creased.

Philip shrugged. "Non, Isabella will not have instant power laid at her feet. My daughter will find it to be an uphill battle."

"Votre Majesté, I can only hope I do not end up fighting against your daughter, for you are putting me in a most precarious situation—"

"Do not worry. The only fighting that Isabella is likely to do is against this…this…man called Gaveston. I hope by then you'll be clear of Scotland and peace started between the two countries," decreed the royal. He washed his fingers and then signaled to his retainer who brought forth a piece of parchment with written instructions and orders for the royal coffers to provide Comte de Strasbourg with his needs.

Richard read his orders then passed it to Philippe who scrutinized each word before carefully folding the parchment and placing it inside his waist pouch.

"All is well with your orders?" the king asked.

"Most well," Richard answered, for even if he didn't agree, there was nothing he could do.

His majesty stood. "I pray for an expeditious journey. And France wishes you God speed and a safe return."

4 The Pardon

Falconshire, England
November 1307

It was cold—so terribly cold and the meager fire burning in the constable's outer chamber didn't begin to reach the bedchamber where Deirdre lay. Having gone into labor while in the cage, the guards had ignored her cries for help until it was almost too late. When they became aware that their most prized political prisoner was about to give birth, they lowered the wooden structure and carried her to Constable's Warren's chambers where his wife Maude was skilled as a mid-wife.

Like a strutting cock, the Earl of Wrothbury waited in the constable's outer chambers. He waited to take his child, but most of all, waited to see if Deirdre was ready to become a dutiful wife. It mattered not that his rape of her was the result of the babe, for his act of force appeared long forgotten. When her time drew near, he'd journeyed to Falconshire to be present for the grand occasion.

He stood in front of the meager fire, his hands clasped behind his back and thought back to last August when summoned by Deirdre, a curt message that told him he had gotten her with child and she needed coin and essentials to survive her imprisonment. Only the thoughts of having a son stirred him into action. He started sending coin for her care by messenger.

Upon this grand and long awaited news, Wrothbury had ridden post-haste to London and Westminster. His intent was to procure a pardon for her. His liege King Edward had died in July at Lanercost, and it felt strange to see his son Edward sitting on the throne. But not so strange since Wrothbury spent several months enjoying the current king's hospitality before he deemed it was time to journey to Falconshire.

When he and his retinue arrived at Falconshire after the sun had set, they pounded on the gates and insisted they allow him entry. He refused to meet with his wife in the cell they kept her in at night and insisted they bring her to the constable's chambers. Once there, wearing filthy rags, yet standing tall and defiant, his wife stared at him with wary, hate-filled eyes.

Putting on a grand display, he gleefully produced a rolled up missive from his waist pouch and read it out loud.

'Be it known on this day, September the eighth, the year 1307, that I, Edward II, King of England do rescind said proclamation of one Edward I, imprisoning Countess Deirdre Brodie Wrothbury. On this day, I, King Edward, degree that Countess Wrothbury is free from her present imprisonment.'

Her loud gasp echoed in the small chamber and he enjoyed bringing forth such a reaction.

She was a free woman.

No matter what, the edict so ordered.

When Deirdre reached for the document, he selfishly held it aloft, putting his hand out like a barrier.

"Not so fast, wife. I've conditions you must first meet. One is to publicly denounce Robert the Bruce and swear loyalty to the king who generously gives you your freedom. The second is to proclaim England as your country and me as the husband you love. Only then will I take you from this pest hole."

"The edict does not require that I do so. It simply says I'm free. Is this King's Edward's requirements, or yours?" she spat out.

"Mine." He gloated.

His gaze took in her body that was round and large with his child. Curious as to what it felt like, he placed his hand over her protruding abdomen. She drew away as fast as a viper's strike.

"Who knows of this edict?" she asked. "Who else has read it? Constable Warren perhaps?"

Their thoughts were exactly alike. The more people that knew about the pardon then all the better for her. But he was much too cunning.

"Three only. His majesty, me, and you my lovely wife. Hmmm, four if one counts the scribe that inked the parchment." His mouth formed a sly smile that matched his eyes. "This document is mine to do as I see fit."

Elation and despair flickered across Deirdre's face. "I canna believe the king would issue such and not mean for ye to have me freed. Mayhap if he hears that ye play games with me, he will force his edict to be followed to the word."

Wrothbury scoffed. "He is most busy with issues that are more important, like preparing to continue his father's campaign against your people." He flashed the document at her. "Madame?" When she didn't reply, he folded the parchment and put it inside his waist pouch.

She turned and reaching the door, paused. "There is nothing more to say. Ye will be notified when I give birth so that ye may come for this child." She walked away.

Refusing to scream and give the earl the satisfaction of hearing her pain, Deirdre gulped in air, the inside of her body was being shredded by knives. Leaning back on her elbows, she watched Maude Warren, the constable's wife, who was between her splayed thighs waiting for the baby's head to crown. Mary Clair, who accompanied Wrothbury to Falconshire, knelt behind Deirdre holding her head. She wiped perspiration from Deirdre's face, and tried her best to be encouraging.

Deirdre's lips drew back in a grimace as she bore down, trying to rid herself of the pain tearing though her body. She hated the babe in her womb. She squirmed, wanting to be free of Wrothbury's baby, convinced the bairn would come out with horns and hooves, certainly a spawn of the devil, and one that she was prepared never to see.

"Bear down, milady! That's it—push—push! I see its head," Maude exclaimed.

She obeyed, she pushed, she strained, the baby squirted from her body. The pain eased the moment Maude placed the squalling babe on her stomach.

"Where did I put those scissors?" Maude said, and turned to search for them.

Deirdre stared blindly at the ceiling and didn't dare look upon the infant. She groped for the baby's face. Slipping her hand across its nose and mouth, she wanted to snuff its life and fool everyone that it was stillborn. But her baby chose that moment to squirm, and moving its head let out a soft mewing sound. Deirdre's finger accidentally slipped inside its mouth, feeling the warm moist tongue. She snatched her hand back just as Maude turned around and with a quick snip of the scissors, severed the cord.

"Be quick, Mary Clair, get the wee one washed before it freezes to death," Maude urged, and then handed the baby to the handmaiden who immediately started to bathe it in a small tub of warm rosewater.

Mary Clair cooed and sang to the babe while Maude took care of Deirdre. She sponged her body and changed her gown. Deirdre, no longer able to suppress her curiosity, asked, "Is the bairn male or female? Does it have all its toes and fingers—is it deformed in anyway?"

"I thought ye did not want to know a thing about it," Maude softly reminded her.

"Tell me," Deirdre pleaded, her resolve at not looking or wanting the child fast receding. She watched Mary Clair approach and the tiny arm that stole from the woolen blanket.

Mary Clair grinned and her eyes twinkled as she gave over her bundled joy into Deirdre's outstretched arms. Deirdre unbound the baby. She had a daughter. The wee baby was like a new leaf still folded with her legs pulled up about her stomach, her tiny fingers questing. She was a perfect little girl with ten perfect toes and ten perfect fingers. Deirdre eagerly perused her little mouth stretched into a yawn.

"We fought hard, aye." Knowing her milk wasn't in yet, Deirdre put her babe to her breast and gazed at the tiny rosebud of a mouth latch onto her nipple. Each pull of the babe's mouth tugged at Deirdre's heart, her mind. How could she live without this little one? Deirdre swore that the wizened little eyes looking up at her dared her not to love her.

Deirdre ran her fingers over the little miracle, and could see nothing of Wrothbury in her. The babe was a miniature of Deirdre. Like the fluff on a baby duck the baby's wispy reddish-brown curls wrapped around her finger. Tracing a finger along the tiny shell of an ear, Deirdre didn't think to ever see such a wee little life. The baby's hand kneaded the flesh of Deirdre's breast, the feeling like being stroked by a downy feather.

"Milady," Mary Clair said, "shall I tell the earl he has a daughter?"

"Nay—not yet. Allow me time with her, please." Like a mother lion protecting her cub, she would swear fealty to the devil himself to get out of this imprisonment. The thought of her wee daughter raised by Wrothbury and his twisted mind was beyond her grasp. Nay, he wouldna have her child. "Look at her Maude, is she no' a sweet bairn?"

Maude, having finished cleaning up after the birth, leaned over to beam at the sweet babe's face. "Aye, milady, I think she is quite fine. And being born in this place that is no better than a stable, I would say she is like the Lord Jesus. Mayhap ye will call her Mary?"

"I think to name her Colleen after my mam."

A pounding on the door startled them. "Is my child born yet?" Wrothbury bellowed through the door.

"Nay, Milord, we will come and tell ye when it is." Maude was quick to say, "Moan, milady, moan as if in labor."

Deirdre, recalling her recent pain, began to moan quite convincingly.

The deceit was played out several times, giving Deirdre time to explore her baby from front to back and toe to head. When she placed a kiss on the fat wrinkle at the back of her neck, the rose scent of the baby came wafting up and Deirdre thought her heart to burst with so much love. Her mind firmed with the intent to leave here with her daughter.

When the earl would knock again and Deirdre played out the farce, baby Colleen let out a cry causing Wrothbury to throw open the door and boldly enter. Maude Warren slipped from the room while Mary Clair discreetly stayed across the chamber.

Unable to hide his anticipation, he slowly approached, dragging and limping in his usual gait. Clasping his hands behind his back, he leaned over to peer down at the baby Deirdre held protectively in her arms.

"Do I have a son?" he asked in a hopeful voice. "Is it straight of limb?"

Deirdre's arms tightened on the baby. "Nay, no son. Ye have a perfectly formed daughter."

"I see," he said, unable to hide his disappointment. "It would have been too much to ask that this be a son. You couldn't give me the satisfaction of such a joy, now could you?"

"Then if ye loathe her so, I ask that ye let me keep her. Dinna take her from me." Deirdre kissed the tiny forehead, pleading, her eyes never left Wrothbury's who returned a chilling gaze, his mouth a firm slit.

"I do not remember saying I loathed her, and be it a son or daughter, no child of mine will be in this dung hole longer than necessary."

"Then show my pardon to Constable Warren. Let me go with ye and be with Colleen. Please, she needs my love, my nurturing."

Wrothbury appeared taken aback. "One thing at a time, madam. Colleen? You think to call her Colleen?"

"Aye, after my own mam who died when I was but five."

"Well...I think to call her Joanna," he said, his face going stern, the lines around his mouth deepening. He held out his hands for the child, but Deirdre wouldn't give her up.

"'Tis a certain then, we can call her Joanna Colleen, aye?" Deirdre suggested, and from the speculative look on his face could tell he was seriously considering it.

With a shrug of his shoulders, he surprisingly agreed. "Joanna Colleen Dufray, it is. Now, about you begging to return to Wrothbury Castle. Sweet words…wife. I assume you're willing to go in front of Falconshire and submit yourself and new cause to them."

"I would give up my life fer my wee bairn," she said most fierce.

"Careful what you say, Countess, as that I can oblige most willingly. But . . . alas, I'm no longer prepared to take you back to my home. I do not believe you're contrite enough, that you are lying to be with the child," his words were as lashing as his fists could be. He gloated, his cruelty again unleashed.

"Nay…dinna do this. Dinna take what the Lord has so kindly placed in my hands. Dinna take away the reason fer me to live. Joanna needs my breasts, my milk…please."

But Deirdre's words might as well be spoken on the wind. He was unyielding and her heart tore when he belligerently held out his hands for baby Joanna.

Deirdre kissed her daughter's cheeks and mouth. She memorized every feature of Joanna's sweet face. And with hot tears blinding her, she handed him the child.

She glared in dismay as Wrothbury held Joanna who had started to cry. When Deirdre struggled to get out of bed, he placed a hand on her chest and shoved her back down. He cautioned her not to try anything. Awkwardly holding the baby against his chest, he turned to leave.

"Wait!" Deirdre called out, stopping him. "Will ye bring her back to see me?"

Wrothbury shook his head and started to leave when she loudly said, "Wrothbury, ye leave me here illegally. I'm going to write the king and tell him that ye will not show the edict so I can be released."

"And which king is that, Madame? For certes you do not recognize

England's Edward as your king. And, there will be no writing to Robert the Bruce to tell him about me when he did not ink the edict. Nay, you cook in a broth of your own making. Mary Clair, here, take the child, and come with me."

"Wrothbury, promise me ye will no' harm Joanna?"

"Madam, why would I harm what I've coveted from your womb since that day at Foxlair? I just did not know that it would take almost two years to achieve. To be sure, I'll treat her as though she is a queen." And with that said, he walked from the room and shut the door.

Joanna's faint cries echoed down the hallway and faded.

Deirdre eyeballed the door and then her empty arms.

"Maude!" she cried. And watched with relief as the woman's stout body slipped back into the room. Maude knelt to enclose her into her warm arms, extending kindness, and kindling the start of a strong friendship this day.

"There now...milady," she crooned, trying to give comfort. "We must be careful. If my acts of kindness to ye are discovered, my Thomas will replace me with an uncaring guard."

Deirdre sobbed against the woman's bosom.

Once again, someone she loved was taken away from her, making her wonder if she was truly cursed. Had God placed her on this earth to constantly burden her with grief? The injustice weighed heavily. She thought back over her entire life, and could rightfully say she'd done nothing wrong to bring any of this upon herself. The only thing was being born Scottish and on the wrong side of an invisible border.

Deirdre seethed. She silently swore at Christ Jesus—she would get Joanna back, with or without his help.

5 Endure Boldly

Falconshire, Northern England
March 1308

The wind, strong enough to rock Deirdre's cage and bite through her cloak had her wrapping the meager cloth about her body. The gesture was useless, nothing helped to ward off the cold.

She had been in prison fourteen months, the last eight of them illegally so. After Joanna's birth, Wrothbury made good his threat and withheld coin for Deirdre's food and necessities. He'd also kept Mary Clair from visiting and bringing word of Joanna.

Deirdre's clothing was becoming threadbare. The constable groused that no coin had crossed his palms since the birth of her daughter. Her plight turned for the worse, and Wrothbury waited out her will, thinking to subdue her.

She told Constable Warren about the pardon, that the Earl of Wrothbury had an edict from King Edward saying she was a free woman. But the constable told her he needed proof. That he would have to see the document of which she spoke of, a document that he didn't believe existed. She couldn't come up with a way to show proof, making the constable scorn her even more. The only thing that helped Deirdre endure her imprisonment was the knowledge that Mary Clair was taking care of Joanna.

Deirdre and her jailers had long settled into a reluctant routine. Early in the morning they would take her to the cage where she would remain until evening. Before darkness fell, they lowered the cage and escorted her back to her cell to spend the night. They had become lax in feeding her during the day so she carefully hoarded something from breakfast, a piece of bread or cheese, by tucking it into her embroidery basket for later. Maude Warren would bring her evening meal and try to cheer her with gossip, but the news Deirdre always craved was never forthcoming. Maude claimed that Thomas hadn't received word from Wrothbury either. Deirdre believed her.

She could say her survival depended on being inside at night. Even though the cell was filthy, it afforded some protection from the elements and allowed her to write letters. And write them she did. Pleading her cause to the English King, she'd given letter after letter to the guards and could only pray they delivered them. Not ignoring Wrothbury, she also sent letters to him, though no answer was forthcoming. Constable Warren complained about the amount of parchment she was using, and without Wrothbury's coin to purchase more, ordered her inkhorn, quill, and parchment removed. Effectively taking away from her any means to get away from her confinement.

And flexing their might even further, for the past two nights they had left her outside. Nor had any food been forthcoming making her wonder why Maude hadn't insisted they feed her. Deirdre figured that Constable Warren warned his wife not to interfere, that he was following the earl's orders to starve her into submission.

This night, she was relieved that they were leaving her out again. Their actions had forced a decision from her, and that was to escape. She reached into her basket and removed the long cloth she embroidered on. That sturdy cloth, now yards long would become her means of escape. She'd been looking at it and concluded that it would get her close enough to the ground that she could easily drop the rest of the way. She remembered well each stitch that created a colorful flower, or people doing everyday things, images of what she used to do before abducted.

Deirdre craned her neck to see past the solid top of the cage. The rope that raised and lowered the cage disappeared into the darkness. Unable to see the top of the battlements, she found it strange that the guards hadn't lit the torches that usually blazed the battlement's perimeter. She wondered the whereabouts of Miles Woodstock, a guard with a vile attitude, and one that mirrored Wrothbury's mistreatment of her.

All was quiet.

She foraged in her embroidery basket and took out a pair of scissors. Sitting on the cage floor she dangled her legs through the bar openings. Using the sharp tip as a chisel, Deirdre started chipping away at one of the wooden bars, working close to the base where it seated inside the hole. The loud scratching sound seemed to echo around the area and she tried to work in silence. Satisfied that the bar was loose enough, she began to turn the wooden shaft then pushed against the wood, forcing it to break free from the hole that held it firmly in place. She sat the bar down and started on the next one in line.

Her thoughts inevitably turned to Joanna who was now five months old. Was the color of her hair dark or light? Did her wee bairn have sky blue eyes like hers or the cold gray of Wrothbury's? But even gray eyes would be acceptable for she just knew Joanna's would have a twinkle behind those cloudy depths. Did anyone play with her or did they let her cry unheeded in her crib? Certainly, Mary Clair would make faces at her and tickle her feet. The more she thought about Joanna the more determined she became. She wanted to see her baby grow, but most off all, she wanted Joanna to know that she was her mam.

Knowing there was a decree from the king opening her cell door and that Wrothbury kept it to himself rankled Deirdre beyond acceptance. Her jaw firmed, once free from here, she would go to London to see the king. She would beg and plead for another copy of her pardon.

Finished with the last bar, she placed it next to the others. Certain that her thin body would fit through the opening, she grabbed the embroidery cloth and prayed the long narrow length would help her reach the ground. Securely tying one end of the cloth to the bar, she then tossed the rest out of the cage. The white fabric fluttered like a flag before disappearing into the darkness.

Lying on her stomach and dangling her legs through the opening, she gripped the cloth in one hand and held fast to one of the upright bars with the other. "Damn ye, Wrothbury—I hope Satan pulls ye into hell!"

Pushing away from the cage, and going hand-over-hand, she started to work her way down. Although the night air was chilling and a clinging mist had already started to cloak the township, sweat beaded her face and body, staining her bodice dark. Her damp palms soaked into the cloth. "Deedee...ye fool," she moaned and thought herself extremely foolhardy to attempt this.

She slid down the fabric and was over a body length away from the cage when the low growls and snarling started below her.

"Wolves. God—no!" a desperate moan escaped her.

The wild stench of them drifted upwards, almost overpowering. With the wolves snapping at her feet, her escape was doomed. Her heart thudded so loud she thought they could hear it clear upon the battlements. She tightened her hold on the cloth, but her hands started to shake from the strain. The cloth began to tear and a scream erupted from her, echoing around the still night like an alarm bell. The beasts played with the cloth, shaking it, ripping it from her hands.

She dangled.

Not wanting to be torn apart by the wolves propelled her into action. She pulled herself upward, grabbed a bar, and hauled herself into the cage. Prostrate on the cage floor, she panted, her heart pounded so fast, it hurt. Did she really think her foolhardy attempt would succeed? That she would never leave this pesthole without Wrothbury first opening the door.

"Are ye having trouble with yer furry friends?" A voice, low and menacing floated out of the dark. "Perhaps we should give 'em some-thin' to eat? What say ye, Countess? Ye…perhaps?" Miles Woodstock laughed.

Torches flared above on the battlements, biting into the darkness, yet not quite reaching her cage. They'd discovered her pitiful attempt. Miles, the despicable guard, had probably been watching all along.

"Oh…gore!" Frantic, Deirdre rolled over and rapidly pulled the embroidery cloth up into the cage and shoved its long length back into the basket.

The cage was slowly being lowered.

Yellow eyes glowed up at her. Working in haste, she tried to replace one of the bars, but her shaking hands betrayed her and it wouldn't seat. A sliver pierced her finger making her drop the bar that rolled close to the edge. She snatched it back just in time.

"Miles dinna lower me. The wolves—the wolves. Please, Miles," she shouted eyeing the gaping hole they could fit through with ease.

The cage jerked to a stop. "What is the matter, Countess? D'ye not want to be eaten tonight?" Miles snickered, "The cage will protect ye, will it not?"

No, it would not. Deirdre snapped another bar in place and had one more to go. The cage hit the ground. Eye-to-eye with the wolves, frantic, she tried to seat the last shaft in place when one of the large beasts leaped at her. Its body slammed against the cage almost lodging its head inside the hole. It bared sharp fangs that dripped with saliva. The impact made the loosened bars strain but they held.

She screamed, and grabbed up the last shaft of wood. She pounded the wolf's head. Lightning fast, a paw shot out and clawed her hand.

"Damn ye—beast of Satan!" She fought back, whacking its nose, drawing blood. The wolf yelped and backed off. Deirdre swung repeatedly. "Go—away!" The wood cut the air. "Go—away!"

A flaming torch careened down amidst the two wolves, scattering them, sending them to slink off toward the forest.

Shouts and commotion came from up above and she recognized

constable's Warren's voice as he ordered Miles to raise the cage.

Deirdre sank to her knees and glancing upward yelled into the dark, "Thomas Warren—take me inside. I'm hurt—I bleed."

"Not this night, Countess. Ye will stay where ye are."

"Please, Constable...."

The cage was raised.

Vapor rose in ghostly wisps from amongst the tall trees of the forest. The sun formed the vertical bars into dark wavy shadows that crept across the cage floor. Deirdre lay on her side and pulled her mantle around her, but it offered little in the way of warmth and protection against the biting cold.

The township was starting to stir and loud voices came from within the walled city. Wood smoke coiled above the high wall, carrying with it the smell of cooking. Her growling stomach reminded her that she hadn't eaten for several days.

Deirdre got stiffly to her feet. Her joints ached and her throat burned. Needing to relieve herself, she eyed the small-lidded piss-pot overturned in the corner. She hated to use it, but gave in.

She wished for a pail of water, not only to drink, but also to have a quick wash-up. She hoped to receive the daily bucket of cold water allowed her. Trying to keep up her appearance, she unbraided her long plait and used her fingers as a comb.

When Deirdre's imprisonment was new, the Constable forbade the citizens to talk to her. But as her pregnancy advanced, he relaxed his rigid stance and she was able to make friends with some of the townspeople and guards. She liked the company of Arless Crowther, wife to Emerson a guard on the battlements. After the birth of Joanna, Deirdre was quick to form a binding friendship with Maude Warren who had helped her through the ensuing grief of losing Joanna. Maude would slip occasional treats in her meals. Honey cakes being one of them. More often than not, Maude would visit with Deirdre while she ate.

The sound of horses nickering caused her to stop braiding her hair. She peered south in the direction they were coming from and could see that three men rode in a hastened pace. Their cloaks flapped out behind them like wings of the hawks taking flight from the tall trees in the forest. They rode as though they couldn't reach Falconshire fast enough. What was their mission? Her blood ran cold. Nay, it could not be. Wrothbury wouldn't be sending someone to harm her, would he?

6 This I Promise

Deirdre watched with dread as one of the riders reined in his war-horse.

"Saladin—whoa!" He stared up at the cage. A multitude of emotions changed his features, leaving him looking perplexed. The man moved closer to the cage that was lower to the ground than normal. Gawking, he rudely pointed at her, and she feeling like a wild beast on display, turned her back to them.

"*Mon Dieu*...a woman," one of them exclaimed. His deep voice and French accent sounded familiar to her. She turned her head slightly, allowing her to better hear their words that drifted upward.

"A most strange sight," said the same voice. "I've never looked upon such. Gordon, do you know of this?"

"Aye," another man piped up. "Something nags at me about this. I understand this was a favorite punishment of England's old king. He even caged the King of Scotland's sister as thus." The man now speaking was definitely Scottish. "Let us continue into the township as I crave food as much as I need a good piss."

"One moment," said the Frenchman. "Gordon, Bertrand, go on, I'll follow shortly."

"We canna tarry here."

"And I say we are stopping to eat. Take thy piss you so covet. Go and seek a warm meal. As I said, I'll be close behind."

From the fading sound of the horses, Deirdre knew two of them had left. She could sense that one remained. Could feel his eyes boring into her back. Angry, she shot from her chair and within three brisk steps gripped the bars. She glowered down at the man's dust-covered face.

"Do I have horns? Perhaps a tail? Fer ye look like yer staring at the devil himself," she bristled out, her low raspy voice made even more so by her temper. A voice once heard, not easily forgotten. "Be off with ye—I'm not fer yer amusement." Her scowl deepened, but the insolent man refused to budge. Instead, he had the gall to grin.

"Nor would I ever be so bold to think of you as an amusement for me, Deirdre Brodie," he decreed.

His words, so meaningful, surprised her, melted her scowl, and snapped her mouth shut. She squinted down at the man, searching, trying to think. "How d'ye know...."

The breeze tossed his hair across his face, and in a most familiar movement, he flicked his head to remove the strands. Deirdre found herself staring into friendly eyes that she'd vowed never to forget. And she hadn't. Excitement made her flesh bump and her mouth hang open like a village idiot.

She found her voice. "Richard de Laci, Count of Strasbourg?" His name rolled from her tongue with ease. "Then ye are no' dead." Joy and elation spread through her and nestled into the depths of her being.

He laughed at her words. His grin gleamed white through the travel dust on his face. Spreading his arms wide, he scrutinized himself. "Non, milady, I'm truly in the flesh, and looking upon a woman that I never thought to see again. And one who appears to have gotten herself into a most horrible predicament."

She laughed out loud for the first time in months. Happy for a brief time, she forgot her misery, forgot all but the man below. He surprised her by maneuvering his horse directly below the cage. Kicking free of his stirrups and with boyish enthusiasm, he climbed upon the saddle. He squat, and then shot upwards and grabbed the bars. He fought to still the swaying cage that threatened to knock him over backwards. At last, it stilled. His boots were firmly planted on the leather of his saddle.

"Oh…gore," she said, and sat on the cage floor in front of him. He was close enough that she could see the flecks of gold amidst the green of his eyes, and the lines that formed around his mouth when he smiled at her. He had aged somewhat since she'd been in his arms. His raven black hair held a few threads of gray, and the start of his beard held interesting patterns of gray and black.

Remembering her own sad appearance, she fingered her unfinished braid, and asked herself what could it possibly matter what she looked like to this man? Besides, he had an established life that probably included a wife and child. She was married and an imprisoned woman at that. She shivered at the thought of Wrothbury.

"Mademoiselle, I see that you are cold." Without pause, and holding onto the bar with one hand, he whipped off his fur-lined cloak and shoved it through the bars. "Voila pour vous, Deirdre Brodie."

When their hands touched, she allowed her fingers to linger a little longer than necessary. Their gazes met. She pulled the cloak around her. It felt like a caress, enveloping her. "Mmmm…." She nuzzled against the fur, cocooning herself as she sank into it. The warmth from his body still lingered inside warming hers. Oh…gore…his scent was still there, spicy, woodsy, male.

"Count Strasbourg, ye must leave. It is forbidden to talk to me," she whispered, trying not to draw attention.

He merely smiled. "It pleasures me to talk with you, Deirdre Brodie. No guards will prevent me from doing so."

"My Lord, I'm no longer called Deirdre Brodie."

When he started to speak, a guard yelled down from the battlements interrupting what he would say.

"You—down there! Get away from the prisoner!"

Deirdre saw that Miles Woodstock was fast approaching, sneaking up behind Richard. "Count—" Before she could finish the warning, Miles grabbed the reins and pulled the horse forward, leaving Richard dangling from the rails. His feet sliced empty air, searching for a foothold that was no longer there.

"Jesú!" Richard's grip tightened on the bars. He glanced at Deirdre at the same time the wood made a cracking sound.

"Let go of the bars, they are…" Deirdre's remaining words caught in her throat.

"What?" Richard yelled just as the rail broke and fell to the ground. He grasped the next shaft over. With the cage wildly swinging, the shaft in his right hand broke and Deirdre found her voice at last.

"Loose—they are—"

"Now you say!" Both bars pulled away sending Richard crashing to the ground where he landed flat on his back. Air whooshed from his lungs leaving him in intense pain. The cage gyrated, propelling Deirdre through the gaping hole. He tried to break her fall, but she slammed against his body with enough force to break a few ribs.

"Dieu…" he managed to choke out, in spite of airless lungs.

"Och…see what ye've gone and done." She lay on top of him, her face inches from his and spearing him with a blue-eyed gaze.

"What I have done? Certainly you jest?" Richard bristled. Wasn't he the one flat on his back with this long bodied female pinning him down?

"Constable Warren willna like that I'm out of the cage and—" her words were abruptly cut off as the guards hauled her to her feet.

When Richard started to rise, a long spear was pushed against his throat and he wisely stayed put. But not for long, as two guards seized his long dagger and sword before yanking him upright.

"Unhand me—and do so now." Offended at the rough treatment, Richard tried to pull free, but could not. The guards jerked him about and tightened their hold on each arm. He assessed his chances of escape and concluded it foolhardy to try. He glanced over at Deirdre who returned his stare.

"Miles Woodstock—please. He didna plan to take me from the cage. 'Twas merely curiosity that stayed him to chat."

"Shut yer mouth…Coun…tess," Miles sneered and then shoved her backwards, toppling her to the ground.

Wanting to help her and with the name *Countess* sticking in his mind, Richard started forward but found the spear's sharp point against his neck a goodly deterrent.

Deirdre scrambled to her feet. "Dinna hurt him. 'Tis as I say, he only stopped to talk."

Richard could tell she was trying to draw attention away from him, but he didn't required help to fight his battles, especially female help. Feeling blood trickle down his neck meant they would kill him before asking the truth of the matter. In no position to do otherwise, he wisely checked his anger. He narrowed a look of contempt at the guard named Miles Woodstock. Dressed in the township's livery, a conical helmet framed the man's pudgy face. His chest armor strained to encase his corpulent body.

"Ye are not allowed to talk to Countess Wrothbury." Miles Woodstock's mouth twisted into a smile, showing teeth blackened with decay.

"Countess Wrothbury?" Richard was loathed to learn Deirdre was attached to Wrothbury by marriage. The excited feeling he had upon seeing her was gone. She belonged to another man, his old adversary. If she was bound to Wrothbury, why was she caged like a wild beast? He was going to find out the truth of it. Richard noticed his squire Bertrand Damours and his guide Gordon Bryce, stood alongside several guards. Richard glanced over to see that Deirdre was looking at him with a worried expression.

"They have cut yer neck, does it hurt?" she asked in that deep rich Scottish brogue he so liked to hear.

"Non, Countess Wrothbury, I assure you I'm most fine." The name Wrothbury inflamed him, stuck in his craw.

Richard's guide, Gordon, moved in front of the guard called Miles.

"Count Strasbourg travels through Falconshire only. We stopped for food and if this is yer way of giving succor to weary travelers then we should have given this place a wide berth. I suggest ye release Count Strasbourg and do so now."

Appearing undaunted by Gordon's threats and with enough guards present to make him appear brave, Miles walked over to Gordon and Richard. "Aye? Sure ye both were not trying to help Countess Wrothbury?" He glared at Gordon. "Yer Scottish. She's Scottish. Makes sense." He pointed his pike at Richard. "But you, a Frenchman in Falconshire does not. I say ye are up to mischief, Scottish mischief."

Gordon's hand went for his claymore, his voice deadly. "Watch what ye accuse us of. I think to split yer tongue in two, for it spits forth dung. I...we support the English crown, so do not associate us with this—this traitorous bitch, or Scotland."

Richard flinched at Gordon's harsh words and watched with caution as Deirdre's expression went from concern to distain. But Gordon's words were forgotten when Richard's attention was garnered by another group of armed men approaching.

A tall, thin man leading the soldiers stepped forward and stared. "I'm Thomas Warren, constable of this city and jailer of Countess Wrothbury, who is no longer in her cage." The man's hooded gaze rested on Richard as he spoke. "You must be the one who tried to help the countess escape?"

"Non, I'm being accused unjustly. I was talking to Countess Wrothbury when your man pulled my horse away. The bars simply broke putting us both on the ground." Richard took in the man's dull chest armor, his helmet that set askew on his head, and knew he'd been summoned in haste.

"'Tis forbidden to talk to her. Did she not tell ye that?"

"Oui, she did, but I chose to ignore what she said," he blustered, knowing instantly he'd erred.

"That was most unwise of ye. Ye'll be jailed until we can find out the truth of this matter."

"I'm a friend of the Earl of Wrothbury," Richard said.

"What proof do ye have of such?" The constable challenged.

"My word should be proof enough," Richard said, his anger rising. "I'm a warlord, and an old acquaintance of the Countess and the Earl of Wrothbury. Besides I do not know why Countess Wrothbury is confined as thus. That cage is a most heinous punishment and I wonder what madame could have possibly done to warrant such."

"She is there because the King of England ordered her so," the constable snapped his words, and then asked, "If yer a friend of the Earl of Wrothbury, why do ye not know of this?"

"I've only recently returned to England. I'm on my way to visit with Wrothbury. I would ask that you reconsider putting me in jail," Richard ordered, and could see his request surprised them all.

"Watch him, Thomas," Miles said. "For he appears most crafty. I say ye should jail him."

"I am watching him, Miles, but in all truthfulness he's done nothing to be arrested for." The constable's eyes narrowed and his hand went to his sword. "What name did ye give?"

"I didn't. I'm Comte de Strasbourg from France." Richard's rank was so high that few nobles stood between him and the throne. He heard the sharp intake of breath by all those around him.

Weapons were sheathed. They took in his clothing, seeing what they hadn't bothered to notice before. Even though plain, his garments were of a rich texture, foretelling that he was a wealthy man. Richard remained undaunted and smiled at Gordon and Bertrand.

"I insist on taking Countess Wrothbury where I can converse with her in private. Do you have such a place?"

"But...but," sputtered the constable, "she is a pris—"

"Do not worry." Richard remained nonplus as he studied the posturing constable. "You can post guards. But know this, I went into battle with the Earl of Wrothbury and your good King Edward, God rest his soul." Looking pious and at the heavens, Richard crossed himself and prayed Deirdre would see through his ruse. But a quick glance at her stormy face convinced him that once he was alone with her, he had some fast-talking to do.

Gordon's gaze was sharp with understanding, while a secretive smile creased Bertrand's mouth.

A small crowd of curious onlookers had started to gather and the constable ordered the guards to disperse them. One lone woman approached the constable and leveled a hard stare at him. "What is happening here, Thomas?"

"Nothing that needs you out here. Go back inside and finish your chores." He then turned back to the problem at hand.

However, the woman ignored Thomas, and went to stand next to Deirdre. "Are you well, milady? Where ye hurt during the fall?"

"Nay, Maude, I wasna hurt. Count Strasbourg was gracious enough to catch me," she said with just a touch of humor.

Richard caught the faint curve of Deirdre's mouth and thought perhaps she'd forgiven their strong words calling her a traitor. "Has Countess Wrothbury been fed today?" he thought to ask. When the guards and Maude shook their heads, he ordered, "I want to make sure she gets a meal fitting a countess."

The constable came forward, his hand on the hilt of his sword. "Aye, take her to the tavern, but I will be beside ye and so will my guards."

Richard bent down and picked up the cloak he'd given her. Giving it a quick snap, and with everyone gawking at him, he stood in front of Deirdre and wrapped the cloak around her shoulders. He then took Deirdre Brodie's hand, a woman he'd never forgotten, and now knew why.

Her hand gripped his and from the way she nervously felt her hair and ducked her head, he realized she was embarrassed at her appearance. But to him, she never looked lovelier. She was taller than his remembered vision, and although much too thin, he recalled the shapely body he'd held in his arms that terrible day. She cast a curious blue-eyed glance at him. And he in all thoughtfulness, said, "Would you like to have some personal time to collect yourself, madame?"

Her smile for him was bright. "Aye, that I would, Count Strasbourg." She turned toward Thomas Warren who walked behind them. "Constable Warren, would that I be allowed to cleanse myself?"

"Of course ye can," Maude answered.

They escorted Deirdre inside the dungeon, and left Richard waiting by the doorway. She stepped inside the cell where someone had brought a pail of hot water for her. Her cheeks were warm and her throat hurt to swallow.

Intent on not letting anything keep her from Richard's side, she was quick to use the chamber pot. Unlacing her gown, she pushed it down around her waist, and then dipped a cloth into the water. She took a hoarded piece of lavender soap, and after soaping the cloth, scrubbed her face and entire upper body. She became lightheaded and grabbed the edge of the bucket, steadying herself, and thought it was because she hadn't eaten in several days. Finally the dizziness passed and she dried off and laced her gown back up.

She was careful to wrap her soap and stow it. Not having a mirror to see with, she could only guess at the condition of her hair as she combed and re-braided it. No longer having a decent veil to cover her hair with, she went without.

The Scotsman's words that Richard's sympathies were with the English stuck in her mind. Thinking back to when she first met him during her capture, she was never told his true reasons for being with the English king. That this man who she put such glowing faith these past years might not be as he appears overwhelmed her. In despair, she sat down on the filthy pallet.

She didn't hear Richard enter, but certainly heard the sharp intake of his breath as he exclaimed something vague in French.

He approached her and spoke in very clear English. "This is your cell?" He glanced around the room now in shadow from the flickering candles and took in the filthy straw pallet on the floor, one lone chair, a small wooden chest, and an overflowing piss-pot in the far corner. The stench was horrendous.

"The air is…is…heavy in here." No sooner spoken, he regretted his words. She must realize what he was trying not to say. She did.

"Aye…it smells in here, but the stench of this cell is preferable over the stench of one who supports the English crown. All these years I've thought differently of ye. I thought ye a kind and gentle man. The pedestal that I've had ye on was so tall that ye stood next to God himself. And now I hear that ye side with the English after all." Her words cut through the air like a knife.

Richard recoiled. "I'm not an English sympathizer—I can explain—"

"Why did the man called Gordon say ye side with the English?"

"He said that to turn curiosity away from us. Certainly you could see that I had a spear pushing at my neck, oui?" He watched her debating his words, wondering whether he spoke the truth. He strived to convince her otherwise, to make her think he wasn't a beast that walked with the English. "I cannot explain myself, nor my mission, but understand this, I'm a Frenchman who cares not for the politics of England. Nor do I uphold the ambitions of Edward's whelp, England's present king. Madame, if I sided with the English, why would I have risked King Edward's wrath and tried to help you the day of the invasion?"

"Then d'ye speak in favor of Scotland? Is that what I hear ye say?" Her words were fraught with hope as her eyes searched his face.

He could say no more for fear of betraying himself and his mission. He saw the dried blood on her hand and thinking to change the subject, took her hand within his. He carefully traced the long cuts. "These are fresh. When did this happen?" She tried pulling away, but he held firm. "Tell me."

"Last night." Her gaze met his.

"They leave you out at night?" His jaw clenched in anger.

She nodded and told him the story about her attempted escape.

He released her hand, and paced. His anger at her situation was almost uncontrollable by the time she finished. "Just where did you plan to go?"

"It matters not. I didna plan well and I failed miserably. But since ye broke the bars, I'll not be able to try again. They will secure them even more so."

"Indeed! You keep saying I broke the bars." He bristled, his voice challenging, "Madame, I find that ironic since I was the one dumped on my backside by the shafts that you loosened."

"Count Strasbourg, I dinna ask ye to poke yer nose in my cage, did I? Ye were the one who wanted to look at the fey, did ye no'?" She jabbed him hard in the chest, her fingertip as sharp as a weapon.

Richard glared and rubbed the spot she'd poked. "I was relieved to know *you* still lived, and to find out why *you* were in the cage. If this is how *you* treat people trying to help you, 'tis no wonder *you* are in a cage. I have business at hand instead of being stuck in this damn smelly cell, with a feisty, Scottish—"

"Why ye fobbing…ill-nurtured…hedge-pig! 'Tis sorry I be that I canna offer ye a clean cell to chat with me in."

Richard's mind raced. Mon Dieu, what was wrong with him? He never argued with women, and certainly should not be doing so with the one woman who has haunted him these past years. Already he regretted his harsh words and wondered how he could make amends.

"Countess, I'm sorry to have offended you. It was not my intent, nor do I usually speak in anger like I just did."

She turned to face him, her hands demurely clasped in front of her. "And I'm most sorry to have called ye a hedge-pig." A smile softened her mouth. "But ye bristle like a hedge-pig when yer angry."

"I have been called worse." His laughter rumbled forth. It was contagious and Deirdre joined in. Their moods lightened considerably.

"I had quite forgotten how feisty you are, madame. Let us not keep the Constable waiting any longer than we already have." He stood directly in front of her and wrapped his cloak around her shoulders. With her face so close, all he had to do was dip his head to meet her lips. But she belonged to another man. And yet as he continued to study her, he wondered what she'd do if he kissed her here and now.

People gawked and pointed as Deirdre and her male companions were led across the township square. Not used to seeing the countess walking about, everyone paused and whispered. Deirdre stared back with equal curiosity. Even when taken to and from the cage, and with the dungeon close to the gated entry, she was never in this area of the township. She took in the bustle and vivid colors of the peoples clothing. Some of the wooden buildings that lined against the stone walls were either open stalls for selling, or closed dwellings for living. The smithy was a large open stall with a bright fire burning in the forge. The blacksmith banged his hammer against metal.

Two heavily armed guards escorted the small retinue into the alehouse. Upon entering the dark room, they all paused to let their eyes adjust before they could see to find a table. Guttering tallow candles sparingly placed around the room helped to lighten the dark corners, while a lit torch in a single wall sconce also fought the dark of the windowless room. The smell of fermenting ale was strong as it mingled with wood smoke and unwashed bodies. Bare trestle tables were placed haphazardly about.

The proprietor along with his serving wench appeared busy counting barrels of ale and wine. Both of their heads popped up to see who had entered and stopped the customer's usual chatter.

"Enid," the proprietor said loud enough for all to hear, "Look—'tis the countess. Ye best see to 'em and be quick."

Deirdre couldn't help but notice that everyone stopped talking, and with mouths agape stared at her.

Richard put his hand against the small of her back and pointed at the fireplace. "I'll sit there with the countess. The rest of you will please sit apart from us." He indicated another table for the constable, Bertrand, Gordon and others.

Richard picked the table next to the fireplace that belched out more smoke into the room than up the chimney, but a fire crackled and its meager blaze already beckoned Deirdre. Richard must have been think-ing of her when he picked the table. She immediately went to warm her hands by the flame and couldn't remember when last she'd done so. With reluctance she pulled herself from the warmth and took a seat next to Richard.

Enid, the serving maid, tucked stray hairs back into her headdress as she dropped a short curtsy to the newcomers. She smiled at Deirdre.

"Welcome, Milady. 'Tis a certain I never thought to see ye in here. Ye be right welcome, I say. I'm always tellin' Ralph that ye could use a good meal to fatten your bones. It weren't long after ye had yer baby that ye started looking right poorly, aye, that is what I told 'em. 'Twas bad enough that ye were locked up, but having to give up yer child made it appear God had abandoned ye." Enid, having no idea that she'd practi-cally told Deirdre's story to Richard, grinned and wiping reddened hands on her soiled overtunic kept talking, "Would ye like a hot mead to warm yer innards? We have mutton pie to serve as well. What say ye? Are ye both thirsty and hungry?"

"Oui, serve both tables the hot mead and food," Richard said.

Deirdre hadn't missed the shock on his face when the serving wench mentioned her baby.

"You gave Wrothbury an heir. That is why he coveted you at Fox-lair," he stated. His stoic face gave notice that he wasn't prepared to like or accept anything from Wrothbury.

"My wee daughter is over four months of age, and it has been that long since I have seen her sweet face...I..." she said, unable to utter another word. The stabbing pain of losing Joanna once again slammed through her. She fidgeted with the laces of her bodice, fighting back tears, and it was with great relief when Enid chose that moment to place the hot mead in front of them. Enid then turned to the other table to do the same.

"D'ye have children of yer own?" Deirdre asked of him.

"I'm not married."

To know that he was free to take a wife somehow bothered Deirdre. It was as if the fates strived to keep them apart. Why she felt thus about a man she hardly knew made her pause. Perhaps it's because this man was different than any she'd known. Deirdre observed that Thomas Warren and Miles appeared to be more interested in what went on be-tween her and Richard than they did at their own table where Richard's two companions sat talking.

"Where is your child?" Richard asked.

"Wrothbury took her from me the verra day I gave birth to her. Jo-anna Colleen is her name. My sweet Joanna, who I crave to hold each day, is the verra reason I tried to escape. And that is not all, Count Stras-bourg. I have been pardoned by the present King Edward II, but Wrothbury keeps the edict to himself." She reached up and wiped a droplet of perspiration that tickled her temple.

Richard spoke above a whisper, "What say you, madam? Are you tell-ing me you are a free woman and yet are not free?"

His eyes narrowed in thought as they met hers and feeling as if she was drowning in their cool green depths, she answered, "Aye, the edict was dated the eighth day of September this past year. The earl asked of me things he knew I would hate to do. He rejoiced in telling me that since I recognized only Robert de Brus as my king, then what the King of England had written on the parchment couldna possibly be recognized by me. When he would take wee Joanna from my arms, I begged him not to take her. That I'd do what he asked. I would swear fealty if only he'd let me be with my child. But he just laughed at me and took her away. 'Tis a certain the earl is Satan in disguise. Count Strasbourg, ye must be careful as this township is under Wrothbury's control."

"Ah…that explains the abhorrent actions of the townspeople toward you. He has cowered them to do his bidding. "Where is Wrothbury?"

"At Wrothbury Castle."

"And where is that to be?"

"West of here, several days ride at the most."

Enid brought the hot pies that smelled of leeks and mutton, but Deirdre didn't think she could manage a bite.

"You must eat, try to get your strength back," he urged.

Deirdre brought the first bit to her mouth and tried to chew. The pie formed a lump in the back of her throat. She took a sip of the ale, but that too didn't appeal.

Richard leaned close to her and whispered, "My lady, I'm going to get your child for you, and your pardon which I'll bring here and place under the constable's nose. But listen to me and listen well. Please be patient, for 'twill take time. I have an assignment that must be carried out. I will get your Joanna for you."

So great was Deirdre's elation, that without thinking she gripped Richard's forearm in a most intimate hold. His hand automatically covered hers and squeezed as he smiled. His honest face was close enough to kiss.

"D'ye promise?" She could hardly talk, her voice so full of hope.

"Oui, Milady." He brought her hand to his lips. "I promise."

She managed a weak smile, her elation beginning to ebb as she became lightheaded. Her food would not settle in her stomach. Looking down at her lap, she dabbed at the tiny beads of moisture forming on her upper lip.

Richard lifted her chin and turned her face to his. "Are you unwell, Countess?" He placed his palm on her forehead. "Dieu, you are burning up. Why have you not spoken up sooner," he exclaimed, and motioned for his squire.

She was vaguely aware that the men were starting towards her but the room wavered and she slumped in a dead faint.

Alarmed, Richard caught her and gathered her against his chest. Perspiration trickled down her temple, matting wayward hair against her face.

"Milord, let me help." Bertrand bumped elbows with Richard and helped hold Deirdre while Richard got to his feet. Bertrand lifted Deirdre and placed her in Richard's arms. Gordon was quick to open the door.

The constable and guards were right next to them, their hands on their swords and acting like Richard was up to trickery.

"Have you a clean chamber? I'll not take her back to that pest-hole you've been making her live in." Richard barked over his shoulder at the constable.

"Aye, somewhat."

"Then send one of your guards to prepare it. I demand a healer for Countess Wrothbury." Richard shifted her weight in his arms and could feel just how thin she was.

Constable Warren hurried ahead. He held the door open leading to the dungeon cells. Richard followed the constable until he paused to let Richard enter the open chamber. Being most gentle, Richard laid Deirdre on the pallet and was pleased to see it was plump with goose down. He covered her with clean wool blankets. A quick glance around the chamber assured him that it was a vast improvement.

"Have you sent for the healer?" Richard asked.

"Aye, milord," Thomas answered, his gaunt face wary as he folded his arms across his chest as if to guard himself against the warlord's wrath.

Miles scoffed. "Ye be wasting a healer's time on that bitch. She is about done for, and good riddance I say. She is like a boil on my arse that needs lanced. Let her hang in the cage until the carrion birds pick her b—"

Miles words gurgled in his mouth as Richard picked him up by the throat, propelled him backwards, and slammed him against the stone wall. He put his arm across the guard's windpipe and leaned in with all his weight. "Shut your mouth—you filthy scut! You are the boil on my backside and I'm about to lance it," he whispered his mouth close to Miles' ear. "If you ever think to abuse her—ever—I will cut from your body what you think to please a woman with." To solidify his meaning, Richard unsheathed his dagger and cut the material next to Miles' crotch. "Mayhap—I'll just lance these boils now, understand?"

Wild-eyed, Miles nodded and clawed at Richard's hold on his neck.

"What say you?" Richard pushed hard against the guard's windpipe. "Oui, perhaps?"

Miles, his face a bright red, beat at Richard's arm. He struggled to speak and managed to croak, "Aye…"

Short of killing the guard, Richard released Miles who collapsed onto his knees coughing and gagging. Finally, holding his throat, the man arose and scurried out the door.

"What has happened to the coin that Wrothbury should be sending for her care?" Richard asked the constable.

Constable Warren merely shrugged. His attitude showed he had better things to do. "The earl says he will no longer pay for her care."

Richard pushed the issue. "Countess Wrothbury told me the King of England has pardoned her. The edict with his signature was dated September of last year and resides with Wrothbury. Has she mentioned this to you?" Richard waited for the constable's reply.

"Aye, she told me of such. I think she lies. Why would Wrothbury keep her imprisoned if she is truly free?"

Richard kept his council and didn't say that Wrothbury had always let his hate overcome good judgment. Instead, he asked, "What has happened to her letters written to King Edward telling him that she has not been released. Do you know of this?"

Once again, the constable nodded. "I sent the letters to the Earl of Wrothbury."

"You sent letters intended for the king to Wrothbury? Why?"

"Because the earl told me to."

Richard was about to ask another question when a tall man dressed in a long black tunic entered and stared at Deirdre. He wore a leather pouch over his shoulder.

"I'm the healer. And I find it most uncommon to be summoned here to look after a prisoner." He turned a hawk-like face toward Richard. "Are you the one who sent for me?" Not waiting for an answer, he leaned over and brushed his hand across Deirdre's forehead. "She is feverish," he announced, and then wiped his hand on his long robe, implying the mere touch of her might sicken him as well.

"Oui, this I know. How will you help her?"

"I can only give her medicine," the healer said and removed a chalice from his pouch and used the water vessel to fill it. He then sprinkled herbs into the water. "Mayhap this potion of lemon balm and chamomile will reduce her fever and cough." He offered the chalice that gave off a tangy odor of lemon.

Richard accepted the healer's medicine. He knelt next to Deirdre, slipped his arm beneath her shoulder and lifted. "Chéri, awaken." Relieved to see her eyelids flutter open, he coaxed, "You must drink this."

"What is it?" she whispered, her eyes red-rimmed with fever appeared anxious.

"Chéri…'tis medicine. Please, drink." Richard held the chalice and was disappointed that she could only take a small amount of the liquid. He dabbed at the dribble on her chin. "Healer, is there nothing more you can do for her?"

"Keep giving her the herbs, and try hot broth. My business is done here." And before anyone could do or say otherwise, he left.

"Is there no one that can take care of the countess?" Richard, his temper flaring at the lack of compassion for Deirdre, stood and faced down the constable.

Thomas, becoming brave and belligerent, spoke, "Need I remind you that she is a prisoner? Imprisoned by old King Edward himself?"

"And need I remind you that if his son, the present king, has issued a pardon for Countess Wrothbury and it has not been adhered to, you will be in dire trouble."

Thomas blustered, "How can I be at fault?"

"How can she be at fault or imprisoned if she has been pardoned?"

"Bring me the edict and I will release the countess."

"Milord?" A woman's subtle voice interrupted.

"Oui?" Richard turned to see the stout matron that had been present earlier during the commotion by the cage. She stood in the doorway and held a small metal washbasin and several cloths for washing. Behind her, a young boy shifted from foot to foot holding a heavy pail of water with both hands, sloshing some of contents on the floor.

"May I help with Countess Wrothbury?" She went to stand beside the constable and cast a nervous smile at Richard. Her brown eyes took in those around her.

"And you are?"

"Maude Warren. Thomas's wife. I'm a friend of Countess Wrothbury." She pushed away strands of hair that escaped the sides of her wimple headdress. "I'm here to take care of her." And with that said, she knelt at Deirdre's side, and signaled the lad to pour water into the basin. She dipped the cloth into the water and began wiping Deirdre's face, cooling her.

Richard felt great relief that this woman, so different from her husband, was willing to help Deirdre. He fingered his whiskers, while staring at the constable, and asked. "Do you know how to keep accounts?"

The constable leaned back against the wall. "Milord, I'm a learned man. I keep the prison ledgers. Have to show the mayor and good citizens of Falconshire where their tax coin is spent."

"That is most good to hear, for I'm about to ask a boon of you." He needed to trust the man and didn't know if he could. Loyalty would have to be bought, for Wrothbury had dug his talons deep into the people of Falconshire. Richard opened his waist pouch and taking out a small bag of coins placed it in the constable's hand.

Thomas weighed the bag with his hand as emotions played across his face, foretelling an inner struggle.

"Open it," Richard urged.

Nodding, Thomas slipped the leather drawstring and after peering inside shook several shiny coins into his palm. Maude gasped as Thomas continued to stare questioningly, yet Richard could see the gleam, the temptation that money brought to a man.

"That is enough coin to keep Countess Wrothbury for a good many months." Richard ran his finger across his mouth, his mind racing, thinking what more could he do to insure Deirdre's safety after he left. "What are you paid as constable?"

"One shilling per day."

"I'll pay you one crown a day to be in my employment and take care of Countess Wrothbury. What say you?" Richard was more than relieved when Thomas nodded in agreement. "Do not brag of your good fortune to anyone. And you are not to inform Wrothbury of this. I'll be seeing the man within a few days, and plan on telling him myself." After getting another nod from Thomas who appeared dazed by his good fortune, Richard instructed. "Countess Wrothbury is to have hot meals, baths, and walks. Since you can keep ledgers, I demand an itemized account of every ha'penny spent on her. In time, you will receive more coin." He pointed at Thomas. "If you play me false, I promise you will be the one hanging in the cage. Nor do I ever want to hear that she's been left outside in that damnable cage overnight. Agreed?"

Maude spoke up from beside Deirdre, "Aye, Count Strasbourg, Thomas and I'll see to her."

Gordon Bryce entered the chamber and standing beside Richard, whispered, "Count Strasbourg, are ye ready to continue north?"

"Oui, I'm almost finished here. Wait by the horses."

The guide left to do as told. Richard moved over to the desk where he sat and opening the only drawer, was pleased to find writing supplies. He pulled a piece of parchment out of the desk and dipping the quill into the ink horn, began to write. When finished, he rolled it up and then fumbling around in his waist pouch pulled out his sealing wax and seal. He glanced up to see the Warren's questioning stares as he melted the wax and pressed his insignia into it.

"This missive is for Countess Wrothbury. Make sure she knows of it." After placing the missive inside the lone desk drawer, he went to stand in front of the couple.

"I must leave. Yet, I find comfort in knowing that you'll see to her needs. Try and get some broth down her. She didn't eat but a few morsels in the alehouse." Richard studied Maude's friendly brown eyes. "Were you present when Countess Wrothbury gave birth?"

"Aye, I brought the wee little girl into the world."

Richard started to ask of the babe when he glanced down at Deirdre and was surprised to see her watching him.

Maude seeing this as well, smiled, and said, "I think ye wish to be alone with the countess, aye? Come along then, Thomas."

"Richard...Count..." Deirdre muttered and struggled to rise but he knelt down to prevent her from doing so. "Please...take me with you..." She pushed at him, trying to stand, but he held her down and taking her flushed face between his hands, he thumbed her cheeks most gently.

"I cannot." And it was of great importance to him that she understood his words, and that he would indeed return for her. "Madame...ah...Deirdre, do you understand what I say?"

"Nay..." she whispered, her eyes searched his face, her own masked with despair. "All I know is that ye are leaving me. What of my baby? Will ye bring her back?"

"Milady, as ill as you are, you would not survive long on such a journey. I do not want your death. I want you to live. Get well for your daughter's sake. Please try to endure this place until I return. Deirdre, with the pardon's existence, there is hope."

Tears squeezed from the corners of her eyes then down the side of her face to form tiny wet spots on the pallet next to her head. He traced their path.

"Count!" Gordon burst into the room. He approached and whispered. "We have to leave. Soldiers ride this way."

"How close?"

"They are almost upon the township."

Richard embraced Deirdre. He placed a kiss on her forehead, her skin hot and damp beneath his lips. And not ready to stop just yet, he tenderly cupped her face, his thumbs outlining her parted lips before his mouth brushed against them. She clung to him and it was with bitter reluctance that he helped her to lie back down and arranged the wool blanket over her. Her eyes that stared at him were like a child's, trusting, yet frightened.

"Chéri, remember your promise. Please live for me." She was entrenched in his soul and he prayed the memories of her would no longer torture but instead give him hope. He stood, and darting one last glance her way, left the chamber before he changed his mind. Gordon was fast on his heels.

The day was starting to wane when Richard and his companions crossed into Scotland. As far as Richard was concerned, he was going the wrong way. He should be heading to Wrothbury Castle and put an end to the man's life that made Deirdre's so miserable. But it was more than

Wrothbury's treatment of Deirdre. The very fact that he stumbled upon her today had to mean something, and he took it as an omen. He thought long and hard of the fact that he coveted another man's wife. But more so, he was going to kill the bastard to have her.

Richard compared himself to King David in the old biblical stories that had the king lusting after Bathsheba. King David made sure the husband was killed in battle so he could have Bathsheba. Well, so be it. Richard would make Wrothbury die a slow death, like the slow death of the cage he kept Deirdre in. Seeing Deirdre Brodie had rekindled Richard's desire for her. Not a lust filled desire, but a desire filled with a craving to walk next to her, hear her laugh, hold her hand, show her that life could be good, give her peace and happiness. He did not know if she had any feelings for him. She'd admitted she had him on a pedestal and he'd seen something in her eyes, tenderness, want, perhaps yearning. He didn't know what it was and tried not to put false hope inside his heart.

And there was a baby to consider. He hadn't missed the light in Deirdre's eyes when she mentioned her child. He also didn't know how he felt about a child born from Wrothbury's loins. But the infant was half Deirdre, and that side had to prevail over Wrothbury's evil.

Torn between his duty for his King Philip and his promise to Deirdre, he tried to figure out how he was going to satisfy the one without letting down the other.

"Milord." Bertrand maneuvered his horse next to Richard's. "This Countess Wrothbury is the same woman that you helped when last we were in Scotland, is that not true?"

Richard nodded at his young squire. "Oui, that is true."

"I'll never forget what happened that day. I didn't think you would leave there alive. I remember being most frightened of what would happen to me if something happened to you."

"Then, Bertrand, I'm most glad I'm still here and looking out for your welfare."

Gordon pointed at a copse of trees at the base of a steep hillside.

"We should be meetin' with the Scots soon. The place is just ahead."

Richard could see movement, shadows of men that appeared to be milling around the trees.

The three rode up to the camp where a group of ten or more rough looking men hunkered down around a fire that held rabbits on a spit. Coming to their feet, they silently watched Richard dismount. Armed with claymores, dirks, and long daggers, Richard was glad he would be joining these men and not fighting against them. They spoke Gaelic amongst themselves, but hushed as Richard approached.

Gordon's angular face creased into a broad grin as his dark eyes teased. "D'ye have enough for the three of us as well? Those are mighty skinny looking rabbits. Could ye no' do better?"

"Watch yer tongue, Gordon, or ye might be the one roasting on the spit." One of the Scots teased back as he came forward. His eyes locked onto Richard. "'Tis glad I be to make yer acquaintance. I'm Macadie Gunn, here to take ye into the bowels of Scotland to meet up with the man that's waitin' for ye." His gaze was shrewd as he clasped Richard's forearm with his big paw.

Richard couldn't help but take in the wild mane of graying brown hair and the bushy beard that enclosed the man's lined face. He was of medium height and slender build. In place of chest armor, the warrior wore a thick-plated leather jerkin that fit around his upper torso and over a long tunic shirt. His breeks were a coarse material, while a dark plaid cloth draped over one shoulder and secured in place by his dagger belt and a thick leather holster that held his deadly claymore.

"I'm Richard de Laci, Comte de Strasbourg, but you already know that, oui?"

The grizzled leader gave a curt nod. "Aye, Coont, we've been told that ye fight against England fer yer King of France." His gray eyes twinkled from under dark bushy brows, and a broad grin displayed a gap between his two upper front teeth. "Hear that ye can siege a castle and reduce it to rubble in no time."

"Both my brother Philippe and I can do so."

Richard looked at the others. Some merely nodded at him not bothering to leave the comfort of the fire. The Scots persona was of warriors. Men used to fighting hard, fast, running, and living off the land.

Several men came forward to introduce themselves.

"Count Strasbourg, Graham Buchanan is my name." Graham, a bear of a man clasped Richard's arm in a biting grip. He wore his forelock braided and opposite the braid, a scar ran down the right side of his face from hairline to jaw. Another inch and it would have dissected his face; instead, it cut through his eye leaving a scarred opaque pupil. He turned his attention to Richard's guide. "Gordon Bryce, 'tis gude to see ya. I havna seen ya fer a year or more."

"Aye," Gordon grinned at his compatriots. "Before I led the count here from London, the Brus had me in Ireland trying to recruit men fer the cause."

Graham slapped Gordon on the back. "Gude work—gude work." He then addressed Richard once again by signaling forth another man. "This young pup here is Macadie's nephew, Conner Kincaid. Count Strasbourg, ye willna find better fighters than the men before ya."

Conner, tall and handsome, launched into a cocky grin. "We will teach ye to wield a two handed claymore. Takes a man's head off with one slice," he said, knifing his hand across his throat.

"Oui, as does my sword." For effect, Richard mimicked the young Scot, knifing his hand across his own throat. His other hand automatically covered the hilt, and he prayed to God that he would never have to draw it against these men.

"Conner, ye cocky whelp, cease with this talk before the Coont shows ye a thing or two about parting a man's head from his body." Macadie glared at his nephew, trying to subdue him, but Conner only laughed, his youthful brashness allowing him to joke.

Graham picked up a water bladder and offered it to Richard. "Yer army is several days ride north, awaiting yer arrival. They slipped ashore with no trouble. But yer brother Philippe was put out. He said the channel crossing wasna gude."

"Something must have gone wrong." Richard worried, for Philippe usually never voice problems, especially when it came to a clandestine mission as this.

Macadie said, "Aye, well, if those French and Flemish mercenary soldiers he has with him fight as nasty as they look, we'll win this war faster than it took yer brother to bring them from France."

Richard smiled, for he could well imagine the type of army that Philippe pulled together. Men who fought for coin, enjoyed killing, and didn't care what country they spilt blood in.

Macadie took the rabbits from the fire and leaned the sticks against a log so the meat could cool somewhat. "Did ye stop in Falconshire?"

"Oui. Spent more time there than planned," Richard answered and took in the stoic faces that stood next to the fire and eyeing the rabbits.

"Did ye see Countess Wrothbury…ah…Deirdre Brodie to us?" Macadie asked.

Richard's easy smile faded, his relaxed stance becoming rigid, causing all those around him to tense. "You know of Countess Wrothbury?"

"Aye," Macadie answered. "She is a Scottish lass. One of our own. We all know of her."

To hear that her own people had abandoned Deirdre made Richard's ire rise. "She is a fellow Scot, and you let her wallow in that cage. Is she not worthy enough for you to rescue her?" Unable to contain his anger now directed at Macadie, his voice got louder.

"Aye," said Macadie, "but ye have no call to get riled at me, Coont. We have been too busy fightin'—stayin' alive—to help her out. But dinna think we have forgotten the Lady Deirdre. Her own brother, David Brodie, is with Scotland's King Robert de Brus and busy attackin' English castles. David tried gettin' her out last fall, but failed."

"Her brother? That's right. I'd forgotten she has a brother." Richard remembered the man who had thrown a rock at the king and made it to safety. He wondered why Deirdre didn't speak of him.

"Coont, if ye've tamper down yer anger a wee bit, have some rabbit," Macadie said. "Since Gordon thinks 'tis puny fare, mayhap we willna give him any." His grin became wide and easy.

Gordon chuckled.

Conner handed his uncle the sticks. Macadie pulled the rabbits off, and after tearing himself a leg, handed them to the others.

They talked of war and Richard's army that was coming to the Bruce's aid. Men that could help turn the tide in Scotland's favor. After taking the edge off their hunger, it was time to move on.

They broke camp.

Gordon and Conner pissed on the fire while the rest mounted their steeds. Richard gave Saladin a strong pat and the faithful horse shook his great head. They headed deeper into Scotland, taking Richard further away from Deirdre and from his destination with Wrothbury.

7 Suffer

Falconshire, England

Hovering somewhere between lucidness and the dark void of un-consciousness, Deirdre fought against being pulled back into reali-ty. Three days had passed since Richard had left. Three days that she'd spent fighting for her life against the fever that raged through her.

At last, she opened her eyes and peered over the blanket. Accus-tomed to being in the dim squalor of her cell, she looked around. This one was different, cleaner. Candles placed around the room made her aware that she was now in a chamber close to where the Warren's lived. Her eyes lingered on a small desk that held a burning candle, quill pen, and inkhorn.

Deirdre sat up. The room began to spin, forcing her to close her eyes. When at last, the dizziness passed she opened her eyes. She pushed on the feather-filled pallet underneath her. Even her clothing had changed. She ran her hand over her bosom and the material of the chemise she wore, loving the fine feel of it. The chemise was finer than anything she ever owned.

Spotting a clothes chest placed against the wall close to where she sat, she scooted over to it and opened the lid to reveal the count's beautiful fur lined cloak, neatly folded. She removed it and rubbed the thick black fur against her cheek.

Richard.

The cloak reminded her of him.

Promises made.

Promises to keep.

Promises to get her daughter, the pardon, and to return for her.

Promises made to get well.

It would be easy to keep hers, but much harder for Richard to keep his. Knowing Wrothbury's cunningness and ability to seize an enemy before the enemy could strike, unsettled her. Richard had two men with him—two. He couldn't get past the gates at Wrothbury Castle with just two. Now she had Richard to worry about, but oh what glorious worries.

The key grating in the lock had her staring with trepidation at the heavy door. Expecting Miles, she held her breath, but was pleasantly surprised to see Maude enter with a tray of food.

The smell of hot porridge wafted before Maude, and over to where Deirdre sat.

Maude flashed a warm smile her way. "Och...milady...'tis good to see ye awake and looking to join the living. Praise the Lord for his healin' powers, do ye not agree?"

Still behind bars, Deirdre didn't know if she wanted to thank anyone with divine powers, especially the Lord. But her stomach let her know it would be thankful for the food that Maude held.

"Mistress Warren, how long have I been sick?" She enjoyed Maude's cheerful outlook and accepted it no matter the cause.

"Don't ye think ye best be callin' me Maude? And ye have been ill for three days. I fear ye'll be going back to the cage, but only when yer better. Methinks ye can make yerself sick for a few more days, can ye not? Milady, d'ye remember Count Strasbourg who helped ye?" Her cheeks widened with a grin that revealed slightly crooked teeth.

"Aye," Deirdre blushed. How could she possibly forget Richard's kindness? And didn't he already dominate her every thought? "I remember him well. Is he gone then?"

"Aye, and the two with him. Count Strasbourg is a right fair man, handsome indeed. Why, he made me own heart flutter—that he did!" Maude rolled her eyes and rapidly patted her chest in jest.

Deirdre giggled at the thoughts of Maude getting excited about a man. "Maude, did he say where he was going?" She took her time eating, and was careful to take a small spoonful of the porridge and wash it down with a sip of goat's milk. Goat's milk. To be sure, she hadn't tasted milk since before giving birth to Joanna. She swished it around in her mouth and could swear it was still warm from the teat.

"Milady, 'tis fer certain ye spent more time with Count Strasbourg than any other person. What with him taking ye to the alehouse and all. I thought my Thomas to have a fit." Maude relaxed on the pallet next to Deirdre.

"I was so sick when he left, I thought perhaps he told ye where he was going." She buttered her bread then nibbled at it.

When Maude shrugged and shook her head, Deirdre smiled a teasing smile, and said, "He does have kind eyes does he no'? Green with gold flecks—"

Maude cackled. "If ye noticed his eyes and those gold flecks, perhaps ye were not all that sick, lass."

"Oh bugger on, Maude. When I fell from the cage and landed on top of him I couldna help but see those gold flecks. And… er well there are many other arresting qualities about the man," she rattled out.

"Yer right, milady, I'm sure he has many favorable qualities about him. And with ye on top of him ye just might share that experience with me, aye?" Maude gave an all-knowing grin. "Oh, and I do not know if he told ye this but he is a rich nobleman from France and has left coin to take care of ye."

Deirdre frowned at Maude's news, and wondered what it meant for her future. "Coin to take care of me? Then he fattens the townships coffers with coin that the earl by rights should be paying fer me. The count is indeed most generous." She became queasy and feeling lightheaded stopped eating.

"Milady, he was right put out with Thomas and me. Mad he was about the filthy cell and cage. Said ye were never to be left outside at night. And about that...he is right. He ordered Thomas to keep a ledger on every ha'penny spent on ye. 'Tis with shame in me own heart that I sit here and ask for forgiveness. I've not been the best of friend to ye."

Deirdre leaned back against the wall and shut her eyes. "Dinna fret yourself. Ye were doing as ordered by your man. Right or wrong, it was ordered."

Wanting to know more about Richard's intentions, she whispered in hesitation, "Maude, did the count tell ye he planned to return?" Deirdre was thinking of Foxlair when he was forced to leave her. Now her fears were different. No king was here to threaten him this time. Yet he was gone and she was still caged. Nay, that wasn't true, she argued with herself, circumstances forced him to leave her. This time he would return.

"Oh...aye, milady, he did. He ordered Thomas to be true with his money or he would put Thomas in the cage." Maude chuckled making her bosom bounce with mirth. But her laughter soon faded and she became serious. "Milady?"

"Aye?"

"I'll have to fight for every kindness I can show ye. Dinna be angry at me when I can show none." Maude worried her hands together as her eyes pleaded with Deirdre's.

From the sad expression on Maude's face, Deirdre understood she spoke the truth. She patted Maude's hand. "Aye, Maude...I understand." She also knew Maude was her only ally amongst those at Falconshire that wished her ill. And those that wished her ill were allies of the Earl of Wrothbury.

"Are ye finished with yer meal then?" Maude started to pick up the tray.

Deirdre no more than nodded when the door burst open and Thomas entered. "Well now, Countess Wrothbury, 'tis back in the cage for ye."

"Please…Thomas, what could it hurt for her to remain in here for a few more days and get her strength back? Ye know that is what Count Strasbourg would want." Maude beseeched him, never before arguing against her husband's wishes.

Appearing surprised that his wife defied him, he became firm. "Maude, do ye need me to show ye the king's proclamation concerning the countess and her being caged?"

"Nay, there's no need to remind me what's written on that parchment. I just thought ye could find kindness in your heart—"

"She goes to the cage—now," he interrupted, his lips thinned into a flat line.

"But…."

"I have spoken. She goes to the cage. I'm still the constable, am I not?" Thomas cut his eyes down at Deirdre then glanced around the chamber.

Maude acquiesced as her gaze sought Deirdre's. "'Tis sorry I be, milady. Perhaps with warmer clothes, it willna be so bad. 'Tis springtime and getting warmer."

"Make her ready, Maude. I'll return shortly." He left the two women alone.

Maude helped her dress in a warm woolen gown and then dug into the chest and handed her Richard's cloak. "I think yer ready."

Deirdre grabbed up the leftover bread, boiled egg, and nested the food alongside the tattered embroidery cloth that looked like it had been used for a war banner leading the charge.

With dread, Deirdre approached the lowered cage. New bars of wood replaced the broken ones. Despite Richard's generosity and orders concerning her, her imprisonment was going to be made unbearable by guards who hated the count, and hated her even more.

"Ah...Miles...here ye be." Thomas acknowledged the guard. "Secure Countess Wrothbury in the cage."

"Aye, Constable Warren." Miles gripped Deirdre's arm tighter than necessary.

He released her to open the cage door, and then stood in the opening, forcing her to brush against his body when she entered. She immediately sought the chair and kept a wary eye on Miles while placing her sewing basket down beside her.

Miles entered the cage and made a great pretense of shaking the repaired bars to see how they held. He glanced her way. "Think yer safe with that French Count holding money over our heads? Beware, Countess, for I dislike ye even more. I hear tell the man's a long way from here. Certainly much further away than Wrothbury, yer husband."

"Ye needn't remind me of my husband," she snapped.

"And why is that? Yer husband's coin mighten cross my palms iffen he found out about the time ye spent with that there Frenchman. Mayhap I should tell him." He loomed over her and grabbing her face, his fingers bit into her cheeks. He pointed to the bruises on his neck. "See this bruise? 'Tis from that damn Frenchman, given on yer behalf. Methinks ye owe me for this."

She tried turning away from his rancid breath but he held tight. "Ye owe me...Countess." He ran his hand over her bodice, feeling, pinching her breasts. "I'll get at thee. Mark my word."

Wanting nothing more than to scratch his eyes out, she remained calm, and returned his malicious gaze with one of her own. It disquieted him enough that he stepped out of the cage and snapped the lock in place. He signaled the guards on the battlement to raise the cage. Had Wrothbury's coin paid Miles to make her life miserable? Certainly, they were both cut from the same cloth.

The ratcheting sound of her cage being raised echoed around the township. They raised her higher than usual. Higher even than the battlements. Bile rose in her throat and she barely made it to the bars before retching. She rested her face against the strong wood. No one could possibly help her this high up, certainly that was their intent. She slumped onto the floor and wrapped Richard's cloak tightly around her. The gentle swaying lulled her to sleep…

…*"Davey…Davey wait for me!" Deirdre, her little legs pumping, ran up the hillside and stopped to look around. When she couldn't find her older brother, her lower lip quivered, but not for long as she was distracted by the heather growing in the cracks between the stones. She began picking the heady flowers when suddenly a head popped from behind a giant boulder.*

"Scat…scat fraidy cat!" David jumped out at her trying his best to scare her with his eyes crossed and tongue dangling.

She squeaked and dropped her bouquet. She fought back tears, determined that he wouldn't see her cry.

"Davey, 'tis bad scarin' me so," she scolded.

His dark eyes were bright as he bent down to retrieve the dropped flowers.

"Here." He thrusts them at her. "'Tis tired I be of a wee sister followin' me about. Makes me look like a nursemaid to ye…aye it do."

Deirdre knew he had reasons to be put out with her. She was a pest.

He pointed at a rabbit scampering across the rocks, and quickly taking aim with his bow and arrow, shot, and missed.

Deirdre was relieved the rabbit went unscathed. But Davey was quick to blame her for his bad shot. "There now, see what ye made me do. I missed it."

They sat side by side on their hillside and looked down at their ancestral home that appeared tiny from their favorite niche. Foxlair Castle built from solid stone gave off a feeling of security to all who lived and worked in its shadows. Built with their ancestor's blood and sweat, Foxlair was in truth a large stone keep that boasted no crenellated towers.

Davey pointed to the island in the middle of the inlet. "See—a deer swims to the island. I'll tell Papa, mayhap he will hunt it."

Shading her eyes, she could barely make out the dark head of the deer cutting through water that the sun turned into glittering silver. Below them, men and women from the clan toiled in the fields of barley and wheat.

It was her turn to point. "Tis the foxes." And they both watched the pair of foxes creeping up the hillside. Their coats a beautiful burnish-red against the low growing vegetation gave them away. They paused to sniff the air with their long snouts and getting wind of the children, quickly scurried out of sight.

"Aye, their lair's around here, but it canna be found. They be most clever, the foxes."

Dismissing the animals, they laid back and gazed up at the blue sky dotted by an occasional cloud that appeared close enough to be plucked from the sky with little or no effort. The steady drone of crickets filled the air.

"Davey, where do dead people go?"

He slanted a glance her way, his youthful eyes narrowing in thought. "To heaven or hell. Ye know that."

"Papa says Mam's in heaven. Can she see us d'ye think?"

"Aye, to be sure she can."

Deirdre thought her brother most smart and took his answer as the absolute truth. And looking at the puffy clouds thought something so pretty had to be part of heaven.

They fell asleep and awoke when the sun's warmth was broken by shadows. Deirdre opened her eyes to see the tall body of her father standing over them blotting out the sun's bright rays.

Andrew bent and scooped her into his arms then nudged Davey with his foot. "David...lad...'tis time ye awaken and head back." He reached out a hand and pulled his sleepy son to his feet. "And ye, Deedee, will have to start learning the duties of a lassie and take care of our home."

"Aye, Papa..." She slipped her arm around his neck then gave him a quick peck on his whiskered cheek. "Papa..."

"...Papa!" Deirdre awoke with a start and realized she'd spoken out loud. She sat up. Her dream most vivid, made her dispirited and sad. How unhappy Papa would be to see her in a cage. If he still lived, he would have rescued her long ago.

The day was long and it was a great relief to her when the cage was lowered and Thomas stood at the ready to escort her back inside. He coughed a dry hacking cough with each step. His body always slim was becoming even more so, and this alarmed Deirdre.

"Thomas, ye must take medicines for yer cough."

"Perhaps."

Still weak from her illness she tried her best to keep up. "Thomas, must the cage be so high? The wind blows something fierce. Without this cloak that Count Strasbourg gave me, I would surely freeze. Please…Thomas…not so high?"

"Aye, Countess, I noticed. 'Twill be lower tomorrow." He opened the chamber door and allowed her to pass. "Maude will be bringing yer food in good time. Light the candle before I close the door."

Smiling and feeling spirited about having coins to buy more, she lit several candles and vaguely heard the door close and the key rattle in the lock. Moving one of the candles to the desk, she sat down and trailing her hands over the smooth wooden surface, realized how much she'd missed having a desk and writing tools. How spoilt she might become with Richard's help.

Curious, she opened the drawer and spotted a rolled up parchment. Picking it up, she turned it over and studied the sealing wax and the insignia pressed into it. Holding it closer to the candlelight she could make out twin leopards with a crown around their necks. Recognizing it to be Richard's insignia, she slid her finger under the seal and lifted the round red blob from the parchment.

'Madam, Do not forget your promise to me, and that is to make yourself well. I too, remember my promise to you and that is to return with your daughter and the pardon. I will take you from the cage. Destroy this. Richard de Laci, Comte de Strasbourg.'

A short note written in bold masculine strokes, his name signed with a flourish. She shivered with excitement. For the first time in years, she had hope. She remembered images of Richard, from when he'd first plucked her from the burning fields of Brodie land, to just three short days ago. The way he held her in his strong arms and made her promise to live. Oh aye, she remembered.

She read the missive several times, and finally put it to flame.

As the parchment curled and turned black, her mind churned with wants and dislikes, love and hatred. She fell to her knees on the cold stone floor. In prayer she asked God's forgiveness for wishing her unwanted husband dead.

8 Do Not Forget

Scotland

Philippe de Laci, standing amongst his soldiers, used his hand to shadow his eyes against the sun, now low in the sky. Several months had passed since last he'd seen Richard. When Richard left for London to ferret out information concerning England's intentions toward Scotland, Philippe, so ordered by his king, had pulled together an army. Not the type of fighters he was used to leading, but a force of vicious Flemings, Frenchmen, even Norwegians, and some snarling Germans.

Crossing the channel was no easy feat with legions of men and war machines. The ship Philippe was on floundered before it had even left French soil behind. He stood here now by the grace of God.

Etienne Grimoult, the de Laci's sergeant, approached and gave a report that riders were approaching. They were the Scots that had left to go meet Richard.

"Is my brother amongst them?" Philippe grinned, and already knew the answer from the smile Etienne wore.

"Oui, he is."

Both Philippe and Etienne turned around to gaze at the gentle rise in the terrain. Expectantly, Philippe stared at the hillcrest until he could see the dark specs of heads and then bodies as they came into view. When the riders reined in their horses at the top of the rise, Philippe could pick out Richard from the way he sat his horse and the toss of his head to get the hair out of his eyes.

The soldiers appeared to be making camp. Some unsaddled horses, others cooked, and Richard could hear the melodious voices of so many in one place.

"There ye be, Coont." Macadie pointed. "From the way yer brother is watchin', I'd say he waits fer ye." From the moment they'd met and shared rabbit, Macadie had usurped Gordon's place next to Richard and appointed himself personal guide and the one to keep Richard apprised of the Bruce's movements and the war with England.

"My brother was long aware of us. I've noticed Philippe's scouts following us for about the last five miles or more." From his viewpoint, Richard watched his brother walk away from the camp. "Most of my soldiers remain in France guarding my domain that is on the Rhine River across from the Germanic lands. I live in a tempestuous area that is home to poachers and rogue warriors who like to strike at my home and then cross the river to hide like cur dogs."

"Jest like the English, aye?" Macadie said.

"Oui. I'll meet you in camp, Macadie." Spurring Saladin into a swift gallop, Richard rode toward Philippe who stood with folded arms. He thrust himself from the saddle, and stood grinning at his brother.

"Philippe, 'tis good to see you." He clapped his brother on the shoulder.

"Oui, and you, Richard."

Richard released his brother and stood back to appraise him. "The Scotsman, Macadie Gunn, said there was trouble crossing the channel. What happened?"

Philippe's face appeared thunderous. "You almost lost me—that is what happened." He poked himself in the chest none too gently.

"What say you?" Alarmed, Richard grabbed Philippe's arm.

"That I almost drowned. The ship I was on floundered within sight of the land we'd just left. Twenty men drowned. We lost fifteen horses, mine included. Armor, weapons, my ship was loaded with supplies. I managed to keep from drowning by grabbing a chest floating by."

Richard's gut clinched at the close call his brother had, and of the men and horses lost. "Were you injured?"

Philippe shook his head. "Merely cuts and bruises. But losing my warhorse Jezebel and my armor will take some getting past."

"You're still vexed about it."

Philippe nodded in agreement. "As any man would be. I think next time we cross a sea, you can be the one in charge of moving the army. It is hard work, and not very rewarding when one loses lives. Not to mention we were half-crazed from being on board ships for so long since we had to sail up England's coastline until we reached Scottish soil."

"Philippe, I understand why you are upset, but how can this accident be any different than losing men on the battlefield? Loyal men who are hacked to pieces before your very eyes? I think not," Richard said in a mindful voice.

"Oui, perhaps. But to know that horses are closed up inside the hull of a ship and cannot escape is something I'll not easily forget, especially their neighs of terror that sounded like screams. I can still hear the sound in my sleep." Philippe shuddered, his eyes still seeing the carnage.

"Nor should you forget. You are most caring, and if you were not, you would not be a true de Laci," Richard said with conviction and sympathy. "Was the king's treasurer with you?"

"Yes, he was, but I fished him out. He was so upset that he said he'd tell King Philip to finance whatever the Bruce needed, because he wasn't stepping foot on another ship. The last I saw of him, he was riding toward Paris. Good riddance I say. He would be nothing but trouble. The man could hardly ride a horse without falling off."

Richard started laughing. "Philippe, you did not drown because you had so much hot air in your lungs that it kept you afloat. Mmmph!" Richard took an elbow in the gut.

"You think you have wit? Well, I do not," Philippe said, a scowl furrowing his brow.

Still grinning, Richard said, "I, too, have tales to tell, but they can wait. What of Valentin and Pernelle? Any news from home?"

"Ah…always the elder and always worrying about things you shouldn't. Valentin and Pernelle are well. I would think that Valentin being twenty is old enough to watch out for our interests while we are away." Philippe's mood lightened. "We know our duties and can carry them out with or without you." Chuckling, he shook his head. "Will your concern for us never cease?"

"Philippe, I am…as Perri calls me, 'mon frère de papa.' She constantly tells me I act like her father. Thus my duties as such give me no ease of concern about your welfare. Allow me that indulgence please. And be most glad I'm not otherwise and care naught for each of you."

Appearing to accept his answer with good humor, Philippe glanced past him and at the approaching riders who stopped their horses and dismounted. "Ah…here is your escort."

Richard motioned the men forward. "I believe you've already met." His hand swept the circle of travel weary men.

The skin next to Macadie's eyes crinkled into deep furrows as he grasped Philippe's forearm. "Tell me, milord, is yer brother always so serious? He dinna crack a smile the whole journey."

"Always. Richard finds little to smile about."

The men made their way to the fire to get warm and loosen up sore muscles from being in the saddle so long. When the French squires offered their Lords and the Scots drinks from metal cups, amused, the Scots took the offered chalices of wine and joked about drinking from tin chalices, no less. But they indulged in toasting to the future and asked that God give them victories in all battles.

"Milord, let me remove your chest armor." Bertrand began unbuckling Richard's armor. "I'll see to Saladin as well."

"Merci, Bertrand." Richard took a long drink then tried to loosen up muscles that were tight from being restricted underneath hot, heavy armor. He studied the ruby liquid in his cup and thinking about Deirdre made plans. "Tell me, Macadie, is there someone that can deliver a message to Falconshire? I'll be needing a trustworthy messenger, one to take the missive both ways, and be cunning enough not to get caught by the English."

"I'm thinkin' Conner's the man ye need fer this."

"Conner? I'm sure you know best.

"Coont, yer a good man to help the Lady Deirdre. I think there is more to yer feelings in all this."

"Oui, there is. But I'm not at liberty to speak of it." Richard yawned, tired from his journey and still upset with the thought that Philippe had come so close to dying. He stood and stretched. Pausing to address the surrounding group, he said, "Men, we break camp at sunrise. Until then."

Richard followed Philippe into the tent where sleeping pallets were tossed on the ground. Thankfully, Richard plopped down on one.

While Richard got comfortable, his brother poked through his saddlebag and finally produced a couple of missives that he stuffed into Richard's hand. "Those are from Pernelle and Valentin. You can read them later. Right now, I'm most curious about this countess that you and Macadie had such a lively conversation about. Who is she and what is she to you?"

Richard immediately envisioned big blue eyes staring at him from between wooden bars. "Remember the story I told you when I returned from Scotland?"

Philippe grimaced. "The horrors that happened at Foxlair, the clan, and the laird's daughter, Deirdre Brodie?"

"Oui, she is the countess to whom I'm sending a missive." Richard told Philippe Deirdre's story, about her illegal confinement, her child, and Wrothbury's immeasurable cruelties.

"Then you think to assuage your guilt by helping her? Richard, you have never had anything to feel guilty about. What good would it had done for you to reveal your true business to King Edward? You would have brought down England's wrath on France and our King. Your head would have adorned a pike. Non, you did the right thing, which was nothing." Philippe nudged Richard's shoulder. "True?"

"True. But I plan to go after Wrothbury and get Deirdre's child and her pardon."

"Richard, there is no way to do that and fight for Robert le Bruce. We must follow King Philip's orders."

"This I realize. How ironic that following my king's orders in the past introduced me to Deirdre. Now his orders are once again keeping me from helping her. I should have gotten her away to safety that day at Foxlair. Five days ago I should have taken her from Falconshire and would have if she wasn't so ill."

Philippe scoffed. "I disagree. At Foxlair, you wouldn't have taken two steps before England's King would have ordered you gutted. As it was, you ended up unconscious, tied over your horse, and sent away from Edward's army. Cease with this self-destruction, for it does you no good. Besides, it sounds like Countess Wrothbury was left with better conditions than when you found her. She is out of the cage, oui?"

"Non, she will still be in the cage during the day. At night, she's supposed to be inside. But I plan to get her out of such confinement."

"How do you plan to do this?"

"I intend to kill her husband. Find the pardon he hides from everyone, and then rescue her."

Philippe's face became stormy. "Christ Jesus—Richard. You do not jest, oui?"

"Non, I do not jest."

"I see. Tell me…just when do you think to kill this man?"

"Tomorrow, I leave with a small band of men and travel to Wrothbury's castle."

Philippe's eyes glinted in the low candlelight. "God's blood—Richard. So, I'm to take the army to Dundee whilst you go back to England and kill a man whose wife you covet? Nothing good will come from this. You act the fool. One cannot go kill an Englishman who is in good standing with England's King."

"Calm yourself. I'm going to do this deed. I cannot abide a man who treats women as this man has treated Countess Wrothbury."

"There is no changing your mind?"

"Non, Philippe."

"Then I will honor your decision and do as commanded."

Richard nodded as he popped the seal on Valentin's missive and read it. "It appears Valentin is having trouble with poachers. He says they steal our sheep, but that he will get them back. Mayhap, Valentin cannot handle this as expected. Perhaps I should write to Ditmar and asked that he help our brother."

Philippe let out a long sigh. "Valentin was not to write you of this. And I'm sure our brother is capable of flushing out poachers. I would surmise that Ditmar's sheep have been pouched and he helps Valentin get them back. Read your missive from Pernelle. She will lighten your mood."

Mon frère. I ride your warhorse, Kashmir, to keep him trim and exercised. He is headstrong, but I gentle him. King Philip of France, along with your approval, has seen fit to make a match for me. He has sent Julien Quesnel who thinks to be my betrothed. This man makes himself at home here and presses Valentin to plan the wedding. I need your council on such matters. Please return safely to us. Your sister, Pernelle de Laci."

Richard grumbled and said, "This does little to lighten my mood. Valentin cannot sign betrothal papers. This…this Julien Quesnel must know I'm the head of our house. How can I tend to such when I sit on Scottish soil? Jesú. And…and, she should not be riding Kashmir."

"Who said the oldest son gets all the glory?" Philippe chuckled and yawned out a goodnight.

Restless and unable to sleep, Richard finally got up and went outside to piss. Seeking nearby bushes, he relieved himself. Philippe's words that no good would come of coveting another man's wife assailed him. But more than that, would his strong convictions allow him to end the man's life? Any other man, perhaps not, but Wrothbury, oui, that he could.

His thoughts wrapped around a low raspy voice and the bluest eyes he'd ever looked at. God had seen fit to put her in his life again. He admired her burning defiance, her loyalty to her king. What had engrained such a strong fortitude in her? A fortitude so strong it allowed her to endure Wrothbury as his wife, and then confined and enceinte with a child nine of those months.

Richard headed to the fire and nodded at several soldiers who talked amongst themselves. He sat on a fallen log and picked up twigs to toss into the crackling fire. A slight breeze swirled smoke around. He waved it away from his face. This was Deirdre's homeland, her country. What was her life like before Wrothbury took her? Like most women, she ran Foxlair, was in charge of the meals. Andrew Brodie had told King Edward that she was to be married within two days. How altered her life had become.

He felt a presence standing next to him and glanced up to see Macadie holding a wine bladder. "Here, Coont. Take the dust off yer tongue."

Richard took a long swig and found its tastes not bad. "Macadie?"

"Och, must be serious from the look on yer face. What is it yer wantin' to know?"

"Tell me about Deirdre Brodie."

"What d'ye want to know about her?"

"All that can be told."

"Then move over and let me share some of that log with ye." He settled in next to Richard, and pulled his plaid around his shoulders. "Weel,

I only met the lass a few years ago. All I know is from her brother. Deirdre's now a legend, and legends grow tales. Deirdre is the second child born to Andrew and Colleen Brodie. Colleen died when the Brodie children were but wee things. Andrew was laird of the Brodie clan. David is now laird."

Richard sighed and tossed a twig onto the fire. "Tell me more."

"When Deirdre turned seventeen, Andrew, against his better judgment, agreed that she could marry young Bonnar Cameron whom she loved. But several days before the weddin', Edward the King, rode through Andrew's domain looking for Robert de Brus. That day was nasty. The day Andrew was killed. Deirdre was forced to marry an Englishman called the Earl of Wrothbury. Young David joined the Brus. The English have put a price on David's head."

"I was there that day, Macadie."

"What say ye? Where—what day?"

"The day Edward killed Andrew Brodie." Richard felt his friend's body stiffen.

"Ah…I remember. Deirdre Brodie told us about ye when we stopped at Wrothbury Castle. She said ye tried to help her. Mayhap ye can explain why ye rode with the English. For I dinna understand why ye were there with the king at all." His voice usually fraught with mirth carried an edge.

"It is not as you think. I had been at Edward's court the better part of a year, spying for my King Philip. Edward planned to invade France, and King Philip was interested in keeping the English king busy with Scotland. But the Welsh and Scots didn't need France's help to keep the king busy. Robert le Bruce was doing that all by himself. Edward insisted that I accompany him on his mission to capture the Bruce. I was appalled at the atrocities the English king committed against the Scots, especially on Brodie land. I tried to help Deirdre Brodie, but was stopped by the king. My mind has been left in torture these past years because I failed her. But this time will be different. I will prevail and let no man stop me, husband or otherwise." The more Richard learned about Deirdre, the more his heart became locked in the cage with her.

"'Tis glad I be that ye were no' a traitor." Macadie's eyes glittered in the firelight. "I've fought until I'm tired of fightin', for it has been one battle after another. The English killed my wife and daughter four years ago while I was away fightin' for the Brus. My wife Forba had a gentle soul. The Lord blessed us with Iseabail, our daughter. Issy was everything to us. A lassie with curls the color of me own hair. She was but five years of age when my home was attacked. They left nothing standing. My revenge is for my Forba, my Issy. That is what I fight fer. We all suffer in this…" his voice trailed off in anguish.

Richard listened with his heart and with Macadie's sharing of his loss, came a new bond of friendship, one that Richard needed in this rugged land, someone to share heartache and laughter with. Knowing his words were of little comfort, he spoke to his friend, "I'm most sorry about your wife and child."

"I often think of takin' another wife, for I'm lonely. I would like a son. But a child born in Scotland is a child born to grief."

Silence prevailed between the two. Richard couldn't help but compare the armies he'd led against other countries. Unease settled about him, with the similarities between his conquests and those of the English between the Scots. Macadie had said it was the Scots way of life, the constant struggle. For Richard it was the same, only he was the aggressor.

Needing to clear his mind, Richard asked, "What about this Bonnar Cameron? Where is he?"

"Bonnar is with David Brodie. They are like brothers. Bonnar also has a price on his head."

Richard lifted the wine bladder and took a deep drink. "You should know that tomorrow I do not go with my brother. He takes the army to Robert le Bruce."

Macadie's face glowed red in the firelight. "Where are ye goin'?"

"To England and Wrothbury's castle. I'm after Deirdre Brodie's pardon and her child."

Macadie coughed with surprise and then grinned. "Weel...ye best be gettin' some rest for tomorrow will hold none for ye if yer bent on traveling to make amends. I'll be goin' with ye."

Morning found Richard with little sleep and in a quarrelsome mood. He snapped at both Bertrand and Philippe. He accidentally knocked over the inkhorn, spilling the precious ink onto the ground. The quill wouldn't hold a nib and he grumbled that he might have to kill a bird so he could make a decent writing quill, but didn't see any birds nearby. When finished with the missive he burnt his finger on hot sealing wax, and questioned what else would go wrong this day, for he was only an hour into it. "Merde," he cursed and sucked his finger. He glanced up to see Philippe looking just a little put out as he stood with folded arms glaring down at him.

"Now what is amiss?"

"I could ask the same of you. Are you ready to join us?"

Richard relaxed into a laugh. "Oui, let us go break our fast."

The brothers approached the fire where Richard acknowledged Macadie who stood and accepted the missive from him.

"Conner, over here." Macadie beckoned his nephew who approached the group. "Here is the Coont's missive that I told ye about." He handed it to Conner and turned to Richard. "Conner's me sister's lad. She has entrusted his safety to me."

"Should you be sending him then?" Richard having second thoughts about the young man.

"Oh...aye, he'll be right slippery when it comes to the English. If ye wanted him to, he could get into the countess's cell. Ye did ask that she reply, aye?"

"Oui, I did." Richard eyed Conner. "You will miss fighting the English for a while. What say you to that?"

Young and brash, Conner shrugged. "The English will always be there. It doesna matter if I fight them or deliver missives amongst them. 'Tis all the same to me."

Macadie scoffed, "Ye mighten brag a little less, Conner."

"Be most careful, lad," Richard cautioned. "I want that missive given to Mistress Warren, the constable's wife. She will make sure that Deirdre Brodie gets it. You know what to do if you're discovered?"

"Aye. I'll make out fine, Count Strasbourg. Ye need not worrit about me."

Richard was relieved that this young warrior took his assignment to heart.

Macadie gave his nephew an affectionate shake. "Off with ye, Conner. Ye can find us traveling toward Wrothbury's castle."

Feeling relieved and secure with his plan to send Conner to Deirdre, Richard observed the young man until he crested the hill and dropped out of sight.

After parting company with Philippe, Richard rode alongside Macadie. The look on Philippe's face wasn't one Richard would soon forget. He was letting his brother down, that he should be riding alongside him and helping to command the army. But, Richard could not turn away from the mission he'd taken upon himself. A mission to him that was more important than Scotland's war with the English. At Philippe's insistence, Richard had hand-picked some of the Flemish soldiers to accompany him. Counting his squire Bertrand and their guide Gordon, they numbered a dozen men.

They rode across land with a rugged sweeping beauty that made an impression on Richard. After a day of traveling over steep hillsides and valleys, they rode next to a river that meandered across the land.

"The place we cross is hereabouts, Coont. 'Tis been a bit since I've come this way." Macadie wore a troubled frown as he guided Richard slowly along the riverbank.

Their horses cut through the dense foliage as Richard studied the water close to the opposite riverbank. The setting sun cast the opposite bank into inky black shadows and the darkening foliage edging it was foreboding.

"Would that you find your crossing soon, Macadie, for I would like to keep going before we stop for nightfall."

They continued along the bank lined with heavy branched conifer trees.

"Here we be, Coont. This is the spot." Macadie quickly reined in his horse.

"Macadie, what is amiss?"

"I'm not sure…go ahead and lead yer men across while I check over there." He pointed at the foliage a little further down.

Richard studied the water and hoped it wouldn't come past his stirrups at the deepest point. Signaling Bertrand to join him, they started to cross. Saladin nickered and hesitated, but Richard spurred him on. Once he plowed into the frigid water he realized why Saladin baulked and couldn't blame the horse. By the time the water reached Richard's thighs he was swearing. As both men neared the other side, the water level slowly dropped past their knees. Again Saladin balked and shied away from the bank.

"Saladin." Richard tried to control his steed and hastened a puzzled glance over at Bertrand whose mount was also giving him trouble. "Bertrand? What in the—?"

Without warning, a naked body flashed through the air as a man dropped out of a tree and knocked Bertrand off his horse. They disappeared under water. Richard struggled to control his mount whose eyes rolled white with fear. Suddenly a man surged up out of the water with such force that water swooshed off his naked body and over Richard's thigh. Saladin reared, his great hooves striking air as the man grabbed Richard out of his saddle and buried him head first into the muddy ooze that made up the riverbed.

Richard's air choked off as mire filled his helmet, his nostrils and mouth. He held his breath and pushed his hands deep into the mud, seeking leverage, anything to help him squirm out of his assailant's grasp. But strong hands held him down. Just when his brain felt to explode from lack of air, someone grabbed the neck of his chest armor and lifted him out of the silt. Dragged onto the bank he was dumped on dry ground. Fighting to breathe, Richard tore his helmet off. Someone wiped the mud from his face.

Richard rolled over on all fours and vomited silt.

"Can ye breathe, Coont?"

He nodded, sucking in air.

"Let's get ye out of this armor," Macadie said, and removed Richard's chest armor. Macadie then used the tail of Richard's tunic to wipe the mud from his eyes.

Able to see again, Richard glared up at the man who not only pulled him off his horse but also had the gall to stand there with his claymore pointing at him.

"Get thy weapon out of my face," Richard growled, his anger resonating in his voice, his teeth gritted against the dirt still in his mouth. "Vous plaisàntez trap souvent!" He roared to his feet and then half lifting, half shoving his assailant, he pushed the big man backwards into the river. When the man rose up out of the water, Richard smashed his fist against the man's jaw. "Bâtard! You think to drown me?" He pulled the man up out of the water and hit him again.

"Christ's blood—!" The man who so far had not hit Richard back, now did so.

He landed a knuckle-cracking blow against Richard's chin. Richard tackled him. They both went underwater, tussling, and rolling about. The water churned like an angry sea with their surfacing bodies. Richard hit him again, the blow snapping the man's head backwards. The big man's fist plowed a bruising blow against Richard's mouth, splitting his lip, the tastes of blood strong.

Macadie and Gordon rushed in and tried pulling them apart, which was no easy feat as their fight was going strong. Macadie grabbed Richard's arm that was poised to launch another blow. "'Tis enough—Coont. Ye be hitting David Brodie—Deirdre's brother."

Amidst a barrage of swear words, both men were dragged from the water. Richard, taking in David Brodie's size, was thankful the man's fists hadn't launched his head off his shoulders. He glanced over to see Bertrand standing on shore next to the very man who had taken him off his horse. Everyone stared at Richard with an amused look.

Richard stood shivering. His sojourn in the river had cleansed most of the mud from his face and he glared at the Scots who milled together and said nothing. Richard was glad of the silence as he didn't think he could be civil to David Brodie who almost succeeded in drowning him.

Someone built a fire, and with Bertrand's help, Richard stripped off his clothing. He hastened a glance at Macadie who was over talking with David and the other man who had jumped from the tree. Both men were dressing and shot occasional glances his way as they conversed in Gaelic.

Richard handed his weapons belt to Bertrand who had a grin tugging the corners of his mouth. Bertrand hummed and averted his eyes. He wiped the sheath dry and then hung it on a tree branch. When Richard started to hand him his wet clothes, a chuckle escaped Bertrand.

"What say you, Bertrand?" Richard tongued his bruised and bleeding lip that throbbed.

"Nothing—milord." Air fizzed out of him. No longer able to contain himself, Bertrand bent over in gales of laughter.

"Are you finding humor in me getting buried head first?" Trying to cower his young squire, Richard leveled him with a glare.

However, Bertrand was beyond chastising, and unable to contain himself, he stuttered, "N...n...non, milord. But—but—if you could see what I did...what we all did...when your legs flew up in the air and your head went under water...for a moment you actually stuck that way...like an arrow!"

"You saw all that from almost being drowned yourself?"

"My assailant didn't try to kill me. Your fight was longer than ours." His mouth parted in a wide grin.

All the men slowly started to laugh and soon deep laughter resonated into the night.

Thoroughly chilled, the night air giving up little to a man without dry clothes, Richard pulled his blanket from his saddlebag then warmed it by the fire before wrapping it around his middle. Bertrand had lightened everyone's mood with his laughter. Even Richard cracked a smile, hurting his injured lip, thinking indeed he must have been a comical sight. But he still held less than congenial thoughts for the man, David Brodie, who had so efficiently dunked him, outsmarted him, and made him feel like a fool.

The two Scots had finished dressing by wrapping their kilts around their hips and throwing the rest over their shoulders. They used their sheaths to anchor the material in place. David, sitting on the ground while pulling on his boots, occasioned a glance at Richard. David's companion had finished dressing and now waited beside him.

Richard hunkered down next to the fire and opened the front of his blanket to allow the warmth at his legs and privates. Running his tongue over his cut lip, his thoughts turned to Conner. Had the young warrior reached Falconshire yet? If so, Richard prayed that he delivered the missive to Deirdre without interference. He hastened a sideways glance at David Brodie, and then stood to pull the blanket around his shoulders. This certainly was not how he'd envisioned meeting Deirdre's brother, but then it was not the preferred way to meet neither friend nor foe.

Macadie approached and offered a wine bladder to Richard. "Here ye be. Have ye unruffled enough to meet David Brodie and Bonnar Cameron?"

"That man with David Brodie is Bonnar Cameron?" Richard swore to himself.

"Now, Coont, dinna fret yerself. That was a long time ago between Bonnar and Deirdre...over two years."

"Oui," Richard snapped, "and most of that time she's been caged like a wild beast, has she not." Usually easy going, he'd lost his temper more today than he cared to think about.

David approached to warm his hands over the fire. Richard was glad to see the man also had a cut on his lip to equal his own.

Trying to grin at Richard, David flinched. "Ye have a hard fist, Count Strasbourg. I'm honored to make yer acquaintance and feel verra sheepish for pulling ye into the river. We've been scouting for Robert de Brus." And not waiting for Richard's reaction, he turned and motioned Bonnar to join them. "Count Strasbourg, meet my good friend, Bonnar Cameron."

Having no choice, Richard acknowledged both and sized them up. Bonnar was of medium height, blond, and well-muscled. David, taller by a head then all the men in camp, wore his long black hair tied back, his dark eyes sharp and raven like. His whole persona reminded Richard of the way Andrew Brodie had looked that day. Those dark eyes of David's searched Richard's face, seemingly for signs of malice.

"We had a minor skirmish with English soldiers and were bathin' the blood from our bodies when we heard horses. Thinkin' ye to be English, we grabbed our claymores and hid. I cut a reed and went into the water. Bonnar climbed the nearby tree. Bonnar was the smart one. I swear the water was so cold it was stopping me heart, and I was just about to come out of it when yer horse's hooves stepped within inches of me face."

"I go with what David says." Bonnar's brown eyes twinkled. "'Tis sorry I am that I took yer man down. No harm done, aye?" He turned to Bertrand who joined them and actually smiled at the Scot who had bested him.

Richard wrapped his blanket tighter and accepted David's apology. "Oui, as you say, no harm done, only my mouth will be a reminder." Forgetting his lip, he started to grin making the cut bleed and sting again.

Cursing to himself as he wiped blood on the back of his hand, he spoke, "David, I've met your sister, Deirdre."

David's brow creased in puzzlement. "What d'ye know of my sister?"

"I know that she was delivered of a baby girl this past November, and that Wrothbury took the infant from her. I know she is still imprisoned," Richard said.

Taking this news with silence, David hunkered down by the fire and put his hands dangerously close to the flames to warm them. The fire cast his face in an orange glow. "Did Deirdre tell ye about feeding and allowing de Brus to rest in Wrothbury's castle?"

"Oui, she told me all."

"Ye canna know how many times I have blamed meself fer not taking her away. She has suffered greatly at the hands of Wrothbury. God smite the man. Not long after my sister was caged, I tried to rescue her. Someone must have warned the constable we were coming. I could see Deirdre in that damn cage. The soldiers manned the battlements like locust. Some of us were wounded, me included." David's jaw firmed. "Each day she's in the cage is like a thorn under my skin that keeps festering. Count Strasbourg, I remember ye from the day my clan was attacked, Deirdre taken. Why were ye ridin' with the English?" David's gaze was filled with questions.

Macadie started to answer when Richard shook his head. "I was a spy for my King of France. That's all I'm inclined to say."

Bonnar knelt next to Richard and reached out to the fires warmth. Keeping his gaze locked onto the fire he spoke to no one in particular. "The crown of Scotland wobbles on the Brus's head, and he sets about fightin' to keep it and prove that he is the one true leader of Scotland. Not the English. Not Edward's whelp," he emphasized with venom, giving testimony to how they all felt.

David picked up a piece of wood and tossed it on the fire that sent sparks scattering into the night sky before winking out. An owl hooted.

Getting to his feet, Richard spoke to both David and Bonnar. "I've left coin to make Countess Wrothbury's life more bearable. She's been moved into a cleaner cell. The constable has been paid wages for her care. But the both of you listen well to what I say. I am going to get Deirdre's child from Wrothbury, and then I'm going to steal Deirdre from the cage." Richard dared them to say otherwise, but no one did. Bonnar's face tightened when Richard spoke of helping Deirdre, then the mask slipped back into place again. Had Richard not been looking at the man, he would have missed it.

"David, we need to talk away from the others," Richard said.

David followed Richard from the warm fire and waited patiently until the count finally turned to address him.

"David, your sister has been pardoned by England's present King Edward."

This took David unaware, as it was the last thing he expected to hear. "What d'ye say?" he asked in an incredulous voice.

"Your sister told me that Wrothbury came to her before the baby was born and had an edict pardoning her. But when Deirdre defied him, Wrothbury decided to punish her and refused to share it with the constable of Falconshire. Instead, he waited for the child's birth and extended Deirdre's punishment by denying her freedom. He took the baby girl away."

David's temper flared and he vented by slamming his fist against his palm. "I would like nothing better than to castrate Wrothbury and make him eat his tarse, which would be a small nibble. Then I would choke the pardon from the man." If anyone were to try and take David's three bairns, he would kill them on the spot. His life before theirs, always.

"David, I also have a vendetta against Wrothbury. My brother Philippe takes our army to the Bruce. Please keep that Scottish temper of yours from putting my plans in jeopardy."

"Dinna worried, Count, I willna spoil yer plans. But I'll be goin' with ye to get Deirdre's wee bairn. So, dinna think to try this without me."

"You may join me, but not Bonnar Cameron. I think it best he seeks out my brother Philippe de Laci and join the army Philippe takes to Dundee Castle and your king."

"Bonnar means ye no harm. If ye want him away from ye, then he'll go." David put his hand on Richard's forearm. "I have a question. What d'ye have to do with Deirdre?"

"I care about your sister. I'll leave it at that."

David suddenly remembered his sister asking about Count Strasbourg when he supped at her table in Wrothbury Castle. She said that the man showed her kindness when their clan was attacked. The only thing David could remember about that day was his sire's death, and Deirdre's kidnapping.

Wrothbury left his chamber with the intent to join several English Barons who awaited him in the great hall. Holding his gloves in one hand, he slapped them against the palm of the other. He anticipated breaking his morning fast with a hearty meal and lively conversation about his recent sojourn into Scotland. After that, he planned a full day of hunting using his prized falcons to impress his guests.

Dressed in an ermine-trimmed tunic of black, with black hose covering his legs, his clothes helped to disguise his deformity somewhat. But nothing could disguise the constant knife-sharp pain in his crippled leg, or his aching back, now more hunched than ever. His pains made him think that maybe his time in the saddle and charging into battle was almost done. Certainly the king couldn't fault him if he decided to forgo the actual fight and simply command battles from a field tent. After all, he groused, since England's King refuses to leave the side of his male whore to mount a campaign against Scotland, how could he possibly criticize Wrothbury's aching body?

As he hitched down the hallway, he couldn't help but notice the door to the baby's room was open. Curious, he paused on the threshold and peered in to find the room empty of Mary Clair and the wet nurse. A warm fire crackled in the large fireplace, and a chair faced the fire. He'd noticed from time to time that was where the wet nurse sat while feeding the child.

Wondering if the baby was here, he approached the tall wooden cradle in the center of the room. The infant was indeed there, sound asleep and snuggled under a brown woolen blanket. Wishing she'd been born a male, he felt no love for his daughter. She was simply a means to bring his wife to heel. Like a worm dangling on a hook, he meant to use her as bait. A wife who made his manhood turgid just to think of her, a wife that he was going to bring home as soon as he deemed she had learned her lesson well. She'd do anything to be with the child…anything at all. He considered Deirdre to be in the frame of mind where he wanted her to be. Yes, it was almost time to bring her home.

Used to giving the baby a mere glance now and then, he leaned close to peer at her face. She resembled her mother. But her fine baby hair was a much brighter shade of red. Without thought, he reached down and stroked her round cheek which was warm and soft. She jerked from his touch. He recoiled. His child was just like her mother who flinched at his very touch. A most distinctive resemblance, his lip curled in distaste at the comparison.

Her mouth moved in a sucking motion before a yawn made it gap wide and then her eyes slowly opened. Her eyes looking up at him were the color of dark gray clouds, exactly like his. She grinned at him, and this was surprising. He never received smiles from anyone. When he leaned closer for a better look, she waved her arms and cooed, sounding like the pigeons in the woods. He started to capture her tiny fist within his when the low rustle of a skirt sounded behind him. His hand fell to his side.

"Milord, I've been sent to seek you out." Mary Clair joined him next to the cradle. Looking down at Joanna, the maid's face lit with joy. "She is such a good babe and hardly ever cries. Why, Joanna's almost six months of age and it's been that long since Countess Wrothbury held her. It isn't good to keep a mother from her daughter."

The babe now forgotten, Wrothbury stared at the pretty maid. "Perhaps, you could replace my wife and warm my bed. You have already become like the child's mother." He took her by surprise and ran his finger across her lips.

Gasping, Mary Clair moved out of his reach. Her dark eyes widened as her hand went to her mouth. She nimbly moved around to the other side of the cradle and darted him a glance. "I'm mother to Joanna only because you've kept her own mother locked away." She nervously straightened the blanket covering the infant.

"And my bed? Will you not warm my bed?" He leered at her across the crib, knowing his touch sickened her. Enjoying her discomfort, he started around the crib when she stated in a hurry.

"Oh! I almost forgot the true reason I sought you. This was delivered from Falconshire."

"And the messenger?" he asked, accepting the rolled up parchment.

"Being fed and awaiting your answer should there be one."

He broke the seal and began to read. His smile was sly and contented. "It sounds as if my wife begs for my company. She can wait." Laughing, he crumpled the parchment and threw it to the floor. Again, he eyed the pretty maid and reached across the cradle for her. His actions sent the cradle into a wild rocking motion making Joanna cry.

"Milord, your guests await and ask that you join them," she said in a rush of words. "Will there be a return message for Countess Wrothbury?"

The maiden's words made him pause. "No reply is necessary." He pointed his finger at Mary Clair. "Be forewarned, I'm not done with you, not done at all."

Joanna's crying became wails as she waved her arms about.

"Keep that child silent." He limped from the room.

Mary Clair bent to retrieve the message. She un-wadded the parchment and began to read the letter she'd penned before giving it to Wrothbury. *'To the Earl of Wrothbury. Yer wife begs for yer company. She is said to now favor ye.'*

Glancing toward the door to make sure the earl was truly gone, Mary Clair removed the messenger's original missive from her bodice and read it again. *'To the Earl of Wrothbury, ye need to be apprised that a Count Strasbourg champions yer wife.'* Not many words, but enough. Countess Wrothbury had told Mary Clair of this man's kindness to her at Foxlair castle. Somehow he must have returned and found the caged countess.

Smiling with pleasure, she went to throw both of the letters into the fire. How easily the parchment burned, and in a blink of the eye they no longer existed. She shuddered, thinking that if the earl ever found out that she replaced the missive with words of her own, for certes she would be put to death. But maybe now Countess Wrothbury would beg for leniency from the earl and come home to be with Joanna.

She hurried over to pick Joanna up. "Shh baby, don't cry."

9 Patience Conquers

Falconshire

The morning sun chased away the cold that settled about the cage. Deirdre, to her own surprise, was looking forward to the day, the last of April. Not that her existence wasn't wretched, but now Constable Warren treated her more like a royal prisoner than a scourge.

After word spread of Count Strasbourg's interference on her behalf, the townspeople became more tolerant as well. There was rumor of the pardon, and if true then Countess Wrothbury's imprisonment was illegal. Someone around Falconshire appeared to be working in her favor spreading the truth. At first, little things began to appear in her cell, a comb, a ribbon, a head veil, and a sturdy gown of blue. An item a day kept appearing and when questioned, Maude Warren feigned innocence to the originator.

"Good morning, milady." A man passing by in a wagon filled with jostling barrels nodded up at her, startling her when he spoke, but delighting her that he did.

She smiled back, and called down. "Tell me good sire, what d'ye carry in your cart?"

"'Tis wine from France. They be unloadin' ships at anchor on the river." He took off his hat and wiped his forehead. "It be a right fine day, d'ye agree?"

"Aye…that I do. Ye can trust me to know for certes how the weather is going to be."

"Good day to ye then, milady. Walk on horse." He flicked the reins against the roan colored rump and sent the horse trotting toward the city gates to blend in with the other bustling people entering and leaving.

Deirdre returned to her embroidery, nimbly pulling the white thread through the material to form a flower on the neckline of the blue gown given her. However the activity of the township drew her attention away from her sewing. She enjoyed watching the comings and goings of the people. Some, like the man in the cart, stopped to talk to her while others scurried by without a glance. So, it was a surprise to her when a wadded up piece of parchment pinged off her forehead and fell onto her lap.

Startled, she picked up the missive and scanned the area. A young blond-haired man leaning against the township wall acknowledged her by tapping two fingers of his left hand against his forehead, a subtle gesture letting her know that indeed he was the one who threw the missive. She couldn't help but smile down at him.

Cautious, she smoothed out the parchment on her lap. A brief glimpse showed Richard de Laci's bold flourish. Her heart quickened. She glanced to where the young man still relaxed against the wall, and again tried to smooth out the crinkles.

"Deirdre, I hope I do not offend by using your given name. It is with haste that I write this, and pray this missive finds you recovered from your illness and regaining your strength, for it is most imperative that you do so. Chéri, remember your promise to me, as I remember mine to you. I will meet with your brother David Brodie and inform him how you fared when last we met. Destroy this missive, and all others that I send. Richard."

Again, a coveted peek assured her the man was still there. She folded the missive and stuffed it inside her embroidery basket. The young man then left to mingle with the throng of people jostling and converging through the township gates.

A group of women and children came out of the city gates. Playing tag with one another, the children ran ahead of the women who strolled along swinging empty baskets. They laughed and chattered amongst themselves.

Only Arless Crowther paused under the cage and shouted up at her. "Milady, we are going to meet the tinker's wagon. D'ye need medicines or anything else he might carry? I can give it to Maude for ye." Smiling and without malice, the woman tucked her dark hair beneath her head-dress.

Slowly Deirdre nodded. "If it be no trouble for ye, 'tis a certain I could use some parchment. Would that ye give it to Maude Warren?"

"Aye, but surely there is more ye need?" Arless urged.

Deirdre tapped her finger against her cheek, thinking. "Well…I could do with some lavender soap. Mayhap some herbs fer medicines. Oh…and could ye get me tooth powder, the kind made from cuttlefish and oyster shell?" Her list grew fast.

"That I can," Arless said, and hurried to catch up with the rest.

The day was overly long for Deirdre. As the cage started it slow descent to the ground she searched about, but found no sign of the young man. Her patience was vexed as the pulley squeaked and groaned, the sound echoing around the wall. Drop a little, squeak—squeak—drop some more, squeak—squeak. Deirdre's foot tapped with impatience when the cage finally hit the ground. Her guards walked at a snail's pace as they escorted her inside, making her want to scurry ahead.

Maude kept up a constant chatter when she brought in the food tray. "Milady, there must be more than the few simple things ye asked Arless to bring ye?" She handed the package to Deirdre.

"Aye, Maude, did ye pay Arless fer these fine things?"

"That I did. She said to tell ye that her husband Emerson has been made a township guard. He might be escorting ye to and from the cage."

"'Tis gude to hear. Emerson appears to be most kind," Deirdre volunteered. Indeed, Emerson was one of the rare guards who would smile at her instead of sneer or turn away.

"Quite pleasant indeed and a welcome change from Miles' hateful ways. Remember, milady, Count Strasbourg's coin is for ye to buy what ye need, so tell Maudie if there's something else ye be wanting from the tinker."

"Maude, I canna believe all the people that speak to me. It must be because of Count Strasbourg's influence." A warm smile creased Deirdre's mouth and she grew hot with a blush.

Maude perceived it too, and said, "Oh...aye, milady, to be sure it is the man's coin that has changed things fer ye. At least yer belly's full and ye have warm clothing, baths, and even that there parchment ye asked for."

Deirdre eyes narrowed as she began to pace. "Something niggles at me, Maude. Now that things have improved for me, I canna help but think that the earl's ugly self will reappear. 'Tis fer certes he canna be through makin' me grovel at his feet."

"Perhaps ye speak the truth of it and I pray that ye are wrong." Maude's easy smile faded, and she said in a nervous voice, "I worry for my Thomas. He is feeling poorly and speaks naught of it, but his cough worsens."

An unsettling feeling flashed through Deirdre's mind. Her fortune, having turned to the good, depended on Thomas who indeed showed a kinder heart toward her. If something happened to Thomas, Miles would become his replacement. She grimaced at the thought and hoped Richard would soon bring the pardon.

"Maude, have ye asked the healer to help Thomas?"

"That I have. He has bled Thomas and given him medicine for the cough. But Thomas has a strange yellow color about his skin."

"Then ye must purchase the best medicine for Thomas. Use the money that Count Strasbourg left for me."

"Milady, we have no need of his money. We have the coin to pay for Thomas' care. Count Strasbourg pays Thomas a wage to take better care of ye."

This news surprised Deirdre. At least she wouldn't have to worry about Thomas betraying her. "Then we must help Thomas get well, d'ye understand?"

Maude nodded with understanding. "Miles will be constable if something happens to Thomas. And I canna blame the fear I see in yer eyes at such a thought. But for certes, we are doing all we can."

Deirdre waited until Maude left before sitting down to her meal. She tried the soup and found to her delight that it had chunks of meat in it, deer meat from the taste of it. Taking the round loaf of bread, she tore it in two, and dipping a piece of it in the broth, ate with gusto, savoring every bite and washing it down with goat's milk. Even this meal was purchased with Richard's coin. Gore...when would she gaze upon his handsome face again?

When at last she was full, she moved to the desk and removed a piece of parchment from the drawer. Dipping the quill into the inkhorn to wet its tip, she thought but a moment before beginning to write.

'R.' She wrote his initial with a flourish that would rival his, and using care, she authored her missive. Except for several cleverly placed words that would alert him to what was going on around her, she kept it light-hearted. She tried not to push him about her wee child, knowing he would keep his promise to her. When finished, and with no means to seal it, she folded the parchment into a small square.

After dressing for bed, she unwound the braids coiled over her ears and while stroking the brush through chestnut kinks, all she could think about was Richard. She chided herself. If she didn't stop with such thoughts, she'd be back on her knees praying for forgiveness. But her mind wouldn't stop, and once she was in bed, she tossed around like wheat in the wind until at long last she settled on her back and flung an arm over her forehead. Gore...how forceful he was when he made her promise to live for him. She slowly ran the back of her hand up her neck, following the path his mouth had taken. Using a fingertip, she outlined her mouth, remembering his feathery kiss, the tickle of his mustache and the heat from his lips. Oh…gore…his lips. How could she possibly forget the hard feel of his long body under hers when she landed on him? He had made her feel like a delicate flower when he embraced her. She wanted his hands caressing her, making love to her.

Her eyes popped open, Saints above! What brought on his acts of kindness to her? Why would he not covet a rounded maiden with meat on her bones?

Deirdre needed to ask Maude to purchase something important from the tinker. Something she did indeed want.

Morning found her being escorted to the cage by William and Emerson. Walking between the guards she stole a glance at Emerson who was pleasant to look at with shaggy blond hair that fell below his helmet. His uniform hung loose on his slim body. When he caught her staring at him, he winked at her with twinkling blue eyes. William, much older, had white hair and lines on his face that reminded Deirdre of a broken spider web.

"In ye go, Countess Wrothbury." William held the door for her and snapped the padlock into place.

She sat on her chair as William and Emerson went to take up their positions at the gate.

The cage was raised. When it didn't stop at the normal level, she tried to get the soldiers attention. "Roger, is that ye? Please dinna raise the cage so high. Could ye lower me back so I'm out of the wind?"

Deirdre gasped when Miles turned around and grinned down at her. "Oh…is yer highness too high and the wind too cold for yer skinny bones?"

"Thomas says not to raise me this high," she stammered.

"Well Thomas is not here—now is he? But if her highness wants to be lowered, then let me oblige." Releasing the brake on the pulley and giving the handle a strong spin, he sent the cage plummeting toward the ground. Joined by Roger, they both stood laughing.

Deirdre screamed as the cage rapidly dropped.

When it was within a couple of feet from the ground, the cage jerked to a stop.

Deirdre spilled onto the cage floor, and the chair overturned on top of her.

As though materializing out of nowhere, the young man from yesterday was next to the cage before anyone else. He reached through the bars trying to help her. "Are ye injured, milady?" he asked and then whispered, "My name is Conner Kincaid. D'ye have a missive for the count?"

Still on her backside and trying to regain her feet, she reached into her bodice and quickly handed him the missive. "'Tis no broken bones I have this time." Pleased that Richard had sent a fellow Scotsman, her words tumbled out, "D'ye know my brother David Brodie?"

"Hey you—get away from her," Miles shouted, and started to raise the cage.

Conner shrugged and shading his eyes glanced up at the guards. He yelled, "Jest making sure she wasna hurt. 'Twas a bad spill she took." He whispered to Deirdre, "Aye, I fight beside David. He is well."

"When ye see David, tell him I ask about him," her words rushed out. "And tell Count Strasbourg, I promise."

Again Miles shouted for him to leave.

Conner's brows drew together as he started to slowly back away. "Ye must be speakin' of something between ye and Count Strasbourg, aye?"

Deirdre nodded and wanted to say more when Miles bellowed down as both he and Roger stopped winding. "I said get away from her!"

When Miles disappeared down the tower stairwell, she warned the young man to leave and be quick about it. He disappeared around the outer wall. Deirdre watched with trepidation as Miles bounded out of the tower door and looked around for the young man who was nowhere in sight.

"Whom were ye talking to? Yer not to talk to anyone."

"But…but the town folk are starting to talk to me. And that should be allowed. I am, after all—a Countess," she said, being forceful.

"That man was not from Falconshire. Who was he?"

"He wasna?" Meekly, she looked at Miles. "How am I to know otherwise?" She beseeched him. "He only said good morning and asked if I was hurt when the cage fell."

Miles started to reply but instead moved closer. "Yer still too skinny for my liking, but yer pretty enough." He ran a dirt-encrusted finger over her face.

Conner was forgotten.

Loathing the man and his stench, she jerked out of his reach. There was no doubting what his touch predicted. Recoiling, Deirdre sat on her chair and prayed that Thomas would get well soon. The joy had gone out of the day.

Maude brought Deirdre's evening meal and handed her a package wrapped in parchment. "Here's what ye asked for, milady, but it took a bit of coin. Best be careful with yer money."

"How is Thomas? I sorely missed him today when Miles tried to hurt me by dropping my cage on purpose. At least Thomas would brook no pranks like that from Miles."

"He is better to be sure. I think the medicines help him somewhat. Mayhap he will be back to himself in no time. I'll tell Thomas what Miles did."

"Nay. Say nothing about it," Deirdre cautioned.

"'Tis sure ye be, milady?"

"Aye, say nothing."

Maude left Deirdre alone with her food and the package.

The aroma-filled soup had fish in it, and tasting most delicious Deirdre scraped the bowl clean. The bread was another matter, unable to break old habits; she broke it apart, saving some for later. She still found it hard to accept such acts of kindness when she'd suffered such brutal misery for so long. Richard was indeed most powerful.

She went to her clothes chest and fetched the small package that Arless had brought her the other day. The soap's lavender scent filled her senses as she inhaled its heady aroma. With diligence, she smoothed out the parchment wrap saving it to use later. Perhaps a scented missive to Richard would be sure to remind him of her.

But it was the bigger package that enticed her. Before unwrapping it, she took the soap and gave her body a good wash. When finished, and as though the package held a rare jewel, she slowly unwrapped it, and lacking courage to go any further, held the lone contents tight against her chest.

"Sweet Virgin Mary and Christ—Deirdre. Dinna be such a fraidy cat."

She brought her purchase, a hand mirror, slowly in front of her face and studied herself for the first time in over a year. The mirror, made of copper and hammered into a slim piece of metal, gave her a true reflection. She stared for the longest time. Who was this woman staring back? An anguished sound escaped her lips. She groped for the chair and blindly sat down. Again, she took up the mirror. Her mouth, always wide and full, was too big for her face. She traced fingers over cheeks that once glowed with good health but were now drained of color. Her eyes that once sparkled like jewels were dull and listless.

Fearing to do so, she grimaced and examined her teeth. Her gums were somewhat red, but her teeth were white and a tug on each one proved none was loose. A sob of relief escaped her. Next, she opened a small leather pouch and poured a tiny amount of tooth powder onto her left palm. Wetting her fingertip, she dabbed it into the finely ground powder, and then carefully rubbed it over her teeth and gums.

When finished, she again looked into the mirror and with a lift of her chin, bargained with herself. She would make herself well. With or without the pardon, with or without Richard's help, she was getting out of this imprisonment. When that happened, she was going after Joanna.

Weariness closed her eyes as silent tears slipped beneath her lashes. She was somewhat comforted that Mary Clair was with Joanna. But Mary Clair was young, she'd be married off someday and leave Wrothbury Castle. Then who would be with Joanna? Deirdre compared the short five years she'd had with her own mam to the brief time she had with Joanna, less than an hour.

All that remained in Deirdre's mind of her mam was one of a tall woman with russet colored hair, and the smell of flowers when she held Deirdre close. She remembered Athey, her nursemaid the most. Old Athey's gnarled hands that coddled her, made sure she ate. Athey taught her about life, told her stories. It was Athey's soft bosom Deirdre buried her head against when she'd cried and needed comforting. Joanna wouldn't even have faded memories. She would have nothing, and that was more disturbing than anything to Deirdre. She didn't want that for her daughter.

10 He Who Leads

Southern Scotland

Richard's journey to get Deirdre's daughter was slow going. Not only was the weather against his small band of men, but they kept running into English patrols. Some they either dispatched with ease, or if the patrols were too large, they would hide until the way was clear. His men had become used to these short forays as Richard now called them. The Scots liked to hide, kill, and then retreat, or in their case, go forward, constantly edging closer to England and Richard's destination, Wrothbury Castle.

Having fought alongside these Scots and mercenaries for close to a month, Richard formed a strong admiration for them. He'd also forged a mutual friendship with Macadie Gunn. Fifteen years older than Richard, Macadie at forty-four, had proved himself an able fighter.

Less than a fortnight ago Richard received a lengthy missive from his brother Philippe that he had delivered the army to Scotland's king. Philippe reported that at first the Bruce was vexed that Richard wasn't present. But once explained that Richard sought Countess Wrothbury's pardon, her child, and to do battle with the Earl of Wrothbury, Scotland's king reluctantly accepted Richard's absence. The Bruce, Philippe wrote, had campaigned throughout the winter in northwest Scotland and annihilated quite a few of the English garrisons that dotted the country-side. Philippe's new orders were to clear the border of the English, and to cleanse its mighty castles of the Scottish barons that sided with England's king. At present, the Bruce was on his way to take the port of Aberdeen. Philippe was heading toward the southern border territory and the Castle of Blackadder of which he would siege until it surrendered...

...Richard's horse, along with the rest, struggled against the road turned into a muddy quagmire created by a spring downpour. They cursed at their mounts, and at each other, their misery getting the best of them. The men, miserable as they continued on, urged by Richard who traveled as though the devil himself plotted his course. The rain abated some, allowing muted sunshine to break through the dark clouds, giving Richard a respite from forcing his men to keep going in wretched conditions.

Movement up ahead drew Richard's attention. He held up a hand stopping everyone as one of his outriders, along with another man, labored to get to them.

"Look," Richard said to Macadie, and pointed. "I send out one man and two returns."

Guarded, they pulled their swords and waited.

Once in front of Richard and his troops, both men sharply reined in their horses. The outrider acknowledged Richard with a brief nod. He then gave way to the other traveler.

Macadie chuckled. "Ah...'tis Conner. We can rest easy." He stepped forward to greet his nephew who was so mud spattered he was hardly recognizable.

Conner Kincaid, trying to get his breath, pointed back to the way he'd come. "Uncle, a troop of English soldiers are on me tail. I happened upon yer outrider who brought me here."

Alarmed, Richard addressed the young fighter. "How far behind? "

"Less than an hour."

"I see." Taking in the warning, Richard said, "I've been most concerned about your welfare."

"Dinna worrit about me, Count Strasbourg. I'm able to take care of myself. Traveling alone even more so." Conner searched inside his tunic and withdrew the missive. "Here ye be, Count Strasbourg. 'Tis from the Lady Deirdre." He wiped water droplets from his face and stared expectantly at Richard.

Wanting to read Deirdre's letter immediately, Richard forced himself to secure the parchment inside his waist pouch. "We'll talk later. Right now we have the English to fight."

"Count Strasbourg," David said and pointed at the embankment and the hillside. "Up there is a gude place for an ambush, aye?"

Macadie protested. "I dinna like it."

Richard disagreed. "It looks most likely."

He led them back the way they had come, and like goats, they started climbing the backside of the hill. Once they reached the top, they hurried to chop saplings into poles of which were used to work loose some of the larger boulders.

Richard was next to Macadie on a large outcropping boulder slick with the rain that was back with a vengeance. They watched the columned progression of English soldiers struggling in the mud.

Seeing that the size of the retinue was larger than he liked, Richard prayed the soggy hillside wouldn't give way and send them crashing down to land amongst the English. Movement from David caught his eye as the warrior pulled his plaid cloth around his shoulders and tried to stay out of the small streams of muddy water coursing down the hill.

Richard motioned his men to readiness. They scurried to pick up the long poles and took up their positions next to the large boulders they had ready to dislodge.

Macadie, in a hurry to get into place, lost his foothold. He started sliding down alongside the rocks and loose gravel. Frantically grabbing for bushes, anything to stop his fall, he tried to get a toehold, but couldn't. Unable to call out for fear of revealing their location Macadie reached for Richard's outstretched hands. Richard sitting on his behind had a death grip on Macadie, but he too was being pulled forward in the slippery mud, and both men were in danger of falling amongst the English. Suddenly, strong hands went around Richard's waist. David pulled them both to safety.

"Are ye gude?" David asked in a whisper.

"Aye, laddie, gude. And the English?"

"Almost here," Richard said and helped Macadie to his feet.

Sounds from the advancing English became louder as they cursed and urged their mounts through the slippery mud.

Richard raised his hand up and quickly knifed it down, signaling to start. Putting their weight against the poles, muscles strained as they grunted and pushed. David put his massive strength into rocking the thick shaft, trying to loosen the stubborn giant rock. Richard, along with the rest, did the same. Slowly the boulders shifted and started to topple down the hillside, picking up speed as they rolled.

The English looked up in wide-eyed horror to see boulders hurtling down at them. Some spurred their mounts and got out of the way. Others, not so fortunate, were crushed. Screams echoed up the hillside.

Macadie along with the rest rushed to mount their horses. Then with a battle cry that would scare a man's soul to running away, the Scots, led by Conner and Macadie, galloped down the embankment to rush into battle. Swinging their claymores with both hands, they made short work of the wounded.

Richard and his men took out after the English that were getting away. David charged past him and reined in his horse as the English turned to fight. He stood in his stirrups, screamed his war cry, and swung his claymore in a vicious arc, wounding the first man, then without pause, hacked the next man from neck to heart.

Another soldier turned to face him. He bore a spiked mace in one hand and a shield in the other. Meeting him head on, David, unwound his own chained-mace from his saddle. Both men swung at the other, causing sparks to fly as the balled ends wrapped together. Grunting, David yanked with all his might and unseated the man who landed on his backside. The man quickly regained his feet and running next to David's horse managed to jerk David to the ground. Grabbing his claymore, David scrambled upright and attacked. Their swords clanged together, the sound loud, until David went on the defensive and drove the man backwards, slicing his arm from shoulder to forearm. Blood spurted in a red arc. The soldier screamed and grabbed at his arm.

A hot piercing nudge stung David's back. Stunned, he swung around just in time to glimpse a soldier hastily riding away. He tried, but couldn't reach the dagger protruding from his back. He swirled back around to see the soldier he'd just wounded advancing toward him. Richard jumped in front of David finishing the soldier off.

David groped for and sat on a boulder. "Did ye get the scut that stabbed me in the back?" Still breathing heavy, he asked Macadie and Richard who approached.

"Gordon's gone after 'em." Macadie dismounted in a flash. Looking at David's back, he said, "Hold on laddie." Taking the knife by the handle, he pulled it out, releasing a trail of blood as he did so.

David swore like a peasant being led to the gallows. "How bad?"

Macadie unwrapped David's plaid and removed his tunic shirt. Perusing David's back, the older Scot tore a piece of plaid and pressed it against the cut. "Och, not verra bad at all. The wound's deep, but no real damage done. Ye should be used to getting little nicks like this, aye? If ye had yer leine croich on, mayhap a blade wouldna find yer body. Coont, can Bertrand stitch him up?"

"Oui." Richard studied the cut, then handed David the water flagon. He motioned Bertrand over.

David took Richard's offered flask and drank deep from it. Rain pelted David's hair and face, picking up dirt as it rivulet off.

Bertrand threaded his needle and without warning started stitching David's back.

"God's blood!" David growled out, almost jumping from the rock he sat on, the sting from the needle now more painful than the cut.

Conner approached and stood grimacing at David's wound.

A horse's whinny drew their attention toward a boulder and Gordon who rode around it. Behind Gordon and dangling across his saddle like a discarded sack of grain was a dead Englishman. Gordon stopped in front of David.

"Here is the filthy scut whose dagger meant to take ye out, David," Gordon said. Reaching behind his saddle he grabbed the soldier by his breastplate and unmercifully dumped the man to the ground. The soldier flopped over onto his back driving the dagger in deeper.

"It is good that he didn't get away to warn others. You've done well, Gordon." Richard liked the young man who was so willing to take orders and not question them, but more so, the Scotsman was dependable, another characteristic Richard favored. He retrieved Gordon's knife and handed it to him.

Macadie winced as Bertrand poured wine over the stitches.

"Damn!" David roared to his feet. "That burns like hades. I would rather be pourin' that down my gullet than on me back. Give it here." Grabbing the bladder from a startled Bertrand, he poured a steady stream into his mouth before tossing it to Richard who gladly accepted the drink.

"Gordon, you and the others strip the dead of weapons and armor. Take any supplies we might need. Have the men dig a pit and bury them," Richard ordered.

"Aye, milord, 'twill be done. What of the ones under the boulders?"

"Leave them." Richard motioned for Conner to join him. David and Macadie also came to listen.

"How did Countess Wrothbury appear to you, Conner?" Richard asked.

"Not knowin' how bad she looked before, 'tis fer certes she be a skinny thing. She was in the cage the first day I got there. And without a means to get your missive to her I balled it up and tossed it through the bars, I—"

"You were told to give the missive to Maude Warren," Richard reminded.

"I didna see her. When I asked the whereabouts of Mistress Warren, I was told she was inside somewhere. I didna want to go into the dungeon seeking her. I wanted to get rid of yer letter as soon as I could. I motioned to the countess it was me who threw it. Some of the townspeople talked to her."

Accepting Conner's account of what happened, Richard was pleased that some people's attitudes were changing toward her. "That is good to hear."

"The next mornin' I watched as they brought her out to the cage. The soldiers raised it up past the city wall. Too high it was. She asked that it be lowered out of the wind. One of the soldiers, nasty man he be, flipped the brake and the cage came this close to hitting the ground before it was stopped." Conner spaced his hands two-feet apart.

Concern etched Richard's face. He gripped Conner's forearm. "What of Countess Wrothbury, was she hurt?"

"She was knocked off her chair and onto the floor, but appeared unhurt. When I ran over to her, she handed me a missive for ye. Still flat on her back she was. A soldier yelled at me to get away from her and came down from the battlements to run me off. I slipped away before he got there. I looked back to see him botherin' her. He is a mean one for sure."

David's brow furrowed and he said, "That is Deirdre, brave even when it would be better fer her to cower in the face of her enemy."

Richard asked Conner, "Did you see Thomas Warren, the constable?"

"Nay, heard tell he has the ague." Conner paused for a moment. "I believe yer worries are with that soldier, Miles."

Richard wished that while back in Falconshire when he threatened to emasculate the guard that he'd ripped the man's sacs from his body. He'd be a threat to no one then.

"D'ye have anythin' to eat?" Conner asked hopefully. "I havna supped since yesterday."

David reached into his pouch and offered Conner some salted beef. "'Tis sparse, I know. But we have little left to us."

Conner nodded and accepted the food from David.

Richard slowly unfolded the parchment and read Deirdre's words.

'Count Strasbourg, I am growing stronger. I try to be patient knowing that ye will be bringing me my sweet Joanna and my pardon. With both in hand, I will leave this confinement. I do admit that not knowing your plans concerning Joanna and myself keeps me in a constant state of wondering. Ye are in my mind and prayers. Ride with God beside ye. Deirdre'

He could well imagine the bright smile she would have for him as he shared his good news that he was on his way to take back what was rightfully hers. He couldn't help but grin at that vision. "Conner, I've an important message for you to deliver to the countess as soon as humanly possible. 'Twill be your last, nor do I expect an answer."

Richard handed David the missive to read. "Your sister writes a fine hand for a woman."

"Our sire insisted she learn alongside me. Deirdre can do her numbers as well as she reads and writes."

Conner spoke up. "Count Strasbourg, in all the excitement, I almost forgot. Countess Wrothbury said to tell ye she promises."

11 Either To Do Or Die

Falconshire

Deirdre sat watching young Caleb Crowther playing a game of bandy ball with some other youngsters. The rain had stopped several days ago. Today the sun spread its warmth, drying up the mud, and allowing the children to come out and play. When the ball escaped their wild kicks and rolled toward her cage they stopped playing. Caleb ran over to retrieve it.

"Ye play gude for a youngster," Deirdre called down to him. She liked Caleb. Unlike the others, he was never cruel to her. Perhaps it was because his mother Arless had taught him better.

Caleb's chest puffed out and Deirdre could see that he was proud at being praised. He kicked the ball back toward his companions then hesitated, looking up at her.

"Milady?"

"Aye, Caleb?" She watched him struggle to find the right words.

"D'ye think ye'll get out o' the cage? Yer not a...er...witch as some say, but a fine person like my mam says."

"Caleb," Arless called from the township gate and then spotting him, approached. She shaded her eyes and smiled up at Deirdre. "Milady, ye be right pretty this fine day."

Deirdre, although still slim, had put on weight defining her bosom and hips, and making her face less gaunt. Her attitude of hopelessness had been replaced with one of strength. "Arless, ye canna know how pleased I am to have Caleb talk to me. 'Tis for certain it helps pass the day."

"Then 'tis glad I am that young Caleb be a pleasure to ye, and not be deviling ye." She reached for her son's hand. "Come along lad, 'tis time to prepare our meal."

"And a good day to the both of ye." Laughing, Deirdre's gaze was drawn to a person who had just leaned against the wall next to the gate. Her heart lurched when she realized it was the Scotsman Conner Kincaid. Giving her a quick nod, he simply joined those entering the open gates by walking right behind Arless and Caleb. Deirdre's heart practically stopped as the Scotsman went past the township guards as if he were from Falconshire.

Deirdre anxiously grasped the bars as the cage was being lowered. When it finally thumped against the ground, Emerson opened the door, his wide grin crinkled the skin around his blue eyes.

"Milady, Mistress Warren asked that we take you for a walk before returning you to yer chamber," William volunteered.

Reluctant to do so, Deirdre vacillated. Today of all days why did Maude want her to walk around? With Conner Kincaid here, she desperately wanted to know where he went. Did he talk with Richard? Did he have another missive for her?

"Then we shall do so," she acquiesced.

Emerson removed his helmet and pushed at sweaty blond bangs pressed against his forehead. "Countess Wrothbury, Mistress Warren is not the only one ye can call friend. Ye have others amongst yer guards."

Deirdre hesitated no more and walked between the two. Emerson's words stuck in her mind. She was glad that not all the men at Falconshire took orders from Wrothbury. They walked opposite the city wall toward the sparse forest, and across the road that was packed into hardpan but deeply grooved from the wagon traffic. Carefully lifting the hem of her gown, she jumped across the ruts.

White daisies clumped here and there, and she resisted the urge to pick them. The fresh scent of evergreens, moss, lichen, and rich loam wafted about her as she inhaled deeply of the intoxicating smells. Emerson pointed at a squirrel that darted across an upper branch.

The squirrel stopped to chatter down at them as though scolding them while its tail did a fast swish. It scampered away, disappearing further up the tree.

Emerson cleared his throat and blurted, "I do not think ye should be in the cage. There is rumor that ye have been pardoned, but 'twas not shown to the constable."

Astonished at his remark, she started to tell them that she was a free woman, but held her council. "Do more guards hear the rumor and share your sentiment but canna speak of it for fear of reprisal?"

William shifted uncomfortably. "If ye be asking if they are afraid of being punished, the answer is aye, milady. Some of the guards would like to treat ye better, but stand in fear of Miles. Roger Hackward is the only one who calls Miles friend."

"I see. So my misery has been imposed by Miles as well." Deirdre, not knowing whom she could really trust, thought it best to end the conversation. "Emerson, would that ye cut me that small branch?" She pointed to a new branch that was low to the ground but higher than she could reach. "I think to take the smell of the outdoors into my cell."

Taking his dagger, Emerson sliced the evergreen branch and handed it to her. She put it to her nose and breathed deeply of its sharp pungent odor. "I've missed this smell. It reminds me of the trees around my home at Foxlair." She bent over to study the new growth breaking through the ground and where small tightly rolled fronds were pushing through the center of the ferns. "I miss seeing spring unfold. For it is a new beginning, is it not?"

After they left Emerson at the gate to take up his duties, William continued escorting Deirdre. The bright sun faded as they stepped inside and started down the small flight of stairs dimly lit only by oil wall sconces that constantly burned. The smell of the oil having long permeated the walls as black wisps of smoke coiled from the flames layering a coat of black soot on the walls. They came out into a corridor where the pine scent in her basket fought with the smell of urine, vomit and sweat. As they walked past the constable's area, she heard voices.

Maude with a secretive smile on her face stepped out to join Deirdre and William.

Thomas stood, and using his desk top for support, gave them a strained look. "Maude, is it time to feed Countess Wrothbury?" he asked as though the day had somehow slipped away.

Maude glanced over at her husband. "Aye, Thomas, that it is. I'm thinking to stay and visit with milady for a spell."

Thomas nodded and Deirdre couldn't help but notice his wince of pain when he sat back down.

Maude hastily dismissed William at the door, saying she'd already brought Deirdre's meal and that she would be sure to lock up when the countess was done eating. Maude no sooner had Deirdre inside the cell and the door secured when Conner who was waiting on the chair, sprung to his feet. He acknowledged her.

"Conner Kincaid? Maude," she whispered, unable to believe that anyone else knew about the young man risking his life to bring Richard's missives. Yet here he was inside her cell. Knowing how much Maude risked to get him here stymied Deirdre. "My word, how d'ye ever get—"

"Do not fret yerself, milady. Today, this young lad sought me out. I have been secretly helping the count. Not even Thomas knows of this." Maude's smile was so broad that Deirdre couldn't help but smile back. "As for ye, Conner Kincaid, I'll return for ye shortly." Opening the door mere inches, Maude peered out. Satisfied it was safe, she stepped out and eased the door shut behind her.

Deirdre offered the chair to Conner but he declined and took the pallet. "Yer right pretty. Taller than I thought."

She sat on the chair. "I see Maude has brought two bowls filled with venison soup. She certainly intended fer ye to eat as well."

"Aye, I've been smelling it as I waited fer ye. Thought ye'd never get here." He appreciatively sniffed the air filled with venison aroma. "It smells gude." He tore the bread in two.

"Rightly so," she agreed and handed him a bowl of the enticing sustenance. When she could no longer contain her curiosity, she asked, "D'ye have news from Count Strasbourg? Or my brother?" It felt strange to be next to the young man who had become her link to Richard and David.

"I do."

When no other words followed, Deirdre's mouth fell open as he tore off a chunk of bread and dipping it into the broth, continued to eat. Watching him concentrate on his food, and ignoring her, she thought to throw her own food in his face, but that probably wouldn't stop him from eating, he'd just lick it off with his tongue.

"Conner—if ye dinna tell me what Count Strasbourg has to say, for certes I'm going to clot ye upside the head." When he raised a mischievous looking face to hers, she said, "Gore, ye tease me, aye?"

"Aye, a little. I'm mighty hungry. This food is better than what I've been gettin' in the alehouses." He reached into his waist pack, and rifling around, handed her the missive.

"That is the last one I deliver. Ye should be out of here within a fortnight. The plans are being made for ye, milady. The count is a good man. A brave warrior. Ye need to be ready for him."

"Ye act like ye willna be seeing Count Strasbourg again."

"I go in a different direction when I leave here. I seek out the Brus and join him."

"Conner, tell me something of yerself, for I know little about ye. Are ye from the Kincaid clan?"

"Milady, that I am. Me mam, my Uncle Macadie's sister, married my father who is laird of the Kincaid clan."

"Then ye will be laird someday as well."

With his mouth full of meat, Conner could only nod and wipe the juice from his chin.

Too excited to eat and talk anymore, Deirdre ignored her food and quickly turned the missive in her hand. Breaking the wax seal, several gold coins tumbled from the parchment landing in the well of her skirt.

'Deirdre, I write this in haste while riding to Wrothbury Castle. As always, you are foremost in my thoughts, and I pray this finds you in good health. I had a most interesting introduction to your brother, of which you'll learn about someday. Your brother rides with me, as do other Scotsmen. I will not be able to correspond for a time. Look for me at Falconshire with your child and pardon in hand. Destroy this. R.'

Her mind was rattled by his words that held future promises. He was bringing Joanna. Too excited to sit still, she rose from the chair. "Oh…gore. He is going to get my wee bairn, isn't he?" she exclaimed out loud.

Conner's nod confirmed all. Richard would soon be here. "What of my brother, David Brodie? Is he well? Richard speaks of meeting him. He says that David along with other Scotsmen have joined him. Who else rides with Count Strasbourg?"

"Aye, David's well. He, along with my Uncle Macadie and Gordon Bryce, travels with the count. I dinna think ye know the others. They are men that Count Strasbourg brought with him from France." He drained the broth from his bowl and setting it aside, belched loud.

"Does Bonnar Cameron ride with Count Strasbourg?" She shouldn't care, and yet she had to know about him.

"Nay, he rides with Philippe de Laci."

"Philippe de Laci?"

"Aye, the count's brother. They brought a huge army with them from France. The Brus divided it up." Realizing that he'd just chattered on about things he shouldn't Conner lost his nonchalant attitude. "Milady—

I jest said too much."

"Nay, Conner, for what ye say will go no further than myself. And indeed, be assured that Count Strasbourg will appreciate your words of enlightenment to me." She no sooner got the words out when the door swung open and banged against the wall.

Miles walked in.

Shocked, all three glanced at each other as if they were caught poaching the king's stags. Jumping to her feet, Deirdre gasped as her plans to leave this place tumbled about her.

Conner stood.

Miles pulled his sword and went into a crouch. Keeping his eyes on Conner he said, "Heard a man's voice. Looks like I've caught meself a Scotsman."

Deirdre could see Conner looking around the small cell, gauging his chances. She blurted out without thinking, "Go—Conner—get away."

But Conner having regained his composure, and with the cockiness of youth, or just being a warrior used to fighting, he unsheathed his long dagger that he'd kept hidden.

"Milady, stand over there." Conner motioned Deirdre to get against the wall.

She quickly obliged.

No longer the teasing Scotsman who had just shared her meal, he was ready for battle. "Fight me, ye fat fart of a man," Conner said.

Crouched in a deadly stance, his weapon out in front of him, it was hard for Deirdre not to compare the two men, one gone to flab with ill-fitting armor, the other wearing no armor but honed from the battlefield. Pressed against the wall with her eyes on the combatants, Deirdre didn't know how this was going to come out, but no matter what, she was going to lose.

Deirdre glanced over to see a wide-eyed Maude standing in the open doorway, her hands covering her mouth to silence a scream. She twirled around and ran down the hall.

Miles banged at Conner's long dagger like he was chopping wood. Conner gracefully dodged every blow. At times, their blades came close enough to her that Deirdre could feel the wind they made. She was quick to duck away. Miles's chest heaved in and out with exertion. Sweat poured down the sides of his face. Conner didn't appear to be under any duress at all.

Miles, in a rush of vengeance and missing Conner who jumped aside, brought his sword down and smite the bed pallet. The savage tear sent goose feathers into the air. With both men on the pallet, forcing the white fluff out of the gash, it looked like a snowstorm had erupted. With an angry yell, Miles sliced at Conner who jumped backward and prompt- ly fell over the desk. He rode the desk to the floor. His sword clattered next to his feet. The bowl of stew splashed onto the floor where meat and vegetables mixed with the black ink from the spilled inkhorn. As Conner tried to regain his feet, Miles quickly thrust his sword, piercing Conner's shoulder.

"Conner!" Deirdre screamed.

Conner grimaced as his hand went to the wound where blood imme- diately stained his white tunic red.

Advancing for the kill, Miles stepped in the wooden bowl, lodging his foot tight, sending the bowl to skid on the floor slick with spilt stew. "Christ on a cross," he swore as his legs split under him sending him to crash on his backside.

Conner jumped up. Casting a quick smile at Deirdre and moving like lightning, Conner bolted for the door. He shot past Thomas and Maude, who barely stepped out of his way.

"Stop him—Thomas." A struggling Miles kicked the bowl away and made it to his feet. He started after Conner.

Deirdre put her foot out and tripped him. He hit the floor in a loud grunt of jiggling fat, and more than a few feathers shot into the air.

Thomas ran after Conner.

Miles got to his hands and knees and heaving himself upright didn't give chase. Sweat coursed down his fat creases. Trying to catch his breath, he stood glaring at Deirdre. "That was the same Scotsman that was here several fortnights ago. Who is he—how did he get in yer cell?" His voice an agitated high-pitched squeal as he held out his hand. "Give me the missive—Countess."

In all the excitement, Deirdre forgot that she still held Richard's letter. She shook her head and backed away.

Holding out his hand he was within inches of her. "Give it to me. Now!" His face fused red.

She crammed the missive into her mouth and began to chew. She tried to swallow the round ball of parchment that was getting bigger with each chomp. Gagging, she finally got it down. When Miles tried forcing her mouth open, she bit his fingers hard enough to make them bleed.

"Ow—ye Scottish bitch." He cuffed her hard against the side of the head, knocking her to the pallet where once again feathers lazily floated. Some landed on the top of Miles' head. Before leaving, he pointed a finger at her. "Ye have much to answer for," he prophesized, and limped away.

Thomas managed to chase Conner into the town center when a thousand daggers let loose inside Thomas and the pain took him down to his knees. The Scotsman glanced back at him. Thomas, without the breath to call out and stop him, tried to point to a few stragglers going about their business. One man putting out a fire under a large kettle turned to see what the commotion was. Again, Thomas pointed at the escaping Scotsman who stopped running and walked through the gates as though he owned them. Thomas was going to be the foil in all this and at this moment he cared not. Unable to do anything different, he lay on the hard cobblestones of the town square, his face pressed against the rough stones and the weeds that grew between them. All he wanted to do was sleep. He found himself being turned over. He gasped and stared skyward at the circle of concerned faces peering down at him. Maude's being one, and his wife, bless her, took control.

"Quick—carry him to our chambers," she ordered.

Strong hands picked him up and started running with him. His heart faltered, his lungs were heavy. Above him the faded blue sky was replaced with the dark of the corridor, making him wonder if this was how dark Hell would be.

Maude hovered over Thomas's bed. His skin was the color of mustard spice, even the whites of his eyes where yellow and his legs no longer the skinny sticks of always, were swollen stretching the skin tight.

Earlier, the healer seeing to Thomas had left behind a potion for pain. He'd told Maude that Thomas hadn't long to live. With her husband's demise in the near future, Maude thought about the hemlock tucked away in a jar hidden in her clothes chest.

She took his dry withered hand within hers. He opened his eyes to give her a pain-filled gaze. "The Scotsman...yer doing..."

"Aye, husband. I didn't mean to betray ye." And then she urged, "Thomas, ye need to let Countess Wrothbury go. What harm if the cell door is left ajar, or the cage unlocked? If there is truth in her pardon, then ye do no wrong. Fer certes the Heavenly Father will look upon ye with a kinder heart."

Thomas sighed. "Maude...Wrothbury's vengeance will out reach any kindness the Lord might place on me fer letting her go. And there is ye to consider. All will know 'twas ye who slipped the Scotsman inside her cell. I...suspect there is a pardon...that Wrothbury has kept it from me—"

"Then all the more reason to release her. She cannot wait for Count Strasbourg to return."

A wry smile creased his mouth. "Ye've been a busy woman. I fear what will happen to ye when I'm gone—"

"As well as I. Miles will turn me out before yer cold in the ground."

Thomas turned his face away, waiting his fate.

Conner, riding without stopping, finally managed to elude the soldiers that followed him. He wouldn't have wagered that he would get out of Falconshire alive, but owed his luck to the constable collapsing.

The fat guard surprised him. Although the man lacked skills for fighting with a sword, he had tenacity and a hate to see him dead. The man's sword caught him high on the left shoulder. In great pain he reined in his horse. Tearing his tunic, he pressed it against the wound. Unable to stop the bleeding he needed help. Instead of continuing toward Scotland, he headed for Kiltsbury Abbey and the friars who would know what to do.

Deirdre, looking around at the carnage her cell was in, wondered what punishment was going to be meted out to her. Would the earl be told about the young warrior? But most of all would Richard reach her before Wrothbury was sent for? She righted her desk and picked up the inkhorn that held but a drop of ink.

The door to her cell squeaked open. Afraid that Miles had returned, she backed away. But it wasn't Miles. Maude entered with a broom and two lads who were lugging a new pallet between them.

Emerson stood by the door.

"Well now, milady, I thought ye might be needin' a new pallet," Maude said with a ghost of a smile as the lads bent over and started rolling up the damaged mattress. An occasional feather still flew in defiance.

From Maude's demeanor, Deirdre could tell something dire had happened. Her mind wanted to resists the worried thoughts that ran rampant. "Maude, is it Thomas? Was he hurt this eve?"

Maude didn't say anything as she used a broom to try and capture the feathers that was almost a losing battle. Finally having corralled most of the white fluff, Maude gave the bucket to one of the lads to take away.

"Countess Wrothbury?" Emerson spoke up, "Ye were not hurt in all the fighting, aye?"

"Nay, Emerson. I'm well. But how does Miles fare?" She couldn't help but notice Emerson's smile, his eyes twinkling with mirth.

"He has a swollen foot that will keep him off of it for a few days."

"I pray 'tis more than a few days," Deirdre said.

Emerson nodded and took his leave.

Deirdre insisted that Maude sit beside her on the new pallet.

"Was Thomas hurt when he chased Conner?"

"I wouldna say it was from chasing Conner." Worrying her overtunic in her hands, Maude turned soulful brown eyes on Deirdre. "He already complained of having a deep pain that gnaws at his innards. He even said he wanted to take a dagger to himself and be done with it."

Taking Maude's hand within hers, Deirdre tried to be reassuring. "Thomas mustn't think that way. What does the healer say?"

"That Thomas hasn't long to live." Maude's face was a mask of apprehension. "He says Thomas is swollen inside and that a cancer eats away at him. When Thomas dies, I might as well be buried with him, as I can see no hope for me here in Falconshire. I depend on his employment. Like the lot of most women, I've nothing to call my own. My lady, I worry so."

"Maudie, dinna worrit. Mayhap Thomas will start feeling better. Ye know how the warm spring months can make our aching bones go away. It makes a person wonder what all the complaining was about. He'll soon feel like his old self, ye'll see."

"Milady, ye give hope where there is none, and I thank ye for it. Miles bellows at our good mayor that ye are going to try and escape. Ye might be kept inside as well and not taken to the cage."

"Gore, d'ye think that Wrothbury has been sent for?"

"I dinna know, milady, perhaps." She wished Deirdre a good eve.

12 Through Difficulties

Northern England
Wrothbury Castle

The first of May found the villeins hard at work in the fields belonging to the Earl of Wrothbury. A dozen men and women, wearing gray woolen clothing and large hats, bent laboriously with hoes in hand, digging at the weeds that threatened to overtake and starve out the rye and oats plants that stood a good half-foot tall. Nearby, a small group of children played on a cart that held tools. A horse still harnessed to the cart grazed at the weeds growing at its feet, slowly pulling the cart forward as it munched.

An unusual amount of people were coming and going through the castle's open gates. Since Robert the Bruce had been inside Wrothbury's castle, Wrothbury had tightened its defenses. No one was admitted without first having their papers checked by the gate guards, who would do a little heckling here and there. Despite being checked, the people appeared in a jovial mood.

Richard, wearing chest armor, his long sword, a flowing cape with a few holes in it, was dressed as a poor knight; a disguise he prayed would get him through the gate. With Bertrand beside him, they followed behind a wagon loaded with wine barrels, and being driven by Friar Macadie. The blessed order remained rich by taking money from the wealthy, so it was without any qualms that Richard had stolen a friar's robe upon his departure. His only problem had been to keep the men from getting drunk on the wine as they made their way here from the abbey. Well, that and selecting the person who was going to be the friar.

Looking at the back of Macadie's tonsured dome, Richard couldn't help but cringe at all the scabbed-over cuts that he'd put there. He smiled at the remembrance of how they all deemed that Macadie would make the best friar. All but Macadie that is. He'd pulled his claymore and poked it at them, yelling they would never put him in a gown. He jabbed at them making them jump backwards, again shouting he was too thin to be a friar. David worked his way behind Macadie and wrestled him to the ground and sat on him while Richard cut his hair in the style worn by friars. Macadie's violent struggles caused Richard's knife to slip and make a few unwanted cuts to the scalp. He'd even shaved off Macadie's bristly beard...

...The wagons loud rumbling stopped Richard's musing as the barrels jostled and clattered together with every rut the wheels hit. Approaching the castle's entry, Macadie pulled on the reins to slow the wagon to a crawl. Two sentries crossed their pikes, the noise of metal hitting together rang out and around the courtyard.

"Whoa up—horse," Macadie said and scratched his chest. "Is milord to home? I deliver the best wine that Wickam Abbey has made. These casks have fermented all winter. The abbot sends them as gifts fer the Earl of Wrothbury's generosity to us."

One of the guards approached. "Wine, ye say? Generosity, ye say? The Earl of Wrothbury?" His homely face creased into a crooked-tooth grin for the man of God. He scratched his flaxen-colored hair then gravitated down to his armpits like a dog after fleas.

Listening to the exchange, even Richard thought Macadie was going a little too far in speaking of generosity.

"Aye, most generous in the name of his daughter, Joanna. The earl gives us a gift, the abbey gives one back. How does the Earl of Wrothbury and his blessed child fare?"

"He isn't here, good Father. Gone to London town, aye. Expect him home soon. He tries to rally King Edward against the Scots. Which seems most unlikely since the young king isn't prone to battle," this said by the other older guard who chuckled at his own wit.

So far, it had been easy and going according to plan. But when the guards started pushing against the barrels, closing in on the ones in the center that were empty, Richard looped his reins over the saddle's pommel and like a hawk watched the scene in front of him. Hoping that nothing would go wrong, he put his hand on the hilt of his sword.

"Wine ye say? I don't think the earl would mind if we have a taste. What say ye John Ward, a simple taste?" said the younger guard.

"If ye wish to have a drop of the nectar, how could his lordship begrudge ye?" Friar Macadie hopped down and tripping over his long frock, grabbed up the offending length and accidentally flashed Richard a glimpse of darkened plaid.

Richard coughed and signaled Macadie that his plaid was showing.

Macadie quickly dropped the skirt of his coarse brown frock, and tightened the rope belt around his middle to keep all in place. He approached the back of the wagon and signaled the guard forward.

The man called John Ward stared at Macadie with a sharp gaze. "Ye look familiar."

"'Tis me first time here at Wrothbury Castle. I just returned from a pilgrimage to the holy lands." Macadie lied. He'd been here with the Bruce and David to see the Lady Deirdre.

Richard prayed Macadie's disguise would hold up.

"Have ye been to Wickam Abbey?" Macadie asked the guard.

John Ward wagged his head. "Nay. Let me have a taste of that wine." His mind on the drink, he removed his helmet and bent to place his mouth under the spigot.

Macadie turned the spigot to let the wine spill out. John Ward opened his mouth allowing the ruby liquid to flow into his mouth and over his chin. He rapidly gulped, trying to capture as much of the prized liquid as he could.

The other guard impatiently elbowed John Ward. "Let me have a little taste. Ye needn't make a pig of yerself."

John Ward stopped drinking. He stepped aside and used his sleeve to wipe his mouth and the pink stains in his blondish-gray beard. He let out a loud belch. The other guard helped himself and tried to guzzle as much as possible.

Friar Macadie finally turned off the spigot, a wide grin forming across his mouth. "Ah…yes, and me good men, did I not say this was nectar from the heavens? Mayhap, I'll jest leave this barrel in the stable fer ye to enjoy. Since the Earl of Wrothbury is not here, he will not know how many barrels the abbot sent, and we won't be a tellin' now will we." Snorting a laugh, the friar conspiringly elbowed the one called John Ward in the gut.

Richard rolled his eyes and thought Macadie a big windbag who was going to get them caught if he didn't cease with this.

The guards nodded, and conversing between themselves, finally pointed. "Leave us a barrel by the stables. Take the rest around to the kitchen tower. Be sure and eat. Food is being served in the great hall."

Nodding most humbly at the two men, Macadie climbed in and flicked the reins. "Walk on—horse." The horse ambled forward, the wooden wheels clattered loud against the cobblestone entry.

Richard, next in line to be questioned, moved forward and brought out papers that he placed into the hand of a most agreeable and happiest of guards, their eyes a little glazed with fulfillment.

"I wish to speak with the Earl of Wrothbury. I'm a mercenary knight and I offer my sword and myself in his service of dispatching the Scots." Richard didn't think the guard could even read which became apparent from the puzzled frown on his face before handing them back to Richard.

"Who are you?" he asked, his voice somewhat slurred.

"I'm Renaud d'Ordec. This is my squire, Bertrand."

"A Frenchie. Thought as much." He hiccupped. "Well, his lordship is not around. But ye can take a respite if ye like. Put yer horses in the stable for some oats." John Ward signaled them by and was already looking past Richard to the next group of people.

After meeting with Macadie in the stable and sending him on ahead to search the upper floors, Richard and Bertrand went to the great hall which was filled with people being fed a midday meal. Smoke from the giant fireplace clouded the room and mingled with the odor of baked bread, cooked fish and meats. Soldiers dressed in armor sat alongside men, women, and children wearing colorful clothes.

Richard wondered what was happening here, for he'd been told that the earl usually had a subdued castle with very little activity. Right now, a place no sooner emptied at a table when it was snatched up. When a man and a woman started to take two empty spots, Richard flicked his hand at them warning them off. He and Bertrand took the chairs at a long trestle table.

A young dark-haired maiden was already seated when Bertrand scooted in next to her.

Richard leaned forward and smiled at the young woman. "The castle appears busy today. Is there a festival? I understand the Earl of Wrothbury is not in residence."

The young woman stopped eating and thoughtfully chewed her food before responding. Wiping her mouth with a white linen cloth, she met Richard's stare. "The earl opens his castle to travelers one day a year, and this is that day. He gives away a loaf of bread to each of his villagers. At present, he also readies a small army to go north into Scotland." She sipped her wine, her dark eyes sweeping over both men.

"I understand the Earl of Wrothbury has an infant daughter?" Richard asked, trying to ferret out information.

"Aye, that he does." The young maiden put her goblet down and stared directly at Richard. "And who might ye be?"

Richard introduced himself as Renaud d'Ordec, and Bertrand as his squire. When he would ask more about the castle, an empty wooden trencher to share with Bertrand was placed between them. A servant hurriedly slopped ale into cups.

Using his knife, Bertrand speared pieces of fish and eel and placed them on the trencher. He then sliced a large piece of mutton and grabbed a rounded loaf of bread. Not waiting for Richard, he started stuffing the hot food into his mouth as though it was his last meal. Several honey cakes soon followed. At last he swallowed, and running his tongue around his lips, he turned his attention to the maiden who could only stare with amusement.

"Ye eat as though ye haven't had a good meal in a long time."

"Indeed I have not had a good meal since leaving France. The food here in England is…is…how do you say…lacking in taste?"

Her thin brows pulled together in a most becoming frown while her lips formed a reddened pout. "I would say ye are not having problems with English fare, for ye act the pig."

Not taking offense, Bertrand only laughed and winked at her. "Would mademoiselle like something else?" He offered the maiden a loaf of bread.

"Nay, I'm most full and must excuse myself," she said sweetly and tossed a little flirtatious smile at Bertrand whose chest swelled with the attention.

"Your name…I would know your name," Bertrand blurted out.

"Mary Clair," she replied and left.

She was the maid that Deirdre told Richard about. His luck was holding, and he waited patiently while she crossed the room and ducked through a side door. They hastened after her, and listened to her footfalls echoing back down a spiral staircase that led to the upper chambers.

Richard cautioned Bertrand to be silent as they slowly moved up the stone stairs. "Go and search for the pardon while I seek the infant. Leave no chest unopened, but be most careful."

In searching for the baby's room, Richard found Wrothbury's chambers and started going through a large ornate chest that held the earl's richly textured clothing, all in the color black that Wrothbury so favored. He went through everything possible in the chamber with no success. Hearing loud voices, he came back into the hallway and drawing his short dagger slowly eased down the candlelit corridor.

"Ow," Macadie's voice carried out into the hall. "Ow—ow!"

Richard rounded the doorway to see Macadie in his friar's robe holding an infant. The young woman called Mary Clair was hitting him with the bellows from the fireplace. The blows echoed around the room.

"Give—me—the—baby!" She whacked Macadie a good one with each emphasized word. Flinching with each blow, Macadie quickly relinquished the infant back to her. "How dare ye think to take this child." She held her precious bundle tight against her bosom as the frightened baby started to cry.

Taking in the scene, Richard quickly went to Macadie's side. Macadie who was bleeding from a cut over his right eye mumbled under his breath about his head taking too much abuse here lately.

"Mademoiselle, we mean no harm to the infant. I've come to take the child to her mother, Countess Wrothbury." Richard reached for the child but the maiden backed up putting distance between them. It was obvious she would give up her life for Deirdre's child.

"How do I know ye have not come to harm Joanna?" She menaced them with the bellows, prepared to attack anyone who tried to come near.

"Because I'm Richard de Laci, Comte de Strasbourg. I have promised to help Countess Wrothbury."

"That is not the name given downstairs," she said belligerently.

"Oui…it…"

Bertrand at that moment entered and said, "Comte Strasbourg, I cannot find the pardon. Did any of you have better luck?"

"Nay," Macadie said.

"The pardon?" Mary Clair looked at them like they'd lost their minds. "It isn't here. The Earl of Wrothbury keeps the pardon on him, in his waist pouch. And he is gone from here."

Richard approached and held out his hands for the baby. This muddied his plans, as he would have to take Deirdre from the cage, find Wrothbury, and get the pardon later.

Mary Clair reluctantly placed the baby in his arms. He studied the little infant. Her reddish-brown hair curled wispily about her face. She sucked on two fingers, her little and the one next to it, while her remaining fingers curled over the tip of her nose. With tears still welled below her eyes, she leveled a rounded gray-eyed gaze up at him. She resembled Deirdre so much that he was amazed. As he kept staring at her, the baby pulled something else from him. Fatherhood perhaps? She was a reminder that he had no issue of his own and that he needed heirs.

Macadie moved next to Richard. He smiled an all-knowing smile while clucking the baby under the chin. "There is no denying that this is Deirdre Brodie's bairn. She looks jest like her mam. Coont, we canna stay here any longer."

Alarmed, Mary Clair blurted out, "Wait, ye can't leave me here. When the earl returns and finds out that you have taken his child, he will harm me or worse."

"Then get your belongings, and the bébé's. Be quick. We must be away," Richard urged and no sooner spoke when a young blonde woman appeared in the room. She warily looked around and said to Mary Clair, "'Tis time for me to feed little Joanna."

"Aye, Una," Mary Clair said and approached the young wet nurse. Taking her hand, she pulled her over to Richard. "Milord, Una is here to feed Joanna." And taking the child from his arms, she gave her to Una. "These men are friends of Wrothbury's. They have come to join his cause. Alas, the good friar upon delivering wine from the abbey has asked to see Joanna and give her a blessing."

Appearing relaxed at learning the strangers intentions, Una nodded at the men. Going to the lone chair next to the fire, she settled comfortably on it, and baring her breasts, put Joanna's mouth to the nipple. Una hummed to the child.

Richard motioned everyone out of the room and they stood in the hallway, waiting for Joanna to finish nursing. "This is good that the baby is fed before we leave."

"Milord, what about the wet-nurse? How will Joanna be fed during the journey?" Mary Clair said with worry.

A question Richard couldn't answer for he had never in his life traveled with a baby.

Macadie spoke. "We canna bring the wet nurse, so make sure ye bring a drink bladder. She will have to feed from that. We will have to stop along the way and get milk from a cow or goat."

Richard nodded, realizing that it wasn't going to be easy taking the baby. Oh…taking the baby was easy, he argued with himself, but getting where they had to go with her was going to take some ingenuity. What man amongst them besides David and Macadie had been around babies? No one, and both of them had always been off fighting while their wives did the raising of the children. Richard's plan just fell apart. Mayhap they should take Una with them.

"Bertrand, go with Mary Clair to help gather both hers and the child's belongings. Make haste. And…er…Mary Clair we must bring the wet nurse with us."

"Ye cannot do that."

"Why not?"

"She has a child of her own. That is why she is feeding Joanna. Ye can't take her away from her own children and husband."

This was becoming complicated. Richard in a hurry to be on his way could see that they would not be traveling as fast as needed. He walked back into the room to wait with Macadie who stood with his arms folded. The Scotsman was thinking the same as he.

Mary Clair returned with a bundle and dismissed Una, saying she would change the baby's soiled wrap and began to do so. This was yet another thing that Richard hadn't thought about. Messes—baby messes. He and the men could slip off their horses and piss against a tree, disappear in the forest to do other business, but the baby would need to be changed. Also Mary Clair would have to stop the retinue and daintily make her way into the woods. A detail overlooked.

Mary Clair no sooner had the baby ready and they turned to leave when John Ward along with two soldiers walked into the room. Albeit a bit too much into the wine to immediately sense what was happening, John Ward tried to draw his sword that got stuck in his weapons belt. Macadie and Bertrand drew theirs, and begin fighting with the other two guards. Finally freeing his weapon, John Ward advanced toward Richard. Seeing no advantage in fighting a man drunk on wine, Richard tried to avoid the man's blows, but drunk or not he was still deadly. Finally, Richard knocked John Ward's sword from his hand and started to pierce the man's heart.

"Nay!" Mary Clair screamed. "He is my father—do not kill him!"

Stunned at this jolting news, and with no other choice, Richard knocked the man in the head to slump to the floor. "Your sire? This man is your sire? Then mademoiselle, I cannot take you with us. How do I know you're not a traitor?"

"Because I care for milady more than I care for this man. Although he is my sire, he has shown me no love or even admission at times that I am his issue. Ye will not leave me here. Either I go with Joanna, or I turn and run screaming down the hallway. With the gathering army around the castle, ye will not get far at all." When her back went rigid, her stance militant, and her lips set in a firm line, Richard had met his match.

They gagged and bound the soldiers, then dragged them into the garderobe. Mary Clair led them down and out the back way. Without incident, they reached the shed and the wagon. Handing Joanna to Richard, Mary Clair climbed into the back of the cart and lay down.

"Be silent until we leave the castle behind," Richard cautioned the maid and handed Joanna back to her. He covered them with a blanket.

To his surprise they made it away from the castle without further incident. Richard was able to join David Brodie and the rest of his men that waited several miles to the west.

Richard tried moving his small band in haste, but it just wasn't happening. The only thing cooperating was the weather with clear blue skies. They had to stop to feed Joanna, but before they could do that, he had to send either Gordon or Macadie to find a tenant farmer with a cow or goat. He even ventured forth himself and along with Macadie had tried to milk a cow. Richard had never milked a cow, and Macadie for certes was better at fighting then pulling a teat.

They all took turns carrying Joanna. David had devised a sling from cloth that was worn around the neck and shoulder, nestling Joanna against the chest. So, several times a day she would bounce against a different chest, which she didn't appear to mind. Richard couldn't wait to see Deirdre's face when he placed her child back in her arms.

If Richard's plans went well, day after tomorrow they would arrive in the evening and make camp close to Falconshire. But being a man of many battles things could go wrong in a heartbeat. How he planned to take her from the cage was another matter, one that went through his mind with each step of his horse. A fake pardon? Impossible to do without the king's scal. Attack the township? A possibility with planning.

It was Richard's turn to carry the child who now bounced against his chest. He cut his eyes down at Joanna who was awake and giving him an intense stare. She had forgone sucking her fingers to blowing spit-bubbles. Right now, she made cooing sounds at him. Richard, unable to help himself began making faces at her by sticking his tongue out and wagging it. A wide grin spread across her face, pushing her fat cheeks out, showing her toothless grin. Richard wondered when babies got their teeth. He had no idea about babies at all. He glanced over at David's broad grin and knew he looked the fool for making faces at a baby.

Gordon was riding next to Mary Clair, as he was wont to do since they had first met. But Bertrand, having met her first at the castle, and not about to be put off, rode on the other side of the pretty maiden. Richard hoped the two men wouldn't start fighting over her. This was also new to him, traveling with two lovesick men.

Richard figured that Wrothbury would be fast to find him when he discovered his child had been taken. He also knew how Deirdre felt when the babe was snatched from her arms, as this little girl had already wormed her way into his heart.

Joanna was a good baby and seldom cried. Mary Clair tried feeding her from a bladder and she took the milk, but to Richard's dismay she sometimes brought it back up, and those seemed to be the times when he had her with him, like now. He was wiping off slobbers when Macadie rode up beside him. The Scot's haircut brought a smile to Richard.

"Coont, we are not moving fast enough. I think we best try to put more landscape between us and Wrothbury Castle."

"I agree, Macadie," he said studying the terrain. Joanna at that moment gripped his tunic within her tiny fist. She chortled at him, her legs kicking in delight. He would protect Deirdre's child no matter what.

Leaving his army to camp outside the castle, the Earl of Wrothbury rode through the gates of his home. The sunny weather did little to relieve his sour mood. He could have saved himself the trip to London and the sore knees he got from bowing and scraping before the young and very stupid king. The fool, the blustering, posturing, mincing, pompous ass of a ruler. He couldn't help but wonder how someone like the great Edward could have fathered such a spineless, effeminate fop. For certes, Edward's true issue must have died at birth and this ill-begotten thing on the throne a sad replacement.

He tried to convince the king that the time to strike the Scots was now. But the king's companion Piers Gaveston was always whispering in his ear, turning the king's ear away from sound advice. Edward had promised an invasion of Scotland, but he dawdled, being content to let his baron's try and roust the Scottish heathens. And while he dawdled, Robert the Bruce made great strides by taking back Northern Scotland, razing his own peoples' castles to keep the English from garrisoning in them. Rumors abounded that French re-enforcements had landed in Scotland. That one Wrothbury refused to believe since the English King was married to the King of France's daughter.

He patted his waist pouch thinking of the pardon inside. It was time to go claim his wife. There was no doubt in his mind that wanting Joanna as much as Countess Wrothbury did, that she would do anything he asked. And he intended to ask away. Didn't her last missive to him say as much? His cock stirred with some of the visions that popped into his mind. It was enough to make him want to tumble the nearest maid.

His horse no sooner clattered into the courtyard and the young groom scrambled to take his reins when Wrothbury sensed something was wrong. Even more so when John Ward bowed and then met his stare with a blackened eye and bruised face. Wrothbury looked to see that several other guards wore bruises.

"Did the war start in my own domain and I know nothing of it?" Wrothbury said, his eyes narrowing at John Ward who looked like he wished to be anywhere but here.

"Milord, we…ah…well we…"

"What are you trying to say? Be out with it John Ward or feel the back of my hand." Wrothbury's anger was mounting, something dire had gone on in his absence.

John blurted out. "Your daughter and my daughter are both gone, milord." This time John went to his knees, his eyes closed. All those around waited, holding their breath, waiting for the terrible vengeance they knew to come.

"What do you mean our daughters are gone? What nonsense is this?

Has your mind wandered away from your head?"

"A Frenchman that claimed to be a mercenary soldier wanting to work for ye took both your child and my daughter." John kept his face down, facing the ground, not daring to rise, not daring to do anything at the present but wait.

"What did this Frenchman look like? Stand John Ward as I tire of talking to your back."

John scrambled to his feet and keeping his head bowed described Richard. "Tall, dark hair, poor looking. Had his squire with him. Believe he called him Bernard or something like that. Don't remember. There was another dressed like a monk."

"A monk? A French knight?" Wrothbury felt as though someone had him by the throat choking him. His cheek began to tick spasmodically as he fully grasped what had occurred in his absence. Richard de Laci had brazenly entered his castle and taken Joanna. No doubt, he intended to take the babe to Falconshire where Deirdre awaited them both. The traitorous bastard, he should have killed him that day at Foxlair. Over his dead body, he swore, no one would have Deirdre. He would kill her first. And no one but he would have his child.

"How long ago?" he asked his guard, and not receiving an answer fast enough, screamed, "How long ago?" He backhanded John Ward hard against the head knocking him to the ground.

John rolled over onto his knees. "Two days, mayhap less."

Wrothbury's mind was already making plans. "We can catch them. They are not that far ahead. Saddle your horses and be ready to ride within the hour." Muttering to himself he limped inside the castle. As he made his way up the staircase, his insides were like a cauldron, churning, burning hot.

Standing over the empty cradle as if to make sure John spoke the truth, Wrothbury surprised himself with the feelings he had at the loss of his daughter. Empty. A great emptiness that had followed him around all his life.

In this very chamber his own mother had shunned him at birth. One look at his crippled leg and foot had her screaming for his father to take the squirming child and dash his brains out against the wall. The boy had the mark of the devil about him. His father refused and tried to do right by his son. But his father had flaws of his own. He hated. He taught Wrothbury to hate. He taught him to wield a sword, be a warrior, to be as crippled in his mind as he was in body. An adapt pupil, Wrothbury exceled at being cruel.

Although he'd put it from his mind all these years, he well remembered his mother on her deathbed. Withered from the disease that ate at her, her eyes had widened at the sight of him as he approached her bedside. His foot dragging in the rushes, making rats scurry before him.

"Henry?" she muttered.

He laughed. "So...after twenty years you finally say my given name. A name my father gave me."

She begged him to forgive her for how she had shunned him.

For him, it was too late.

"Why...are...you...here?" she whispered, picking at the bedcover.

"To help you with your journey to hell." He took her scrawny throat within his hands, squeezing. She didn't fight him, her hooded eyes seeing the hate he held for her were resigned.

"Devil." She managed one word before he crushed her windpipe...

...Wrothbury shook his head trying to dispel the image. His father had died two years later leaving Wrothbury to make his way in life. The one and only thing in his life that was truly his, was Joanna. Stolen from him. His wife, Deirdre was never his, even though he tried to make it so. He'd get his daughter back or die trying.

13 Brighter From Darkness

Falconshire

The eerie sound of wailing penetrated Deirdre's subconscious to mix with her dream that a wolf stood howling up at the cage. Trying to hide from the terrible beast, Deirdre pulled the blanket over her head and burrowed deeper into the mattress. When the wolf faded into a wisp of smoke, and the loud wailing continued, Deirdre opened her eyes and groggily listened. It wasn't long before the keening sound again broke the silence.

It was Maude.

Coming up off the pallet in a mad rush, Deirdre started for the door but the blanket wrapped around her leg nearly tripping her. Hopping on one foot until the blanket gave way, she groped blindly for the door and started pounding.

"Maude? Maude—is that ye?" Frustrated, she pounded with both fists. "Maude—is Thomas all right?" She beat on the wood until her hands hurt. "Can no one hear me?"

At long last she could hear footfalls hitting against the stone floor as someone hastened to her door. The bolt was thrown and Emerson holding a flaring torch peered inside. "Shhh…milady. You will awaken all."

"I was awakened," she said grabbing Emerson's arm, practically shaking him. "What is wrong? It sounds like Maude." His face told all. She didn't need words to affirm it, yet she asked, "Thomas is dead, aye?"

Emerson nodded solemnly. "Aye, milady."

"Could ye take me to Maude? For certes 'tis allowed," she begged.

"Change your nightgown." He agreed to her simple plea, and Deirdre was quick to comply.

After dressing, she slipped out to an awaiting Emerson. They hurried down the corridor.

"Did it jest happen?"

"I believe so. Thomas felt poorly this day. Told me he wanted to die, so intense was his pain. He never recovered…er…well ye know…after chasing the Scotsman."

She could only nod, the lump in her throat disallowing words. She had mixed emotions about Thomas Warren, but her concern for Maude overwhelmed any disparaging thoughts she had about the man.

The township held a council meeting after Conner Kincaid escaped and failed to conclude how he'd been let in. Like all Scots, the thief must have stolen the key and without anyone's knowledge slipped in to see the countess. For certes the Warren's were not to blame. Besides, Thomas almost put himself in the grave trying to catch the man. Miles told of seeing the Scotsman hanging around the cage less than a fortnight ago. No, they quickly laid the blame on Deirdre who somehow must have lured the Scotsman into her cell.

Upon entering the Warren's chamber, Deirdre went straight to Maude and put her arms around the grieving woman. "Oh, Maudie, dinna fret yerself so. Thomas is out of pain and is with the Lord."

"Truly, milady?" Maude sniffed. "Ye know how mean he was to ye before Count Strasbourg put a bag of coins in his hand. Only the shine of money made him treat ye better."

"I'm most certain that Thomas Warren is with the Lord in Heaven. And if I forgave him, 'tis a promise the Lord did long before the likes of me." Deirdre peered around Maude to where Thomas Warren lay on the bed, his features holding testament to the sickness that had ravaged his body. "Mighten I help ye lay him out, Maude?"

Emerson joined them, shaking his head, "Nay, milady, I've sent for Arless. She will help Maude whilst I see to the—" his words were stilled by a knock on the door. He opened the door to admit Arless who had the township priest with her. "Emerson, Father Gregory is here."

Maude hastened to the priest's side and blurted, "Father, was Thomas shriven?"

"Aye, and not more than a fortnight ago. Thomas was absolved of all earthly sins. You need not agonize about his soul." The priest stepped around her. Going to Thomas' side, he began to pray in a deep baritone. When finished, he made the sign of the cross over Thomas' forehead then pulled the blanket over his face. The good father didn't bother to offer solace for those that grieved. He was here to serve God, not the living. "Thomas Warren must be buried on the morrow," he said. With a simple nod at Maude and the rest, he took his leave, leaving them all to stare at his retreating back.

Arless poured water into a bowl then started washing Thomas, preparing him for burial. Maude sniffled and tried to help until Arless finally took her by the arms and guided her toward Deirdre. "Milady, would that ye see to Maude. I can finish with Thomas."

Deirdre took Maude by the hand and led her to a chair. "Here now, Maudie, please sit. 'Twill be well." She stood behind Maude giving her shoulders a reassuring squeeze. Deirdre glanced around the sparsely furnished chamber that she'd given birth to Joanna in. Besides the bed, there was a trestle table, a chest, several pegs on the wall holding a few items of clothing, and the lone chair where Maude sat. Deirdre wondered about being married to a man for as long as Maude had been married to Thomas and tried to put herself in Maude's place. But then her marriage to the Earl of Wrothbury was not much different. Wrothbury treated her with the same indifference that Thomas had treated Maude, although she'd never known Thomas to hit Maude. That in itself made Thomas a better man than the earl ever could be.

Maude patted Deirdre's hand before securing it within her own. "Milady, d'ye no see what Thomas' death means for ye? Miles Woodstock will probably replace him, and I'll be turned out of my home like a beggar. And no telling what Miles will be doing to ye. If Thomas had to die, why couldn't he wait until Count Strasbourg returned?"

"Oh Lord—Maude. Ye know not what ye be sayin'. 'Tis bad enough that Thomas is dead, but to wish he could have waited longer to do so isna right." Deirdre's eyes went skyward thinking that indeed God would strike them dead for such blasphemy.

"Emerson?" Maude beckoned him to her side.

"Aye, Mistress Warren?"

"Do ye know where Thomas kept the coin and records for milady?"

"'Tis in the desk drawer next to the dungeon cells."

"Get it before Miles does. Or he will take the coins and destroy the record. We must try to see that Deirdre is still taken care of. We must…." Unable to control herself, she dissolved into tears. "By the Saints…what will happen to us all?" She used the sleeve of her gown to dab the wet from her eyes.

"Maudie—'twill be well," she whispered," Count Strasbourg is on his way."

At this news, Maude shot her a surprised stare. "Conner's missive, aye?"

Deirdre nodded and would have said more, but Arless who had completed her task of preparing the body joined them and took Maude's hand.

"Thomas is ready for ye. Ye can go and sit by him for a while. The men will soon come to take him away."

Maude went to stand next to the bed and willed herself to look at Thomas' face. It had shrunken onto itself, the skin like yellow parchment. His nose, already hawk-shaped, was enhanced even more so by his weight loss. Even death wasn't kind to him. She placed her hand over his and unable to stand the cold dead feel of it had her pulling hers away. Certainly, she should feel something more, be sorry, afraid at being alone, but none of those emotions would come to her. Perhaps later, but not now.

Deirdre approached Maude who turned away from Thomas and said in a low voice, "Ye know, I was married to Thomas when I was fifteen, and I've known no other. By marrying me off, my father had one less mouth to feed, and Thomas was happy to get a young bride to warm his bed. Thomas was a handsome young soldier in King Edward's army, and in truth, he set my heart a flutter. But as he aged, he became bitter. Sometimes he was cruel to me, and yet other times he was kind. Even so, after more than twenty years of marriage, I never knew the man I called husband." Maude looked at Thomas a final time.

On their way back to Deirdre's cell, Emerson paused to search through Thomas' desk. After grabbing up a ledger book and a bag of coins, he hurried her into her cell. He surprised her when he followed her inside and lit a candle.

"I'm going to try to be appointed constable over Miles. But I cannot protect you from him if the mayor determines that he is deserving of the position. Milady, listen to my words. Be most careful not to do anything to rile Miles. He is still angry about the Scotsman, not to mention the indignity of stepping in a bowl of stew during the fight."

She rubbed her forehead, trying to think, knowing just how precarious her position was without Thomas. "Emerson...only Thomas kept Miles away with threats to dismiss him. I dinna know what to do."

"I'll try to protect you if I can, but I have to think of Arless and Caleb." The sound of voices carried to them from down the corridor. "I must go. I'll return on the morrow." He shut the door behind him.

Deirdre couldn't move, it was as though her limbs were weighted down. The thought of Thomas being gone and Miles now in charge was chilling. She was in trouble and prayed that Richard would be here soon. When Maude's loud crying once again carried inside her cell, Deirdre pondered how much of Maude's sorrow was for Thomas, or for Miles, who certainly must be chafing to move into the Warren's chambers.

Deirdre was surprised to see Maude bringing her breakfast tray. Maude's face was still swollen from crying, and her normally neat appearance thrown together.

"Milady, I've convinced Miles to let me stay and keep the chambers clean, and to fix the food for the prisoners, yerself included, at least for a little while. Miles will be comin' to take ye to the cage himself."

"Where is Emerson or William?" Deirdre wished either one would be escorting her.

"They help carry Thomas' coffin to the cemetery."

"Oh, should ye not be there, Maudie?" She put her arms around Maude and gave her a good squeeze. "I've come to care deeply for ye. Yer a true and trusted friend to me."

Maude patted Deirdre's arm and started to speak when Miles, along with Roger Hackward tagging behind him, entered. It was strange to see Roger off the battlements.

"Mistress Warren, leave us." Miles flicked his head toward the door, motioning her out. When Maude hesitated, he pointed and growled, "Out—now."

A knot the size of her fist closed off Deirdre's throat. Roger, stood silently by, his long thin face dark and feral. The man emanated a stench of the unwashed. Deirdre never felt more vulnerable.

"Yer guardian no longer lives. Ye are mine," Miles said moving next to her. "I've bided my time waiting fer Thomas to croak." He cupped her buttocks and pulled her close. "Tonight, Countess, be ready for my visit." She turned her face away from his fetid breath. Laughing, he shoved her toward Roger who caught her, his hands cupping her breasts. His small eyes gleamed. All of a sudden, Roger, always in the shadows, appeared as much a threat as Miles.

"Cage her—Roger." Miles swaggered with importance as he led them from the room before turning into the constable's chambers where he started rifling through Thomas' desk.

One day had passed since Thomas' death. One night of torture as Deirdre lay awake expecting Miles to make good his promise. But apparently, his new duties had kept him away.

Waiting for breakfast, she tried to concentrate on the tear in her favorite gown. She deftly pulled the needle through the material, the thread closing the last of the ragged edge. Forming a final tight knot she used her teeth to cut the thread.

Someone paused outside her cell door. Thinking it to be Miles, she held her breath. The door clattered open and Emerson hurried past her carrying a loaf of bread in one hand and a cloth-wrapped bundle in the other.

"Milady." He placed the bread and bundle on the desk and then unwrapped it, revealing to her delight, a honey cake, boiled eggs, and some cheese. He appeared agitated and acted in a hurry. "Eat half and save the rest for tomorrow. Oh…here is a knife if ye need it." He placed the knife on top of the food making her wonder what he was up to as there was no need to cut a honey cake or bread.

"Emerson, will I not be taken to the cage?" She halved the bread and offered him some, but he shook his head. He quickly picked the knife up from the desk and surprised her by opening the desk drawer and placing it inside.

"I expect not," he said, acting as though putting a knife in a prisoner's desk was something he did all the time. "Miles says that you're to be kept inside for the time being. I cannot argue against him for he has been appointed acting constable."

Deirdre could see the gravity of her situation and met Emerson's kindly stare. "Then what am I to do?"

"Listen well," he said and moved close to her, his voice a conspiring whisper, "Ye need to—"

"Well…and what d'ye talk about standing so close to each other?" Miles stood in the doorway looking at them both. He strolled over and picking up an egg, cracked it and while peeling it let the shells fall on the floor. He took half of it with one bite and talked while chewing, "Is the food not to yer liking?" He approached and stood within inches of her. "What do ye think has happened to the coin the count left Thomas to take care of ye with?" He snorted, showing bits of egg buried in his rotten teeth. "But if yer nice to me, I mighten see that ye have good care without the coin."

Miles ran a dirt-encrusted finger around her face, tracing. He revolted her. Stepping backwards, she cast a beseeching glance at Emerson who watched with narrowed eyes.

Emerson surprised her when he quickly moved next to Miles and tried to nudge him out of the way as he began crowding Deirdre, running his hand suggestively up her arm.

Miles swatted Emerson's hand away. "She is not for ye. Ye have a wife. See to yer duties."

Emerson clasped Miles about the shoulders. "I thought the countess could be shared. Ye be a greedy man, Miles Woodstock, aye—most greedy." But when he started to touch Deirdre again, Miles grabbed his arm.

"Ye need to bank yer own fires at home. She is mine," Miles said belligerently, and then suggested that they go search for Count Strasbourg's coins. Emerson allowed Miles to escort him out of the cell.

The day was overlong to Deirdre, who without being taken to the cage had no way of knowing what was going on around her. At least being in the cage did afford her to see the comings and goings of the people. She would be the first to see Richard's retinue riding in, and with Joanna. Sweet Virgin Mary, how she longed to hold her child. Peer upon her face. But what if Richard wasn't on his way to Falconshire? What if he hadn't been able to get Joanna? The pardon? Wrothbury wielded a long sword, and even though aging, he was still a formidable man. What if…what if…what if. Her mind hurt from all the thinking and she finally readied herself for bed.

She fell into a fitful sleep, only to awaken later with her candle guttering in its wax. Too tired to get up and snuff it, she allowed it to burn itself out. The chamber, in total darkness, made her think of Foxlair and the window slit that let the sun send in colored beams of light and shadows across her walls.

Scrape. The noise so faint she thought she'd imagined it. Again, the same low scraping sound. Someone was entering her room and trying to be secretive about it. Instinct warned her away from the pallet and she quickly rolled off it and went to stand against the wall opposite the door. Pressing her body against the hard stones, the door hinges creaked open. She couldn't tell who slipped in as the corridor's lamps had been extinguished. The door closed, shutting her in with a person who meant to do her harm. But what if it wasn't Miles, what if it was Emerson coming to help her?

With her heart tripping, she called out softly, "Emerson?"

"Ah…ye think me to be Emerson?" Miles voice edged out almost stopping her heart. She dropped to her knees.

"Do ye lay with yer legs spread, waiting fer his cock? Methinks he has been here before, enjoying what I should be enjoying. Ye cannot hide from me ye Scottish bitch. I intend to have ye tonight."

She began moving opposite of him as he knocked against the desk and cursed. She crawled for the door and in her haste wasn't aware that he had sensed her presence and was next to her. He stepped on her hand, pinning her in place.

"Ah…Countess, here you are, at my feet." He reached down and jerked her upright.

She tried to break his hold on her wrist, to no avail, "Let me be,

Miles, or 'twill bode ill fer ye."

"Who's to care? The Frenchman? Emerson? 'Tis for certes not yer husband who wouldn't come to bury your bones if ye rotted in here." He cackled a low laugh sounding like the devil himself. "Nay, Countess, there's no one to do the rescuing of ye."

"Ye've been warned by Count Strasbourg n...n...not to touch me," she stammered, fear spiking through her.

"What of the count? Mayhap ye can tell me about him? What is he to ye?"

"I know not of what ye speak. Let me go, and I'll no' tell anyone ye were here."

"Ye are a prisoner," he snapped. "My prisoner."

"And one who should not be here," she said out of desperation. "The earl carries a pardon in my name, signed by the present King of England, and dated September the eighth of last year. But he is as spiteful as ye are and refuses to give it up—"

"Ye lie. There is no pardon, or we would know of it. Yer trying to put me off."

"Nay, 'tis true." Her voice echoed in the dark chamber.

"Ye may have enjoyed the Frenchman's money but that is over with. As of today, I'm Constable. Any contract between Thomas and Count Strasbourg is nil. I want what ye have been giving Emerson." Pressing her against the wall, he grabbed her face and held it captive.

She fought against him, prying his hands from her face. She swirled away and started for the door. He grabbed her and roughly shoved her against the wall. His tongue skimmed over her mouth. He tried to kiss her but she clamped her mouth shut against his vile invasion. When he started to tear her bodice, she kicked his shin, hard.

He yelped. "Ye slut. Ye piece of Scottish dung." With malice he slapped her hard. His hot breath was fetid against her face as he whispered, "Do not fight me anymore."

He lifted her nightgown and while he fumbled to release himself, she whispered, "Let us go to my pallet." Shuddering with revulsion, she reached down to stroke his swollen cock. "I'll no' fight ye."

He relaxed as she continued to stroke and then in a most seductive lure she pulled him toward her pallet, her arm held out in front of her guiding her in the dark. When she walked against the desk, she wanted to cry with relief. She opened the drawer and began feeling around, her hand closing over the knife.

"What are ye doing?" he asked.

"I search fer my candle. 'Tis fer certes, I like to see the man's face as he strokes inside me." Teasing him with that spicy vision, she turned toward him. Putting her hand behind his neck, she pulled him into a kiss. As he put his tongue inside her mouth she plunged the knife deep into his gut, past quivering flesh.

"Ahh…" Miles moaned and grabbed at the handle trying to pry her hands from the blade.

She held tight and pushed the blade to its hilt. "I want ye to die."

His grip tightened on her shoulders as he tried to remain upright. Unable to break his hold, they slammed down to the floor where his corpulent weight pinned her. The knife's handle pressed hard against her chest as his warm blood spread across her nightdress. Finally, his hold on her arms slackened and she was able to pry his hands loose.

"Miles?"

When he didn't answer, she pushed and inched her way out from under his heavy body. Using the sturdy desk to pull herself up, her hands shook so bad the flint popped loose and fell onto the floor. Going to her knees, she fumbled around until her hand closed on the flint. Standing, she lit the candle. Guarding the flame, she went back over to Miles and knelt down to look at his face that was in shadow. Alive, but barely, his slack mouth gaped like a dark cavern. The knife handle rose and fell with each labored breath.

"Oh sweet Mother Mary of Jesus—he will die," she moaned. "They will hang me." She sat on her chair, thinking to call for help. If Emerson were to come, he'd help her. If Roger were to come, he'd blame her and see that she hung even if Miles lived. She crept back over to peer down at him.

His eyes opened slowly. "Help me…" he moaned.

Now most calm and with a plan in mind, she tried to reassure him. "I'll go fer help." Covering him with her blanket, she then removed her bloody nightdress. With shaking hands almost preventing her from doing so, she managed to dress herself and slip into her shoes. Grabbing her cloak, and not looking back, she left.

No one was about as she stepped into the shadowy corridor and quietly closed the door behind her. Here and there, a wall sconce burnt low, almost flickering out. To her dismay several of the township guards lay sleeping in the corridor. Loud snores attested to their fatigue. A quick peek into the guardroom showed it was filled with traveling soldiers. The door to Maude's chamber was down the hall beyond the soldiers. With her heart in her throat, she began maneuvering around the men. She approached the last guard who turned over. Roger Hackward's eyes briefly slit open, unseeing, then closed again. He snored, his breath tickling her ankle.

Looking back the way she'd come, praying they would remain asleep, she knocked softly on Maude's door. Finally Maude opened it. Peering out with caution and through eyes puffed from crying, Maude's cheek was bruised. She held the candle close to Deirdre's face as if she was dreaming. Maude sucked in a frightened breath and pulled Deirdre into her chambers. She shut the door behind her.

"What happened to your face?" Deirdre asked.

"Miles. He accused me of having the coin the count left for ye. Never mind about me, milady. Why aren't ye in your cell?

"I stabbed Miles," she rasped out in a quivering voice. "He's in my chambers—alive, barely. I must get away. Please get Emerson, he'll help ye. Please—Maudie, can ye do this fer me?"

In a panic, Maude's hands flew to her mouth. "Oh…Milady, nay, it canna be."

"But it is and I must go, now. If I stay here—I die. They will kill me no matter if Miles lives or dies. Look at yerr own face, a testament to how cruel some of the guards can be."

"What about Count Strasbourg? Ye said he is on his way."

"I dinna know where he is. If they find Miles and I am still here, I'll dangle from a rope, Wrothbury's wife or not." She turned to leave. "God bless ye, Maude Warren, God bless ye."

"Wait—Milady. I'm coming with ye."

Maude stunned Deirdre by pulling the cloth covering from a pillow and began throwing her meager belongings into it. She slipped her hands under the hay-stuffed mattress and tipping it up, ripped the outer cloth. She snatched the coins hidden there when Thomas died. For good measure, she took Thomas's dagger and scabbard from the peg and attached it around her waist.

The May night air was slightly chilled. But being cold was the last thing on their minds. They crossed the town center, glancing up at the battlements to gauge where the sentries were. A cat scurried across the center, pausing to hiss and arch its back at a dog that barked and gave chase. Flaring torches helped guide them as they kept close to the buildings and headed for the embrasure and a crumbling hole at the base of the wall made long ago by marauders trying to undermine it. Deirdre, suspended in the cage had watched children use the small hole to scurry in and out of while playing games of hide and go seek. Bending low to the ground, they pushed aside empty barrels and moved a pile of stones until the hole was cleared. Maude went first and then Deirdre shimmied through the opening, coming out close to the cage that loomed in the dark.

Deirdre stood rooted to the spot. She wanted to burn the cage and the hate that was held within its wooden frame. She would fight to the death before ever stepping foot inside it again. If she had to walk to London to get a copy of the pardon from the king, she would do so.

There was no going back.

Maude came up beside her and put her arms around her. "No more, milady, the cage is over with for ye." They started walking when Maude thought to ask, "Where are we going?"

"In the direction of Wrothbury Castle. If Richard de Laci is out there, mayhap he will find us." Deirdre prayed that to be true, but it was a big countryside and the chances of that encounter indeed small.

With Maude fast beside her, Deirdre fled the misery that had engulfed her for so long.

14 The Lost Is Found

The aroma of cooking rabbit filtered into the night air perfuming it with mouth-watering treats to come. Philippe de Laci's soldiers sat around the fire watching several men turn the crudely made spits. Used to dried meat and simple rations, they acted mesmerized by the rabbit juice that sizzled and popped when hitting the flames. Although they were a grubby, filthy looking lot, Philippe had turned them into a brutal fighting force that could deal even the finest English soldiers defeat.

On the morrow they would strike further south, directly above the border, searching for errant Scottish barons and earls who thought to play both sides by changing their allegiance to Scotland as fast as the sun rose and set on a new day.

Philippe worked his way through the camp, pausing to joke with the men who sharpened weapons or tried darning their clothes. At the age of twenty-six and the veteran of many campaigns, he was used to hardships. He had recently fought for and won control of Blackadder Castle. Blackadder was strategic to troop movements and its gain was a boon to Scotland's Bruce. Unprepared for a siege, the castle had quickly fallen under the constant pounding of the massive siege machines. But then Philippe never expected any other outcome, for he hardly lost in war.

What Philippe remembered most about the siege was the caravan of travelers caught in the midst of the battle. Once he'd secured the castle he'd led them to safety inside it. Amongst the travelers was a healer, Gilbert Elphinstone. But it was the healer's redheaded daughter Caitrina, a diminutive mademoiselle, who Philippe found most interesting. Working next to her sire helping with the wounded, her skills at healing were as apparent as her father's. Her eyes, dark and alluring, had lifted briefly to acknowledge him during an introduction by Graham Buchanan.

Thinking to do none other in life than lead armies into battle, he'd never asked Richard to find a wife for him. He'd given thought to go on a crusade, lead King Philip's army to the holy lands, but Scotland's cause had become his cause, and he couldn't see beyond it. During meals at Blackadder Castle, he'd deliberately sat next to the young redheaded maiden, forcing his company on her, whether she wanted it or not. They had shared good conversation, and as her floral perfume distracted, Philippe found that he was becoming interested in more than just siege machines.

Tonight, enjoying their success, the men bantered and joked with each other. For this very day, they had taken out an English patrol. Philippe, to his relief, had lost very few men. Their surprise attacks at least afforded them the luxury of fewer deaths, so he was the first to admit that he rather enjoyed this type of warfare.

Leaving the warmth of the fire, he made his way over to Graham and Etienne. As he approached and started to speak, Graham signaled for silence. Graham slipped off the rock he was sitting on and disappeared into the heavy brush. Following close behind, Philippe and Etienne drew their swords.

Someone crashed through the underbrush in a manner that foretold they didn't care about being spotted. Philippe recognized Conner Kincaid, the young Scot who had delivered messages to Countess Wrothbury for Richard.

Tossing a quick wink at Philippe, Graham jumped out from his hiding place and grabbing Conner, held a dagger to his throat.

"God's blood!" yelped Conner.

"Ye stupid whelp. Dinna ye know better than to come upon an armed camp like that?" Graham scowled at Macadie's nephew while releasing him.

"Well I made it past yer guards jest fine. They knew 'twas me. Besides, I smelled your food way back, 'tis how I found ye."

Etienne shook his head, muttered something about the rabbit being done, and walked off.

Philippe laughed good-naturedly. "They had best challenged you, or I would be gutting them." He guided Conner into camp. "You're in time for roasted rabbit."

"'Tis gude, fer I'm most hungry." Conner joined the eager men around the fire.

Bonnar Cameron tossed a wine flagon to Conner. "'Tis gude to see ye again, Kincaid. Ye look like ye've been in battle with the English." He pointed at the dried blood and tear on Conner's tunic.

"Aye, but one Englishman only. A guard at Falconshire, and we fought in Countess Wrothbury's cell. I was saved by a dead goose and a soup bowl." Conner then told the story of his narrow escape.

All but one of the men laughed at the vision of the fat guard trying to fight with a bowl stuck on his foot. Bonnar didn't.

When Philippe asked about Countess Wrothbury, Conner admitted he didn't know how she fared. This deeply concerned Philippe, wondering if she was being further misused. His plans just changed, for he thought it best to seek out Richard who was traveling between Wrothbury Castle and Falconshire.

"On my way here I spotted an army troop, mayhap fifty or more men riding north toward Falconshire," Conner said.

"What colors do they ride under?" Philippe asked, knowing it wasn't his brother as Richard had with him a small contingent of men. Nor did he fly any banners.

"'Twas unknown heraldry, probably English. Mayhap a fat English lord with coin in his waist pouch."

"Shall we search them out on the morrow?" The skin crinkled around Philippe's eyes. He wore a daring grin, and looking around at all the nodding heads, was pleased to see they were willing. "But you, Conner, I need to send to the Bruce with a missive." When Conner nodded, Philippe then tore off a chunk of rabbit and handed the rest to Conner. After popping the drizzling meat in his mouth, Philippe sucked the juice from his fingers.

Bonnar Cameron hunkered down next to Philippe. "I'm uneasy about Deirdre Brodie," he said.

"And I for my brother."

"Do ye think he will rescue Deedee?" The nickname slipped from Bonnar's lips as though it were his own.

Philippe appraised him. "Why?" he asked, and taking a bite of rabbit used the back of his hand to wipe the juice from his chin whiskers.

"Because, I'm a fellow Scots and have an interest in her," Bonnar answered.

"I would say it is because you still have love for her." Philippe tactfully stared at Bonnar, but the firelight masked his face. "Countess Wrothbury must be truly beautiful, oui?"

"Aye, that she is. But there is something more. She is a woman who puts others and their needs before herself." He kept to himself his memories of how her kisses tasted, and the soft feel of her.

Deirdre, with Maude close beside her, headed toward Wrothbury Castle. They hadn't gone too far when Deirdre stubbed her toe and almost sprawled onto the ground. Fumbling about as they were in the middle of the night, Deirdre prayed they would manage to put distance between them and Falconshire. An owl hooted, and the scurrying noises from the nearby forest caused the flesh on Deirdre's body to ripple. Wrapping her arm within Maude's, they hurried on.

The moon, a mere half of itself, played hide and go seek with drifting clouds. Its meager light helped little in lighting their way. But once their eyes adjusted to the dark, the traveling became somewhat easier.

"Think the wolves are out here, Maude?"

"I think not, 'tis spring and they can find plenty to eat without trying us." She tried unsuccessfully to joke.

"I keep expecting to hear guards from Falconshire after us."

Maude snorted. "Ye know, milady, if Emerson is the one who finds Miles, he will do right by us and wait to sound the alarm."

"I shudder to think otherwise. Pray 'tis Emerson."

After walking most of the night without stopping, Deirdre suggested, "Mayhap we should rest a spell."

"Aye, milady, to be sure me feet aches."

The sharp odor of wood smoke alerted them that someone or something was nearby. Deirdre lifted her head and sniffed.

"Do ye smell that, Maude? Mayhap we near a cottage or township," Deirdre voiced her hope.

As they left the main road and headed toward the smell, a horse's neigh made them stop. The sounds of loud snoring cracked the dark, and a deep rumbling noise surrounded them.

"Gore, this is no peasant's cottage," Deirdre whispered. Her foot hung up, pitching her forward. She sprawled on top of a body.

"Christ above!" he bellowed.

Trying to get to her feet, Deirdre's hand squished his face for leverage, his nose getting the worst of it. His hand captured hers and held her wrist in a bruising grip. They became a flurry of limbs and legs as she tried to get away, but he wasn't letting go. Frantic, she started to roll off him, but he was all over her, grappling with her, gripping her breasts, hurting her.

"Ye thievin' night-crawling bitch." Gripping her around the waist, he flipped her onto her back and yelled, "Thieves! Help!"

Deirdre panicked and when he clamped his hand over her mouth, she bit down on his finger, tearing flesh.

Maude entered the fray. "Release her—I say." She kicked the assailant hard in the side.

"Ow," he yelled and slapped Deirdre upside the head, trying to extract his finger from her mouth. "Light a torch."

She released him and tried to heave him off of her. When she couldn't, she reached between his legs and grabbing a handful of supple flesh, squeezed.

"Saints above…" a shattered groan escaped the man as he sucked in air and rolled off her in one quick motion.

Pandemonium broke out. The hiss of swords being drawn rang out and men started running about.

Torches flared.

"Milady, quick!" Maude, holding her dagger in one hand, yanked Deirdre to her feet. They started to scamper.

Maude's grip was ripped from Deirdre as Maude hit the ground with a loud grunt. Deirdre, too petrified to stop, didn't. She bolted, her long legs carrying her deeper into the forest. Tree branches tore at her face and arms. Someone chased behind her, crashing through the underbrush. Oh gore—the pursuer was right behind her.

His hand seized her shoulder in a strong grip and stopped her so fast they both fell. He landed on top of her, his long masculine body pressing hers into the leafy mold of the forest floor.

"Please dinna hurt me," she managed to blurt out between gasps of air, her chest heaving. The man's weight was heavy on her, making it even harder to breathe.

Like a helpless animal, she was snared.

An easygoing chuckle stilled her pleas. He spoke. "I would never think to hurt you, Deirdre Brodie." The accent was unmistakable, his lips within inches of hers. She relaxed against the dew-wet grass, her heart tripping from excitement.

"Count Strasbourg—Richard? It is ye?" The hands that held her had relaxed into a caressing hold. "How d'ye know 'twas me?"

"I recognized Maude Warren's voice, and then the woman herself from the torch light. But my concern is for you, madam. Once again I think to have found you in a most unusual predicament. I don't even confess to know why you're out here away from Falconshire falling on one of my companions."

He laughed, his long body vibrating against hers and she didn't think she ever wanted him to move. She liked the strength that came from him, the warmth, the security he gave off. Safe, she was safe. It didn't matter who came after her, the guards from Falconshire or Wrothbury himself. Richard was here. A heavy weight lifted from her and for the first time in years, she relaxed and said a silent prayer of gratitude to the Lord for sending this man into her life. She couldn't help but turn her face into his palm, nor could she help but place a kiss within it. Richard followed suit by brushing a gentle kiss across her cheek. His persona was overwhelming.

A torch flared above them, breaking the spell and she selfishly wanted to tell whoever it was to go away, let her have more time with this wonderful man. But looking over Richard's shoulder, she couldn't help but stare up at her brother's face made bright by the torch's flame.

She drew in a deep breath. "David, ye are here as well."

"Aye, that that I am. I dinna know what is before my eyes here, but Count Strasbourg tells me he has plans for ye, so I'll look the other way." He helped them to their feet.

Deirdre, bitter about being in the cage for so long without help from her clan or king, said in a strident voice, "Ye dinna need to look the other way, jest look here at me. Ye must know I've been livin' in a cage like an animal. Where were ye, David Brodie? Where was the mighty Brus?"

He gave his sister a black annoyed look. "I tried to rescue ye and was wounded fer me efforts. I'll do the tellin' of it later. Why are ye not in prison?"

Willing to hear her brother out later, she told about Thomas' death. When she told of stabbing Miles, she couldn't help but see the exchanged looks of apprehension that passed between the two men.

"Then the guard was alive when ye left the chamber?" David asked.

"Aye, he was breathin', barely." No longer wanting to discuss Miles, she was more interested in who was with Richard. Their eyes met as he wrapped his arm around her waist. "Did ye no' go to Wrothbury Castle?" She fished, her insides fluttered with anticipation.

It took him forever to answer. Finally, he grinned and nodded.

"Then d'ye say that ye have Joanna with ye?" She bit her bottom lip, her stomach in knots.

"Oui." One simple word crossed Richard's lips.

His simple yes forced her to her knees. Feelings rushed in, surrounding her mind, her body. The very fact that her child that she'd spent months pining for was within yards of her embrace was too much to bear. Overwhelmed, she covered her face with her hands and sobbed.

"David," said Richard, "return back to camp. I'll bring your sister after she's composed herself."

With another glance at Deirdre and nodding at Richard, David handed him the torch. He disappeared into the dark, the foliage whispering as he went.

Richard's hand rested against the back of her head. "You have a fine daughter, Deirdre. Since leaving Wrothbury Castle she has ridden against my chest daily. I'm afraid with her so close to my heart she has stolen it."

His words were most soothing, but the meaning even greater. Deirdre's sobs turned to hiccups. At long last, she was able to raise her head. She accepted his hand allowing him to pull her to her feet. The torch danced shadows across his face; his eyes that searched hers were full of what? Compassion, friendship, perhaps more? She reached up and ran her fingers down a strand of hair next to his face. She was deeply in love with this man, but while she belonged to another, those words of love could never be voiced.

"Did ye get the pardon?" Her words broke the spell between them. Her eyes, full of hope, searched his face.

Richard thumbed away tears that had pooled below her eyes. "I'm most sorry to have failed in that. Wrothbury carries it in his waist pouch and he was not at his domain." He folded her inside his arms and held her for the longest time. "Madame, I'll get it for you, this I promise."

She nestled against his chest, breathing the strong male scent of him. "I think ye are sent by God, and I would never question God's choice. But without the pardon, I am still caged." Knowing Richard was a man of his word, she wanted to bite her tongue for even sounding ungrateful.

"Please take me to my daughter, Richard. Take me to sweet Joanna."

Richard escorted her out of the woods and to the camp that a rekindled fire now crackled. Everyone, including Maude, stood in a circle around it, looking as if they waited for them to appear. Mary Clair was holding Joanna who was no longer the tiny newborn of Deirdre's memory, but a wee bairn six months of age. She held onto Mary Clair's bodice and sucked on two fingers. The baby's rounded eyes followed Deirdre's approach.

"Oh…milady," Mary Clair said in a quivering voice and started toward her.

A sob burst from Deirdre. She was fast to Mary Clair's side and held her arms out for Joanna. Frightened, the babe turned her back on Deirdre and hid her face against Mary Clair's bosom. Deirdre couldn't help but feel crushed at seeing her little daughter turn away. A lump of disappointment formed in her chest, yet she gave Joanna a big smile.

"Och…ye be a lovely wee bairn." She greedily looked her over and couldn't help but cup the small round head capturing the baby's wispy hair. Her fingers stroked the tiny reddish-gold curls while she wished to God that Joanna would turn and put her arms out to her. The motherly urge to kiss the baby fat of her neck was suppressed.

Richard, standing next to her, spoke. "Deirdre, she has no way of knowing that you are her mother. Give her time and all will be well." At the sound of his voice, Joanna turned and put her arms out to him, and without a thought, he took the baby.

Realizing he spoke the truth, Deirdre could only nod in agreement. Joanna would have to be eased back into her life and she prayed it wouldn't take too long. She couldn't help but notice how right Richard looked holding a child in his arms. Darting a curious gray-eyed look at Deirdre, Joanna widely yawned, and started to fuss.

"How have ye been feeding her?" Deirdre asked.

Mary Clair giggled. "With a drink bladder. 'Tis most amusing to see Macadie and Count Strasbourg trying to milk a cow."

Joanna fell asleep in Richard's arms. Deirdre reached out to uncurl her daughter's fingers from Richard's tunic. Those tiny fingers gripped tightly to Deirdre's. If this is all she could have of her daughter for now, then it was better than visions of a baby only a few hours old. Memories best forgotten, now she had new ones. Richard gave Joanna over to Mary Clair who went to sit on a fir-bough pallet and tuck Joanna under a blanket.

Maude, her eyes glistening with happiness at being amongst friends, went to Deirdre's side. One by one, the men came forward to make themselves known.

Macadie dashed his head down in a brief nod at both her and Maude. His one finger was wrapped with a bloody cloth, yet his eyes gleamed as he cleared his throat and spoke, "Countess, I'm Macadie Gunn. I was the one ye fell on a bit ago."

"Oh." Deirdre's face flamed hot, she stammered, "Macadie Gunn, I dinna mean...that is to say...er...I—"

"Weel, I did have me hands full of yer flesh...and...weel I'm ashamed to say that ye had me genitories and put the squeeze to 'em!" Macadie shot everyone a scowl as muffled chuckles went around the campfire. He fingered his wounded hand.

"Your what?" A chuckle broke from David as laughter ricocheted around the circle of men.

Macadie glared. "Laugh ye bunch of cockered scuts. Have yer face stepped on, and yer dainties squeezed and see how ye feel. And ye, Mistress Warren, I think that to be your shoe that kicked me in the side?"

Maude smiled at him. "'Tis for certes had I known ye to be friends of milady's, I never would have acted the attacker. Tell me, Macadie Gunn, if I may be so forward, that is an odd haircut for one such as ye, aye?"

"We needed a friar to aid in our rescue of baby Joanna. Macadie volunteered," Richard said.

Macadie's disagreeable snort foretold otherwise.

"I'll walk the perimeter," David volunteered

The lighthearted banter went on for some time, until Richard excused himself and went to make a bed for Deirdre close to where Joanna slept. He was on his knees putting down pine boughs when he heard the rustle of her gown and turned to smile up at her. "I've made you a bed next to your daughter." He was rewarded with a dazzling grin that lit her eyes up.

She then surprised him even more when she asked," Where will ye be sleeping?"

"Next to the fire, chéri." It was good to be talking to her, using endearments.

"Would ye place yer pallet next to mine? I dinna mean to sound forward but I'm most comforted when ye are near. With ye on one side of me and my sweet Joanna on the other my comfort will know no bounds."

"How can I argue against such words?" He needed no coaxing and made his bed next to hers.

At long last, everyone was able to settle back down. Maude had been given a spot alongside Mary Clair, and snuggling under the same blanket their mummers carried around the camp.

Sitting next to Deirdre's pallet, Richard smiled while watching her move a sleeping Joanna close to her side. She would constantly touch her daughter, a gentle finger to caress the baby's hand, or a light tracing outline of the delicate ear. She tucked the blanket tight and then rested her hand on the rounded tummy as if to insure that her babe was indeed there.

Richard glanced skyward to gauge the time. The moon was low on the horizon making dawn not far off. He stared into the fire that somebody stoked. A lengthy silence ensued between him and Deirdre until they both turned to the other and started to speak at the same time. They paused, and Deirdre insisted that he speak first. The eyes she turned on him were bright in the firelight, casting spells. He thought she was an enchantress, a fey, and there was nothing he wouldn't do for her.

He edged closer to her. "Try and get some sleep for I know all too well how tired you must be. We break camp at dawn. I do not know when Wrothbury was due back at his castle but according to his sentries, it was soon. If he has arrived and found his daughter gone, then I've unleashed the hound of hell, for he will be fast on our heels."

"Oh gore. Will my life be over before I'm to see the end of him? He is like Satan himself. Always there, always lurking, and I never know what he deems to do next, how he will make my life more of a living hell than he already has. Even now the mere mention of his name spoils things fer me."

"Only if you let him, chéri. Do not let him invade your mind with fear." When she took his hand and kissed his calloused palm, her warm tears tickled his skin making him ask, "Are those tears for me?"

"Aye, Richard, I believe they are. To be with ye again after all this time is more than I can bear. How can I ever forget that ye brought my wee Joanna to me," her voice hitched and her face creased with worry. "Yet my future still looks dim. If Miles dies, I'll be hunted until they have me back."

It was his turn to give solace. "I'll protect you, chéri, always." He tried to squelch her fears.

She ducked her head in a shy gesture that he found enduring, and casting him a gentle nod, said, "Ye have been on my mind ever since ye helped me at Falconshire. Givin' Constable Warren coin made my plight somewhat easier. My thoughts of ye have been...er...well...dreams. They have been most..." her voice faded.

"Are you saying that I more than held you in my arms during your dreams?" he teased. "They say dreams are a doorway into real life happenings."

"Then the doorway into my life is wide open. Richard, we know verra little about each other."

"Oui, chéri, for we are little more than strangers are we not?"

"Perhaps. Yet, sometimes I feel like I've known ye forever. I owe ye more than I ever could express in simple words

"Deirdre." He said nothing more than her name and bent to kiss her hand, holding it captive, caressing it with his thumbs. "Someday." Again, nothing but one word, and yet both knew what the someday meant. He continued to caress her with words. "I want you beside me, my helpmate, the one I turn to in moments of joy and grief. The mother of my children."

She sucked in her breath. His words so fraught with hope almost shattered her. "Richard, I'm still a married woman."

He laughed a most bitter sound. "You tell me nothing I do not already know. I'll never forget that Wrothbury forced you into marrying him. That he raped you and that Joanna was the result of that act. The one good thing to ever come from that man's loins was Joanna. I would protect her until my last breath."

Her mouth quivered, forcing her to nod an answer.

He shifted closer, his thigh touching hers. "I'd like to sleep near you tonight. I'll not touch you. I just want you here beside me." He traced his finger down her cheek.

She nodded. "Aye, I'll lie next to ye. Richard..."

He heard the hesitancy in her voice and was surprised by the overwhelming sadness on her face. "Deirdre, what is amiss?"

"I would ask another favor. But with ye doing so much for me these past months, how can I impose on ye even more?"

"I cannot know what you want until you ask. Please do so."

She clutched his hand as if to steady herself. "Please take me to Brodie land to see my father's grave. Please give me new memories of my home and help to take away the bad ones that linger in my head. Can ye do that for me, Richard, or is it too much to ask of ye when ye've done so much for me already?"

"Is that what you truly want to do? Aren't the memories too painful?" He brought her fingertips to his lips.

"Aye, 'tis what I need to do. And yes the memories are most painful fer me. But with ye by my side, we could make new ones. Mayhap we both need new memories of my homeland."

He hesitantly pushed her gown up to her knees where the firelight revealed the scars that dotted her legs and feet. Scars made when she ran across the smoldering field after her father. He ran his hands over the shiny whorls on her legs and feet and remembered her legs to be beautiful and yet she didn't care about herself, only her father as she ran to him.

"I'll never forget lifting you from that burned-out field, nor what they did to your peré," he said.

"'Tis fer certes that I'll never forget ye were there that day. Other than papa, ye were the only one to try to help me. I keep thinking how different it all to be had we been able to escape from Foxlair."

"I heard you screaming, a scream I could not forget. I rode away from Edward that day, returning to France and never looking back. I didn't care about the English King or his wars. I thought that Wrothbury would use you and then kill you. I had no idea he'd married you until I found you at Falconshire." Richard was through reminiscing, and tilting her face toward his, he said in a voice gone low, "Deirdre, I would steal a kiss if allowed."

"Nay, Richard de Laci, ye canna steal what is freely given." She closed her eyes, willed her heart to remain within her chest and as his lips touched hers, the warmth from them spread into her, his strength filled her, and as his tongue searched and pressed hers she gave herself to this man of her dreams. He ended the kiss with little nips, prolonging the kiss, and she wanted the feel of his lips to never end. Finally, he withdrew to meet her eyes.

"I'll take you to Foxlair," he whispered in a voice husky with desire. "And together, Deirdre, we will make new memories for you…and me."

"D'ye promise?"

"Oui, I promise."

Reluctant to do so, he left her long enough to grab up his cloak and then return. As she lay back on the pallet, he flared the cloak to cover them. He shifted her in front of him, fitting her body next to his. His arm tightened around her waist. Slowly his hand crept up to rest beneath the swell of her breast.

"I think this night to be overly long, chéri."

She giggled. A delightful sound to him, and this night, he fell deeply in love with her. Everything about her was wonderful. It was clear to him what made Bonnar Cameron, and God forbid, Wrothbury to want her still. His hold on her tightened as he kissed her earlobe, the back of her neck, and wanted her so much he thought to die.

Long after everyone slept, Richard lay looking at the dwindling fire that was nothing more than hot coals. Hearing movement in the bushes across the clearing, he went up on an elbow to peer into the dark where the noise came from. Perhaps it was a fox or rabbit, but he didn't think so. Getting to his feet, he unsheathed his sword, and went over to where Macadie slept and nudged him awake. Both men slipped into the trees, searching, seeking, and making sure their companions were safe.

Roger Hackward, the guard from Falconshire hid in dense foliage watching the camp. He had followed Countess Wrothbury and the Warren widow quite easily from the moment they squirmed though the hole in the township wall. From his vantage, he watched and listened to all that had transpired this night. The earl would be most interested to learn of the familiar ways between the countess and the Frenchie. She was bent on returning to her home, Foxlair. Also valuable information that Wrothbury would give much coin to learn of. He spotted a baby amongst them.

Like a snake, he slithered back out of sight and made it to his horse. Leading his horse away from the camp, he walked a goodly pace before daring to mount.

He rode toward Wrothbury Castle.

15 Grip Fast

Unsettled, David stood in the darkness of predawn saddling his horse, Rome. Tightening the cinch around Rome's girth, David was like a bowstring with a notched arrow pulled taunt. He worried not for himself, but for the three women and child with whom they traveled. Twenty men were not enough to keep them safe. Even though close to Scotland, they were still in England that abounded with English garrisons.

They started breaking camp before sunrise, and after Richard told him he thought they were spied upon last night, David wanted to cross into Scotland before the day ended. Richard said that Deirdre had asked him to take her to Foxlair and he'd agreed to escort her. David, hungry to see his wife Seonaid and his children, agreed to go with them. But first order was getting past the English who would be in pursuit.

David, absent from home long lengths of time, left the burden of raising their children to Seonaid. She ordered the planting of the crops and keeping the clan safe as best she could. He would never forget the look of disbelief in her blue eyes when he told her that Robert de Brus summoned him. She'd sullenly turned her back to him that day but was unable to keep it turned. They were constantly drawn to each other and constantly drawn apart. Like crops growing in a field, his life cycled like a stalk of wheat.

He thought how alarmed she'd get when he'd disrobe and she'd see a new scar tracing across his chest, or somewhere else on his body. He always tried to shrug it off and say it was only a scratch, but she knew better. She often cried, and asked how she could raise their three children without him, and he would make promises he could never keep. Again and again, he returned to Seonaid's warm embrace only to face her heartbreak when once again he left.

He was unable to shake the image of Seonaid as she would sneak up behind him and put her arms around his waist, and then ever so teasingly slide her hand inside his breeks. The mere thought of it made him swell. It had been too long since last he'd touched her intimately. With resolve, he put her from his mind and body.

His horse now saddled, he tied his saddle bag next to the saddle horn and gave Rome's neck a few friendly pats. He watched Richard approach.

"Ready?" David asked while adjusting his plaid over his shoulder.

"Oui. We will follow your lead." Richard studied the sky that was starting to lighten. "It looks like clear skies this day. Let us move with haste."

They were no more an hour into the journey when Joanna started crying, letting them know of her hunger, forcing them to stop at a peasant's hovel to purchase milk.

Richard, with Joanna slung across his front and Deirdre's arms around his waist from behind, purposely left off his chest armor. Gordon rode with Mary Clair snug against his back. Maude clung and pulled at Macadie as though she would topple from the back of his giant horse any moment.

Macadie snapped at Maude. "Leddie, can ye no' set a horse?"

"Nay," she snapped back, then leaned forward and whispered, and whatever was said brought a wide smile to Macadie.

Richard, having spent the night snuggled up next to Deirdre was never more aware of her than he was right now. The way her body moved against his, the feel of her breasts pressed against his back and jiggling with the horses gait, made every fiber of his male being known. Looking down at Joanna's sleeping face made him surge with protection for both her and her mother. His desire for Deirdre forced his resolve to do away with Wrothbury even stronger.

"Tell me about your home in France," she suggested.

Glad to have a respite from his less than gallant thoughts, he began telling her about Château Falaise. "Falaise overlooks the Rhine River, and is named for the cliffs it rises from. It looks like a powerful God has taken a chisel and hammer and made it so. I'm the gatekeeper to the Germanic lands beyond. I try to do my king's bidding and keep that part of France safe from marauders. My youngest brother Valentin is in charge whilst Philippe and I are here in Scotland. The youngest of us siblings is my sister Pernelle. She calls me mon frère de papa."

"My brother the papa," Deirdre translated and Richard nodded.

"Oui, she tells me I act more like our papa than her brother. Pernelle is a hellion. Wild as the wind and rides horses like a berserker. She is too strong a woman and must learn to obey." He frowned at the thought.

"Ye dinna approve she uses her mind?"

"I only say she must learn to control it, or her life will not be easy."

"How long have you been like the parent to them?" she asked. Her breath on the back of his neck felt like a soft tickling breeze. Her hand kept sneaking around his waist so she could touch Joanna's foot.

"Ten years. First, my father sickened from the sweating sickness and then my mother took as well. They died within weeks of each other. Pernelle fell ill, but she recovered. I enlarged my domain by land swaps and the king's generosity. We grow grapes for wine, but it's the sheep and their wool that makes my fortune."

Richard glanced down at Joanna who was soundly sleeping, her eyelashes shadowing against rosy cheeks. He turned slightly to the right, shifting in the saddle.

"Madam, your daughter has snared me like a rabbit—"

The arrow came out of nowhere, piercing Richard's left forearm, and missing Joanna's skull by inches. Pain and rage had him yelling out a warning. But the volley of arrows thudding into the ground around them was warning enough.

"Move the women to safety!" Richard wasn't sure where to take them and wheeled Saladin around, trying to see where the adversary was. Grimacing, he pulled the arrow free from his arm, the hot sting sickening familiar.

"Nay. Not again. Not again," Deirdre screamed. "Joanna—how does she fare?" Her words were swallowed amongst the loud roar of the attackers that came flooding out of the trees to the left of them.

Recognizing Wrothbury's heraldry, Richard and the other men who had women with them whipped their horses to gallop away from the oncoming soldiers. They deposited the women on the other side of the glen. Richard handed Joanna down to Deirdre and whipped off the sling.

He unsheathed his dagger and gave it to her. "Hide in the trees. Do not let Wrothbury see you."

"Yer hurt. Milord—ye have no armor."

"I have no choice," he said and left her, spurring his horse to gallop away to join David and the rest who already clashed swords with Wrothbury's men.

Richard, feeling naked without his chest armor, swung his sword at the man riding straight at him. Their swords hit together in jarring blows. The sides of their warhorses butted up against the other. They continued to fight until Richard, with deadly accuracy, sliced the man's shoulder, almost severing his arm. The soldier fell writhing upon the ground. His horse terrorized and uncontrollable trod upon his inert body, finishing what Richard started.

Wrothbury in full armor sat on his horse. The black falcon on his heraldry flag waved defiantly next to him as he shouted orders. "Get my child and wife. Kill Count Strasbourg. Kill them all!"

"Come against me only," Richard taunted. "I say you haven't the courage."

Pointing directly at Richard, Wrothbury shouted, "You'll soon be dead, you meddling bastard."

In a surprising move, Wrothbury galloped forward, swinging his spiked mace in a deadly circle. Richard caught the blow full force with his shield. Again, Wrothbury swung his weapon. Richard trying to shield his body from the deadly spikes was knocked from Saladin. Landing in a bone jarring heap, Richard sucked in air. Hurt, he got to his feet slowly. Clanging metal, anguish cries from men was all around him. He vaguely heard David shouting orders.

Wrothbury kneed his horse and continued his advance, battering at Richard who was hard pressed to parry the blows. Wrothbury leaned in his saddle. Swinging the mace, he brought it upwards, connecting with Richard's shield, ripping it from his hand to sail into the air. Richard glanced around for his sword. Before he could reach it, Wrothbury plowed his warhorse into Richard knocking him to the ground. Landing on his back, Richard rolled out of the way of slicing hooves. Wrothbury tried to trample Richard's prone body. Richard threw his arms up to protect his head. An arrow whizzed by Wrothbury, missing his head by inches. He wheeled his horse about and headed toward Deirdre's hiding place.

Realizing Wrothbury's intent, Richard ran to Saladin and started to swing into the saddle when a man pounced on him and hauled him back to the ground. The tip of the soldier's sword bit into the ground next to Richard's head sending pebbles and dirt across his face. Using his legs as scissors, Richard wrapped them around the warrior's ankles and tripped him. Grabbing up a sword he sprung to his feet and buried the steel into the men's neck. Blood spurted, the man gurgled as Richard leveraged the blade free. He glanced around. David—Macadie and all others were busy trying to stay alive.

Richard yelled out, "Wrothbury's after Deirdre." His words were lost amongst the din of clashing blades.

He turned just in time to see another man advancing. Their swords hit together, sparks flew. He couldn't stop to see if Wrothbury had reached Deirdre. Richard tussled with his opponent. When they were close enough to breathe the same air, Richard head-butted the soldier's face. Stunned, the man staggered backwards and didn't see the blade Richard swung to take his life.

Covered with blood, his chest heaving, Richard gulped in air. He spotted Wrothbury across the meadow searching for Deirdre.

"Gordon. Get to Deirdre before Wrothbury does," Richard shouted at the young Scot still on his horse.

Helpless to get to her, Richard prayed that Deirdre was deep inside the woods. Trying to force his way through grunting, sword swinging men, his mind on Deirdre, he found himself fighting close to Macadie. They were outnumbered and everyone fought desperately. He turned to meet an Englishmen's assault.

"Coont—duck," Macadie yelled.

Richard veered to his right and tried to get out of the way when the sword blade sliced down his back. He opened his mouth to protest against the searing white-hot pain, but nothing came out. He dropped his sword. His knees buckled. The ground came up to meet him as he pitched over onto his face.

Macadie yelled, "Ye English bastard!"

A body fell next to Richard. In a haze, he looked into the unseeing eyes of John Ward. Macadie's battle-ax protruded from the back of the man's head. Richard's mouth moved in silence. Moisture blurred his vision. Wrothbury would win after all. *Deirdre, I've failed....* Blood tickled as it rivulet down his side soaking into his tunic. The faces of his loved ones swirled before him. Someone kneeled beside him.

"Coont—ye canna die. David—help! The coont's hurt bad!"

Deirdre, watching Wrothbury ride toward her, clutched her dagger. "Ye'll not take me again. I'm no longer yours to cage." She became as deadly as the blade she held. He'd never make her cower again.

Joanna, still in the sling against Deirdre's bosom, started to wail.

Ignoring Deirdre's meager attempts to frighten him away, he sneered at her. "Give me my daughter. I plan on killing you and leaving you to rot here with your lover who has lost his last battle. He's dead." He unwound his spiked mace from his saddle horn and pointed at the bloody gristle hanging from it. "That's his brains."

Her mind screamed. "Nay, Richard is not dead." She began backing up. Joanna squirmed and grabbed at the sling.

He urged his horse closer, almost trampling her. She swiped the blade against Wrothbury's deformed leg, cutting him where it was unprotected.

"You Scottish whore!" He swung the mace.

The wind from the weapon lifted Deirdre's hair, missing her head by inches. Joanna's wails echoed around the meadow. Deirdre sprinted out into the opening. Joanna bounced against her chest, making it hard to run. Feeling Wrothbury trailing close, she stopped and turned to face him. But his attention was on the warrior advancing toward him.

Close to Wrothbury, Gordon went on the attack. He swung his claymore at Wrothbury but it was no match for the spiked ball. Wrothbury swung with all his might and knocked Gordon's weapon away. Closing in on Deirdre, Wrothbury cut the air with his mace and almost had her.

Gordon pointed at a small army riding fast, their blades gleaming in the sunlight. "We have help!" he yelled.

Directing his hate at Deirdre, Wrothbury had the last word. "You'll never escape me, nor Falconshire and what you have done there." He kneed his mount and rode to join his soldiers.

Their saviors came screaming into the battle, some giving off Scottish war cries giving credence to the sound alone striking terror into the enemy that hears it. Others fought with the cool arrogance of men who did little else for a living. Their leader smashed into the English, immediately dispatching with two of the cur dogs before they had time to mount their horses.

David stood with his feet planted on each side of Richard's head and fought like a berserker. Just when he thought they had lost and would all be killed, to David's amazement, he watched Wrothbury signal his men, and the English scuts rapidly withdrew. Some of the rescuing soldiers gave chase. The sight made David want to weep.

Both David and Macadie knelt beside Richard, their faces a blur to him as they tore his tunic away and used it to staunch the blood. Richard tried grabbing David's plaid, but couldn't. "Deirdre…."

"Dinna worrit."

A warrior reined in his stead right next to where David knelt. "Where is my brother?" he asked while removing his helmet. He glanced around.

David recognized the man as Richard's brother. David started to point to the count just as Deirdre, holding a screaming Joanna, ran past him and dropped to her knees beside Richard.

"Richard," Deirdre sobbed and removed the sling holding Joanna from around her neck. She laid Joanna on the ground. But a terrified Joanna immediately rolled over onto her stomach. Deirdre turned her attention to Richard. "Richard, dinna fret, we will get ye help." She removed his blood soaked tunic and peered at the wound.

"God in heaven help him. Dinna take him, not now…." she wailed.

"Mon Dieu," exclaimed a warrior who knelt beside Deirdre and who looked amazingly like Richard.

His face contorted with alarm as he stared at Richard's injury. "Merde. How does he live through this?" Blood welled from the gash, and wadding Richard's tunic up, he pressed it against the wound. "Etienne," said the warrior taking control. He glanced up at the surrounding men and barked out orders. "Unload the supply cart and get it over here—make haste! Bonnar Cameron, take our men and make sure that the English are not coming back. You," he said and pointed at Gordon. "Bring Mademoiselles over here to see to the child. Graham, catch some of the dead Englishmen's horses for the women to ride."

Richard tried pulling air into his lungs but the pain was too intense and any kind of movement felt like his head would topple from his shoulders. Flat on his stomach, he heard Deirdre and Philippe talking over him. He must be dreaming—how could Philippe be here?

"Deirdre? Philippe?" he whispered as he was lifted from the ground and being carried.

Macadie jumped into the back of the cart. "Give him to me."

David carefully hoisted Richard into the cart and with Macadie's help laid him on several blankets. Richard was aware of what was happening but little else, so great was his pain that he wanted to die.

"Where are ye taking Richard?" Deirdre asked.

"I'm Richard's brother, Philippe de Laci. We go to Blackadder Castle and the healers that are there," he said and tied Saladin to the cart.

David nodded at the French warrior. "I'm David Brodie, Countess Wrothbury's brother. Isna Blackadder in English hands?"

"No more. The Bruce's banners fly from its parapet," Philippe said. "Mount up." He pointed at the battlefield where carrion birds circled high. "Someone, fetch that woman."

Bertrand turned to where Mary Clair stood over a dead Englishman. "She mourns her sire," he said about the grieving maid.

"I'll get her," Gordon said. Mounting his horse and taking the reins of another, he rode toward Mary Clair.

Maude climbed into the cart with Deirdre, and taking Joanna from her, tried to feed the baby, but she fussed and turned her face away from the milk bladder. Maude sniffed the milk. "'Tis sour, no wonder she turns away. Poor baby. We need milk fer the little one."

"Aye, I'll tell Philippe de Laci when we are away from here." Deirdre peered at Richard who was still unconscious. She prayed with fervor. How could she lose Richard after finding him again? Nay, God wouldna be so cruel. He would not snuff the sun from her life, not now.

"Richard, ye must not let go. Dinna leave me, not so soon, not after finding me again."

Bertrand climbed into the cart with his simple pouch of needles and thread.

They started their journey.

Bertrand leaned over Richard. "Milord?" His voice shook with emotion as well as his hand while trying to thread a needle that the cart's bouncing almost made impossible.

"Stop the cart," Bertrand roared. "I cannot do this whilst we move."

He handed the needle to Deirdre then poured wine over Richard's wound that started on the left side where his neck met his shoulder, then down his back to stop below his shoulder blade. The cut wasn't as deep as feared, but deep enough, and most certainly he would have been killed had Macadie not yelled out a warning. Bertrand, with Deirdre's help, began the arduous task of stitching him and while doing so prayed to all the powers in heaven to please keep Richard alive.

Macadie rode close to the cart. "Bertrand, will he live?"

"I do not know. 'Tis a most grievous wound." He continued to push the needle through the skin and pulled the coarse thread behind it. "I pray we get him to Blackadder and the healers that Philippe de Laci speaks of."

"Richard will not die—this I promise," Deirdre said and continued dabbing at the blood.

At last, Bertrand finished with his crude stitches. Not having anything to wrap the cut with, he covered it with Richard's blood-stiffened tunic.

Richard moaned and tried turning onto his back but Bertrand restrained him.

A soldier driving the cart slapped the reins against the horse's backside and urged it onward.

The cart's constant rattling jarred Deirdre to her very bones, making her wonder how Richard endured the jolting. Seeing that flies were landing on Richard's wound, she fanned at them, to no avail. She motioned at Philippe who was riding next to the cart, his eyes constantly going to his brother's still form.

"Oui, Countess Wrothbury?" He managed a smile.

"Philippe de Laci. Richard spoke often of ye. How long until we reach Blackadder?" It was disconcerting for Deirdre to be looking into eyes the same as Richard's and it not be him.

"On the morrow at the earliest," he answered.

Deirdre couldn't help but gasp. "Oh—gore. I dinna think Richard to live until then. Is there no place closer? Even my wee bairn must have milk. She hasna eaten since this morning."

"Non, madam, there is no place under Scottish control that is closer. Without a wet nurse how have you been feeding the child?"

"Richard used a water bladder. He purchased milk from tenants."

"The milk I can obtain." He smiled.

Thinking of Richard, she asked, "This cart is too hard on his body. Can ye get straw or something soft to put under him?" She spotted a group of men riding their way, the dust whipping into the air behind them. She pointed toward the men, her heart thumping wildly. "Are the English returning?"

He shook his head. "They are your fellow Scots. Men who ride with me. I sent them to make sure the English were indeed gone."

There was something familiar about the way one of the men sat his horse. As they came closer, she watched the man from her past approach. This time she didn't have the battlements of a castle to hide behind.

Bonnar Cameron reined in his mount beside the cart and with interest flicked a look at Richard before his gaze settled on her and stayed there. "Countess Wrothbury," he said. "How fares Count Strasbourg?"

Bonnar, if possible, was even more handsome than she remembered. His grin was still quick as he nodded at her, his brown eyes brazen.

"Count Strasbourg lives, but he is sorely wounded."

Joanna chose that moment to start crying and Deirdre took her from Maude. The babe was hungry and she gladly nestled against Deirdre's bosom, rubbing her face against the cloth of Deirdre's gown. Her two fingers went inside her mouth and she sucked loudly.

"This is my daughter, Joanna."

"She acts like she's starvin'," Bonnar said, a frown furrowed his brow as he shifted in his saddle.

"She is, "Philippe answered. "Can you obtain some milk for her? We must get Richard to the healers at Blackadder."

Bonnar nodded at both Philippe and Deirdre. "I'll find milk for yer wee bairn, Deedee." Her nickname rolled off his tongue with ease. To her relief he rode off taking several men with him.

The cart rattled and lurched, each rotation of the wheels rendered backbreaking jolts. Joanna had finally fallen asleep again, so Deirdre handed her back to Maude. Mary Clair rode a horse next to Gordon. When David wasn't leading the way, Philippe was, and both of the men would take turns to check on Richard. A line of soldiers stretched out behind the cart.

Sweat rivulet down Richard's face and Deirdre wet a cloth with water from the bladder and wiped his face.

He moaned and opened his eyes. "Chéri," he managed to say.

She loved him for the effort but cautioned him. "Richard, dinna try to talk. Yer brother Philippe is here and we journey to Blackadder Castle where he says there are healers. We'll be there on the morrow." She dabbed the cool cloth against his face.

He turned his head into her skirt. "I cannot abide the pain," he moaned.

As she kept watch over him, either sleep or pain claimed him, for he became quiet.

It wasn't long before Bonnar rode up leading a brown milk cow that mooed with each step and fought the rope tied around her neck. Seeing that at long last her daughter was going to have something to drink, Deirdre asked the driver to stop the cart so that Maude could hand the bladder to Bonnar. She heard the cow being milked, and once the bladder was filled, it was handed to Maude.

With Richard's head in her lap, Deirdre observed Maude coaxing Joanna's little rosebud mouth to latch onto the milk bladder. Her daughter drank greedily. Deirdre shut her eyes and wondered of her predicament. Three men wanted her. But the one she desired was fighting for his life. Richard's hand snaked out and grasped her skirt, clutching the material as if it was a lifeline.

She whispered into his ear. "I love ye, Richard de Laci."

He moaned, squeezing her leg, telling her that he heard her words.

The cart's constant bumping laced pain through every part of Richard's body. He winked open one eye to see Deirdre was still next to him, bathing his face with cool water. Unable to stare into a sky orbed by the blinding sun, he closed his eyes tight. Snatches of conversation wafted to him. They were taking him to Blackadder and he despaired of ever getting there.

His wound seeped, the blankets beneath him became sticky with blood, attracting flies. He had to get the sun off of him before he cooked. "Deirdre," he managed to say, "the sun…hot…"

Philippe chose that moment to ride up, and most worried, stared down at him. "Richard—are you awake?" he asked, leaning close as if to satisfy himself that Richard still breathed.

"Philippe de Laci, the sun is burning him. We must shade him somehow," Deirdre said.

"I think I know what might work. But you'll not be able to remain at his side."

The cart was stopped. Bertrand with David's help stretched a blanket across Richard and tied it to all four corners of the cart. It was high enough not to touch him yet did its purpose of shielding him from the sun. Only the heat was left to plague him, for it was captured under the blanket as well.

He started to reach up and wipe the sweat from his brow, but couldn't lift his left arm. "Too hot...too hot..." he muttered. Alone in the cart he missed Deirdre's comforting presence and her cooling cloth.

He slept again and didn't awaken until the coolness of dusk. Sick to his stomach, he retched into the straw that made up his pallet. He sank into oblivion as a fever took over and became delirious.

When the horses started to lather, Philippe stopped the cart and had Richard removed to the cool ground underneath a tree. Again, Deirdre took up her vigil next to him and tried to comfort him. But he no longer knew where he was.

Richard thrashed about, but was restrained by Macadie who had given Deirdre a respite, and had to threaten her to do so. He made good sense when he told her she'd be no good to Richard if she became sick from exhaustion.

Morning found Richard drifting in and out of consciousness as once again they continued their journey. At times, Deirdre's gentle voice urged him to stay with her. In the distance a baby cried. Philippe bullied him, telling him if he died, he'd be sorry.

Late that afternoon, Philippe caught Deirdre's attention and pointed. "Look yonder, madam, we have reached our destination."

Blackadder Castle bustled with people scurrying about. Scaffolding nestled around the tall, stark castle, which was a flurry of activity as masons repaired the damage done to the castle by Philippe's prior siege. The laborers stopped working and soon the whole of Blackadder was welcoming them.

The drawbridge no sooner rattled down when a petite redheaded woman ran across it. She paused to shade her eyes from the morning sun as she searched the group of men and then her dark stare latched onto Philippe de Laci and his onto hers. She moved with grace as she approached his horse.

"'Tis glad I am to see ye are safely back." She smiled up at him, but he didn't have a return smile, instead he pointed at the cart not far behind him. "Mademoiselle Caitrina, my brother is badly wounded."

Caitrina moved with alacrity to the cart that held Philippe's brother along with an exhausted looking woman with dark smudges under her eyes. A baby next to the woman was crying. Caitrina climbed into the cart and kneeling beside Richard peered at his wound.

They clattered under the drawbridge.

Dust rode the air as their retinue filled the courtyard. Stable boys ran to and fro, gathering reins and shooing away yapping dogs.

16 With Fortitude

Blackadder Castle

Richard lay on his stomach with his left arm immobilized against his side. His fingers twitched occasionally belying that he was indeed alive. Since arriving at Blackadder he had drifted in and out of consciousness for days, but was now more often lucid than not. Listening to the inevitable bickering going on over his backside, he prayed the potion for pain recently given to him by the healer, would start to work.

"God's blood—Gilbert," Macadie raised his voice at the healer. "Take those squirming maggots off the Coont's back. Gives me the shivers to see 'em."

"My gude, Macadie, if ye canna stand to see what is taking the poison from Count Strasbourg's wounds, then ye shouldna come in here giving me grief with me healin'."

"Och. Ye be a charlatan and no' a healer, for ye have almost let the Coont die and ye let those squirmy maggots run amuck on him!"

Gilbert Elphinstone drew himself up to his full five feet. His frizzy red-hair that stuck out about his head made him resemble a wild berserker. He glared at Macadie. "D'ye only hear out of one ear? Now ye listen to me—Macadie Gunn. A maggot eats the infection and cleans a wound. Milord Strasbourg's wound is cleansed and that is a gude thing."

He poked his finger against Macadie's' chest. "Mayhap ye can tell me when ye became a healer and know more of medicines than me."

Macadie held up his hands in defense. "Calm yerself—Gilbert, ye'll be fallin' on the floor in a fit. Then what good would ye be to the Coont?"

"Cease with this," Richard whispered as he tried to turn over, but only managed to tangle the linen sheet around his long legs.

"Nay—Coont—ye canna move." Macadie pulled the cover away and rearranged it over Richard's bare backside and legs.

A faint knock preceded the entry of Caitrina. "Papa, I could hear ye and Macadie clear down in the great hall. How can a sick man heal, if ye be yellin' in his ear?"

Gilbert smiled at her approach and exclaimed, "Ah…Macadie, here is me daughter, the elixir of me life." That he doted on his daughter and had taught her well in the art of healing was plain to see.

Caitrina bent to study Richard's wound. "'Tis time to remove the maggots. Their work is done. Papa, did you ready milord by giving him the opium poppy mixed with wine?"

"Aye, daughter, that I did."

She checked the laceration on his forearm made by the arrow. It was healing up nicely. The day they'd brought Count Strasbourg here the wound on his back was already infected stretching the stitches and had the larvae started. She'd cut loose the stitches made by Bertrand.

"Papa, I think to—" Suddenly the door opened and Philippe de Laci followed by David Brodie entered.

"Richard, ah, mon frère, how do you fare this day?" Philippe bent for a closer look as Caitrina removed the maggots. "How in Hades can you stand those things crawling on your back? Do they not itch?" He made a face and rolled his shoulders as if to take away the phantom itch.

"Non, Philippe…I feel nothing."

"Gilbert," David said, "how long till Count Strasbourg can ride?"

Using his pestle and bowl, the diminutive healer continued mixing the salve, his dark eyes squinting in thought. "Mayhap several fortnights or more of proper healing. Caitrina and I can stay that long, but then we must continue our journey to Dundee."

Caitrina continued to cut away dead tissue. "I agree with Papa." She threaded the needle and leaned over Richard. "Milord, I'll be stitching yer wound closed. 'Twill hurt. I pray the potion will dull the pain."

"I pray you are fast with that needle," Richard said, his voice becoming thick from the drug.

"Richard, you're most fortunate to have such fine healers," Philippe said.

As Caitrina leaned over to start the stitches, so did Philippe, and they banged heads.

"Ouch." She straightened and fingered her forehead the same time he straightened and felt his.

"Pardon me, mademoiselle, for I did not mean to do that." His eyes twinkled with beguile.

She sucked in her breath, and holding her needle pinched between her fingers as a weapon, she waved it in front of his face, almost jabbing his nose with it. "Just how d'ye expect me to stitch up yer brother if ye cannot keep yer head outta my work?"

She appeared so indignant that Philippe laughed. "Pardon me, Caitrina...a lovely name, Caitrina."

"Mmmphm," she muttered. "I be thinkin' there are too many bodies in this chamber. Count Strasbourg canna breathe with all the air being sucked out by so many of ye."

Philippe nodded toward the door and said, "Macadie...David, ye heard mademoiselle. Out you go."

"Me? Why ye young pup, who d'ye think has been beside yer brother since his injury?" Macadie scoffed. "Coont, d'ye want me to leave? ...Ah...Coont? "

Caitrina glanced at Richard who appeared to be sleeping. "The potion has taken him beyond this room. 'Tis a blessing. Macadie Gunn, David, I suggest ye go and fetch some broth for milord. But wait until I summon ye to return."

"Come, Macadie." David started guiding Macadie out the door.

The door no sooner closed when Caitrina addressed Philippe. "Yer brother has God on his side, for just a hair closer, I think his head would have toppled from his body, and ye would be head of yer family." She pulled the needle through Richard's skin and started on a new stitch.

Philippe's gaze traveled to her face where a spattering of freckles bridged her nose. Her hair, bright red, was braided and tied to the back of her neck with colorful blue ribbons.

Concentrating on her work, she chewed her lower lip and happened to glance up to meet Philippe's gaze. "What are ye lookin' at? Ye stare as if I have two heads."

"Non, mademoiselle, I stare at a very pretty head, not two, just one." He smiled with delight as she blushed a deep pink.

She tied off the thread, the stitches having started at the base of his neck and ending below his left shoulder blade. His back resembled the laces on a woman's gown.

"Papa is the salve ready?"

"Aye, daughter. Give up yer place and I'll finish." Gilbert slid in next to Caitrina and started spreading salve over the stitches. "Milord, would that ye lift up yer brother so that I can get this wrapped around him?"

Philippe slid a hand under Richard's chest, and then using care rolled him onto his good side and lifted. He continued holding him while Gilbert deftly wrapped the wound with clean linen strips of cloth. He secured Richard's left arm against his side so that he could not use it and pull the stitches loose.

"I'm done, lad," Gilbert announced.

The liquid potion wore off and Richard awoke to a thousand knifes stabbing him. The pain overwhelming, he muttered, "Healer, give me more of the opium drink."

Caitrina held his head and pressed the chalice against his lips.

He gulped down the elixir, spilling it down his chin, draining the cup.

"Mademoiselle, will I have the use of my arm?" Richard asked.

"Oh…aye, Count Strasbourg, that ye will. I've healed worse, and the man is out there fightin' for the Brus."

"Philippe, are you still here?"

"Oui."

Caitrina poured hot water from a bucket into a pewter bowl and after picking up soap and a cloth to wash with, approached Richard. She soaped the washcloth and wringing it out, carefully washed his one arm, his back, and whipping the cover from his body, washed his buttocks and legs.

Philippe offered to help. "Would that I do that for you?"

"If ye'll turn him over I can wash the rest of him," Caitrina ordered as she dried Richard's back. 'Twill make him feel better to have his body clean, d'ye no' see?"

"Mayhap I should wash his front?"

Caitrina gave him a dismissive flutter with her hand. "Och…dinna worrit that I'll see what lies between yer brother's legs, for 'tis plenty tarses I've seen with me healing."

"But…but…." Philippe stuttered.

"Are ye goin' to help me with yer brother or are ye goin' to stand there with yer face the color of me hair?"

Richard, fighting to stay awake, settled the argument when he muttered, "Christ Jesus—Philippe, turn me over."

Catrina dipped the cloth back into the hot water and proceeded to wash what wasn't covered in linen wraps.

From his reclining position, Richard watched his brother hover over him like an anxious mother. Philippe reached to take the cloth that Caitrina held.

"Stop it," she ordered and slapped his hand a good one.

Richard blessed the pain that took precedence over Caitrina washing his manhood. If circumstances were different, he would have laughed at his brother's discomfort and his own predicament.

Finished cleaning Richard's body, Caitrina said to him, "Is it hurtin' ye to lay against yer injury?"

"Oui, but it hurts no matter what position I'm in."

"In a week's time, ye will need to move yer arms about, so that your wound will not tighten up yer muscles and ye be no gude to yerself."

He tried to clear the pain from his mind and concentrate on Philippe. "Any sign of Wrothbury?"

"Non. We have guards posted. Bonnar Cameron and some of my men ride afar searching for him. The earl must have gone on to Falconshire. We will remain here at Blackadder until you're healed."

"An invisible enemy is a deadly one," Richard said. His eyelids drooped, and again the potion did its magic. He slept.

Deirdre opened the door to peer inside. Sunlight from the nearby window slit filtered in to highlight a sleeping Richard. Oil burners on the walls lit the room. Putting her fingers across her lips, she motioned at Macadie who carried a tray loaded with broth, bread, and a chalice of wine with several glasses.

Macadie hurried to place the tray on the table.

Deirdre went over to Richard. His lips were parted, his chest rose up and down with each breath. Worried that he would die, she had kept a constant vigil at his side until Caitrina had ordered her to get some rest. The healers had stressed that his recovery would be long and that he would need her at that time. She reached out to take Richard's hand.

He awoke to stare at her.

"We have brought you food." She squeezed his hand.

Macadie came to stand next to Deirdre. "Ah…Coont, 'tis gude to see ye awake."

Richard managed a nod for his friend but his eyes were on Deirdre. "Is Philippe here?"

"Nay," said Deirdre, "Only ye. They are letting ye rest. Caitrina sent us up with food for ye. She thought broth would be gude."

Richard stretched his good arm out to Macadie. "Help me sit up?"

"Should ye be sittin' up, Coont?" he asked.

"Oui. I can't eat lying flat on my back."

Macadie hurried over to help hold him up, and allow Deirdre to slip a pillow stuffed with goose feathers behind Richard's back.

"Lady Deirdre, would ye like some wine?" Macadie asked.

"Mayhap later," Deirdre said.

"Then I'll leave ya be," Macadie said.

Sitting on the bed next to Richard, she dipped the spoon into the hot, flavorful broth of leeks and fish. He opened his mouth to accept the first spoonful.

"Is it gude?" she asked and gently dabbed juice from his chin.

"As tasty as the one who spoons it."

His honesty amused her.

She held the bread for him to take a bite from. The bread met his approval when he muttered that it was good. She fed him another spoonful. Someone, Caitrina perhaps, had tied his hair back in a queue, and shaved his beard off.

"Ye've been grievously wounded on my account," she said.

"I've been injured in the name of my king more than once. A wound in your name is much more satisfying."

Taking several more bites, he signaled that he'd had enough. After Deirdre set the bowl aside, his hand found hers and brought it to his lips. "You taste better than broth, and smell like the petals on a flower."

Deirdre dipped her head. "Aye, I shared Caitrina's bath water. She puts dried rose petals in it. She let me use her lavender soap of which I'm most thankful."

"I'll buy you scented soaps from Egypt. Lotions from the Dead Sea. I will give you a ring made from the finest jewels. I want you." He rested against the pillow, his face lined with pain.

The sheet covered his lap and nothing else, showing his long, legs. For the first time she truly saw at how well-shaped his body was. Even damaged as thus, he set her heart hammering. His mat of dark chest hair peeked from the linen wraps then trailed down his abdomen to disappear beneath the sheet.

"You like what you see?" he queried, and then continued, "Better than the finest jewels I can offer?"

She whispered softly, "Ye are finer than any jewel, milord." She began placing kisses on his hand, running her tongue over his palm. And being ever so careful, she placed a kiss upon his lips. They parted to contemplate each other.

"Would that I have you beneath me right now, I would make you most delighted. I want you for my wife." He tilted her chin to meet his eyes.

She worried her lip and asked, "Have ye heard anything about my husband's whereabouts?"

"A husband that stands between my having you? Non, he is quiet. Too quiet. And it makes my blood boil to even think in terms of Wrothbury being your husband. I no longer wish to acknowledge him as such." Richard ran his hand up her arm. His face appeared tired yet full of want. "When I'm healed I promise you I—"

Commotion outside the doorway stopped their conversation. The door flew open as Maude carrying Joanna and being followed by Mary Clair and Gordon breezed in.

Gordon peered down at Richard. "Count Strasbourg, 'tis gude to see you're not a memory. The healers say ye will recover in time." He then acknowledged Deirdre with a wide smile.

Maude gave a quick curtsy. "Milady, Joanna's been fussing somewhat, so we thought to search ye out. Count Strasbourg, ye look better today."

Richard smiled in agreement. Philippe, David, Macadie and Bertrand entered. Bertrand hurried over to be next to Mary Clair. Macadie went to stand next to Maude and made faces at Joanna who grinned at him. But her arms stretched out to Deirdre who gladly took her daughter.

"Did ye eat?" Macadie asked.

Richard started to nod his head causing the stitches to pull, "Aïe!" He grimaced as intense pain shot down his neck, nauseating him.

Caitrina entered the room which was filled with people. She forced her way next to Richard and turned to face the small gathering. "I want ye all but Deirdre to leave this chamber—now." She put her hands on her hips and glancing down at Richard's bandages could see slight bleeding at his neck. "Count, ye canna move yer neck. 'Tis bleedin' again." She glared at Philippe. "And, Philippe de Laci, ye should know better than to bring all these people into a sick man's chambers. Now get ye gone—the whole lot of ye."

"Mademoiselle, I'll stay with my brother." Philippe stood his ground, shaky though it was. "That is…if it pleases you—"

"Ye can stay, but the rest of ye out right now." She flicked her hands at Macadie whose mouth twitched with amusement as she shooed everyone out the door. Muttering to herself she turned back to Richard. "Are ye ready to lie back on your stomach? Ye resemble the underbelly of a fish, so white and pasty. Help me to turn him, Philippe. Ye should be ashamed of yerself, lettin' all those people in here, jest what were ye thinkin' of? Not thinkin' would be more like it." Caitrina went to one side of Richard and Philippe to the other and turned him back onto his stomach.

Philippe stared at Caitrina over his brother's backside. "Will you walk with me outside the castle?"

"Oh…aye, that I will."

"You will?"

"Aye, does that surprise ye?"

"Well…er…mayhap."

"Deirdre, I leave Count Strasbourg in yer care and would that ye keep everyone out of this chamber. Lock the door if ye must."

"Philippe," Richard muffled out from his facedown position. "Find where Wrothbury hides."

"Oui, Richard." Philippe escorted Caitrina out the door leaving Richard to wonder if Philippe had heard anything he said.

17 Love Conquers

Blackadder's tiltyard was a bevy of activity as soldiers used it to keep their skills honed. Swords clanged together, arrows released from great bows flew to thud against hay bales. Men holding lances urged their horses on while attacking the quintain. The spinning target unhorsed more than a few to land on their backsides.

Off to one side in the tiltyard, Richard parried with David. Two months had passed since Richard was injured and he had long since shed the bandages and his bed. Gripping the handle of his sword with both hands he never noticed his sword's great weight before, now it felt to weigh five stone or more. He crouched. David crouched. They circled each other, sidestepping, squinting in intimidation. David came at him. Their swords clanged together giving off sparks. Richard knew David was being careful with him, yet gave him a good workout. Their swords hit hard. David pressed, challenged. Beads of sweat popped out on Richard's face. His shoulder muscles pulled in protest. Nauseated, he almost gave up, but instead fought against the pain. David forced Richard back against the wall where the rough stone rubbed against his bare skin.

"I give up," Richard grunted, and allowed his sword to tumble onto the ground.

Macadie who stood with his arms folded, squinted his eyes. "A wee lassie could beat ye, Coont. Ye've a long way to go."

Richard scowled, thinking Macadie impertinent. Macadie bent down to pick up Richard's blade when the guards on the battlements yelled down for the portcullis to be raised. The chains rattled, the iron-gate rose upward, and the thick wooden doors were opened.

Philippe de Laci, along with his soldiers and Bonnar Cameron, were returning from their daily excursions seeking the enemy. Laughter and shouting mingled with the clatter of horses' hooves as they rode across the stone entry. Philippe reined in his steed.

From where he stood, Richard made eye contact with his brother. Philippe tossed his reins to a stable boy, and dismounted.

Richard clasped his brother's arm in greeting. "No English in sight?"

"Non, and that makes me nervous. By now, they should be surrounding us and waging war," Philippe said, and allowed his squire, Henri Grimoult, to remove his chest armor.

Philippe signaled for the young warrior standing next to Bonnar Cameron. "Brother, look who I found riding this way."

Conner Kincaid stepped forward and dipped his head at Richard. He pointed at the scar that coursed down Richard's back. "Milord, yer brother Philippe told me what happened to ye. It looks like ye've been carved by the Devil himself."

"I thought you were with James Douglas, one of the Bruce's commanders." Richard grabbed his tunic shirt off of the post he'd thrown it over, and pulled it on.

"I was. James Douglas sent me here to tell ye that the Earl of Wrothbury bandies your name around as a thief who has stolen his wife and daughter."

"Tell me, nephew, in yer travels have ye heard of Wrothbury's whereabouts?" Macadie asked.

"Nay, Uncle. He disappeared after your battle with him. 'Tis surmised he was wounded, but canna be proved." Conner's easy grin faded as he reached into his waist pouch and pulled out a soiled piece of parchment.

"I found this notice nailed to a tree not far from Blackadder." He gave it to Richard.

As Richard unfolded the parchment, Philippe moved next to him to read over his brother's shoulder.

Richard's brows knit together. "God's blood—the vultures." He drew in a sharp breath and passed the edict to David.

David's face gave nothing away as he read, but his mouth set in a grim line as he gave the edict back to Richard.

"Perhaps you should reconsider journeying to Foxlair and take ship to France instead," Philippe suggested.

"What does it say?" Macadie asked anyone who would listen.

"It bodes ill for Deirdre unless Richard can get her pardon and do so verra soon," David answered. "The English call for her arrest saying she is an escaped felon. They have placed a hefty price on her head. The guard she stabbed while escaping Falconshire has died."

"The pardon holds the key, oui? It will prove she should have been released. Had that been done as the English king ordered, none of this would have happened. This decree is Wrothbury's work," Richard stormed. "Will the man never leave her alone?"

"Aye, when he rots in his grave," David said. "I agree with Philippe, mayhap ye should take my sister to France and be done with all this."

"I've promised Deirdre to take her to Foxlair. My word is my bond. When the time is right I'll tell Deirdre of this edict, until then I ask that you all remain quiet."

"Count Strasbourg, who wounded ye so?" Conner asked.

"One of Wrothbury's men did this to me."

"And the man?"

Macadie laughed with distain. "Dead and rotting on Scottish soil where I put him."

Richard nodded at Macadie's remarks and then said, "When I have Deirdre safely at her homeland, I will seek out Wrothbury. He cannot hide forever."

"Richard," Philippe said, "I cannot accompany you. I have orders to take Crichton Castle. I've tarried here to see how you got on."

"Perhaps a redheaded healer detains you more than I do?" Richard teased. He knew that Philippe was asking for Caitrina's hand in marriage. Even though Richard thought her a miniature berserker, he wholeheartedly approved.

"Richard, you are not ready to fight anyone," Philippe said. "Wrothbury always has a contingent of men with him. That sword of yours will not get past that accursed chained-mace he always swings."

"Your concern will not sway me, Philippe. Nothing will keep me from getting Deirdre's pardon."

"Brother, be most careful coveting another man's wife. Even with circumstances as they are between the earl and the countess. You will have to live with your conscience and the stigma, when, and if, you kill the man."

Richard smirked. "I have no conscience when it comes to Wrothbury." He wished he could ask Deirdre to become his wife, as Philippe was free to do with Caitrina. But having plenty of time on his hands while healing, he'd thought of a most ingenious way to almost call Deirdre wife. He would soon share it with her.

Crunched into a corner in her father's small chambers, Caitrina sat on the floor before an open chest as her father took stock of their medicinal herbs.

Pulling the drawstring on a leather pouch, he would glance into it and then tell Caitrina if they were low on the herb. She then used quill and ink to scribble it down. The strong aroma of dried lemon verbena and marigold was a welcome respite from the normally musty smell of the castle. Hearing a squeak, and the rushes move, she spotted a small mouse scurrying toward the door.

Blackadder, having been through a siege, needed a good scrubbing and the rushes replaced. But there was no time to have it done, nor a lot of servants around to do the deed. Shoring up the outside and repairing the castle walls had priority over the inside. Besides, they'd be leaving soon and this castle's cleanliness or lack of it wasn't their problem.

Waiting to do the next entry, Caitrina gave her father a warm smile as he stroked his reddish gray beard, his mind having obviously drifted. Although he was getting on in years she thought he was most distinguished looking and she loved him dearly. Caitrina was a mere ten years of age when her mam died and remembered her well. Her sire who cured so many, was unable to save his wife from the bleeding and fever that ensued after she'd given birth to a stillborn son. Papa had fallen into a deep depression and thought to give up medicine. But that lasted only as long as it took him to see that his daughter had a knack for healing and was actually taking care of his patients that he'd neglected. Taking it upon herself to do so, she'd planted their garden full of the precious herbs needed in their profession and diligently cultivated the plants, saving the seeds for next year's planting. Keeping a well-stocked apothecary allowed them to make money from selling the herbs as well as using them for their own needs.

"Weel, sweetin, that's the last of it. Some of our stock is low, but we'll make do until we can return home to Dundee."

"Aye, Papa, we have no other choice. I do hope Sophie has kept up our garden. Sometimes she's remiss and lets the cow wander into it."

They grinned, knowing that Caitrina spoke the truth about Sophie, who looked after their home while they went to fairs and on journeys across Scotland.

Caitrina thought how God blessed them with healing and their journeys. This stop at Blackadder was unscheduled. Returning from a fair and taking a shortcut, their caravan stumbled right into the middle of a siege. They had ventured too close to the castle when hordes of men had poured out of the fortress to take on their foe.

A soldier jumped into their cart, and putting the reins to the backside of their horse, had driven them to safety. That soldier, she discovered later, was the commander, Philippe de Laci. Tall, and most handsome, he was the epitome of a warrior.

She'd come to know him quite well in the month they'd tended the wounded at Blackadder. She found herself wishing that Philippe would get a sliver, anything, so that she could doctor him. Whenever she watched as he rode away on a mission, she thought to never see him again. The last time he rode off, he returned less than a fortnight later, bringing his wounded brother with him.

Absentmindedly, she tapped her quill against the parchment sending dark spatters of ink across it. She thought how her heart pounded something fierce when Philippe entered a room. Somehow, she must put this man from her mind. She and Papa had to return home and tend to the Bruce's wounded.

Papa harrumphed. "D'ye get that last herb or are ye still wool-gathering? And ye needin' be telling me just whom ye are gathering that wool with. Am I goin' to lose me sweetin' to a French general?" he teased.

"Oh…Papa, ye needn't worrit about such things. Yer puttin' the cart before the horse, aye?"

"If the looks I see shared between ye and Philippe de Laci are not of a man and woman in love, then I'm that charlatan healer that Macadie accused me of being." He gave her a wry smile.

She started to object when Philippe strode past the open door, and then backed up to peer in.

"Caitrina," he said with genuine delight and wearing a wide grin hastened to her side. "Gilbert, you look well."

Gilbert snorted. "Cart before the horse, eh? I think not." And making his excuses left the two alone.

Philippe and Caitrina stood next to a gentle stream that fed into the river. The water lazily tripped over rocks and was so clear that the bottom of the stream could be seen where baby fish darted around. She had hastily put together a basket with bread and cheese that now set on a rock, forgotten.

They waded into the cool ankle-deep water. Philippe stood with his boots off and breeches rolled up, looking at Caitrina. She had bunched up her gown and tucked it into the girdle that hung around her waist. Laughing, she bent over and pointed at the baby fish nibbling at her toes. The sun flamed her hair into a bright glow. Right now she looked delectable to Philippe whose loins quickened while watching her take delight with the fish. She bent to run her hands through the clear water, scattering the fish to dart away.

Her laughter died as he waded toward her and gathered her against his chest.

"Oh gore...ye take my breath away, Philippe de Laci...aye that ye do," she whispered.

"'Tis more than your breath I'd like to take away right now," he said in a husky voice while tightening his hold and pressing her body close, began kissing her breathless.

"I'll die if ye ride out of my life and not take me with ye," she said, nipping softly at his lips.

Her dark brown eyes looked up at him and he could see the gentleness they held for him. He wanted nothing more than to wake up with her body next to his. He craved the closeness that a wife would bring, someone to talk to. Taking a deep breath, he prepared himself to ask the most important question of his life. "Then mademoiselle, the only way to keep you from dying is to ask you to marry me. May I ask your father for your hand? Will you follow me to France?"

"Oh, aye," her voice hitched and then went ever so soft, "I'll marry ye, Philippe, and I'll follow ye where ever ye go. But to leave my papa when he needs me will be hard to do."

"Your healing skills are still required by the Bruce, oui?"

"Most true."

Philippe felt something tickling at his feet and looked down to see small fish investigating his toes. He kicked his foot causing the fish to dart away. He took hold of her hand and walked her to the foliage covered bank. "I have a missive from the Bruce. He orders me to raze Crichton Castle. After we get your sire's consent, we can be married within a few days. And, Caitrina, we will see what can be done about leaving your sire."

"Aye, Philippe, I'm sure Papa will like having ye fer a son by marriage."

Philippe urged that they immediately seek her father out. "I want to make sure he is willing to give you up."

Wrothbury sat before a roaring fire soaking his feet in a wooden bucket filled with hot water and medicinal herbs. Hunched over in front of the fireplace in his great room with a fur-lined mantle draped around his shoulders, he contemplated his body, his bad foot especially. Pain from it had become unbearable and he was sure he wouldn't be riding much longer. He raised his foot out of the water. Wrinkled and red from the water, it resembled a grotesque appendage, thick with calluses, clubbed, certainly not a human foot, he plunged it back in the water.

Chilled to the bone, he pulled the mantle tighter and signaled for a nearby servant to put more wood on the fire. After bowing to him, the man threw large logs on the fire that took off, the flames crackled shooting sparks up the flue and throwing off heat. Wrothbury's gaze traveled upward toward his heraldry shield mounted on the tall fireplace. With no son to inherit his domain, who would the king bestow Wrothbury's holdings to? Perhaps another who showed valor. He thought to ink an edict naming Joanna as his heir, but knew the king would give all to whom he chose, certainly not a girl child.

He shivered as if someone had walked on his grave. "Warm this cloak," he ordered the servant.

The young man removed Wrothbury's mantle and held it close to the flames, warming it before he replaced it around his master's shoulders.

"There ye go, milord." He bowed.

"What is yer name?" Wrothbury asked.

"Robin Bailey, milord."

He studied the skinny young man. "Tell me, Robin Bailey, do you know how to fight? Do you desire becoming a knight?"

Robin hung his head and said, "Nay, milord. I want to be a farmer."

Wrothbury's mouth pulled down in disgust. "A farmer? I thought every young man wanted to fight for his king, be a soldier, learn how to shoot the great bow."

Again, Robin hung his head and shrugged. "D'ye need anything else, my lord?"

"Nay, leave me," the earl ordered.

He shut his eyes. He brooded about his failed attempt to kill Count Strasbourg. He believed the man was dead, saw him fall with a mortal wound and didn't get up. When told otherwise, he'd slapped the messenger and called him a liar. But too many who fought the battle confirmed the Frenchman still lived. Wrothbury never had so many things go wrong. He'd been but a horse's length from capturing Deirdre and his daughter when an army of Scotsmen ruined all. He later found out that Philippe de Laci, the Count's brother had been the one who led the Scotsmen.

After fleeing from the battle, he and his soldiers took refuge at a monastery. His thigh where Deirdre had stabbed him had become infected and he needed it cared for. Liking how the monks pandered to him, he lengthened his stay and gave freely of his coin.

He'd lost many soldiers that day, John Ward being one of them. He grieved not for the man, only that John, his sergeant at arms and a good dependable soldier was gone. He'd replaced him with Robert Kempe who had yet to prove his loyalty. Kempe's wife, Millicent, was now chatelaine of the castle. The woman, a skinny shrew with several warts on her face, was one that Wrothbury had no trouble staying away from.

Ah, Deirdre, what to do about her? He hated that she preferred the

Frenchman, hated that the Frenchman now had his daughter. Did he truly miss Joanna or was he upset to have lost his bargaining power over her mother.

"Holy Father," he prayed. "Allow me to live long enough to kill the Frenchman and that scab of a woman, Deirdre." He couldn't bring himself to call her wife, the words stank up his mouth.

Deirdre sat basking in the wooden tub. "Oh...gore, I think I could stay in here forever. Maude, would that ye pour just a little more hot water? It feels so good to relax my body."

The steam rose in the air as Maude lathered Deirdre's hair then rinsed the soap from it. "Ye will start looking like a wrinkled old crone if you stay in there much longer."

"Maudie, ye'll have to bathe when I'm finished." A frown creased her brow, and she ventured a question. "What d'ye think happened to Miles after I stabbed him?"

Maude held up a large linen drying cloth. "Step out and let me dry you."

Deirdre stepped out of the tub and stood dripping water. Maude ran the drying cloth over Deirdre's body most vigorously. "Milady, I never thought to say I hope Miles still lives. For if the man is dead from your blade then Falconshire will send out proclamations calling ye a murderess and an escaped felon. Nothing short of your return or death will even this score with the English. If you can produce your pardon then you will be free."

"But if Miles has died, then even the pardon will not help me, will it?" Deirdre stepped into a chemise, her face now a frown of worriment.

"It can be argued that if the Earl of Wrothbury hadn't kept yer pardon from my Thomas and the mayor, then none of it would have happened," Maude said. "Milady, look at the gowns the previous lady of the castle abandoned in her hasty retreat." She beckoned Deirdre to come look. "True, they have been worn a lot...still."

Deirdre peered into the chest and seeing multiple gowns, lifted a gown of blue that unfolded into a deeper blue with gold trim crisscrossing the bodice. The sleeves billowed full to allow an undergarment of pale blue to be worn underneath it.

"Aye, to be sure, the lord of this castle betrayed Scotland and our king, so I'll wear this gown gladly."

She sat in a chair and without a mirror had to depend on Maude's opinion of her. She looked over at Joanna who slept in a borrowed cradle with her little behind up in the air, the side of her face squished against the coverlet. "Joanna is growing so fast. She is crawling most mischievously and I worry she might fall from the cradle. Mayhap I should not leave her."

"Milady," Maude said while braiding strands of golden cord into Deirdre's chestnut colored braids. "The wet nurse will soon be here to feed her and stay with her. I would ask Mary Clair, but with two suitors she canna find the time to do her duties."

"Aye, Bertrand and Gordon fawn over her. The lass will have a difficult choice to make. Either she remains in Scotland with Gordon, or go to France with Bertrand," Deirdre said, and then teasingly raised a lone brow at Maude. "What of ye and Macadie Gunn? The man's eyes undress ye when yer together."

"Ah...milady thinks she is witty this eve. But I have to say that Macadie is most different than Thomas. He is cheerful, and his Scottish self is most...er...." Blushing, Maude chuckled while holding the gown for Deirdre to step into and changed the subject. "Count Strasbourg will see you over all others when ye walk into the great hall."

Deirdre looked down at the gown and ran her hands across the soft material. She'd never worn anything so fine. "Oh...Maudie, I never thought to be as happy as I am right now. Just to be near Richard makes me ache for his touch."

"Here, milady, I have a surprise." She held a narrow girdle made from a heavy golden cloth. Attached to it was a sheathed dagger, the hilt decorated elaborately with gems.

"Maude, is this mine? 'Tis most favorable." She fingered the jeweled hilt.

"Count Strasbourg wanted to surprise you. Still flat in the bed with his wound, he ordered it made by a goldsmith in the nearby village. Said he had promised you jewels. Hold still while I put this on you." Maude fastened the girdle low on Deirdre's hips. "'Tis fer certes, ye will set his heart a flutter this eve."

"I surely hope so." Deirdre bent to look at Joanna whose mouth was fast sucking on an invisible nipple. "She knows I'm her mam, does she no'?" She ran her hand lovingly across Joanna's raised bottom and silently gave thanks for her daughter.

"Oh…aye, milady, she knows ye are her mam."

Deirdre closed the door behind her and turned. She gasped out loud, for she was within inches of Bonnar Cameron's brown eyes. Stepping back, he grasped her upper arms while his gaze ran the length of her.

"Yer a sight to behold tonight, Deedee." From his leather jerkin, his breeks, to the plaid cloth he wore, his own attire of a warrior set off his handsome face and body.

She could see the want in his eyes as she tried to break his hold on her arms. "Let me pass." How dare he touch her after what he'd done? His touch was so achingly familiar, and yet, one of a stranger.

"Deedee, tell me ye remember the day I held ye in my arms. When I kissed yer soft breasts," he urged. "D'ye no' remember our love for each other? God's blood—Deedee, we should be husband and wife. Think of the wee child that should be ours by now." His eyes searched her face.

She knew he desired a sign, anything to tell him she still cared, could love him again. Instead, she lashed out, "Oh aye—I remember that day quite well. I remember ye takin' to the trees with yer tail between yer legs when ye realized that England's king was there. Ye could have gotten me away to the boat, but ye dinna. When Count Strasbourg, the only other person to try and help me was almost killed before my verra eyes, I dinna see ye there. Nor were ye there to stop Wrothbury from marrying me. Where were ye when I was hanging in the cage? So, dinna come here, Bonnar Cameron, and think to have me again. Ye will not. My heart is with Count Strasbourg."

Bonnar's hands dropped woodenly to his sides, his face now ashen. Her words were sharp as a blade. His voice trembled with emotion. "That day at Wrothbury Castle, I would have taken ye away, but ye wouldna speak to me. Am I to crawl before ye on my knees? Is that what ye want?" He started to dip to his knees.

"Stop it," she hissed. "I want ye to stay away from me."

"I love ye, Deirdre Brodie. That will never change. I dinna care what ye say to me here and now. Ye lay in my arms and I watched the sun dapple shade on yer breasts, your hair. I saw myself reflected in yer eyes. Ye took part of my soul that day and I have never been the same since."

She didn't want to walk this path again. "What d'ye think ye took from me that day? Yer memories of me stop in the forest, but my memories go past that day and continue on. The Deirdre you were with died at Brodie land in the flames that devoured Papa. Nay, Bonnar, let me be. 'Tis, gone. Dinna ye understand what I say? There is no us." She pushed him away and hurried down the sconce-lit hallway that bounced in shadows from the flickering torches. Male voices and laughter filtered up the stairwell from the great hall. He caught up with her, his arms enclosed her, his body trapped hers.

"Dinna do this, I beg ye...Bonnar."

He kissed her with desperation, his tongue seeking, trying to rekindle the spark, the love. His mouth was warm, his moustache tickled, and the taste of him the same. Oh, the ease with which she could allow him back. One slight touch with her tongue would do it. But his kiss wasn't Richard's. His touch wasn't Richard's. He wasn't Richard. Again, she pushed him away.

She flew down the spiral staircase. Reaching the bottom, she paused long enough to draw in her breath and stop shaking. When at last she had her composure back, she entered the great hall where the din of conversation droned like bees at a honeycomb and where the large chamber was filled with raucous people.

Her eyes searched the room, seeking one person only.

He stood.

His gaze never wavered from hers as he approached. And then his hand was reaching for hers folding it within his firm grasp. As if they were the only two people in the room, Richard pressed his lips to the back of her palm. His kiss was sensual, his eyes dancing with green-gold devilment as his warm tongue feathered her skin.

"Gore...Count Strasbourg, ye give me nothin' but pleasant thoughts." She drew in her breath as he unknowingly forced Bonnar's misdeeds from her mind.

"My intentions, milady." He lifted her braid, running his hand down the tight coils. He smiled with pleasure as his fingertips feathered her cheek. "Madame, you are enchanting tonight. Every man in this room has his eyes on you right now. I'm most proud to know that I have your heart."

He entwined her arm within his and escorted her to the head table where Philippe, Caitrina, Gilbert, David, and Macadie waited. Richard seated her next to Caitrina and he took the chair next to Deirdre. David and Macadie pulled up chairs facing them. Once seated, she noticed Mary Clair, sat at another table wedged between Bertrand and Gordon. The girl flirted with both men as if they were sweet cakes.

Servants hastened around the table putting down meats, fish, round loaves of bread, and chalices of wine.

David smiled at her. "Ye are looking well this eve, Deirdre Brodie. Verra well, indeed."

"'Tis thanks I be givin' ye, brother."

"Where is Maude?" Macadie asked.

"Watching Joanna. She will join us as soon as the wet nurse comes to feed my wee bairn." Deirdre smiled across the table at the weathered looking Scotsman. "What is yer interest in Maudie?" she teased, and laughed at the gap-toothed grin she received in return.

Maude arrived and took a seat next to Macadie. "Did I hear me name just now?"

Macadie grinned, and using his dirk speared a piece of mutton for her. "Eat, lassie, don't want ye fading away, now do we?"

Deirdre no sooner brought her chalice of wine to her lips when Bonnar slipped into the empty chair next to David and directly across from her. Beside her, Richard straightened in his chair, becoming more alert. She set her wine down before she spilt it.

To her consternation, Bonnar speared a piece of fish with his dirk and plopped it on her trencher. "For ye, Deedee. D'ye still like fish? Remember how we used to fish the inlet at Brodie?" He continued to goad her. "But I remember the woods, more so. Our blanket?" His gaze swept over her, telling what he didn't voice.

Everyone at the table ceased talking. The men became alert.

Deirdre, appalled at Bonnar's boldness, was relieved when Richard's hand sought hers under the table.

He bent his head toward hers, his voice firm. "Would you like me to take care of this uninvited guest?"

Mutely, she shook her head.

Macadie started to stand when Richard signaled for him to sit back down.

David took Bonnar by the arm. "I think ye should leave," he said, keeping his voice low, "Ye've drank too much wine."

"Nay, David...I'm most hungry. Pass that loaf of bread." He claimed the round crusty loaf from David. After tearing it in half, he placed one of the halves on Deirdre's trencher to join the fish. "Remember the bread ye made at Foxlair?"

Deirdre's eyes narrowed, he'd pushed her far enough. Her voice rang out, "Aye, Bonnar, I remember everything about my home. Far more than before ye ever set foot on Brodie soil. And I would like to forget what happened after ye came. But since you're talking remembrances, would ye like me to tell ye about living in a cage like a filthy beast for over a year and nine of those months carrying a babe in my womb?"

Conversation in the great hall stopped. All heads turned to their table.

Bonnar abruptly stood. He drained his chalice and wiped his mouth with the back of his hand. He bowed most ungainly, lost his balance, and palmed the table to steady himself. "Then…I bow at your escape…cage…and leave ye with yer French…is it…lover…paramour? Has he nested between yer legs yet…is—"

Richard shot to his feet, his chair clattered to the floor behind him. Grasping Bonnar's tunic, he jerked him forward until they were almost nose to nose. "You are drunk and letting the wine speak for you. Apologize to Countess Wrothbury, then take your leave. Be most thankful I have my wits about me or you would not be so fortunate, here and now." He released Bonnar as fast as he'd captured him.

Bonnar held up his hands and laughed. "Just talkin' about the past, Count Strasbourg, dinna fret so. Ye remember Foxlair, the day the King of England came callin'? 'Tis true, Deedee. I understand yer Frenchie was there as well. Right next to old Longshanks who came to kill yer clan," his voice cracked as emotion drained from him. "Ye'll stand beside him…but not me. Why?" He turned, swaying as he went

David wiped his mouth with the back of his hand and stood. "I'll make sure Bonnar comes to no harm."

Tears of anger blurred Deirdre's vision as she looked down at her lap. Would the madness never go away? Was it her lot to be tossed around between men like a piece of driftwood in a churning sea? Perhaps she couldn't face Bonnar and deal with the past, not now, not ever. She felt her chin being lifted by a warm strong hand and turned toward the one steady and sure thing in her life. Richard.

"Chéri, do not let what just happened ruin this eve for you. Remember, I'm beside you, always."

"I know, Richard. Mayhap, I canna deal with my ghosts after all."

"Nonsense."

The evening dragged on, minstrels played pipes and drums while mummers put on a play, Scotsmen against the old King Edward of course. Deirdre's spirits drooped like a windless banner. Try as Richard might, nothing could make her happy.

"Madam, if I told you we soon depart for Foxlair would that make you cheerful?"

"Aye," she said perking up. "Do we leave on the morrow?"

"Non, we leave after Philippe and Caitrina are wed. Philippe has been ordered to seize Crichton Castle. Caitrina will travel with us to Foxlair."

"And what of ye? Do you wish to be fighting alongside yer brother?"

Casting a glance her way, he nodded. "Of course, that's how it's always been. The de Laci's, warriors fighting for their king. But now, milady, you have given me an even more important mission. To take you back to Brodie land and then to my home."

18 Open Locked Hearts

Brightly burning oil sconces rimmed the walls of the great hall. The room was festooned with summer flowers of heather. Trestle tables had been pushed to one side to allow for the sweating bodies of the dancers who darted and weaved in a circle dance. Delighted, the women laughed as their arms intertwined with the line of men facing them and they changed off to partner with the man opposite them.

Now man and wife, Philippe and Caitrina sat at the table on a raised dais watching the revelers. Caitrina wore a garland of daisies in her hair. Her dark eyes constantly met Philippe's that never seemed to leave her face. Beside her sat her father. His face beamed. Yet if asked, he would have to admit a certain sadness that his only child would be leaving his hearth.

Sitting at the same table as the happy couple, Richard stood to lift his goblet and spoke in a loud voice. "To Philippe and Caitrina. May God bless your marriage and may He walk beside you always."

"Good health," voiced the guests as all raised their goblets.

Philippe and Caitrina returned the salute by interlocking their arms together as they drank, spilling a few drops down their chins. Philippe licked the wine from his wife's chin and she returned the favor.

Laughing at their antics, Richard turned his attention from the happy couple to the woman next to him, Deirdre. He gazed at her full lips, her rosy cheeks, and for the first time how her hair hung loose with only the sides braided and pulled to the back and tied with golden cord. Her full breasts rose and fell underneath the gown of blue.

"I cannot believe your beauty, my countess," Richard said to her and gave her hand a squeeze. She responded with a tight smile. Despite the merriment going on around them, Deirdre was subdued. "Chéri, is something amiss? Why so sad? Do you wish for Joanna?"

"Richard, I hear whispers about me." She could hardly speak above a whisper herself.

He tilted his head close to hers. "What is it you hear?"

She turned her head, her lips brushing his cheek. "That I'm a felon, and…" she said and swallowed, "there is a price on my head. Miles has died, aye?"

"Have I told you how much I love you, Deirdre?"

"Ye think to change the issue," she challenged. "Ye already know about the edict from Falconshire, aye? Why did ye not tell me about it? This shouldna be kept from me."

"I agree. I should have known that tongues would wag in gossip. I intended to tell you after tonight, for I have plans that I didn't want ruined." He lifted his wine to her mouth of which she took a small sip. He then finished the drink.

After the wedding festivities died down somewhat Richard felt he could leave and not offend his brother and new sister by marriage.

He said to Deirdre. "Chéri, please come with me?"

The curiosity that crossed her face, and her sweet essence that he held so dear, made what he was going to do even more satisfying. Getting to his feet, he helped her to hers. He paused in front of Philippe who was practically eating Caitrina's neck as his kisses raced toward her mouth. She was giggling, and just as Philippe reached her mouth, Richard cleared his throat, interrupting their intended kiss. They both turned flushed faces toward him.

"Ah…brother." Philippe raised his goblet in a salute toward Richard and Deirdre. "'Tis time to do as planned?"

"Oui." Richard answered and took Deirdre's hand. "Follow me, chéri. You and I have something to attend to."

"Why can ye no' tell me now?" she asked, but he remained mum, and pulled her along behind him, weaving through the revelers.

He led her down a corridor and into the small chapel that had earlier hosted Philippe and Caitrina. Deirdre saw that two candles were placed on the alter table and between the candles was a piece of parchment rolled up and sealed with wax. From where she stood, and trying most hard, she couldn't make out the insignia. Had Richard managed to get her pardon? She didn't think so, there was no way, and yet…

Richard put his hand against the small of her back guiding her to stand next to the table. When she looked at him, he returned her stare with a firm smile. His face, a study in handsomeness, made her heart trip. His clothing, a long blue surcoat and tight black breeks, were courtesy of Blackadder's Scottish lord who absconded with the clothes on his back.

"Deirdre, I have brought you here in God's house so the Lord can witness what I'm about to do." And then in elaborate ceremony, Richard picked up the parchment, popped the seal, unrolled it and began to read.

"On this day, the Thirteenth day of July, the year 1308, I, Richard de Laci, Comté de Strasbourg, do hereby plight troth myself to one Deirdre Marie Brodie, Countess of Wrothbury. I'll honor her, take care of her, and should death befall me, this edict insures that Countess Wrothbury is taken care of financially. Said documents detailing this care will reside at Château Falaise, Strasbourg, France, where Countess Wrothbury and her daughter Joanna Colleen Wrothbury are to make their home. When such time occurs that Countess Wrothbury is free to marry with me, she will do so."

Realizing what was being said, that Richard was trying to secure her future with him, Deirdre studied this man who never ceased to bring joy to her. He emanated the man he was, a warlord, a man of honor. "Richard, ye are making a future proposal of marriage to me, 'tis true?"

"Oui, considering present circumstances it's the only way. The document is legal and binding. Will you sign it so that I can truly call you mine in all but name only?"

"Richard, are ye sure ye want to be bound as thus?"

"It is my desire to be bound to you. In truth, I think I'm being selfish to ask you to sign it, for you must live in France to enjoy the comforts of my coin. Hear me when I say that by the time we step foot on French soil I plan on being your true husband."

Knowing Richard was a man of his word, she didn't doubt that she would indeed be his wife someday, but it was that someday that appeared most daunting. "Then my sweet knight, when ye have gone to such trouble, how can I possibly refuse?"

He appeared content as he dipped the quill into the inkhorn and handed it to her. After she signed her name, he inked his. Wearing a wide grin, he rolled the treasured document up and using his insignia ring sealed it with wax.

"Come, my love, we will go and drink to us." He wrapped her arm within his and carried the document.

Richard skirted the great hall that still hosted the wedding guest, and took Deirdre straight up to his chambers where he threw the bolt behind them, securing them into a world of their own.

Deirdre gasped at the many candles placed around the room, giving off flickering light and giving the room a glow. The fireplace held a low burning fire that was lit simply to remove the chill from the room.

Realizing his intent, she asked, "Did ye do this, Richard?"

"Non, Maude and Mary Clair did. And with smiles on their faces I might add."

"The whole of Blackadder will know that...we...er...well..." she stuttered like a new bride, making Richard chuckle. He crossed to the side table and poured wine into two goblets, then turning back to her, placed a drink in her hand.

"Richard, I don't know how to thank ye fer what ye've jest done, yer generosity knows no bounds but shouldn't we go back and join the others?"

"There is no need," he said, and relaxing against the table set his cup down. "Philippe has already given explanations as to our absence. My shoulder aches, and you have gone to be with your daughter. So if we return, 'twill indeed look strange."

Going to her side, he turned her to face him. His eyes tenderly perused her face before he closed them and dipped his head to meet her mouth. His hand slid around to cup her neck and still the kiss lingered. She ran her hands across his wide chest, the rough material of his tunic skimming against her palms. His tongue pressed against hers. She tasted wine, the sweet aftertaste of him. Finally, he pulled away, his eyes green pools of desire.

"Do you say you do not want me?" he murmured.

"'Tis not a matter of want, 'tis a matter of adultery. What ye plan is punishable by death."

Ignoring her protests, he nibbled at her earlobe.

She frowned. "Nay. I carry another man's name. We shouldna."

"We should," he said and kissed across her chin to the other ear where he commenced his nibbling.

"Shouldna."

"I think to seal my pledge…er…bargain."

"I'm not free to do so."

"I am." He grinned, his eyes merry.

Seeing how happy he was, she couldn't help but match his grin, "Are we to make halfway love?"

"Non, I never do anything halfway. I complete every mission I start. But alas, chéri, you are the hardest mission I've ever had in my life. Now come here and let me become that paramour that Bonnar accused me of being."

"And, milord?" She flirted.

"I think I might like the title."

She didn't move, instead she clasped her hands in front of her. "I willna become a woman of loose morals in yer eyes?" She met his embolden gaze, her eyes searching for the truth.

He laughed most heartily, and said, "Never a loose women. I think of you as my wife already. In private, like now, I intend to call you as such. Now come here—wife."

"Just when I think I canna love ye more than I do, ye do something to make that love weak compared to the new love I have fer ye. Whenever happiness finds me, 'tis quickly taken away. I pray this eve that God in all his wisdom will grant me good fortune."

"Chéri, we will have that happiness and fortune you so crave."

She took another drink then closed her eyes as he bent to lick a single droplet of wine from her bottom lip.

"Deirdre, you taste like fine wine."

She tipped her head back and moaned as he continued his kisses, tickling the hollow of her neck, then down across her low cut bodice.

He smiled and removed the forgotten wine goblet that dangled from her hand. Taking a drink, he then held it to her lips allowing her to finish the last of it.

Reluctant to move away from her, but doing so, he sat on the chair to remove his boots. She peered at his feet that were well shaped, the toes long, with tiny hairs on the top of each big toe. "Ye've got nice toes, aye."

Richard threw back his head and laughed, his deep voice vibrating through the room. "I can only hope that you will think I have more than nice toes before this evening is over with." Still chuckling, he stood and untied his breeks.

Blushing, she hastily poured herself another drink. The sweet nectar warmed her and made her just a little bit braver. "Ye make me feel like a maiden, Richard."

"That is my intent. You're so endearing to me as you stand there looking shy and unsure of what to do next. I'm going to make you feel like the woman you are. Before this night is over, we will be joined as never before." He held out his hand, his fingers beckoning. "Come here, sweetheart."

Slowly, he turned her around and began unlacing her gown. His hands fumbled with the unfamiliar task. "'Tis a puzzlement to me why a woman needs so many laces. Could you not pull the gown over your head like a man does his tunic?" He pushed the gown down over creamy shoulders, pausing to kiss her bare flesh as he did so. "Perhaps unlacing your gown isn't so bad after all, and is like opening a gift. I like the surprise I've found beneath it. For a long time I imagined your skin to feel as it does, like the finest silk."

A subtle moan escaped her as his lips brushed against her back. She didn't want his kiss to stop. But it did. He held the gown while she stepped out of it and then tossed it across the chest. He paused to look at her standing in her chemise in front of the fire that outlined her body through the sheer material, revealing her red-gold nether hair. Dazzled, he held out his hand, beckoning her.

"'Tis time to remove yer tunic, dinna ye agree?" She was nervous, and not waiting for his reply, began pulling the shirt over his head. He took it from her and sent it sailing across the room. She ran her hands over his muscled chest, liking the feel of the tiny springy black hairs that curled tightly around her fingers. His excitement was evident as his nipples turned into tiny hard buds under her stroking fingers. "Yer right," she said, "I like yer chest better than yer toes."

"Now we'll have to find something you like better than my chest," he growled, and then taking her hands sucked on the tips of each finger, erotically so.

The candles, some guttering low and almost gone, cast the room, in shadows.

He began unbraiding the tiny plaits that held her hair pulled away from her face, his voice seducing her. "Did I tell you the first thing I noticed about you were your blue eyes? First at Foxlair? Then at Falconshire? Oh, how they blazed at me from the cage. I knew you wanted to tell me to go away, that you hated being stared at."

"Aye, ye were so handsome and I was such a wretch. I was embarrassed to be seen by anyone. But that soon changed to delight when I realized it was truly ye."

"Never be embarrassed, my love." He placed a kiss on each eyelid. Before she had time to react to his kisses, he reached down and caught the hemline of her chemise then whisked it off of her as he straightened.

"Och," she squealed in surprise, now naked before him. Her arms straight at her sides, letting him stare, his body reacting to the mere sight of her. Her breasts, firm, and rosy tipped, brought a smile to his face, as did her curvy hips and pubic bush.

"*Quelle merveille.* You are beautiful, Deirdre."

His desire for her was most evident through his tight fitting breeks. He traced her full lush body with his hands then paused to encircle her waist before capturing her breasts, lifting them. "Your breasts are full and ripe as they should be and are mine to pleasure." Her hands grasped his shoulders as a muted sigh escaped her and she pulled his head against her. He went to his knees and kissed down her ribcage before burying his face against the firm flesh of her stomach.

"I desire you so, Deirdre."

"Come to me, Richard." She slowly helped him to stand and their arms encased each other, holding close what they had dreamed of for so long. His hands wrapped into her luxurious hair as he kissed across her face.

A conspiring smile stretched her mouth. "Richard love, I think ye need to take off yer breeks. See, if ye wore the Scottish cloth wrapped around yer body and no' a thing underneath, I would already be touching yer bare parts." She couldn't help but giggle at the surprise on his face. With relish she peeled his breeks over slender hips, down muscled thighs, and then went to the floor pulling them over his feet. Matching the grin he wore, she made her way up his glorious body with kisses. His was a warrior's body, her Richard. "This scar is something fierce." She ran her finger along the line of puckered flesh, then tiptoed to kiss it, and traced its path with kisses. Over his shoulder and down his back she kissed, and finally ended her kisses where his buttocks began.

"Chéri, I do not remember my wound going quite that low," he rasped out.

"Yer right, it doesna," she said.

Unable to take anymore teasing, he scooped her up and placed her on the bed. Stretching out next to her, he ran his hands over her body, lightly tracing the curves of her hip and leg, then back up her ribs and stopped to cup her breasts. He covered one mound with his mouth and flicked his tongue over the nipple, teasing and pulling at it with his teeth, puckering the rosy end before transferring to the other breast and continuing with his magic. His hands titillated her body. He ran his hand between her legs and laughed with delight when he felt her want for him, his fingers playing, caressing the enticing folds.

She shivered. "Richard, I need ye so. Give me new memories. Take away the pain, make me forget..."

"Deirdre," he said and kissed down to her stomach and lower, making her euphoric. "I'll always be beside you..." His lips pressed against the inside of her thigh. He then nipped his way to the other thigh, taking his time and taking her into a world of swirling love. "Feel me..." he said, and taking her hand, placed it over his hardened length. She stroked him, making circles over the end of his tarse, eliciting a quiver from him.

Again, he ran his hand between her legs and felt her desire for him. "Ah...chéri." He spread her legs with his knee. "Deirdre," he muttered, and treating her like a fragile flower, lowered his weight on her as she guided him into her. "*Vous vous sentez si bon, tout chaud, lisse, juste pour moi…*" His words, most sensual, told her how much he loved her. He groaned as her body sheathed his, and for tantalizing moments, he couldn't move, afraid to, lost in the feel of her.

He claimed her as his own, and showed her the love he'd saved just for her. Masterfully, he brought them both to the brink and back again. He laughed as passion veiled her face and he drove from her any memories of the past, showing her how a man truly loved a woman. He enjoyed her gasp as he worked their bodies, and loved when she gripped his arms daring him to pull away and loving it when he plunged back inside her.

"Deirdre…." He gave himself up to her.

Her arms went around his back and running her hands over smooth skin covered with sweat, she hugged him as tight as she could. "Richard, yer essence fills me up and so strong is my love for ye, that I'll never be the same again."

He rolled off her, trying to catch his breath. She ran her hands over his face to wipe the sweat from him. She pulled him to her and kissed him, her tongue searching his. Suddenly, she found herself being lifted by his strong hands and sat on top of him.

Richard leered at her, cocking one brow higher than the other and said, "Have ye found anythin' ye like better than me toes…me sweet lassie?"

She shook her head in mirth. "I dinna think to ever hear a French warlord try to sound Scottish. Especially with yer accent, Richard." Her laughter bubbled forth, and his laughter joined hers.

"Come here—wench." He rolled her over on the bed and straddled her, then pinning her arms above her head, he commenced to tickle her until she screamed for mercy. Finally, he stopped and became serious.

His gaze met hers with tenderness. "I love you, Deirdre."

"And I love ye so, Richard." She ran her fingers over his chest, watching the tiny damp curls encircle her fingertips. "Richard?"

"Oui?"

"When do we leave for my homeland?"

He brushed hair back from her face and met her serious gaze with one of his own. "Before dawn breaks on the morrow, your baby, Joanna along with Maude, Caitrina, Mary Claire and Gordon will leave here in a tinker's wagon. It's arranged. A colorful wagon will draw less attention than us all leaving at the same time. We will follow suit before dawn the following day, all of us dressed as soldiers. You included." He buried his head against her neck.

She pulled in a sharp breath. "Will Joanna be safe with so little protection? And the others? How will she feed?"

"A small party is bound to attract less attention, especially one selling wares. Have trust in me. Her wet nurse has agreed to travel with us. Deirdre, I never want to lose what I have here with you." He sighed, then rolled onto his side to fit her against him. His hand stroked her hip as she nestled her bottom tightly against his lap.

"Richard?"

"Oui, my love?"

"Protect me always?"

"Always. Now sleep my Scottish lassie."

She muttered, "I still like yer toes."

19 That Torn Down Re-Grows

Foxlair Castle

With David setting a grueling pace, they overtook the tinker's wagon within a day. As planned, they abandoned the wagon and used the two horses pulling it for Mary Clair and Maude to ride. Gordon, who drove the wagon, depended on Richard to bring his horse and one for the wet nurse, Arda, a recent widow whose husband was killed during the siege of Blackadder.

They were deep into Scotland and close to Brodie land and Foxlair Castle. Riding over rugged terrain, the July heat was crushing with its cloudless blue skies and roads kicking up a thick dust that spread a fine coating on the travelers.

Deirdre followed behind her brother and Richard, who moved to her side whenever the trail allowed. The women took turns carrying Joanna in a sling across their chest. Even with her unconventional method of travel, Joanna, at eight months of age, didn't make too much of a fuss. Heavier than when stolen from Wrothbury Castle and more active, she would try to climb out of the sling. Whenever Deirdre carried her daughter slung close to her heart, Deirdre's one joy was to simply gaze upon Joanna's sweet face either awake or sound asleep and sucking on two fingers.

Deirdre glanced over at the wet nurse who carried a sleeping Joanna. Arda smiled at Deirdre. Deirdre then turned in her saddle to glimpse the rest of their retinue. Caitrina met her stare and surrendered a half-hearted smile. That Caitrina missed Philippe was most evident as the normally spirited redhead showed little gaiety. By now, Philippe would be moving part of his army to Crichton Castle to remove the Scottish Earl, Ewan Crichton who had switched sides once too often. The Bruce ordered the castle razed to the ground and a siege could last months. Everyone tried to lift Caitrina's spirits, but she told them the only thing to make her happy was to have Philippe once again by her side.

Maude, riding next to Macadie, cocked her head to one side, listening intently to his chatter. His eyes teased as his hand gestured wildly about. Since meeting each other, Maude and Macadie were becoming fast friends, and Deirdre was glad of it.

Mary Clair was next to Bertrand, who rode his horse as close to hers as possible. Snatches of French being taught went back and forth between them. Gordon, when the two parties met as planned, had left to join Robert the Bruce's army. Scotland's king marched to Inverurie, to bring down Comyn, the Earl of Buchan, another rogue Scotsman. All in all, Bertrand appeared to be taking advantage of Gordon's absence and flirted with Mary Clair.

Bringing up the rear were a few of Richard's trusted soldiers, always on guard, checking to make sure they were not followed.

During their journey, Deirdre discovered little things about the man she loved. She already knew Richard was generous to a fault, yet found out how rigid in his beliefs and habits he was. Affection for his family ran deep and he constantly talked of his sister Pernelle and brother Valentin. He worried of his domain in France, especially if Valentin was keeping everything in good order. He voiced concern about Pernelle's betrothal to a man he didn't know, and prayed that the King of France wouldn't order her marriage to take place until he arrived back home. When they bed down at night, Richard insisted she sleep next to him. He revealed to her how he enjoyed cuddling her tight against him, how he relished exploring her body and she revealed the same to him.

Deirdre knew her protection was foremost in Richard's mind. That he strove to keep her safe. Yet, so far, the English hadn't accosted them, making Deirdre wonder when Wrothbury would reach out to crush her.

Three rough looking Scots, brandishing claymores, approached the party. They were lookout guards on Brodie land. Once they recognized it was David their laird, they returned to their posts.

Shivers of anticipation and excitement started deep inside Deirdre. She'd dreaded seeing her ancestral home and thought the tug at her heart would be unbearable. But now, as she sat on her horse and took in the beauty of the land, perhaps this could be endured after all. The brilliant hues of summer sprung up everywhere. Heather abounded, its brilliant colors trying to steal the beauty from the aqua blue water of the inlet that appeared as smooth as a fine copper mirror.

Everything had changed. The scorched fields were long ago plowed under, moved further east, and the cycle of crop growing had continued. The burnt-out huts of the clan were rebuilt cottages spread further apart. Albeit, not as many stood as before, but the scene before Deirdre was one of tranquility. Smoke lazily fed the sky from open cooking fires. Curious dogs barked at them. People stopped in their labors and turned to stare. Foxlair Castle, her childhood home, loomed in the far distance, and was barely visible past the curve in the inlet and surrounded by a vast wooden stockade.

"Oh…gore…" she whispered, and reached for Richard's hand.

David maneuvered his horse close to hers. "Does it look different to ye?"

"Aye. Ye have managed to be laird of your clan whilst fighting alongside the Brus. Ye've done well brother. D'ye not live in Foxlair?"

"Nay, Seonaid will not go near it. Thinks it's haunted."

Seeing anticipation on his face, she motioned at him. "Go to yer loved ones. We will wait here awhile."

David stood in his stirrups and let out a shrill whistle. Laughing when he received a welcoming whistle in return, he kneed his horse and started down the steep trail leading to his village.

An elderly man cackled and pointed at David. Children, along with nearby adults, gathered. David acknowledged his clan as he rode through the hamlet where smells of smoke, unwashed bodies, and livestock mingled with the fragrant aroma of soups and baked bread being cooked. He nudged his horse in the direction of his home, a large thatched cottage set apart from the others.

The door swung open. Seonaid paused in the doorway warily looking around. When she spotted David, a smile curved her mouth as she visibly relaxed. David's gaze swept over her, and the moment shared between the two did not need words. His face softened as he stared at his mate most fair. She wore a plain gown of green that hid her curves. Her hair, a bright gold, was without a headdress.

His daughter, little Dee pushed past their mam, and upon seeing him, stopped. A smaller dark-haired lad peered around Seonaid's side clutching her skirt.

David dismounted and approached his family. The sight of his children warmed him. He reached out and brought Seonaid against him, his hand cupping her rounded bottom.

"By the Saints—Seonaid, I've missed ye so." He quivered with desire, love, and the need to be held by the woman he carried in his mind and heart day and night. He kissed her, a lingering kiss that to him tasted like honey and home.

Seonaid, her eyes moist with unshed tears pulled back to see his face. "David, ye have wee ones who need to hear yer welcome." She pushed four-year-old Blake forward. But he wasn't ready to meet his sire, instead he kicked David hard on the shin.

Amused, but not showing it, David bent down to stare into Blake's large brown eyes and tried to be firm with a solemn gaze of his own. Undaunted, Blake gave David another kick.

"Och...ye wee devil, has yer mam been teaching ye how to mistreat yer papa?" He grabbed Blake up, and started tickling his bare belly that showed below his tunic shirt. This time Blake giggled as he tried to fend off David's tickling fingers. David was delighted to hear his son's bubbling laughter and tossed him high in the air. David made like he was going to miss, but caught him instead. He set a breathless and laughing Blake back on his feet. He then motioned for little Dee to come to him.

Little Dee shrank next to her mam's side and peered at her sire with wide brown eyes. Her blonde hair escaped their braids making her look like a little hellion. Her gown fit her like a sack and came below her knees and one he was certain that Seonaid had made.

"Where's Andrew?" David asked of his eldest son.

Seonaid's hand went to unclasp her daughter from her side. "Andrew was down by the inlet. He likes to take the rowboat out."

Words no sooner spoken when Andrew came running around the side of the cottage. Trying to catch his breath and upon seeing who was standing there, he stopped and narrowed a dark scowl at David. Not a welcome David expected, but having been gone for over a half of a year, he didn't expect much more.

David met his son's fearless glare and marveled at how much Andrew took after him. Already tall for his age, he had David's dark brown eyes and long unkempt black hair. His breeks were brown, his tunic once white, was a dingy gray with several holes in the sleeves. Belted at his waist was a short dagger.

"Ye must treat yer papa with respect. He willna hurt ye." Seonaid urged the children toward David.

They hesitated, but David quickly gathered all three against his chest. Their warm bodies felt secure, bonding him to them.

"I've missed ye verra much. Never be afraid to come to me, d'ye understand what I say to ye?" He stared at their faces until they nodded. It wasn't long before his daughter's kiss was plastered against his cheek.

"Andrew, yer getting big. It pleases me to know ye are looking after our family whilst I'm away," David said with pride.

"Aye, Papa. I'll be ten soon." Andrew's chest swelled with importance.

Little Dee, over her shyness and not to be outdone by her brother, grabbed David's finger. "I'm seven, Papa," she said with childish importance.

"Indeed. Yer both growin' up before my verra eyes." His heart tugged at his daughter's face that had lost its baby fat and changed so since he'd last seen her. "Andrew?" he tousled his son's hair and said, "We should go hunting fer rabbits in a day or two."

Andrew nodded. "Aye, Papa, I'm gude at hunting rabbits and catching eels."

David smiled at his son's bragging. Unable to stand it any longer, he went to his wife's side and gathered her into his arms. Her breasts were soft and pliable against his chest, his eyes searched.

"Darlin', I dinna think I can wait until tonight, I want ye so."

"Are ye here for a while, David? Or d'ye leave at first light?" Her eyes, blue as the sky above her, held questions.

Seeing she was close to tears, David rested his chin on the top of her head, holding her, trying to reassure her. "I'm here until the Brus summons me. Dinna spoil my homecoming with bitter questions. Just love me, Seonaid."

At the sound of horses neighing and snorting, she pulled away as riders reined in next to the cottage. Leaving David's side, she made her way over to them.

"Deirdre, 'tis ye?" Surprised, she grinned up at Deirdre.

Deirdre slid off the horse in a rapid dismount and unable to hold back escaping sobs, clasped Seonaid within her arms. The two women held each other dearly, until at last and still holding hands they stepped back to stare at the other through tear-filled eyes.

"How happy I am for ye and David. Jest look at yer wee bairns." A smile lit Deirdre's face as her niece and nephews shyly returned her stare. "D'ye remember me? I'm yer Aunt Deedee. Yer papa is my brother." She knelt and putting her arms around them, planted kisses on warm cheeks. "Gore…ye've all grown so much." She cast a beaming glance up at Richard who stood next to her.

Deirdre, seeing Seonaid's questioning smile, introduced Richard to her. "Seonaid, please meet my protector, my champion, Richard de Laci, Count of Strasbourg."

Richard took Seonaid's hand and kissed it. "Enchanté, mistress. David speaks well of you."

"Welcome, Count Strasbourg. How pleasing it is to know that Deirdre is well protected and safe at last from that terrible Englishman who took her."

Young Andrew stood like a fierce warrior. "My name is Andrew," he said to Richard, then pointed at his sister and brother. "That is little Dee, and Blake.

Richard tousled the lad's hair. "The pleasure is mine." He smiled at the children and then beckoned Macadie and the rest to approach.

The two younger children ran back inside the cottage allowing the smell of cooked food to waft out the open door. Andrew, showing self-sufficiency, led the horses toward the shed.

"I couldna believe what I heard about ye being locked in a cage. The old King did the same to Robert de Brus' sister. 'Twas a warm day when Edward died, and even warmer here in Scotland with all the celebrating," Seonaid said.

"His death did little to change my circumstances. Richard did that." Deirdre summoned Arda, the wet nurse. She handed Joanna to Deirdre, who proudly held her up for all to see. Seonaid was drawn to the little babe with the reddish curls and smoke-gray eyes.

"This is Joanna, my daughter by the Earl of Wrothbury." If Seonaid had questions about Wrothbury, she didn't ask. Instead, she tweaked Joanna under the chin making her smile.

"How old is she?" Seonaid asked.

"Eight months of age. I was in the cage when she was born and the earl took her from me," Deirdre said and noticed that Joanna started to fuss and suck her fingers, a sign that she was hungry. "We have brought a wet nurse for her. Arda, take Joanna, she needs feeding."

"Ye can feed her inside," Seonaid said.

Caitrina came forward. "I'm Caitrina de Laci, healer and sister in marriage to Count Strasbourg."

"A healer?" Seonaid sounded surprised.

"Aye, and I dinna think there isna a man amongst us that she hasna stitched," David said.

Deirdre reached for Maude. "This is my close companion, Maude Warren, who helped me whilst I was caged. My other gude friend here is Mary Clair who was with me at Wrothbury Castle."

After being introduced to the men, Seonaid asked David to show the soldiers where they could bunk in the stables. She then motioned all inside the cottage.

Deirdre hung back, and gazed across the inlet at Foxlair.

"Come inside, Deirdre." Richard beckoned.

Deirdre entered her brother's home. Herbs tied in neat bundles hung drying from the rafter beams, the smell of lavender strong. A trestle table was in the middle of the room. Off to one side was a large chest and next to it a ladder leading to the loft and the beds. At one end of the room was a fireplace with a blazing fire heating a large cooking kettle that gave off the delicious smell of mutton stew.

Laughter and conversation merged as they ate their fill of soup, bread, cheese, and ale. While Deirdre spooned some of the broth into Joanna, she observed that David couldn't keep his eyes off Seonaid, but Seonaid couldn't keep her eyes on him.

When it was time to clean up, the women began to help, and Deirdre seeing this propelled Seonaid outside.

"Seonaid, what is amiss? Are ye no' happy to see David?" Concerned, she met her friend's troubled eyes.

"Oh, aye, that I be. Just to look at his handsome self makes me quiver and if it were not for ye all here, we would be in the bed by now." She chewed her bottom lip. "But I'll just get to loving him, havin' him near, and he will leave. Sometimes he isna here long enough for me to even warm his body or warm my love for him. David has missed so much with his bairns. They dinna know him when he comes home, and just when they accept him and call him papa, he is gone again. I've become acting laird in his absence and sometimes there are problems amongst the clan that I dinna know how to deal with."

She turned tear-filled eyes to Deirdre. "'Tis hard to love a man who fights for his beliefs and country. I fear the day when he will never return. Would that he be a simple peasant and come to me each night. But he is laird of this land and tomorrow he will hold court and listen to clan grievances, then after that, perhaps he will have time for me. I pray so."

"Ye knew David was a warrior when ye married him. He has told me of his love for ye and the wee ones. He will be staying longer this time, mayhap through the winter. But listen to me, Seonaid. If a man doesna have his beliefs, then he has nothing. If he doesna own the soil he tills, he has even less. Ye have the love of a good man and yer freedom. Thanks to David and Robert de Brus fighting for our cause, ye can walk the hills, breathe the air, and raise yer bairns without fear of the English. Ye should go and seek out that man ye love and take him to bed. The rest of us will make ourselves scarce." She pulled Seonaid close and gave her a peck on the cheek.

"I thank ye, Deirdre. If ye could endure being locked in a cage, then I can endure David's absences, and 'tis fer certes he will be staying longer this time. 'Tis true?"

"'Tis true." Deirdre put Seonaid's concerns to rest.

Deirdre rode toward Foxlair. If her heart wasn't in her throat, it certainly worked its way there with each stride of the horse, until a beating pulse wedged in the back of it. Richard kept glancing her way. She thought of how he must feel when he remembered the slaughter he'd been forced to endure that awful day. Of Wrothbury.

Her eye caught the outline of the tall Celtic cross in the cemetery next to the small chapel, and she kneed her horse in that direction. David had prepared her, telling her it was there in honor of their father's memory.

Before Richard could help her down, she slipped from her mount and made her way past the scattered grave markers to stand at her father's cross. The cross was carved from wood and halfway down its length it widened into a circle of Celtic knots. Inside the circle, the name Andrew Patrick Brodie was carved and below his name was the clan's motto, Unite.

Horrendous memories pushed into her mind, enveloping her, until she could hear the hooves of the horse galloping, the king shouting, arrows skewering Papa. The remembered sight of his body churning furrows as he was dragged behind the horse shattered her. She grabbed the cross at the same time her legs buckled.

"Oh—God—Papa."

Guttural cries, deep from within, escaped, as she knelt on the ground. She cried until her tears were dry and her sobbing had turned to soft hiccups. Richard, showing restraint and patience, stood back, leaving her alone with her grief. When her hiccups subsided, he helped her stand and wiped the tears from her swollen eyes and face.

"Deirdre…do you need more time here?"

She nested her head against his chest and could hear his heartbeat, strong and reassuring. "Nay, Richard, I've cried enough." She sniffed and searched for something to blow her nose on, and Richard obliged by pulling a piece of cloth from his tunic and held it to her nose.

"If you'd rather not go inside Foxlair, we can go back to David's."

His concern moved her. "Nay, I must face this also. Ye as well must have memories that assail ye?"

"Mine are not as fragile as yours are. With you by my side, much of my guilt from that day has been redeemed." He formed a stirrup with his hands and helped her mount.

Foxlair stood behind the rebuilt wooden stockade like a brooding, silent, gray sentinel. The watchtower guards, that David installed, were in the village, eating with the rest. Little else had been done to restore the keep. Weeds encroached, and chunks of stone lay scattered about from where the English had tried to pull it down. But the keep, partly chiseled from the stone cliff behind it withstood Edward's penetration.

Richard dismounted and surveyed the gloom. "Is this still your desire?"

"Aye," she said. A faint little smile quivered her mouth as he put his hands up to lift her from her horse. A chattering squirrel ran in front of them while the shells crunching under their shoes broke the quiet. They reached the massive front door with its metal trim and large round pulls.

"Deirdre, stand back." Richard pulled his sword and pushed against the door that opened with squeaky reluctance. He pushed it wide enough to let in the light and fresh air. Dust motes swirled and sparkled in the beaming sunlight.

Leading the way, Richard tucked Deirdre behind him. Glancing at the floor revealed small footprints crisscrossing in the dust. Smiling, he pointed. "I think the laird of the castle has been in residence." Satisfied they were in no danger, he sheathed his sword.

Deirdre found several candles on a side table, and using flint left there, lit them. Taking a candle, Richard lit the torch on the wall sconce. With him leading the way, they traversed the spiral stairs, lighting wall sconces as they went. Their bodies danced giant shadows along the stone walls and down the corridor.

She paused by a chamber door. Her fingers flew to cover her mouth as though to suppress her anguish.

He spoke first. "This is where I found you. I wanted to get you to safety."

When she nodded, Richard valiantly entered the dark room. He swept his candle around the room making the bed frame loom large and spindly. Deirdre lit the wall sconce then placed her candles on the floor. Richard did the same.

Deirdre stood where Wrothbury had taken her. The bed, now a frame of sagging ropes void of a mattress, looked different. Even the bed curtains were gone. But the events assailed her as her heart sped up and her mind tried to push that day away. The vision impaled her, the sharp pain of her blistered skin, Wrothbury's invasion of her body. She drew in a ragged breath just as Richard gripped her shoulders and brought her back to reality.

He held her, stroking her hair. "Deirdre, it is over with. The old king Edward is nothing but moldering bones, and I doubt even the worms will have fed on his corrupt body. Let us leave this place."

Her swollen eyes searched his face as she said, "Aye, Richard. Ye speak great wisdom and I honor ye for it. Edward may be dead, but Wrothbury isna. And it is what he did to me here that must be cleansed. He changed my life forever. I have to go through each room. I must close the wound to my mind. D'ye understand?"

He grasped her hands and held them captive, his voice gentle, "Of course, chéri. But I find this place most unwelcoming."

Becoming braver, she led the way to her father's chambers. When they paused in front of the door Richard insisted she get behind him. He pushed open the door and took a step to enter.

Out of the dark came a blood curdling battle cry and a body hurtling at them.

Richard dropped his sword. Deirdre squeaked as her candle hit the floor and flamed out. Childish laughter bubbled in glee.

"Andrew," Deirdre found her voice first. "What are ye doin' here? I thought no one ever stepped foot inside Foxlair." She put her hand over her pounding heart. "Ye gave us a fright."

Richard, having been bested by a lad of nine, cleared his throat. "Oui, Andrew. I would like to know as well."

Andrew stood with his hands on his hips. "This is my castle." Belligerently, he stared up at the adults.

"Yer castle is it?" Deirdre smiled down at her nephew who looked exactly like a young Davey.

"Aye, no one comes here. 'Twill be mine someday."

Richard crouched to his knees to meet Andrew face to face. "You are correct in assuming it is your castle. But right now, I believe your aunt would like to be alone. May we have your permission?"

His young face alight with knowledge, Andrew nodded. "Then ye may use my castle. I need to go hunt rabbits anyway." He picked up the candle and gave it to Deirdre. His laughter rang back at them as he scampered across the hall and out of sight.

"'Tis fer certes he put me one step closer to my grave. And ye my brave knight who dropped his sword," Deirdre said and laughed.

"Oui, he did the same to me. Never tell anyone a young lad bested me, or I'll deny it." Richard shook his head. "He is without fear. When Andrew grows up he will be a warrior to rival his sire."

Deirdre entered the room that was little changed. Even young Andrew's invasion of the chamber had not harmed a thing. Tied back, the dusty bed curtains revealed a large ornately carved four-poster bed with a goose-feather mattress void of blankets. A ledger, a broken quill, and a dried up inkhorn were on the writing desk along with a candle that Andrew had burning. Rushes strewn around camouflaged the trapdoor.

"I would have thought after we were caught in here trying to escape that Edward would have smashed everything, but he didna."

"Mayhap he thought he'd taken enough from your sire. Then you were not invaded here, by Wrothbury?"

"Nay, Richard, not here." She refused to elaborate. Like he'd said, it was time to put it behind them both. She ran her hand lovingly down his cheek, her fingers brushing against his stubble. "Shall we sleep here?"

His mouth pulled down in distaste as he glanced around. "Deirdre, perhaps we could find another place to sleep. I think the hayrick would be preferable."

"Ye dinna understand. I have to make a stand here in Foxlair. That day has never left me, and here all this time Foxlair is mostly an abandoned shell. The rooms so vivid in my memory stand empty. Ghosts dinna walk here. Only a child walking in his grandsire's footsteps has seen fit to break the dust. How fateful can it be that Andrew named after Papa would be the only one unafraid to come here. Think, Richard, you and I, here together. 'Tis an omen." She perused his handsome face, he who had given so much in a quest to make her happy. He drew in a breath. His face relaxed, as the smile she dearly loved broke forth.

He bowed deep and flourished his hand. "I surrender."

"Ye know, I was born in this bed, both Davey and I were. Papa and Mam shared their love in this bed and so shall you and I, Richard de Laci." She smiled, her head tilting in the way of a shy maiden.

Richard pushed on the mattress and in a flash, had her on her back with him on top of her. Dust took to the air making them cough, but they didn't mind.

She traced a finger across his lips. "Richard, how joyous it is to see yer face filled with so much love. 'Tis thanks I be given ye fer bringin' me home."

"Are you the better for it? Can it be over?"

"I believe that to be so."

"Perhaps we will look at the rest of Foxlair later." Teasing, he raised a brow.

"Perhaps..." Her laughter echoed off the walls.

Wrothbury sat at the table and played host to his informant Roger

Hackward, the former guard from Falconshire. No longer needed at Falconshire since Deirdre was gone, Wrothbury had hired Roger to work for him and sent him to seek out the Frenchman and Deirdre. Roger did as told and brought news that the countess was on her way to Scotland and her homeland.

Next to Roger sat the three German mercenaries hired to kill Deirdre. All three were sturdy, stringy-haired, travel stained, and wore chest armor. They tore bread apart, chewed chicken thighs, and slurped wine. After they drained their goblets, they belched, and the young servant, Robin Bailey, was quick with a pitcher to refill their drinks.

"My wife has gone back to that savage land up north that holds her father's bones." Wrothbury's mouth formed a wry grin. He tossed a small leather pouch with a drawstring closure at the mercenaries' leader. "I will give you the rest when you bring me my wife's head."

The leader stopped eating long enough to open the drawstrings. He put a dirt encrusted finger into the bag and moved the coins around. "Ja, 'twill be done." Draining his wine, he wiped his mouth on his sleeve.

"Then cease with stuffing yourselves and be off," Wrothbury ordered.

The three stood and picking up the bread put some of it in their waist pouches. Robin came to escort them out of the castle.

Chuckling, Wrothbury held his chalice to hit against Roger's in a salute, sloshing the ruby liquid onto their hands. Unfazed, the earl licked the spiced beads from his fingers and pealed out a wicked laugh.

"I pray the Germans succeed where I failed."

Roger choked on his wine and wiped his mouth using the end of the tablecloth. "I just heard words I never thought ye to say. Ye just admitted failure." He relaxed against the tall-backed chair, and adjusted his soiled overtunic before spearing a piece of baked fish.

"Countess Wrothbury has chosen her path. I curse them both and will piss on their graves. I'll bring my daughter back here, raise her, and make a fine marriage for her someday." Wrothbury scowled and twirled the stem of his chalice.

"To my friend Miles Woodstock," Roger said and raised his chalice. "The Countess's blade did more damage inside than thought."

"He lingered much too long. My sweet wife is a murderess as well. I'm surprised she did not put a knife into my throat as I slept. When I sought her bed, taking what was so rightfully mine, she could have greeted me as she did your friend Miles." Wrothbury placed coins on the table in front of Roger. "That is just the beginning."

20 Amour Is Constant

Deirdre took up residence in Foxlair. It had been hard at first, her past life never more present as she walked where her family once lived. Her father's booming voice still echoed down the hallways. But good memories were pushing the bad ones aside. After so many years of living in torment, a mellow kind of peace had taken hold of her.

It was time for harvest, and with most of the young men away at war, David put everyone to work, stout, old, able or otherwise.

Laughter rippled from Deirdre who stood close to the grain shed. She had a death grip on her corner of the winnowing cloth to keep it from being ripped out of her hands. It took four women to work the cloth, one holding each corner. Deirdre, Seonaid, Maude and Caitrina gave the cloth a furious snap. The grain shot skyward, the wind did its job, separating the chaff, sending it floating in the air and leaving the heavier grain to fall back onto the large cloth. They repeated the snapping process until there remained little chaff.

Deirdre enjoyed working with the grain. Albeit tiring, the work still felt good, even with the relentless sun beating down on them. The bodices of their gowns turned dark with sweat, the top of their headdresses covered with chaff. To help pass the time they gossiped about their men and families, and shyly, Seonaid asked about Wrothbury, the cage, and how Deirdre survived its hell. Deirdre told about Richard happening upon her and about the intended rescue and how she struggled with Miles. All three women giggled when she told of her escape and the ensuing encounter with Macadie.

Maude snorted. "I don't think ye hurt Macadie's dainties at all. I mean...er...well...now, meself I wouldna know..." Maude stuttered to a stop when the women smiled her way.

"So, Maude, are we soon to be havin' another weddin'?" Caitrina teased.

"Ye know it's too soon after losing me Thomas to think of such, but—"

"Och," said Seonaid. "I say take happiness when and where ye can find it. Ye've got a warm body in Macadie, and yer husband is six feet under. Ye never know when the men will be drawn back into the war. My David should be fighting alongside the Brus right now. If it wasn't fer Deedee comin' home, he would be."

"How about ye, Caitrina, ye must miss Philippe something fierce," Maude said. "Jest lookin' at Count Strasbourg must set yer mind toward yer husband."

"Aye, I plan to join Philippe soon. I had a missive from him saying his siege of Crichton Castle to be long. This castle is little over a day's ride from here, 'tis true, Deirdre?"

"Aye, depending on the man in the saddle, 'tis due southwest," Deirdre said in a vague sort of way.

The women couldn't help but smile at Deirdre whose glaze kept wandering off toward the far fields where Richard was. She couldn't see him, but just knowing he was so close made her shiver. She hoped never to lose that wondrous feeling that he brought about.

"We've shaken this enough dinna ye agree? 'Tis time to dump the grain." Seonaid said as she and Deirdre started walking their side of the cloth toward Maude and Caitrina, folding it as they went, forming a spout. They emptied the grain into the awaiting basket on the ground.

Little Dee scooped up the basket and ran toward the grain shed with it, blonde braids flying behind her.

Deirdre folded her arms across her chest, daydreaming of Richard, her gaze again wandering across the ripened fields.

Seonaid poured another load of grain onto the cloth that was spread open on the ground. When they started to pick the cloth up, she held up her hand stopping them.

"Go find yer man, Deirdre. 'Tis a certain yer mind isna here with us." She raised a lone brow suggestively.

"Nay, I cannot leave the work to ye," Deirdre argued.

"Away with ye, milady," Maude ordered.

Andrew, along with other children, ran up and placed filled baskets of grain on the ground.

Bess, one of the villages many widows, and not too old to enjoy a man's warmth, stepped in to take Deirdre's place.

Delight sparkled in Deirdre's eyes as she eagerly snatched off her headdress allowing a fine dusting of chaff to settle on top of her head. When she turned to leave, Seonaid called after her, "Take David and Richard their meal. Oh…and…cold water from the creek."

"Aye—that I will." Deirdre hurried toward the stable.

Deirdre reined in her horse and stared out over the wheat field, the grain stalks blowing in the wind. Spring had been wet making the crop later than usual and the clan were working extra hard to finish the harvest. Men were lined ten across the field, scythes in hand, briskly cutting. Her mind and eyes sought out one particular male figure in the middle of the field. Richard was working alongside David, slicing the stalks with curved scythes. Both men had stunned the people when they stripped off their tunics, grabbed the sharp scythes, and began cutting wheat. Together, they had struck up a rhythm that helped them move rapidly down the field. The sliced stalks fell to the ground, where not long afterwards, they were bundled by women and children and put in large baskets.

With ease and an occasional nudge of her knees against her horse, Deirdre rode toward the man who made her heart flutter just to be near. A water bladder tied to her saddle horn, dripped cold water, and a food basket dangled from her free hand.

Richard stopped working to watch her approach. She rode a horse as though born in the saddle. His body surged at the sight of her. He had been dubious about bringing her back to the place where so much pain had been inflicted on her and thought the memories would eat away at her, but instead, their time here had been good for her. It had helped her mind to heal, and despite the hard work with the harvest, she glowed with health.

Using the back of his forearm, he wiped sweat from his brow. Swinging the scythe had been good for his damaged muscles and he had full use of his arm. Before now, physical labor wasn't something he would consider doing on his own domain. But here the circumstances were different, every pair of hands were needed to fight against winter starvation.

Deirdre stopped her horse next to Richard and untied the water bladder. "Thought ye might have need of water, aye?"

Accepting the bladder, Richard tilted his head back and gulped the cold liquid, allowing it to spill down his chin and neck. He poured water over his hair and shook himself like a dog, sending droplets to spatter against her leg. The water rivulet down his torso creating tracks in the dust that covered him.

"Would ye like to get wet all over?" Her eyes held promises of things to come.

"And just what do you have in mind, chéri?" Richard brushed against her leg, smiling, and lifted a lone brow in question. He tossed the bladder to David who had approached.

"I want to show ye a special place. I liked to go there when I was little. Davey and I played there. Davey, ye know the place I speak of?"

David had to think for only a moment before a grin whitened his teeth in a dust-coated face. "Aye, I do." Like Richard, he poured the water over his head. His eyes locked onto the food basket. "Would ye have something for me as well, Deedee?"

"Oh, aye. Seonaid sent yer meal along." She separated his food out, and then nudged Richard's arm with her toe. "D'ye want to come with me?" She exaggerated a wipe of sweat from her forehead. "'Tis sorely hot today, is it no'?"

"Oui…that it is. It appears you are going to take me away from my work whether I want to go or not." Kidding with her, he couldn't wait to get away from the dust and heat of the field. He glanced at David who was biting into a chunk of cheese. "We will return before dusk." He whistled for Saladin who slowly meandered over from his shady spot under a tree.

An occasional grasshopper fled before their horses as they ambled along, side by side, their legs not quite touching. She pointed to the hillside. "Up there, Richard, that is where I be taking ye." A smile lit her face as she whipped her horse forward. The trail soon narrowed, forcing Richard to ride behind her.

He perused her backside as he followed her up the hill. She wore a simple green linen gown that hung loose on her frame. The motion of her body as she guided her horse mesmerized him, and knowing what she looked like underneath the gown, he imagined her riding naked. His loins stirred at the thought, making him hope she would soon stop.

They rode around switchbacks thick with ferns, evergreens, tall pines, oaks, and larch trees. The smell of pitch filled the air. Even their approach failed to silence the cricket's steady drone. Startled birds flit between branches. Birds scolded the intruders as they took to the sky.

Deirdre turned her horse off the trail where the roar of water caught up with itself. The trees gave way to a clearing and the clearing gave way to a large pool of water being fed by a furious waterfall. Shading his eyes from the sun that managed to break through some of the foliage he looked up to see where the falls started, where it formed the pool and then continued on down the side of the hill, coursing toward the inlet.

Richard dismounted and helped Deirdre from her saddle. His large hands engulfed her waist. Slowly and deliberately he slid her down his front, pausing only to kiss her nose. "I think milady has more on her mind than eating, 'tis true?"

"'Tis true."

"Here, take this, chéri. He handed her the food basket then grabbed the water bladder and his dagger belt, leaving his sword tied to Saladin's saddle horn. He took care to hobble both horses.

Pulling her close, they stood near the pool of water. The force of the waterfall hitting on the boulders created a fine mist that filtered into the air. Foliage dripped with moisture.

Richard pointed to the rainbow that grew from the mist. "Did you know that if you wish on a rainbow, your wish comes true?"

"'Tis a certain?"

"Oui." He stood behind her and placed his hands over her eyes. "Now wish—wish and 'twill come true." He kissed the back of her neck. "Hmmm…you smell like…wheat." He laughed as she jerked around to face him.

"Oh aye—Richard, and should I tell ye what ye smell like?"

"Non, I know what I smell like. What did you wish for, Deirdre?"

"'Tis my secret, Richard de Laci, and I'll no' be telling ye."

He plucked a piece of wheat stubble from her hair. "You came here often as a child?"

A smile curved her mouth upward, she nodded. "Aye, sometimes with Davey. But when I was older, I came by myself." She rubbed her hand across her face, smearing dirt. Slipping off her shoes, she lifted the hem of her gown and began to wade. "My father met my mam when he was taking cattle to her clan. She was swimming in a river and came up out of the water as naked as the day she was born. Papa fell in love with her as she stood proudly before him and didna run off like a shy maiden."

"A wise man, your sire. Why don't you remove your gown and keep it dry?"

"Are ye having lustful thoughts about me?" she teased as she stepped from the water to join him.

"Most lustful. I want you, Deirdre." He deftly turned her around and unlaced her gown that fell in a puddle around her ankles.

She proudly stood naked before him, then waded into the pool and turned to see what he would do as she backed into the deep water, enticing him.

He studied her while slipping off his boots. Her breasts appeared larger, and the nipples a darker hue. He pulled his tunic over his head and dropped it on the ground.

She continued to back up as he peeled off his breeks and stood naked. "Richard…love, if if ye take notice, ye have a lass who is wonderin' if ye plan to stand there staring all day."

When the water reached her breasts, he ran and dove into the water, the shock of the cold water seized him. He surfaced amongst great splashing and tossing of his hair, and reached for her. "Merde, but this water is cold. You could have said something."

"Och…and keep ye from coming in. I've brought a smidgen of soap with me."

"Pudge, you have the most delectable little dimples right above your arse, mayhap I could—"

She shoved him under water giving him a clear view of her body, and this view he liked even more so. He jerked her legs out from under her and pulled her down to him. His hands cupped her breasts and she could feel his desire poke against her before they broke the surface, each gasping for air.

"There now, what d'ye think ye be doing?" she teased him.

"You know what I be doing. I want you, Deirdre."

She splashed water at him. When he dove for her, she squealed and made her way to the bank. When she started running, he gave chase, his eyes glued to those dimples. Laughing, she ducked into the small cave behind the falls. He did the same and caught her.

"You'll never be able to lose me," he said.

"I dinna want to lose ye, jest lure ye in here." Words spoken with just a leering flash of her brow.

The cave, long ago carved out by some ancient soul, was big enough for two bodies to fit comfortably. The water formed a curtain, cutting them off from the world as it cascaded into the pool. The waters constant roar enveloped them.

She took his hand.

Water beaded then trickled down her body as he stared into the depth of her eyes. The love he read in them for himself was a balm to his soul. His face softened, became most gentle, letting her know he couldn't get enough of her, and never would. He laid her back on the smooth dirt. Mist from the falls sprayed over their bodies, the sides of the cave dripped wet, forming puddles.

"You are lovely," he said. She simply smiled up at him.

He knelt to lick the liquid from her breasts. He traversed her body in a languid motion, going further down to lick her navel then the inside of her thighs. He took tickling little nips and gentle tugs on her delicate skin. Desire surged in waves as she let him have his way. The mere feel of him pleasuring her caused her to soar.

She grasped his hair and pulled him back up to her and as his weight settled the length of her body, she took his hardened shaft within her hand and arched her body up to him. He entered her. He was like a great wild beast that dominated his mate, and she met his domination with a greed that matched his. With wild abandonment, they coupled, and he rode her like never before. Their eyes closed to slits as passion coursed through them, and both reveled in the feel the other induced. When he jerked to a climax, he threw back his head and roared. She moaned in contentment as his seed surged.

She pulled his head close to her face and whispered, "Sometimes, I want to pull ye inside me and never let ye leave me. I love ye so."

He returned her stare as he tenderly wiped water beads from her face. "I would like to be pulled inside you, chéri." He lay next to her, running his hand across her body, the small waist, ample hips, and golden skin. "Once, while in Venice, I saw a statue of a goddess. You look like that goddess." Thoughtfully he stared at her then traced his fingers over the soft tissue of her breasts then around the nipples. "I fear I love you too much, Deirdre. Sometimes God is fearless and thinks to put us mere mortals in our place. My happiness with you is complete, may God grant me a boon and keep it that way."

"Richard, ye frighten me with such talk. Come closer...love."

They laid side by side, lazily running their hands over each other's bodies as if putting them to memory.

"Richard, d'ye ever think about having children of yer own? Ye are so good with Joanna, I wonder of such." Deirdre draped her legs over his, but his serious gaze disquieted her.

"I did not think overly much about children, leastways not until I met you. I want children that legitimately carry my name. Sons to inherit Falaise. I don't want my children to be called bâstards." His jaw firmed.

She stared at the falls. Her mind filled with doubts, her happiness quelled. How could she tell him that her womb already quickened with his child? That she'd conceived at Blackadder the night they signed the parchment declaring that he was hers alone. That she was to be his wife as soon as allowed, and in his eyes already was.

"Chéri, is something amiss? You have turned away from me," he whispered and ran a finger around her breasts, tracing a tiny blue vein that ended at her nipple. She covered his hand with hers, pressing it hard against her breast, changing the subject because she couldn't change his mind. "Richard...love, d'ye want to know my wish?"

"Oui, if you want to tell me so."

"I wished for God to keep ye safe."

"A goodly wish, sweetheart." If possible, he settled her closer to him.

Deirdre ran her hands across his ribs, the muscles tight and firm. She feathered her fingers softly down the front of him, pausing to take his length in her hand, arousing him again. He pulled her over on top of him and settled her onto his hardened shaft. As droplets coursed down and ran between her breasts, he traced the waters path, and then enclosed her breasts, gently squeezing. Rolling her onto her back, he began to make slow love to her. Their eyes locked for but a moment before they shut and both were carried away.

"I think we have been lazy long enough." Reluctantly, Richard rose to his feet and helped her up. He studied her. "Have we succeeded in making better memories for you?"

"Oh, aye, for ye have given me sweet memories of my home. I can go forward now and not dwell on what happened here, for what ye and I just shared, has given me even better ones."

He untied the leather ties on her braids and began to unbraid her hair. When it was released from the tight coils, he let the reddish-brown curls fall through his hand, and then suddenly overwhelmed, he took her in his arms, burying his face against the mass of kinks.

"Deirdre."

They went back to the pool, and using her smidgen of soap, washed each other. Deirdre teased him about smelling like lavender, but he didn't care what he smelled like as long as she was doing the washing. They used the falls strong stream to sluice the soap from their bodies.

After helping the other dress, they spread out their meal. Deirdre silently thanked Seonaid for the cold game hen and cheese that she'd placed in the basket for them.

"Richard love, let me use yer dagger to cut the food." She reached out her hand as he took his dagger from where it was scabbard at his leg, and placed it in her hand. She deftly cut the food for them and handed Richard a piece of the cheese and leg from the bird.

"D'ye have places like this close to your château?" She nibbled on a piece of white meat.

"Oui, and more. The forest is so thick and the tree trunks so large in girth that five men can join hands and barely reach around them."

"I canna imagine a tree that big. I'll see for myself, aye?"

"That you will." He tossed the bones into the nearby foliage and wiped his mouth.

"D'ye think yer brother and sister will like me?"

"Of course, for you are most likable. And besides, they love what I love."

They finished their meal and seeing that the day grew late, he helped her clean up and tie the basket to her horse. He started to un-hobble the horses when Deirdre took his hand.

"Come, I've something to show ye before we leave."

She led him up a path, to the top of the falls where they scanned the spectacular view afforded between the tall trees that surrounded them. "Look at the inlet. See the island? Papa built a hunting cottage there. Ye canna see the cottage from here though, the trees hide it. I'll have to take ye to it sometime. Ye will like it." She shaded her eyes to cut the glare of the sunlight that angled just right on the water.

Richard glanced upward as birds screeched and flushed skyward. For a second he caught the glint of reflected metal through the branches. His skin prickled as his hand went for a sword that wasn't there. He crouched and turned toward Deirdre when an arrow slammed into his thigh almost knocking him off his feet.

"Richard!" Deirdre screamed at the sight of the arrow.

"Get down!" He started to push her out of the way, but slipped in the mud.

An arrow pierced her chest, propelling her backwards. Stunned, she grabbed at the arrow shaft and then at him. Another arrow grazed her temple, snapping her head back.

She reached for his outstretched hand—too late.

She plummeted over the falls.

"Deirdre!"

21 *A Past Love Defends*

Richard leaped into the water after her. The water closed around him as he struggled to find her, but unable to do so, he surfaced. Gulping in air, he quickly dove under again. This time he spotted her hair as it fanned out from her head. His hands cut through the water as he swam to her, his air escaped in a flurry of bubbles. Grabbing her around the waist he pulled her to the surface. With the water fighting against him, he managed to get out of the pool. Slinging her over his shoulder, he crouched low and ran for the dense underbrush where he carefully laid her down.

He put his ear over her heart, trying to hear it over the pounding of his own.

God above—she lived.

Peering slowly over the foliage at Saladin, he gauged the distance to his sword. How could he have been so careless? Looking at Deirdre, he swore under his breath. The front of her bodice soaked up her blood where the arrow entered above her right breast. Blood ran into her hair from the wound to her left temple. Turning her head to see the damage, he was relieved to see a flesh wound.

"Deirdre," he whispered.

Her left forearm above the wrist canted at a strange angle, broken.

Unable to remove the arrow from her chest, Richard snapped the shaft off. Another darting glance over the foliage assured him no one was coming. Turning his attention back to her, he pulled on her arm until the bone snapped back into place. She emitted an anguished groan, yet her eyes remained closed. Tearing the hem from her gown and using the arrow shaft as a splint, he wrapped the strip of material around her arm. He no sooner finished tying it off when voices carried his way.

Unsheathing his dagger, Richard parted the bushes to see two men approach Saladin.

"Look—Neil, the fool has left his sword on his horse. A gift from the heavens that I'll use to kill him," he said to his companion while untying the sword.

An arrow whistled over Richard's head to pierce the stranger's neck. Grabbing at the arrow, his words garbled, blood spurted as he swayed and fell to the ground. The other man drew his sword and focused on his surroundings.

Richard stood and hurled his dagger. His aim was true, for the dagger buried deep into the man's chest, leaving only the hilt to protrude. The assailant fell squirming to the ground. Richard ran over and pulled the dagger from the man's chest. He silenced him with one slice across the throat.

Richard grabbed his sword from Saladin and ran back to Deirdre. He studied the area, trying to see who shot the arrow that killed the mercenary. Was it David? His chest was tight with fear for Deirdre. She needed help—now. He glanced at his thigh. The arrow shaft had broken off leaving a few inches protruding from his leg. He didn't think either one of them would make it out of here alive.

The underbrush behind him quivered as someone came toward them. Richard, brandishing his sword, used his body to protect Deirdre. He was astonished to see both Bonnar Cameron and Gordon Bryce crawl out of the bushes. Bonnar put his finger to his lips for silence.

"Gunther—Neil—where ye be?" The voices called as they came

closer. "Did ye get the Frenchman? Have ye taken the woman's head for proof to the earl that we killed her? Gunther—answer me."

Bonnar signaled Richard to keep down as he scurried behind the giant boulders next to the waterfall and waited.

Richard whispered to Gordon, "I want the one who thinks to take Deirdre's head. Stay with her."

Soon, two men came into sight. Richard and Bonnar waited until they were in the clearing. They both jumped out at the same time, surprising their attackers.

Richard advanced toward the one who stood with his sword drawn, ready to swing. "You want Countess Wrothbury's head as proof of death? Well bâstard—they can have yours instead!" The hireling didn't have time to bring his sword up or take another breath before Richard swirled and holding his sword with both hands severed the man's head from his shoulders. Richard's nostrils flared with anger as he turned to take on the next mercenary who charged at him.

Bonnar was faster and cut the leg out from under the man. The man screamed and fell to the ground. He writhed and tried to stand.

His eyes widened. "Nay," he screamed as Bonnar's claymore hacked through his heart.

Richard and Bonnar stood back-to-back and watched three more men advancing toward them.

Richard growled over his shoulder, "How many more?"

"These three coming on are the rest of them. Gordon—get over here!"

The men advanced toward each other, and the sound of swords clanging together echoed around the hillside, spoiling the serenity yet incongruously blending in with the roar of the waterfall as they quickly dispatched the mercenaries.

Seeing they were safe, Richard ran to Deirdre. Kneeling, he yelled, "Get my horse."

Gordon un-hobbled the horses and brought Richard's to him.

"Where did you two come from?" Richard asked.

"We were bringin' missives from the Brus to David. We noticed these men coming from the direction of Nairn and followed them. We spotted the both of ye standing at the waterfall. So did they. The rest ye know."

In a rush, Richard mounted Saladin, and ordered. "Hand her to me!"

Bonnar obeyed, and using care, lifted an unconscious Deirdre to place her in Richard's arms. Her head flopped back, her arm dangled.

Richard gave Saladin free rein to take them down off the hillside. When they were free of its challenging trails, he urged Saladin into a full gallop. With his escorts fast beside him, he rode as if Satan himself nipped at his heels.

Foxlair never seemed so far away.

Everything was a blur. Saladin's hooves churned up the earth. Richard's chest was tight with fear, he screamed at the Lord, he prayed. "*Le seigner, laissez-la vivant. Ne la prenez pas.* Lord, let her live. Don't take her." He cried. "Don't take her."

Their horses blasted through Foxlair's open stockade. Bonnar leaped from his moving horse and ran ahead to throw open the doors. Richard handed Deirdre down to Gordon and slid from Saladin whose sides were spotted with white lather.

With Deirdre in his arms, Richard rushed inside. A quick glance showed everyone enjoying the eveningtide meal. Their smiles instantly faded at the ruckus. David and Macadie jumped to their feet.

"Caitrina! Help," Richard yelled and dashed up the stairs. "*Sauvez-la— sauvez-la—save her!*"

Caitrina ran after Richard and shouted over her shoulder, "Maude, get my medicine pouch, it's in my chamber. Hurry."

Richard hurried into their chamber and placed Deirdre on the bed. "She's been shot. Her arm's broken." He glanced up to see everyone push into the room. "Mercenaries paid by Wrothbury wanted her head," his voice cracked with emotion.

David looked aghast at both his sister and Richard. "Save her…Caitrina."

Maude hastened in with the medicine pouch followed by Macadie who lugged a bucket of hot water. Caitrina quickly sorted through her pouch until she found her sharp cutting knife. She held it over the candle flame.

Bonnar and Gordon paused in the doorway.

Richard cut Deirdre's gown away and tossed it aside.

Caitrina was fast with her orders. "Get ye all out of this room but Count Strasbourg and Maude. I know ye want to be here, but go." She bent to study the wound. Her forehead creased with a frown, and she asked, "Was it a barbed bodkin tip? If so, I'll have to cut it out."

Richard shook his head. "I don't know, but I have one buried in my leg as well." He tried pulling the arrow free, but it wouldn't budge. He became nauseous from the pain. Blood from his wounds soaked into his breeks and his tunic sleeve.

Caitrina glanced at him. "Richard, dinna try to remove it. For sure 'tis a bodkin tip."

David refused to leave. "Is my sister goin' to live?" He stood next to Richard.

Caitrina flicked a glance at David. "I canna say. Only God knows fer certes." She made a long cut on each side of the arrow shaft. Blood welled out. She parted Deirdre's skin and dug for the arrow tip. "Maude, keep the blood wiped away if ye can."

Maude rinsed the cloth and kept dabbing at the blood.

Richard held out his hand as Caitrina placed the bloodied arrow tip into it.

"Milord, ye did gude in settin' her arm," Caitrina said and continued. "I hope what has happened to Deirdre hasna put the child she carries in peril."

Caitrina's announcement shocked Richard. Holding the sharp arrow tip, he gripped it tight enough to cut his hand as emotions rippled through him.

When he didn't respond, Caitrina glanced up. "Ye didna know?"

"When did she tell you of this?" he said, his mouth gone dry.

"She told me nothing. I'm a healer, but a woman first, and I can tell she is breeding by the changes to her body, the color of her nipples. Besides, she hasna had a menses since we left Blackadder Castle. David, ye, and Maude are to remain silent about this."

"What a fool I've been." Richard admonished himself knowing exactly why she didn't tell him she was enceinte.

"Why has she not told ye of this?" Caitrina asked.

He stared at his love's bruised and bleeding head. He remembered his exact words to her at the pool about not wanting to have bastard children. "Because, Caitrina, I am a fool. I am a man so mired in his stiff beliefs that only a legitimate heir is acceptable. I can only pray she will forgive me."

Caitrina threaded her needle. "Are ye sayin' that if ye can bed her then ye are willing to accept the consequences of such actions? Bastard child or no'?"

"Oui, I am."

Deirdre moaned and turned her head to the side.

Catrina motioned for Richard to sit. "David, hold milord steady so my knife willna slip." She started removing the arrow from his thigh.

David held Richard by the shoulders allowing Catrina to do her work. He talked, trying to keep Richard from passing out. "I'll double the guards to make sure we are secure. Bonnar and Gordon have gone to bury the dead."

"David…" Richard said, barely able to do so. "Find the head that rolled down the hillside. We do not want your children to do so."

The hour was late as Richard sat on the bed watching Deirdre's shallow breathing. She had not gained consciousness since falling. Caitrina told him it was caused by the large lump found on her head. He lifted the coverlet to place his hand on her warm abdomen. His child grew inside, a life from his loins. While at the falls, he figured her wish was to give him a son, and that she had lied and said otherwise.

He berated himself for failing to protect her. He rubbed his brow, his stomach churned at the remembered talks of taking her head.

In the brief time they were together, he'd grown used to having her near, and loved her in ways he never thought possible. How could he not love her quick laugh, loyalty, and feistiness? Her love for Joanna pushed deep into his thoughts. Richard's feelings for his unborn child pushed into his mind. Did Wrothbury have such feelings for Joanna? Love and hate must be driving Wrothbury. Love for his daughter. Hate for Deirdre. Non, Wrothbury wasn't capable of having such feelings. Damn the man to Hades. Damn the man for keeping her pardon a secret.

Today's attack was Wrothbury's hated work, and if he didn't personally wield the sword or shoot the arrows that tried to kill her, then the man's coin crossed the palms of those that did. A ship to France wouldn't keep Deirdre safe. The earl would follow them to the ends of the earth to take back his daughter and put Deirdre in her grave. No longer able to be complacent here at Foxlair, Richard resolved to get to Wrothbury before he got to them.

A soft rap on the door snapped him out of his reverie and he softly called out to enter. Thinking it to be Caitrina, he was surprised to see Bonnar slip into the room and approach the bed. Watching Bonnar, Richard wondered what went through the mind of the man who was to marry her, a man who obviously still loved her. He wasn't all that sure he wanted to know, but Bonnar let him know what was on his mind.

"She is beautiful." He reached out to touch her, hesitated, then pulled his hand back.

"Oui, Deirdre is beautiful, inside as well as out." Signaling Bonnar to join him, Richard strode across the room where he paused next to the table that held a carafe of spiced wine. He filled two chalices, passing one to Bonnar.

"Someday she will be yer wife," Bonnar said over the chalice's rim. "David told me ye are an excellent fighter and strategist. I know ye are rich and have raised yer siblings. This makes yer future marriage to Deedee somewhat easier to accept. Somewhat." Bonnar paused for a moment then continued. "But ye still have to destroy her husband before ye can do the deed, aye? Yer in a strange predicament. Kill Wrothbury and many will think ye did it to have his wife. If ye let the man live until old age takes him, then ye might not marry her fer years and yer children will be bastards. Then there's the pardon. That small piece of parchment that changes all."

"What would you do?" Richard asked.

Bonnar tipped the chalice and drank. He wiped his mouth on his sleeve. "For Deedee, I'd dispatch Wrothbury and not let it cross—"

Holding up his hand, Richard interrupted, "You have let it known how you feel. But Deirdre has made her choice. I've not pushed her into anything she does not want. My regret is that I brought her back to Foxlair. When she was safe at Blackadder, I should have gone after Wrothbury and forced the pardon." Richard slowly sipped his wine.

"I know today is eating at yer insides because ye think ye failed to protect Deedee. Jest like the past several years have eaten at me when I hid in the forest and failed to save her from Wrothbury."

"Oui, my guilt does just that."

"Dinna let it."

"Strange words coming from someone who has not assuaged his own guilt. Agree?"

"Aye, I agree. My guilt still eats away at my verra marrow."

"It appears we travel the same path, non?" Richard tossed down the last of his drink. "Bonnar?"

"Aye?"

"How long before you spotted the mercenaries did you then see Deirdre and I standing at the falls?" Richard had to know that the love he shared with Deirdre was just that, shared between them only, and not shared by the prying eyes of the mercenaries. It should not matter because the men are dead, but it did matter to him.

"They turned off the trail before anyone from the settlement could see them and headed toward the hillside. I think their spotting ye was by chance. We tracked the cowards and when they disappeared into the woods, we spotted ye and Deirdre standing by the upper falls, and knew they had as well."

"Bonnar, you saved our lives today and I'm forever beholden to you. But Deirdre is mine to love, not yours. You must let her go."

Bonnar shook his head. "I need to have her forgiveness for the wrongs I've done her. When I hear those words from her, perhaps I can let it go." He set his chalice down then turned to leave.

"Would you send David to me?" Richard called after him.

When the door closed behind Bonnar, Richard knelt down beside Deirdre and wept racking sobs that shook his shoulders and the bed.

She stirred and moaned slightly. "Richard…."

Richard dashed the tears from his cheeks before standing. "Deirdre? Can you hear me?" He bent closer but she was silent.

A soft knock sounded and David opened the door before Richard could beckon. He came to stand next to the bed where he checked on Deirdre.

Richard spoke first. "I should have protected her, but I did not. I failed your sister. It has been what…four months or more since her freedom? Now look at her. I think she was safer in the cage."

"Nay." David shook his head. "Ye are talkin' out of the side of yer mouth."

Richard rubbed his eyes, trying to wipe away the fatigue that overwhelmed him. His wounds throbbed, yet he would not give into despair. "David, I'm going after Wrothbury. The less who know that I plan murder, the better for it."

David wagged his head. "It isn't murder when one rids the world of vermin."

"I like your logic. I wish God would see it that way." He paused to glance out of the window slit, and at the steep hillside behind Foxlair. Finally, he turned back to David. "Since Deirdre and I cannot marry, I pledged my life to hers. If something happens to me, she is taken care of. She is my wife in all but name. This has been written in a contract and is binding."

It was apparent that David didn't know what to say, but Richard could see respect in David's dark eyes.

"Then ye are as man and wife without it being named so?"

"Oui, as man and wife without my name joined to hers, but joined in body as one. And with my child on the way, she will be Countess de Strasbourg before my child's birth, or I'll be dead."

The torture of throbbing wounds and a sleepless night intensified Richard's precarious position on the chair. Unwilling to leave Deirdre's side, he had pulled a chair next to the bed and used the bed to prop his feet up. His body cried out in protest as he shifted around, and finally giving up, cracked his eyes open to look at Deirdre who astonished him by returning his stare.

"Deirdre?" Slowly, he removed his feet from the bed, and then even more slowly he stood from his chair and bent over her. "Deirdre?" He clasped her good hand as relief to see her awake and lucid almost overpowered him. A brief smile quivered across his mouth.

"Richard...water...so thirsty." She licked at her dry lips.

He poured water into a chalice and lifted her head with care. "Not too much, chéri." He controlled the chalice, allowing the smallest of sips before he set it down. Taking her hand within his, he sat next to her. "'Tis a joy to see you awake. I've been afraid."

"What happened?" She coughed, grimaced, her hand gripped his even tighter. "The pain..." She shut her eyes as tears made their way out of the corners. "Richard…my chest burns. My arm."

"Your arm is broken. Try not to move it," he cautioned.

When she started to touch her temple, he stopped her. "Non, do not touch yourself. That's where the arrow grazed you." Guilt and remorse etched new lines into his face, his voice was raw with emotion, "My love, I failed you. Can you ever forgive me for not protecting you?"

"Dinna blame yerself for this." Her eyes hollowed with pain, sought his.

Before he could answer, Caitrina breezed into the room holding a pitcher in one hand and a candle in the other. She set both down on the side table.

"Och. There ye be, Deirdre, awake and talkin'. It means yer brain wasna damaged when ye fell." She pulled the covers away and proceeded to cut the wraps away from Deirdre's chest. Dried blood stuck to the linen strips. "This looks gude. 'Tis needin' more salve." She studied the cut on Deirdre's temple, and then smeared fresh salve on both wounds. "Richard, hold Deirdre up so I can wrap her chest."

Richard lifted her up enough to allow Caitrina room to wrap the bandage. Caitrina gave Deirdre a potion made of lemon balm and chamomile mixed in goat's milk. When Deirdre finished drinking it, Caitrina turned to Richard.

"'Tis yer turn, Richard. Drop yer breeks and let me see to yer leg."

"Non, I need no coddling."

"I said—drop yer breeks." Her hands went to her hips, elbows straight out.

Her stance reminded Richard of a general he'd campaigned against. With a resigned sigh and knowing he'd lost the battle, he wisely did as told. Caitrina unwound the linen strips from his thigh and examined the wound. "Gude—'tis gude. No discoloration to suggest infection." She applied fresh salve and rewrapped it. "I'm thinking yer the only person I've stitched so much since knowin'."

"I wish it otherwise." Richard smirked, the irony of the whole situation not lost on him. Warily, he eyed Caitrina as she approached with a potion mixed with goat's milk. "What is that?"

"Medicine to keep away infection and fever."

"I do not drink anything that comes from a goat. Mix the potion in wine…er…if—"

"Drink this."

"Non."

"I said drink this. D'ye want to get infection or a fever? Jest what gude would ye be to Deirdre and yerself if ye did so?"

When he refused to cooperate she grabbed his head and held the chalice against lips that were tightly clinched. A sharp pinch on the back of his neck had him opening his mouth. Caitrina tilted the chalice. He gagged and choked the warm milk down. Some of it dribbled down his chin and onto his tunic.

"By the Saints—now I'll smell like a rancid goat," he sputtered.

"Nay, more like clabbered milk unless ye change yer tunic."

"Do you always treat people this way?" He scowled at her while wiping the milk from his face and tunic. "And to think there is no getting away from you since you have married into my family. For the life of me, I cannot see what Philippe sees in your bossy behavior and temperament of—of—a shrew."

"D'ye two always fight like this?" Deirdre rasped.

Caitrina laughed. "I didna think we were fightin'. But milord is quite stubborn. Ye both need to rest. 'Tis verra early in the morn. I suggest ye crawl under the covers next to Deirdre for ye canna have slept well in that chair." She paused at the door. "And ye best get used to me, Richard de Laci, for I'm yer brother's wife for keeps."

She no sooner left the room when Richard stared at his loincloth, shrugged, and thought since he was already undressed, why not? After removing his soiled tunic and tossing it aside, he pulled back the coverlet and slipped in. He tried to distance himself from Deirdre, but unable to do so, he snuggled close to her body. Soon his arm snaked over her hip.

Her good hand sought his, and when she interlaced her fingers within his and squeezed, his guilt began to lift, somewhat.

Deirdre grabbed at the dagger that Wrothbury pushed deeper into her chest. Blood spurted coating her in a blanket of red. Close by, Richard reached for her, he yelled, but no sound came out. Fire spread throughout her chest, the dagger broke through her back impaling her against the ground. The pain, the pain...her eyes popped opened...

She stared directly into the faces of her niece and nephews. Little Dee, Blake, and Andrew returned her intense stare with the utmost concentration. When she managed a weak smile, grins dimpled their faces. Blake patted the bed.

"Climb up." She beckoned with her good hand.

Andrew boosted both his siblings onto the bed, but he remained standing next to it. Their jostling made Deirdre wince, but a moment later the pain abated some. They sat side-by-side at the foot of the bed, sinking into the down-filled mattress.

Andrew moved closer to her side. "D'ye hurt bad, aunt?" He leaned forward, his face puckered into a frown "Uncle Bonnar and milord Richard cut off the mercenaries' heads. Did ye see their heads?"

"Nay, I didna see any heads. I'm told I fell from the top of the falls into the water. Tell me about yer Uncle Bonnar fighting the men who tried to kill me."

"I heard him tell Da that him and Uncle Gordon followed the men who tried to kill ye. He fought next to the count and they chopped off arms and legs from the mean men. They threw their heads down the hillside." Andrew's arm flayed the air in pretense of wielding a sword.

"Be ye sure of that, Andrew? I dinna think any heads were thrown down the hill."

His face flushed pink. He hung his head for only a moment, but then he was back with more of his story. "I heard Uncle Bonnar tell Da that his love for ye is killing him." His young face screwed up with thought.

"What is love that it can kill ye?"

She couldn't help but smile at his innocent question, yet what he said about Bonnar bothered her in many ways. "Andrew, ye shouldna repeat what ye hear grown-ups say. Promise me ye'll never repeat what ye just told me, not to anyone. D'ye understand?"

He nodded most solemnly, his dark-brown eyes big in his face.

Blake, trying to get her attention, patted her foot and pointed at her with a stubby finger. "D'ye hurt, Auntie?"

"Aye, wee Blake, it hurts verra much. And ye, young Deedee, look just like yer mam, that ye do."

Her namesake nodded. "Mam says ye were put in a cage by England's king. 'Tis true?" she asked in a high little voice while pushing wayward strands of blond hair off her forehead.

"'Tis true, and a long tale. How does my Joanna fare?"

Andrew gave his opinion. "She's gude. Maude waits to bring her fer a visit. Says ye need to be able to hold Joanna. Milord Strasbourg leaves for London in a few days."

"What say ye, Andrew? Richard leaves fer London?" Deirdre was puzzled.

"Aye, I heard the men talkin' downstairs and milord is goin' to London with Macadie."

Deirdre smiled as Andrew's chest puffed out with importance at telling her his news. Inside, she was dying.

Already bored, Andrew piped up. "I'm gonna search for those heads."

Before she could say otherwise, Andrew left. Deedee and Blake crawled across the bed and got on each side of her. It wasn't long before they were fast asleep, leaving Deirdre to worry over the news that Richard was going to London.

Richard watched Deirdre and the two little ones as they slept, and thought how natural it was for Deirdre to have children around her. But it wasn't long before Caitrina, Seonaid, and Mary Clair carrying Joanna, pushed in behind him and chuckled when they saw the sleeping occupants on the bed.

Joanna's chubby arms stretched out for Richard, and without thought, he gathered her close. She smelled of milk. He nuzzled a kiss against her rosy cheek, and was rewarded with one of her sweet grins. He handed her back to Mary Clair.

"I see you are without Bertrand," he teased and made her blush.

"Aye, he cleans yer armor and sharpens your weapons."

"And Gordon?"

This time she blushed a deeper scarlet. "He is about."

Seonaid bent over the bed and gently shook her bairns awake. "Come now, wee ones, dinna wake yer Aunt Deedee."

Richard picked Blake up and set him on the floor. He then did the same with Little Dee who yawned and knuckled her eyes.

"Thank ye, Count Strasbourg," Seonaid said.

"Seonaid, you may call me Richard as do the others."

"Richard." She smiled at his words and saying her goodbyes, led the children from the room.

"Mary Clair?" he said, stopping her before she reached the door "Please bring Joanna back later to visit with her mother."

"Aye, milord." She did a quick curtsy, and then asked. "Is France as wondrous as Bertrand claims?"

"More so." Richard thought perhaps Gordon to lose this one.

Deirdre was jostled awake by Caitrina removing the dressing from her chest. "Ah...ye took my bed partners away. They kept me warm, that they did." She tilted her head to see the fine stitches.

Caitrina studied the wound. "Deirdre, can ye tell me how it feels inside to ye?"

"It hurts—it hurts to take a deep breath," she said.

"The arrow went in verra deep and I had to cut it out. Damnable bodkin tips. They are for piercing armor, no' a woman's chest. But with God's grace, ye will heal."

"I give thanks to God above that ye are here. Foxlair has no healer, at least not as ye heal." Deirdre sought out Richard. "Are ye well, my love? Does yer leg wound hurt much?"

He took her good hand. "Non, my worry is for you."

Caitrina picked up the vessel with salve in it. Using two fingers, she scooped out some salve and rubbed it across Deirdre's stitches.

"Here, milord, put this on her temple."

Richard gently dabbed a small amount of salve on her left temple. Deirdre watched him work. Their eyes met, and without thought, he leaned forward and kissed her.

Caitrina laughed, teasing them. "Mayhap his way will heal ye faster than mine. Here now, let me get her chest wrapped."

"You are very knowledgeable about medicines and sickness." He smiled, thinking when Caitrina wasn't so bossy she was somewhat pleasant.

"Papa taught me at an early age. He is verra learned in the art of medicines."

"You must miss yer sire," Richard said.

"Aye, it was verra hard fer me to leave Papa. But he was most relieved that I had married a man such as Philippe. Papa's at Dundee taking care of king Robert's wounded." Caitrina smiled affectionately at Deirdre. "We will keep yer arm splinted for three fortnights. Do not try to do anything with it or ye might move the bones out of place. Richard did a fine job of setting it, and with the mercenaries breathing down his neck as he did so. Here, drink this potion. 'Twill make ye heal faster." She held the chalice against Deirdre's lips. "Richard, d'ye need yer dressing changed?"

"Non, perhaps later." He sat next to Deirdre and neither was aware when Caitrina left the room. He kissed her palm and searched her face, seeing the purple smudges under her eyes. "Milady has too much company and not enough rest." His hand dwarfed hers, overlapping her tapering fingers. "God's blood, but you are a delicate thing."

"Milord, when d'ye leave for London?"

Surprised by the question, he asked, "Who told you of this?"

"Wee ears hear more than grown-ups think they do."

"Ah...so they overheard and thought their aunt needed to know all, oui?"

"Ye have made another ache in me heart, Richard. Dinna go." She grasped at him with her good hand.

"Deirdre, my fear of losing you is far greater than anything I know, and I cannot imagine life without you. I'm going to see King Edward and hopefully obtain a copy of your pardon and take it to Falconshire."

"And then what d'ye plan?" Agitated, she plucked at the coverlet.

He pushed back a stray hair from her face, seeking a warm smile from her, but even he couldn't break through her barrier of worry. "I want you free to marry, and that is all you need to know."

"Ye must not go. All has changed since that pardon was issued. What about Mile's death? I no longer believe the pardon will free me."

"I do. It was never complied with. The argument is sound. If the pardon had been given to Constable Warren and you freed, Miles would still live."

She conceded her dispute was futile. She barely had enough energy to squeeze his hand let alone disagree with his logic. "I hear that Bonnar and Gordon helped ye fight the mercenaries. According to Andrew, ye had heads rolling down the hillside."

Richard was amused. "Little ears have big mouths, do they not?" He drew in a breath. "Oui, both Bonnar and Gordon helped save us, for I could not have fought all the mercenaries at once. Only one was beheaded." His smile faded. "Deirdre, Bonnar needs to talk with you."

She nodded. "Aye. Ye can be here when he does so."

He traced his finger down her cheek. "Non. If I'm here, he will not be able to speak his mind. I'm secure knowing your heart is wrapped around mine."

"Then knowing it is truly well with ye, I'll speak with him."

Richard still didn't like having Bonnar around but they'd forged an unspoken admiration during the fight for Deidre's life. Richard knew how much it took Bonnar to admit his failure, how guilt consumed him, for he' done a grievous injury to Deirdre when he hid from the English. Richard found it hard to compare Bonnar from that long ago day to the man who had since entered battle after battle for Scotland, and who didn't hesitate two days ago to help him fight the mercenaries. It was strange how they both loved Deirdre. Their lives forever altered on the same day and by the same king. And both had their thoughts anchored to the same happenstance from the past. But Richard, the victor, had been able to assuage his guilt, while Bonnar had not.

"I've asked Gordon to stay here at Foxlair and protect you whilst I'm gone."

Her voice was but a whisper, "When d'ye leave?"

Angst lay thick between them.

"Not for weeks, perhaps a month. I would not even think to leave until you're better." He stood, and straightened the coverlet about her. "Rest my love, I'll return later."

Bonnar knocked on Deirdre's door, and not hearing her call out, eased into the room. He shut the door and leaned against it. His heart slammed so loud he was certain she must hear it. Warily, he approached the bed. She slept. Her face relaxed in sleep, looked youthful, like it did that day they'd met in the woods. He shut his eyes and thought of her laying in his arms. Would that vision never leave him? Nay, he'd never give it up. It was his vision to keep, his memory of her. She'd been so innocent. She gave her love to him, was willing to become his mate, and in a heartbeat, he'd failed her. He still tried to work the images and day in his mind. It was like a giant hand had rooted him to the spot. He wasn't a coward as accused. What made him fail her that day still puzzled him as much as everyone else.

Deirdre stirred. She opened her eyes to see Bonnar standing next to the bed. Startled that he was here and that he stood over her as she slept, she ask, "Bonnar…have ye been here long?"

"Nay, I just arrived," he said.

"Richard told me ye want to talk with me."

"Aye." His brow creased, he paused for a moment and then his words tumbled out like fast moving water. "I've lived with the day Wrothbury took ye until I want to take a knife and cut the memory from my mind. I dinna know what happened to me, mayhap I thought to be killed as well."

"I suppose Papa felt the same way. I'm sure he dinna choose to die from a barrage of arrows." Memories surfaced, churned, he'd said the wrong thing, making matters worse.

He started to reach for her hand but paused midair. "Deedee, when I realized something was amiss and heard the English, I tried to figure the distance between you, the water, and myself. Jest as I was starting for ye, Wrothbury crested the hill. I knew I couldna get to ye. Edward's arrows would have taken us out." He sat on the chair.

Her eyes became moist as she listened to his words, the pleading in his voice, and the torture on his face. "Please…Bonnar, forget that day."

He shook his head, violently. "I canna. Not until ye say ye forgive me and mean it."

"Ye dinna know how many times I wished I died that day. For an arrow would have been better than marriage to Wrothbury, years of hell it was. And then the cage. Ye didna come for me when I was in the cage. Wrothbury had taken my wee Joanna from me and left me to rot. When Count Strasbourg happened upon me, I was in great despair. He gave me his warm cloak and left coin fer me. But most of all, he promised to get Joanna and come back fer me." She struggled to sit up.

Alarmed, he jumped to his feet and forced her to lay back down

"Please dinna upset yerself." He leaned over her, afraid she'd try again. "Ye've got to forgive me, for my guilt is eatin' away at my soul until there is nothin' left." He groped for her hand.

She allowed him to hold it. "Richard tells me both ye and Gordon saved us. I thank ye for my life." She winced with pain. "Please get Caitrina…I dinna feel verra well."

And yet, she didn't say the words he craved to hear.

He stood, and then acting on impulse, bent and kissed her on the mouth and murmured against her lips, "I'll never forget ye, Deedee. I love ye." He straightened and before she could utter another word, left.

22 False Pretenses

Richard, on his way to see Deirdre, was reading a missive he'd just received from Philippe. Caitrina also received one as well and immediately sought privacy to read her husband's words. Philippe expected a long siege at Crichton Castle as it was well fortified. The earl, Ewan Crichton, who commanded it, was no fool. Upon reading that, Richard smirked. The man was fool enough to turn against the Bruce and side with the English. In Richard's eyes, that was not only being a big fool, but breaking honor and duty to the king he should be serving. But Philippe was referring to the cunning leadership ability of the confined earl, and not his stupidity.

There was no doubt in Richard's mind that Philippe would be the victor. No matter how well fortified a castle was, they would run out of supplies. Philippe had time on his side to starve the garrison out. He also had the know how to undermine a castle's wall and cause it to collapse.

Folding his missive and tucking it inside his waist pouch, he wondered about the talk between Bonnar and Deirdre. Even though curious as to their conversation, he'd purposely not asked about it, and so far, she didn't speak of it. Richard peeked into the room and found her telling a story to Blake and little Dee. Maude sat by the bed embroidering. Deirdre was propped up against her pillows, and to Richard she never looked prettier. She wore a white linen nightgown and had her hair braided and coiled over her ears. Joanna slept next to her.

"…And this witch had two faces, a face like ye and I right here in the front, and another face in the back of her head, why she could see people coming at her and going away from her! Neither man nor beast could sneak upon her and slay her."

Little Dee and Blake's eyes were enormous, their mouths rounded, as they listened to every word Deirdre said.

"Gore, Aunt Deedee, is two-faced witches here?" Little Dee's high-pitched voice wavered as she nervously plucked at her braid.

"Nay, for yer papa wouldna allow a witch here," Deirdre said. "Jest let me tell ye how this witch gets around. No horse for this witch will do, because no horse would want her on their backs!"

"Does she walk?" Little Dee whispered as Blake gripped her hand.

"Nay. Ye know the broom yer mam sweeps her floor with?"

They both nodded slowly, their faces most fearful.

"Well the witch rides around in the air on a broom, jest like your mams' broom. But not jest like yer mam's broom. The witches broom has fire coming out the sweepy part."

"Fire?" Blake's voice quivered.

"Oh aye—fire. And, ye know what happens next?"

"Nay," screeched Blake.

"Tell us," begged Little Dee.

Deirdre made her eyes as wide as the children's. "Well…the witch comes for the village laird. She rides her broom low setting fire to the village huts. She yells for the laird to come out and calls him a coward. 'Tis known throughout the land that the laird can't hit a rabbit with his bow and arrow. He runs out of his burnin' hut. She's comin' right at him. He's shaking so bad he almost drops his arrow. He shoots, he hits the witch right in the heart. Poof, she disappears in a ball of smoke."

Richard laughed as he approached the bed. "You will be giving them nightmares and frightened to walk past their mother's broom."

Maude chuckled and shook her head, "She has already given me nightmares. Imagine, a two-faced witch. Here now, children, yer Aunt Deedee has finished her story."

When the children started to protest, Richard picked up Blake and tossed him high in the air. He acted like he was going to miss the little boy and let him drop, but he quickly caught him instead. Giggles erupted from Blake as Richard handily set him on the floor and ruffled his dark hair. And knowing how Little Dee couldn't be left out, Richard scooped her up and tossed her high, playing the same game as he did with Blake.

"Count Strasbourg, 'tis a certain ye need children of yer own," Maude said while leaning over and picking up Joanna who didn't blink a lash. "Come children, let us go find yer mam." She herded the children in front of her.

"Richard, where ever did ye learn to do that?" Deirdre asked.

"What?"

"Throw the children into the air then act like yer not going to catch them."

"Why, did I do something out of favor?"

"Nay, 'twas what papa did to me. I always knew he would catch me."

"I see." Richard didn't know why he did it or where he'd learned to do so, only that it felt natural to play with the children as thus. "Well my love, as much as I hate to do this, it's time to remove your stitches."

He unsheathed his dagger and held it over the hot flames of the burning brazier. When he deemed it hot enough, he removed it and set it aside to cool. Now beside her, he unlaced her bodice, spreading the material wide. He perused the wound that was healing nicely. Putting a hand on her back and holding her good arm, he helped her to lie flat on the bed. Taking the knife in hand, he bent close to her chest and cut away the first stitch.

Her color paled to ashen and she worried her bottom lip.

He paused. "Shall I continue or get Caitrina?"

"They have to come out, and ye can do it as well as Caitrina."

He used the tip of his blade, and as he did so, he learned words he never thought to pass her lips. Finally, and with great relief, he was done.

"What of yer stitches?" she asked as he laced her gown closed.

"I cut them out earlier today. Would you like to sit up?"

Seeing her nod, he helped her up and made her comfortable leaning back against the massive wooden headboard. Needing to slack his thirst and wanting to talk with Deirdre, he walked to the table and splashed wine in two goblets.

"Would you like yer medicine in it?" When she nodded, he carefully measured the medicinal herbs into it and returned to her.

Taking a seat on the bed next to her, he downed his own drink in a hurry, the fine taste of the spiced wine not to be enjoyed at this time. She slowly sipped hers, making a face at the bitter taste of the medicines. He held his empty goblet and looking at the plain metal as though studying it, he began to roll it between his palms.

At last Deirdre said, "My love, ye be acting mighty strange. Are ye leaving on the morrow fer London and ye canna tell me so?"

"Non." Not knowing any other way to say it, he blurted, "Deirdre, I know that you carry my child."

Surprised, she frowned. "How d'ye know? Did I talk in my delirium?"

"It makes no difference how I know. What matters is that I do."

"Are ye angry with me? Ye are so staunch about not having a bastard child. Maybe a child born of such love between us could make ye forget it will be so."

Her worry over his reaction to such news was apparent. He smiled and tried to calm her fears. "I could never be angry with you, chéri. And since I have begotten a child upon you, then all the more reason for me to seek out your pardon, Wrothbury, and do what I must."

"That's part of the reason I kept my secret. Please stay with me," she pleaded, her voice breaking.

"I've promised you that I'll not go until you are well enough for me to do so. My word is solid."

Deirdre sometimes wished she was still abed, and thought if that would keep Richard at her side, then so be it. But she'd steadily healed and been back on her feet since the end of September. Now the country-side flamed with the hot colors of mid-October. The splints and wraps were gone from her arm and she could finally hold Joanna in a loving squeeze, and put them around Richard in a warm embrace.

She poured hot water into a medium-sized wooden tub to mix with the cold water. After testing it with her fingers, she picked up Joanna who was standing and holding on tight to the skirt of Deirdre's gown. Her daughter was already splashing before her wee bottom was settled in the tub. Joanna at eleven months would pull herself up by holding onto something solid and try to walk. As she toddled around, Mary Clair was kept in a constant run to keep Joanna from hurting herself.

Using a large gourd, Deirdre dipped water and poured it over Joan-na's head, making her laugh. Deirdre took great joy in bathing Joanna, playing with her as she dressed her, but nothing compared at seeing Jo-anna's eyes light up with recognition the minute she entered the room.

"Ye know, Joanna, my mam loved the water. Papa told me that mam swam like a silkie, aye that she did. Think ye will swim like a silkie?"

Joanna jabbered, "Wa wa." She grinned, pushing her cheeks wide showing tiny pearls of teeth. Using a bar of lavender soap that Richard had brought her, Deirdre washed Joanna's face and body. When Joanna splashed water on Deirdre, she laughed and kissed her daughter's wet cheeks.

"Ye be a little hooligan, Joanna," she said.

Richard slipped up behind her. "I'd like to wash you all over."

"I would like that verra much," she said and turned her head to slightly rest against his warm neck, allowing him to nibble at her earlobe, his stubble rubbing against her cheek. "I dinna hear ye come in the room."

"That's because you were talking to Joanna."

Deirdre tilted Joanna backwards and carefully rinsed her hair. Joanna slapped the water getting both Deirdre and Richard wet.

"Oh…gore, Richard, I canna wait until she calls me mam."

"And me mon père."

"Truly, Richard? Ye would let her call ye father?" Deirdre asked in hope.

"She will know no other." His hands slipped around to cup her breasts as he kissed the back of her neck, before claiming her earlobes. "Your gown is wet, chéri."

"Richard," she said and leaned back against him. "We canna, hmmm…" she let out a long soft moan, finding his touch hard to resist. He tugged her laces open and then his hands slipped inside her gown, caressing the swell of her abdomen. The baby moved, forcing a grunt of surprise from Richard.

"Mon Dieu," he exclaimed. "What was that?"

"That was yer son, milord, telling his sire that he is alive in his mam's womb."

"Christ Jesus, did it hurt?"

She couldn't help but chuckle at his innocence. "Nay…silly, it feels like a feather brushing against my insides." Deirdre wasn't ashamed to be carrying a baby out of wedlock, but wished it could be different. Yet, with all of Wrothbury's cruelty, she tried not to aspire for his death for fear God's revenge would smite her unborn child. Whenever her thoughts went dark and she wished for things she shouldn't, her lips moved silently with words of atonement.

Since her recovery, Richard courted her every day, never letting her forget they were pledged to the other. He would take her for rides, mostly to the inlet where they would slip off their shoes and walk the beach. He would appear from a darkened niche to pull her into it and kiss her breathless. He would carry her to their bed where he would kiss down her body until both their bodies screamed for release.

"Let Maude care for Joanna. Let's row out to the island where you can show me the hut." He pulled her tightly against him and she could feel his hardened tarse pressed against her backside, as his hand slipped between her thighs. "I've something to tell you. Let us go somewhere private," he urged in a soft cajoling voice.

Weak-kneed from his intent, she acquiesced by taking Joanna from the bath. She dried and dressed Joanna in leggings and a linen gown. Richard picked up Joanna's doll of cloth from the coffer and made the doll act like a puppet, talking to her and grabbing Joanna's nose.

"Bebé." Laughing, Joanna captured the doll and held tight.

They sought out Maude who was with Macadie in the great hall trying to teach him how to play chess. As they approached, Maude slapped Macadie's hand and was chastising him for trying to cheat.

"Macadie, ye cannot use your king to simply ride over the knights and other player and knock my king off the board. Ye must go by the rules of chess."

"Och…I like my rules. I think my king here is Robert the Bruce and yer king is Edward. That gives me leave to smash yer king if I want."

Maude shook her head at Macadie's reasoning and grinned at Deirdre and Richard.

"Maude, d'ye mind sitting with Joanna? Richard and I are going to row over to the island. He wants to see the hut."

"See the hut…does he now?" Maude's brown eyes twinkled in an all-knowing look. "Aye, milady, I'll take care of wee Joanna whilst ye show the waddle and dab of the hut to milord." She chuckled, making Deirdre grin.

Knowing how much Macadie liked children, Deirdre placed Joanna in his lap. She laughed when Joanna immediately scooped up a chess piece and waved it in the air before throwing it down.

"Here now, ye wee bit of a lass, ye'll be making me lose to Maudie."

Maude snorted, "Ye've already lost to me, Macadie Gunn. Ye just don't know it."

Macadie's tonsured haircut had grown back in enough that he no longer looked a comical monk. Nodding, he shot a wide grin up at Richard. "'Tis well and gude I let her think that, aye, Coont?" He grabbed up the fallen knight and replaced it back on the board.

Wholeheartedly agreeing with Macadie, Richard told him they would be back before nightfall. Richard and Deirdre no sooner reached the courtyard when a messenger came galloping past the gate guards who were shouting after him to stop. The man reined in so suddenly that his mount reared up. With a hasty dismount, the sweaty, dusty soldier approached Richard.

"I seek the Count of Strasbourg," he said in a deep Scottish brogue while bowing his grizzled head.

"I'm he." Richard's hand automatically went to his long dagger as he shielded Deirdre behind his body.

"This is fer thee." The stranger thrust a missive toward Richard.

Richard's fingers closed around the sweat-stained parchment and squinting, he recognized Philippe's seal. He glanced over at the man who wore Robert the Bruce's heraldry on his tunic.

"You appear to be in a great hurry. Is something wrong in my brother's camp?"

"Aye, Milord. I suggest you read fer yerself." The man ducked his head toward the missive.

"Richard," Deirdre said and squeezed his arm, "Read it whilst I instruct this good soldier to find water and food in the kitchen."

"Nay, I must continue on," the messenger said.

Before Deirdre could say otherwise, he started to mount his steed but Richard gripped the man's forearm and stopped him. "Remain where you are."

With the horse's reins draped loosely in his hands, the messenger stood waiting. Richard broke the seal on the missive and began to read. His eyes widened as a curse slipped from his mouth. "This says my brother has been wounded. How bad is he?"

"'Tis bad, milord. They were firing the trebuchet when the sling broke and the boulder fell. Commander de Laci and others were hit. Some were killed. Yer brother asks that ye hurry to him."

"I'll ride with you back to Crichton Castle."

"Milord, I already had a missive from your brother that was to be delivered to Robert the Bruce. I go opposite of yer brother's camp." He opened his waist pouch and removing a missive with Philippe's seal, offered it to Richard. But upon seeing his brother's seal, Richard, simply nodded, and watched the missive replaced.

"Do you need food or water?" Richard asked.

"Nay, I'm well supplied." Giving Richard a nod of reverence, the messenger mounted, and whipping his reins was well on his way.

Richard turned to go back inside and rapidly took the stairs two at a time. Alarmed, Deirdre tried to keep up with him, her long legs moving in lengthened strides to match his even longer ones. "Richard, who wrote to ye? Philippe? Mayhap all is not as bad as it seems."

"Etienne says otherwise. He beseeches me to come to Crichton Castle." Richard bounded inside, almost tripping in his haste.

"Oh...gore, I'll get Caitrina. Philippe must want ye to command the siege, aye?" But the look of dread on Richard's face unsettled her more than anything.

"Perhaps...perhaps not." Fear was in Richard's every breath, the same fear that always dwelled in the back of his mind that someday Philippe might be killed while fighting the battle that Richard was meant to fight. This didn't set well with Richard...not at all.

They entered the great hall so fast that their mere presence startled everyone who thought they were on their way to the hut. Richard spotted Caitrina who was holding Joanna and helping her walk.

He was quick to her side, and giving no thought as how to tell her about this, he simply blurted, "Caitrina, I have word that Philippe has been wounded—make haste for I leave shortly."

The color drained from Caitrina's face. "I'll pack me medicine pouch and be right down." She handed Joanna to Mary Clair. And just like that, Caitrina was out the chamber and gone from their sight.

Richard turned his attention to his squire Bertrand. "Hasten to the stables and have our mounts saddled. I want two more soldiers with us. See to it and be quick!"

"Coont, I'll be going with ye." Macadie stood and tweaked Maude under the chin. "Dinna look so worrit, fer I'll return shortly."

"Well, those be words I expect ye to live by, Macadie Gunn. And now, let us go and pack your saddlebag." They followed Richard and Deirdre from the chamber.

Holding her skirt off the floor, Deirdre swiftly padded alongside Richard, the fresh rushes crunching beneath her shoes. "Mayhap, I should come with ye?"

"Non, I want you to remain here so that I'll not have to worry about you as well as Philippe. David is here. So is Gordon who is your protector until I return. Guards are posted."

Deirdre took one of Richard's spare tunic shirts from the clothes chest and rolled it into a tight roll. When finished, she handed it to Richard, who along with a few other personal items crammed everything into his saddlebag. He glanced at her as he fastened his leather weapons belt about his waist.

"Chéri, do not worry, for I'll be safe."

"I dinna worry about myself. 'Tis ye that makes my heart sad. Both ye and Philippe will be in my prayers. Would that ye come back as soon as ye can?"

"Oui, I do not know what I face. Perhaps Philippe is not wounded very bad and I can bring him back here to heal." But in his mind, his brother was dying and he couldn't shake the image.

They met at the stables. Macadie hurried over to his mount and tied his saddlebag to the back of the saddle. His horse, a brown gelding, nosed his shoulder. Macadie ran a quick hand down the horse's white star. He then removed his weapons holster and secured it to the saddle's pommel.

Richard did the same to Saladin. And when finished he turned to Deirdre. She was trying to be brave, but he could read the angst in her eyes. Pushing all other thoughts from his mind but her, he clasped her body against his. Nestling his cheek against the side of her face, he drew in the lavender floral scent of her hair, putting it to mind for future re-membrances of this woman he so loved. His hands framed the sides of her face as he stared into her eyes.

"Crichton Castle is but a hard days ride from here. As soon as I arrive and appraise the situation, I'll send you a message." Richard dipped his head to claim a kiss from her. Their lips met as the taste of the other embedded deep into their minds.

"Richard?" she hesitated. "What was it ye wanted to tell me when I was bathing Joanna? I dinna think I can let ye go and not know the full of it."

"I meant to tell you that I was leaving to go after your pardon, and Wrothbury. But that too will have to wait," he said with irony.

"One would think that ye two will be apart fer years instead of sever-al days," Caitrina said with a smile, but her eyes betrayed the unease she was feeling for her own husband.

Realizing this, Deirdre left Richard's side and approached Caitrina who was waiting beside her mare. Giving Caitrina a strong hug, Deirdre tried to sooth her fears.

"Yer man will be well, I deem it so. Philippe's as strong as Richard, ye know that, aye."

"Aye, I pray 'twill be so," Caitrina said in a firm believing voice.

Macadie approached to help Caitrina mount. "Here ye be, Trina, lass," he said, and forming a stirrup with his hands he lifted her up into the saddle. While he secured her medicine bag, she took the reins within her hands.

Deirdre walked alongside Richard's horse until they were halfway to the clan's village. Richard leaned from Saladin to tilt her chin up and force a smile from her. "I'll return soon. Keep Philippe and all of us in your prayers." He kneed Saladin urging him into a fast gallop.

A trace of dust lifted behind Richard's small party as they rode into a day of bright blue sky and russet hues. Deirdre stood watching. When they crested the sloping rise, Richard turned in his saddle and waved. She lifted her arm high in return before he dropped from view.

His dust was still in the air when loneliness settled around her like a shroud. A feeling she hadn't dealt with since her time in the cage. The cage brought Wrothbury to mind, a man she'd rather not think about. She wanted happiness, not hell. And happiness meant the child in her womb. It meant her daily life with Richard, Joanna, loved ones, and friends.

Deirdre wanted to tell her brother about Philippe de Laci. Continuing on to David's, Deirdre caressed the bulge of her stomach, feeling the child move. Carrying Richard's child of love was so different than when she carried Joanna. Her guilt over hating Joanna while in her womb was long gone. God had forgiven her for such vile feelings, and blessed her with a beautiful daughter.

Smoke drifted from the many cooking fires next to the cottages and an occasional woman or man called out hello. Several hounds ran over to greet her, barking as they came on. Bess stood in front of the community oven removing loaves of baked bread. The smell was mouthwatering. She smiled and waving Deirdre over, gave her a loaf. It wouldn't be long before they had to abandon the outdoor fires and turn to their indoor fireplaces. Seonaid already had.

Her brother, with Gordon's help, had been hunting daily, trying to get enough meat into the larders for the winter. They would bring in rabbits and the occasional deer. Some of the hogs had been slaughtered and were hanging in the rafters of the main smokehouse. Harvest had been good. They had flour in barrels, salt, and honey combs from the clan's hives.

She knocked on David's door and was welcomed by cooking smells and Seonaid's wide smile. "Hello, Seonaid. This is from Bess." She handed the loaf to her sister by marriage. David was sitting in his chair removing his boots and appeared as content as a cat eating a bird. Gordon, looking surprised to see Deirdre alone, stood.

Deirdre entered the warm home of her family and shut the door behind her.

Wrothbury couldn't have been more pleased with himself if he'd put on a mummers show for the King of England and it had come off without a hitch. He chuckled with glee at how easy this plan was. If one wanted something done right, then they best get off their arse and take part in the planning and the participation. He'd done just that.

Watching from the steep hillside all that went on at Foxlair and the village, he fought not to give himself too much credit. With a sly wide smile, he glanced at his two companions. Hawk, the Scotsman, and Roger Hackward. Hawk had been at Philippe de Laci's siege, and was the very man who just hours ago had been a most effective messenger in getting rid of Richard de Laci, Wrothbury's French adversary.

Roger turned out to be a beast of a man who didn't care who he killed, never challenged the earl's orders, and had turned out to be more efficient than John Ward ever was.

Wrothbury watched his wife riding behind a young Scotsman as they headed toward the castle. The same warrior, he noticed, was always around snooping here and there, trailing his wife like a cocklebur stuck to wool. Another small obstacle to get rid of. A mere flea on the dog. It wasn't long before Deirdre and her companion disappeared around the bend and out of sight. And, it wouldn't be long before he had Joanna back at Wrothbury Castle where she belonged. His heir, the only person in this wretched life he could rightly say held a place in his heart. He snickered…that is…if he had a heart, for many thought his chest was bare of such an organ.

Upon Wrothbury's orders, they turned their horses around and headed back to the place under a giant tree where they'd made camp a few hours before. Thinking of this as his last campaign, he craved rest. His leg pained him, sent slices of agony up his body until he wanted to cut it off. He would post a guard to make sure that Count Strasbourg wouldn't be coming back anytime soon. There would be no saviors this time, no one to take the head from his hired men. Time was on his side.

Philippe ordered an archer up, and the man stood close by, waiting as a message was being wrapped around the arrow's shaft. On Philippe's order, he fired the arrow to arc high over the battlement. The wait began to see if Ewan Crichton, the Lord of Crichton Castle would concede defeat and give into Philippe's concessions written on the parchment. The wait wasn't very long in coming when an answering arrow with the missive now in flames was sent back, landing within feet of Philippe. And then as if that wasn't sufficient of an answer, a volley of arrows hissed over the wall and Philippe's men scrambled to take cover. Some were not so fortunate and their loud screams ricochet around the castle grounds.

Philippe, not to be deterred, and determined to end the siege this day, returned the earl's answer with one even more deadly. He ordered the trebuchets loaded and the battering ram brought forth.

"Fire!" Etienne yelled. The trebuchets let loose with giant boulders that sailed skyward, arching high, the logistics figured correctly as the boulders smashed against the stone walls, shaking the castle, crumbling the stout crenellations that fell off in large chunks. Scaling ladders, not yet used, were scattered around the ground.

Philippe could hardly breathe for the foul stench that corrupted the air. Nothing could mask the devastation wrought by the siege. The scorched ground smoldered. All the nearby foliage had been ripped from the earth and the trees cut down to create fires for his troops. Open latrines and the decaying dead from inside and outside the castle turned the air thick with a putrid stench that made stomachs churn.

For the better part of the month, some of his soldiers had been tunneling underneath one of the castle's four towers. Those men had scrambled back out of the tunnel to safety. They grouped around Philippe and stood as if holding their breath. Suddenly the stones holding the great tower started to give. Slowly and methodically, it started with small creaks and groans. The tower started sinking, leaning at an odd angle. Soldiers manning the tower's battlements screamed and tumbled over the edge plunging to their deaths. Stones crumbled as the tower cracked open in a rush of flying debris. Dust created a thick haze, blinding and choking those nearby.

Smelling victory, a smile creased the dirt on Philippe's mouth.

Soldiers brought the battering ram into position as its giant wheels rumbled across the terrain. From his horse, Philippe pointed to Etienne as to the placement of the ram with its deadly point of steel. His soldiers took up position, six on each side of the wagon, awaiting his orders. Philippe signaled the men next to the battering ram. The Earl's men on the castle's front battlement and in a heroic effort to defend the dying castle, began firing arrows at the men around the ram. Expecting this halfhearted volley of arrows, they quickly threw up their shields.

The ram, made with French sophistication was free floating with pulleys and chains, allowing the ram to be swung heavily against the thick gates of wood and metal. The steel covered tip jarred the very countryside as it pounded the gate. But the large thick gate withstood battering after battering until Philippe began yelling at the men to swing the ram harder and faster. The battering jarred Philippe to his very core until with a great rending of wood, the gate finally caved in. Philippe, with his sword pulled, allowed his men to swarm around him, and like the hordes from Hell, enter the castle grounds, taking on and bringing to ground the earl's soldiers still braving it to the end. But the fight was short-lived as the remaining garrison laid down their weapons.

Philippe barked out commands concerning the hapless people left within the castle during the siege. He ordered the inhabitants rounded up, dividing women and children from the men and tried to make sure the children were not hurt.

Soldiers carried forth a man's limp corpse and unceremoniously dumped it amidst the rubble of the courtyard. The wound to his chest bled through the gash in his armor. His arms splayed out beside him as though he was nailed to the cross. From the man's heraldry, Philippe recognized Ewan Crichton. A man who wouldn't be dead if he'd aligned himself with the Bruce and stayed true.

A fitting end for a traitor, Philippe thought.

Dark smoke roiled out from the castle's keep to add to the already dusk darkening day. Philippe's men were making it uninhabitable for any English that thought to try and re-garrison it. They had moved the battering ram inside and were effectively using it to pound holes in the inner walls. Only two towers remained as testimony of the castle's once mighty fortifications.

Leaving Etienne in charge, Philippe was at long last able to ride back to his tent where he peeled back the flap and quickly closed it against the foul smell that permeated everything around the castle. He thought to never get the smell out of his nostrils. Henri, his squire, had already lit a crescent oil lamp that hung from the center pole. The lamp's meager flame barely lit the interior, but it was better than sitting in the dark. Henri approached him with a goblet of spiced wine of which Philippe thankfully accepted. He sank down upon the campstool. Quickly downing the drink, he held the goblet out for more.

"Milord, let me remove your armor."

"One moment, Henri," Philippe said as his eyes slid shut with fatigue.

"Perhaps a quick wash-up will make you feel somewhat better, oui?" Henri offered.

Although wanting to cleanse the blood from his face and hands Philippe couldn't move. As darkness surrounded his small tent, he slipped into a sound sleep and didn't hear the horses approaching.

"Philippe," Richard bellowed, thrusting open the tent flap.

Henri already had his sword pulled, but recognizing Count Strasbourg promptly leaned it against the side of the tent.

"How bad are you hurt—Christ Jesus, the fear that rode with me has been most heavy. Philippe?" Richard grabbed Philippe by the arm and shook him. "Are you wounded or is the blood on you from the siege?"

Philippe shot Richard a puzzled look, his mind unable to accept the fact that his brother now stood before him.

Caitrina entered the tent and hurried to Philippe's side where she felt every place there was blood. "My love is not wounded. His blood is from others." She let out a long sigh of relief and sagged against him.

"Chéri, what are you doing here?" he asked, glancing at them both. "What has happened, Richard, to bring you and my wife to this pest hole?" He clasped Caitrina against him.

"Philippe—I received this message from Etienne saying you were wounded and asking for me. I brought Caitrina with me, so she could be by your side." He handed the message to his brother.

"This can't be from Etienne, he wouldn't send an untruth."

Realization slammed into Richard with chilling force. "Jesú. I've been duped. Wrothbury has done this—he's lured me away from Deirdre."

Richard started for the tent flap when Philippe shot to his feet and stopped him from barreling outside. Richard struggled against his brother's strong grip, but Philippe put his weight into his hold and prevented Richard from making a mad dash into the dark night.

"Richard—sit down and talk to me," Philippe ordered, and was relieved when Richard obeyed.

Macadie, along with Bertrand and Etienne, entered the tent. Caitrina, standing next to Philippe listened to Richard telling about the man that delivered the missive. When finished, Philippe put the note into Etienne's outstretched hand.

A quick glance had Etienne shaking his head. "Milord," he said. "I know but a few words to write in my native French. Nor do I understand this heathen English that has been yelled down at me from the castle's battlements for these past months."

Richard rubbed his forehead, shaking his head in disbelief at his own stupidity. But he didn't mire himself in self-recrimination for long. He couldn't afford to. Instead, he got to his feet and focused on Philippe.

"Give me a fast horse. Saladin's been ridden into the ground. If I leave now, I can reach Foxlair before noon on the morrow. How I fell for this ruse, I cannot explain."

"Could it be because you are a mere mortal who has the failings of men since God created mankind?" Philippe gave him a wry smile. "I'll supply you with torches to guide your way. How about soldiers? Wrothbury is hardly ever without an army of sorts. Is David Brodie with the Bruce?"

"Nay, he's at Foxlair. I ordered Gordon Bryce to keep Deirdre secure."

Caitrina spoke up. "Deirdre's in gude hands. Both men would give their life for her."

Richard nodded. "I agree…but still. Philippe, give me whatever men you can spare. I must leave now—and pray to God that I'm not too late." Richard clasped his brother's hand within his and took his leave from Philippe.

Richard, Macadie, and Bertrand followed Henri to the supply tent for torches. Etienne went to round up some men.

Philippe, with Caitrina gathered close to him, watched the flames from Richard's torches grow smaller, and finally the flames winked out of sight to leave them staring into inky blackness.

"I should have gone with my brother, but I have much to do here. I pray that all is well. I'm most unsettled that he was lured away with false pretenses that I was wounded. Someone here stole one of my wax seals and devised a well thought-out plan." Reaching the tent, he opened the flap and allowed Caitrina to pass in front of him.

Caitrina turned to offer him a sweet smile. "Och…Philippe de Laci, ye had me afraid that I was going to be a widow before our time together was verra long."

He sat on the campstool and pulled her onto his lap, situating her to his liking. "I know that I stink and am filthy, but nothing would please me more than for you to give me a kiss, and then a good wash-up. Oui?"

"Aye, that would please me. Just tell me where the water is." When she started to scurry from his lap, he held her tight. "Not so fast, wife, how about that kiss I so desire? And Henri can bring the water."

She gave him his desire with a kiss that enflamed him, made him crave more and wish to the Heavens he was not sitting in a tent with the stench of the siege clinging to him like the brambles from a bush. He finally let her go and order his squire to bring the water.

It wasn't long before Henri handed Catrina a bucket of brackish looking water. Philippe gave himself up to his wife's fussing hands, basking in the feel of the rough washcloth on his face as she tried to clean the worst of it away.

"Wife, the Bruce makes plans to head for Galloway and attack it. He could use me beside him. I know Richard wants me to return to France with him, but—"

"Are ye saying that ye do not know what to do? France or Scotland?"

"You are most wise. Falaise is Richard's home. He has been generous with Valentin and me by allowing…no…insisting that we live there. By rights, we have no claim. I long for something of my own."

"Ye want yer own hearth, aye?"

"Oui. Besides, Scotland still needs me."

"Philippe de Laci, I'll go where ye go, and be the happier for it. But right now, we need to pray for Deirdre and Richard." She cradled his head against her bosom.

Richard's arm felt to break from holding the torch, its flame showing him the way. His eyes were constantly on Macadie's back who was in front of him, leading their small party, taking them in an unfamiliar but shorter route to Foxlair. A missive, not even in Etienne's handwriting, but one of a stranger had hooked him like a fish. A lure with the pretense of a wounded loved one. Not only a fool did he feel, but his fear for Deirdre and others at the village had settled about him like the dark that cloaked them, slowing their progress, and at times hobbling their horses to a crawl.

He switched hands, moving the torch to his left and the reins to his right. "Macadie, I'm lost. I'm not so sure about this shortcut, what good will it do if you are the only one who knows the way? What if we're separated? I'll be like a leaf bobbing away in a stream. Can we not move any faster?"

"Oh—aye, Coont. I'm supposing if I could fly like a night owl, I would. But fer now yer jest goin' to have to depend on me to get ye back to Foxlair before the sun rises. Ye can always look at the stars and know we head due north"

The only sound was the horses' hooves striking the ground, their heavy breathing, and the torch flames that spewed black smoke from the tips. Philippe's loaned soldiers struggled to stay with the group but they kept lagging behind.

His arm now trembling with the effort of holding the torch aloft, Richard started to switch hands again when Macadie simply disappeared in front of his eyes, making Richard blink and stop his horse.

"Dinna come this way…" Macadie yelled out, to be followed by loud crashing, loud swearing, and the shrill neighing of his terrified horse.

But the warning came too late for Bertrand, who half asleep in the saddle, plummeted down the embankment. "Merde!" he roared as the sound of breaking foliage and rolling rocks accompanied his journey.

Richard was fast off the borrowed gelding, and threw himself to the ground to peer down the embankment.

Macadie held his torch aloft as he peered back up. "I dinna remember this being here, a flood must have made it," he said sheepishly and pulled gold colored leaves and twigs from his hair.

Rubbing his hip and shoulder, Bertrand limped over to stand next to Macadie. "Milord, I'm hurt and my horse has a broken leg."

"Coont, ye must go on. Take some of the soldiers and leave others to help pull us out. We'll catch up."

"Then I leave you to follow." Richard was quick to take him up on his offer and would never think to do so had it not been for Deirdre and his haste to get to her.

With only the stars to guide him, Richard continued his mad journey through the dark night.

23 Beware Evil Is Present

Deirdre, along with Gordon who practically dogged her every step, came out of the castle and into the garden area. Gordon, her appointed protector, took his duty seriously. After Richard rode away yesterday, Gordon informed her that she wasn't to go anywhere outside by herself.

She hadn't slept well having been jarred out of her sleep by a nightmare that ripped a loud scream from her. She was dead and floating in a pond. Wrothbury sat gloating on the bank holding Joanna and making her wave goodbye at Deirdre. Richard was nowhere to be seen. She shivered at the remembrance, praying it wasn't an omen, and pulled her cloak tighter. A quick glance at Gordon who leaned against a nearby tree trunk made her feel silly especially when he grinned at her and nonchalantly crossed his arms.

Deirdre aimlessly strolled around the pebbled path. Years ago the area next to the path held the herb garden that gave off heady fragrances. Despite the tall stockade that skirted Foxlair's three sides, the garden area had yet a smaller fence to keep out the animals, both domesticated and wild, that could come down the steep hillside behind the castle. Located on the west side of Foxlair, the garden could be gotten to by several different ways. One of them was coming out a little used side door, another was to come through the stockade and go past the stables.

She glanced around the barren garden that had once been hers to plant and tend. Neglected and never planted since Wrothbury took her, it was a sad looking site. She would have to ask Seonaid for some dried Lavender to sprinkle amidst the newly strewn rushes.

Deirdre picked a burnished leaf from the tree. Finding its brilliant red color fascinating, she twirled the leaf by the stem.

The baby moved within her, small fluttery movements that reminded her of a butterfly's wings, but ones that brought a soft smile to her face. She prayed to give Richard a son. Daughters could follow, but for him to have the heir he so longed for was a nightly prayer for her. "Ah, my wee bairn, I hope that yer papa will return safely and soon." She already longed to touch Richard. To gaze into his eyes that mirrored back his love for her.

"Milady." Mary Clair joined her, breaking into her musing. "I think ye need to go back inside. The day is chilly even with your heavy cloak." Shivering, she reached out and fussed with Deirdre's cloak, adjusting it, pulling it tight.

Deirdre grabbed the woman's hands that fidgeted about her. "Nay, Mary Clair, I do enjoy being out here so much. See, the sky is clear and 'tis truly warm this day. Is that not right, Gordon?"

"Aye, most pleasant. 'Tis gude hunting weather." Gordon had moved from the tree to stand next to Mary Clair.

"Is Maudie with Joanna? Ye know she will not stay abed now and gets into everything. It willna be long before she will be running down the halls."

"Maude is with her. Joanna is a joy to us all is she not?"

Mary Clair gave Gordon a flirty little look that made Deirdre wonder if Richard's squire, Bertrand, was truly the right choice for her. Deirdre's gaze went between the two, recognizing love in the smile Mary Clair had for him. And the same for Gordon, whose feelings shone in the sparkle of his eyes as they roamed over the pretty maiden. Deirdre believed a talk was in order. She would tell Mary Clair that if Gordon was the man she truly loved then she should remain here in Scotland with him. Deirdre wanted the maid to follow her heart.

Deirdre sat on the bench that her father had made for her mam so long ago. Voices filtered over the gate just as David pushed it open, allowing Andrew and Blake past him. Blake rode a stick hobbyhorse that had a fine tassel of red hitting against its forehead.

Gordon grinned, watching them enter. "Hello, David."

"Gordon," David said. "Gude to see ye out here with Deedee."

Deirdre smiled as Blake pulled his horse up next to her and made a big pretense of dismounting. The horse clattered to the ground. Blake got on the bench beside Deirdre. Andrew took his place on the other side of her and got comfortable.

Andrew shyly pointed at her stomach. "Will the babe be here soon, Aunt Deedee?"

His curiosity brought a smile to Deirdre. Seonaid had just recently delighted everyone when she shared that she was also with child and due around two months after Deirdre. "Not until spring, Andrew. Ye must have patience. And just think, yer going to have a baby brother or sister."

"Nay—I dinna want another. Deedee and Blake are always followin' me."

"Not me, Andrew," Blake defended himself as he broke into an engaging grin.

Deirdre put her arms around the dark-haired boys and laughingly pulled them close. "Ye sound like yer papa. I used to follow him everywhere and he grumbled something fierce."

"'Tis true, Aunt Deedee?"

"Oh—aye, 'tis true. Just ask yer papa."

"Yer aunt was a pest, that is fer sure." David winked at her.

"Aye, he thinks so. Yer papa even blamed me when he couldna hit a rabbit with his bow and arrow. A standing rabbit at that." Deirdre giggled at David's look of betrayal, and the amused grin on Andrew's.

Gordon grinned at Mary Clair before turning to Deirdre. "Milady, since David is here to watch out for ye, I'm going to check around the castle to make sure all is secure. But mayhap I should stay here, if what ye say about David's aim is true." He laughed at David's scowl, his barb hitting home.

"Yer a wit, Gordon, or ye try to be." David clapped his friend on the back. "Thanks for yer help. Being inside a warm castle is better than laying siege to castles with Scotland's king, dinna ye agree?"

Gordon nodded and smiled. "Fer certes." He sheathed his claymore and walked away.

"Milady, I would like to go visit Seonaid. Would that be all right to do?" Mary Clair asked.

"Aye. Please tell Seonaid that Bess has weaved enough wool to cut David a new vest."

"That I will."

David picked Blake up off the bench and placed him next to his stick horse. He spoke to the maid. "Mary Clair, take Blake with ye. Andrew, go along with them."

"Ah...Papa. Let me stay," Andrew pleaded.

David relented. "All right, this time only."

"Let me stay too, Papa," Blake whined.

David shook his head. "Andrew is older and can do things ye can't."

Blake pushed Andrew. "Stop it, Blake," Andrew said and pushed him back.

"Come, Blake. Stop fightin' with yer brother." Mary Clair said holding out her hand to him. "Get your play pony. Let's go see if your mam has a honey cake."

Blake picked up his wooden horse and dragged it by its cloth mane. When they started for the gate, Blake stuck his tongue out at Andrew. His young voice bounced back confirming that indeed his mam had honey cakes in the larder.

But not even the lure of a proposed honey cake could make Andrew leave his spot next to Deirdre.

David sat next to her and stretched out his long legs. "I can only hope that Philippe de Laci isna hurt too bad. He is a goodly man."

"I wish I could have gone with Richard. He did promise to return in a few days. D'ye think that to be true?"

Her brother stroked his dark whiskers and shrugged. "'Tis hard to say. War is war. And if ye have never fought a battle, ye will never know what I speak of. A siege is even more savage than men fighting on an open battlefield."

"Davey, I canna think of being in a worse situation then the day our clan was attacked. I was waged war upon that day as well as every man that stood here fighting, aye?"

"Yer right."

"But certainly there is no sign that he…" her words trailed off as the gate creaked open, and Bonnar entered.

"Uncle Bonnar." Andrew hopped off the bench and was next to Bonnar in an instant.

Bonnar ruffled Andrew's dark hair. "How are ye, Andrew."

The last she'd seen of Bonnar was when she was wounded and he'd tried to put things right with her about that day, that horrible day that was so etched in everyone's mind. Perhaps they could talk. Perhaps she had it in her heart to forgive him at last. He did save her life and Richard's at the waterfall. She was happy. Why shouldn't Bonnar be the same? He looked tired, his clothing stained like he'd been traveling without rest. The lines next to his mouth were deeply grooved, making him appear older. He chose that moment to flash a grin at them. Suddenly he was the handsome Bonnar of old.

Delighted, David stood to greet his friend. "I expect the Brus has sent ye to bring me back into the fold, has he no'?"

"Aye, our king now controls most of the castles in the south of Scotland. He is planning to attack Galloway and sends for you. The Brus's brother has captured Rutherglen." He gaze met Deirdre's. "Deirdre, ye look verra well."

"Bonnar." Deirdre held out her hand and welcomed him but couldn't help but notice how his brows pinched together when his gaze dropped to her thickening waist. He took the empty place next to her on the bench.

"Ye've recovered from yer attack, aye?" he said to her.

"That I have. But we received word yesterday that Philippe de Laci's been injured. Richard has left to join him at Crichton Castle."

"How bad?"

Deirdre told Bonnar about the messenger and that was all they really knew.

"Then Count Strasbourg hasn't gone to take back yer pardon from Wrothbury, 'tis true?"

At the mention of Wrothbury's name her flesh rose on her skin. "Aye. But Richard has given that up. He plans to go to London and put my case before the king and to tell him that Wrothbury has withheld my pardon. Alas, every time Richard tries to leave for England something happens to pull him in a different direction. The English call me a murderess. Damn the English to Hell, and damn Wrothbury for ever starting this," she spewed out her words in great agitation.

"There now, Deedee, dinna get yerself riled," David said. "Ye are as safe here as anywhere. Gordon is with ye. Richard will return soon. Bonnar, tell me more of the Brus."

"Our king has been a verra busy man. He has routed the Lord of Argyll and took his castle, Dunstaffnage. John Macdougall still paying homage to Edward, England's king, tried to ambush the Brus at the Pass of Brander. Our king was ready and had them surrounded before they knew what was about." Bonnar smashed his one fist loudly against his palm. "Stopped them dead."

"He has both the Macdougall's, then?" David asked.

"Nay, they signed a truce with the Brus but high tailed it to Ireland before the ink was dry. I wonder when our king will learn he canna trust the Scots who have been against him from the start."

"Ye mean Scotsmen fight against Scotsmen?" Andrew asked, his voice filled with disbelief.

"Aye, lad, sorry to say there is, and just when ye think they are friend they turn out to be foe. Yer King Robert is hard put to tell the difference at times," Bonnar said.

"What of the English King Edward?" Deirdre broke into their conversation.

Bonnar's dark eyes glanced her way. "Rumor has it that he keeps putting off a campaign against us. England's young king has not the stomach or prowess to fight like his father. He leaves Scotland's own earls and barons to fight against our crown."

"Then, the fighting will never cease will it? I dinna think none of us to see a free and peaceful Scotland," Deirdre said.

The two men could only meet each other's stare; each knowing Deirdre spoke the truth. Their life would be none other, and they would no doubt die in a field covered with blood, and all for a cause that was written in the wind and carried from man to man until Scotland was bled dry of her young and willing.

Andrew, apparently hearing enough grownup talk, popped to his feet with the agility of youth and said he was going to find Uncle Gordon. He clanged the gate behind him.

Yawning, David stood and stretched his long body. "Come then, Bonnar, let us go hunting and see what meat we can flush out for Seonaid to cook. Deedee, ye go in the keep. Dinna come outside without Gordon. D'ye understand what I say? Send Andrew home as well."

"Aye, Davey. Ye know I go nowhere without Gordon. Good day to ye, Bonnar."

They waited until she made her way to the side door that led into the castle. Upon opening the heavy door, she waved at them. She stepped inside the castle's comforting warmth that Richard had turned it into. He had organized Foxlair into a working demesne, and had suggested to

David to make the most of the sheep, raise more, and sell the wool produced from them. Richard hired servants for the castle, a good cook being one of them. He'd set up a working structure within the castle where everyone knew his or her duties.

The women of the clan had recently taken over a small chamber, and would gather to work on their sewing where they weaved wool and cut cloth for winter clothing. Richard told her of the beautiful materials that he imported from the Far East, and of the fine wool that was made at Falaise. He promised once they were back at Falaise, he would have gowns made for her from the finest silk material found in the Orient.

Oh…Gore, Richard love.

The mouthwatering smell of fish and leeks was strong and Deirdre thought to get a bowl of stew, but first she wanted to check on Joanna. Hastening to the back stairwell, she lifted her skirt and started up the stairs. She'd barely reached the top step when a muffled cry echoed up to her. Pausing to listen, and thinking it to be Joanna, she quickly went down the hallway to her chamber where she sought Joanna's cradle. Finding it empty, she thought that either Maude or the wet nurse must have her. Joanna was eating solids and she'd developed a taste for hot porridge, perhaps they were feeding her.

In a hurry to join them, she removed her cloak and hung it on a wall peg. Deirdre was almost to the bottom of the spiral staircase when she heard a different noise, but most familiar. A soft swish, the sound of an armored soldier. Gordon wore no chain mail, none of the Scots did. The familiar prick of fear goose fleshed her skin. Her hand covered her mouth and her limbs went numb. Something made her remain silent.

Where was Gordon?

The stairs gradual spiral blocked any view of the main floor. Easing her foot down onto the bottom step, she paused to peer around the wall of mortar and stone. Not seeing anything out of the ordinary, she made her way into the great hall that was empty. Usually someone was there, chatting, playing chess, or eating a cold meal. But then without Richard,

Caitrina, Macadie, and all the others gone, only a handful of women remained. And most of them were now at David's visiting with Seonaid.

Deirdre started toward the kitchen when she gasped and suppressed her scream. Maude's sprawled body blocked the doorway. Bowls of spilt porridge and stew soaked into her skirt. The floor became slick around her. She bled from a cut above her left temple. Gasping in fear, praying that her friend wasn't dead, Deirdre quickly dropped to her knees.

"Maude," she whispered in her friend's ear, "Maudie, can ye hear me?"

Maude's eyes fluttered open, their brown depths glazed with pain. "Milady," she moaned, "Roger Hackward…here…inside…"

"Shh…Maude, can ye get to yer feet?" She put a hand under Maude's head.

"Nay. Get Joanna…go to David's…"

"Where is Joanna? Ye need help."

"I hid her inside the chest. Over there…hurry…"

Placing Maude's head back down, Deirdre said, "I'll get help." With a last glance at Maude, Deirdre hurried to the chest and opened the lid. Joanna's eyes lit up and she giggled at her mam.

"Mam," she squealed.

Deirdre tried to hush her. "Shhh, baby, mam's here with ye."

Joanna didn't understand and laughed loud enough to alert Roger of their whereabouts.

Snatching Joanna up, and again hearing the faint chink of chain mail close by, she put her hand over Joanna's mouth and swiftly went into the kitchen and out the door that led to the ovens that were kept apart from the main structure. Knowing if she wanted to live she had to keep her wits about her and couldn't allow herself to panic. One glance at Joanna's bobbing curls and her large curious eyes, made Deirdre move with haste. She left the castle through the door normally used only by the cook, and came out in the opposite direction of the village.

Sitting Joanna down on the ground, Deirdre crouched behind a large shrub and peered around it. A man eased through the door. He paused to remove his helmet. Mother of God, Deirdre gulped. Maude was right, it was Roger Hackward. He studied the area then went in the opposite direction of her.

Joanna started to crawl away but Deirdre captured her back. In terror, she clutched Joanna hard against her bosom. Fleeing through the rear gate, she tripped and fell over something hard. Her arms clamped tight around Joanna, keeping her from getting hurt. Deirdre bounced directly on her pelvis. Pain laced up her back. She suppressed the scream that wanted to tear from her. She'd fallen over Gordon's body. His face was a mask of surprise, his blue eyes glazed. Her gown soaked up Gordon's blood that had drained out through the savage slit across his throat.

Uttering a prayer, she reached over and shut his eyelids. Somehow, she managed to drag to her feet and lift Joanna into her arms. The pain in her back was unbearable. But one look at Joanna's rounded eyes, made Deirdre determined to get them both to safety.

Joanna must have felt Deirdre's fear, for her face screwed up and her mouth started to quiver. Deirdre made a face at her trying to keep her from crying.

Suddenly, Andrew whom she'd forgotten about was beside her and whispered in a trembling voice, "Auntie Dee, what can I do?" His normal bravado squelched by the severity of the situation. Tears cut through the dirt on his cheeks.

Her hand groped his arm as she urged, "Andrew—Sweet Jesus! Run—lad—run! Get yer father and Bonnar. They left to go hunting—hurry."

"What of ye, Auntie?"

"I'll be right behind ye, but ye can move much faster without me. Go!"

Being a child of Scotland, Andrew didn't need to be told again. Running in a low crouch, he scurried toward home.

Deirdre prayed he'd bring help and soon.

With Joanna clinging to her like a burr, Deirdre ran down the road, her feet striking against the ground. The village never looked so far away. She glanced over her shoulder to see that Roger was gaining on her. Another man had joined him. She recognized him to be the messenger from yesterday. He'd falsely lured Richard away from her.

She tried outdistancing them. But carrying Joanna who had a strangle hold around her neck, and the pain radiating up her back proved too much. She was forced to slow down.

Knowing they wanted her and not Joanna, Deirdre veered off the road. She plopped Joanna down amidst a thick pile of leaves at the base of a tree.

"Stay here baby, stay here," she cautioned.

Joanna stretched her arms toward Deirdre and puckered up. Deirdre turned her back on her daughter and ran. The pain in her side became intense. She prayed for the babe in her womb.

They caught up with her on the road. Hemming her in with their horses, Roger was in front of her while the messenger was behind her, his horse's breath hot against her neck. Using their horses as weapons they pushed menacingly close to her.

"David—help me," she screamed.

Deirdre glanced to see a shrieking Joanna crawling toward her. Her daughter's hands and knees plowed through the leaves, sending red and gold into the air.

"Dinna do this—Roger—I beg ye."

His answer was to un-loop his battle-ax from the pommel and raise it high. "Wrothbury has asked for your head," he shouted. "I'll deliver it to him along with that spawn ye carry in yer belly."

Joanna, innocent of the danger surrounding her, continued to crawl, until, crying, she sat in the road and waved her arms up and down.

"Mam...mam...mam," she sobbed.

Seeing that Joanna was in danger of being trampled by the anxious horses, Deirdre pointed at Joanna and yelled. "Roger Hackward, watch what ye do. Harm Wrothbury's wee daughter, he'll have yer heads.''

The men glanced around for the baby. Deirdre used the distraction to surprise Roger and ducked between the two mounts. She scooped up Joanna. She walked backwards, keeping her eyes on the men who menacingly urged their horses toward her. In despair and with no other options, she sat Joanna back down and away from their horses.

Like a rabbit trying to evade a fox, she darted around the trees using them as shields, until finally, she ran out of trees. Her chest heaved with pain. She turned to face Roger, praying his blow would be swift and that Joanna would never remember this day.

Her baby moved within her womb. Richard would never see his child and that thought was as sharp as the blade coming at her.

Richard…oh God…Richard.

She stood with her head high, tears hot on her cheeks. She looked beyond Roger's flashing blade to see Joanna trying to stand amongst the russet leaves. On wobbly legs Joanna took one step, two, holding out her arms, the sun haloing her red-gold hair.

Deirdre squeezed her eyes shut and waited for the ax to strike. Praying it would be fast and his aim true.

"No—!" A scream penetrated the air.

Her eyes popped open to see Bonnar's horse collide with Roger's. Bonnar leaped at Roger taking him to the ground. Their grunts loud as they rolled in the dirt and leaves.

Deirdre tried to see what was happening, but the frightened horses kept shifting, blocking her view. She glimpsed Bonnar on his feet and fighting. When he turned to block a swing from Roger's ax, his tunic was rent and covered with blood. Too much blood. The red stain kept spreading. He pressed his hand against his middle and tried to hold his claymore with one hand. Roger easily knocked it away. Bonnar's knees buckled under him and he went down. For a moment his eyes locked onto hers, pleading, and then he fell forward, flat on the ground.

"Bonnar," Deirdre screamed, her air chocked off with fear.

Not bothering to deal Bonnar a final chop, Roger turned toward her. She stared at him. "Why?"

"Because I work for your husband. I do as he bids. I owe Miles yer death." Roger advanced toward her. He held his bloody ax aloft with both hands. Just as he started to swing, an arrow hissed through the air piercing his neck. Roger gurgled, his hands fought the arrow. He glared at Deirdre before pitching face first into dead leaves and thick grass.

A second shot took the fleeing messenger off his horse to land on the road. David rode up, his eyes shifting between both men. He held his bow and arrow still strung for another shot. Andrew, with his arms wrapped tight around David's waist, peeked around his da's body.

"Andrew, get Joanna," David ordered. Reaching behind him he grasped Andrew by the arm and dropped him to the ground. David dismounted in haste and was quick to his sister's side. "Are ye hurt?"

"Nay...but Bonnar is," she said, still shaking from her ordeal.

They knelt beside Bonnar who opened his eyes and stared at both sister and brother. His gaze lingered on Deirdre.

Tears blurred her vision. "Bonnar, ye saved my life, and the life of my wee bairn...I'll never forget ye for this." Her hand caressed his cheek.

A trickle of blood crept from the corner of his mouth as he fought to speak, "...forgive me...that day...Deedee?" he whispered.

"Aye, Bonnar...I forgive ye...I forgive ye. I wanted to tell ye so back in the garden," she babbled and cried at the same time. "Dinna die..." She pressed her lips to his, felt the soft rush of his warm breath against her mouth. He was gone. She opened her eyes to meet his. The sky and her face were reflected in his lifeless eyes.

She cradled Bonnar's head against her bosom, unable to believe he was gone. She prayed for his soul. With tenderness she closed his eyes and pushed his hair off his forehead. Memories of their time together rushed through her mind, the first meeting, the bonfire dance, his seeking her body, his loving her, his proposal of marriage, his engaging grin, his cockiness. She pushed away that awful day when her and his world changed forever.

David took Bonnar from her arms and hugged his friend to his chest. He wept and railed, "God…why d'ye take the gude…" His voice broke into sobs, his grief intense for his friend who was as close as a brother.

Andrew approached and stood holding Joanna who was a burden almost too big for him. Joanna held fast to her cousin's neck, and both children stared wide-eyed at the adults.

They remained as they were for a long time, until finally, David stood. He helped Deirdre to her feet, then leaned over to pull Bonnar's plaid loose and used it to cover him.

He peered at Deirdre. "D'ye feel well? The bairn wasna jarred with all the running ye did? Andrew told me about Gordon."

"Aye, Roger killed Gordon. I fell over his body and hurt myself. I feel no pain coming from the babe I carry, only my back. Gordon must have been killed right after leaving us in the garden," her voice hitched and she could hardly continue. "This day God had rendered his vengeance on me. Everyone who gets close to me suffers fer it. Two deaths—two deaths and they are my fault. Maude! God in Heaven, I've forgotten Maude! She was wounded and needs our help." She collapsed with grief and guilt when David shook her hard.

"Stop—it, Deirdre. Wrothbury has done this, not ye, and not God."

"Ye are wrong. It is my fault fer living in sin with Richard. God strikes a terrible wrath." She wiped hot tears. The devastation of this day embedded deep into her mind. She could not believe Gordon and Bonnar were gone.

David relieved Andrew of Joanna. He nestled the little girl close to his chest and pulled leaves from her hair. Soiled and dirty, she hiccupped from crying.

Deirdre went down on her knees in front of Andrew and hugged him dearly. Despite his protest, she rained kisses on his dirty cheeks.

"Andrew, ye are like the grandsire ye are named after. He wouldn't have hesitated to save my life and neither did ye. I thank ye fer my life and the life of Richard's child. Ye will walk well in yer grandsire's footsteps, dinna ye agree, Davey?"

David handed Joanna to her, and getting down on his haunches put his hands on his son's shoulders. "Ye have become the man of the house whilst I'm away. Today ye have shown yerself to be even more of a man. I'm proud of ye, Andrew Brodie, most proud."

Seeing Andrew's prideful smile was reward enough for Deirdre and David.

"It is gude that Aunt Deirdre is safe, but not gude that Uncle Bonnar and Uncle Gordon are dead. Are they in heaven with all the others, Papa?" His eyes filled with tears for the two men he loved enough to call Uncle.

"A special place in heaven, Andrew. They all look down upon us with favor. Now can I send ye off on my horse to bring more help? Get yer mam and Mary Clair. Also some of the men folk. Have them bring weapons and wagons."

"Rome? Ye'll let me ride Rome by meself?" His grief eased somewhat with youthful exuberance of being allowed to do the unthinkable.

David lifted Andrew up into the saddle. Handing his son the reins, David swatted Rome's backside and sent him galloping down the road. Andrew's legs stuck straight out, his feet far from reaching the stirrups.

Wrothbury worked his way down the steep hillside behind Foxlair. On foot, exposed roots tripped him up, and loosened rocks under his boots put him on his backside more than once. Panting from exertion, he finally reached the opening to the secret passageway that led into the upper chamber. Looking around, he scanned the area making sure he hadn't been spotted. All was quiet. The fools, this would have been the first place he would have posted guards. Putting his upper weight against the heavy door, he pushed, it resisted. Again he pushed, cursing under his breath, thinking his mission ended and him so close. Nay, he refused to think thus, and picking up a broken tree branch, he dug around the base of the door, clearing it of dirt and debris. Again, he put his shoulder against the wood struggling until it gave. Light filtered in from outside showing a torch lying on the ground inside the opening. Picking it up, he felt the end to see if it was dry. He knelt in the dirt, his bones popping as he did so. Searching in his waist pouch for his flint, he came across the pardon of which he stared at. After today, he'd no longer have use for it. He started to toss it but decided not to. Finding the flint, he stuffed the parchment back into the pouch and proceeded to light the torch.

Holding the smoking torch aloft, he crept around built up debris that almost blocked the tunnel in places. Cobwebs strung across his face. He brushed them away. The torch danced his shadow on the wall making him look like a hunched-back troll. He curled his nostrils at the dank smell of soil, thinking this would be a good place to bury Deirdre's body once he killed her.

Reaching the stairs that led to the trapdoor and the chamber, he started up them when the muffled voices of women could be heard coming from the other side. He paused. He placed the torch in the holder on the wall and sat down on the stairs to wait and listen.

Concerned and chattering women filled Deirdre's chamber. Bess took care of Maude's wound, wrapping her head with a strip of white cloth. Mary Clair had bathed and changed Joanna who was fast asleep in her crib. Seonaid fawned over Deirdre, cleaning her scratches, watching for telltale signs that Deirdre was losing the baby. So far, despite her back pain, all was well.

Seonaid hovered over Deidre, deep concern showed. "Ye have endured enough fer a thousand souls." She placed her hand on Deirdre's forehead. "Having carried three wee bairns myself, I think yer bairn to wait until it's ready to meet the world."

Deirdre had no words. Two deaths weighed heavily on her. The security and sanctuary of her home had been violated and all under the noses of guards. The duplicity of it all.

Mary Clair came to stand by Deirdre who couldn't help but see her young maid was racked with grief. "Mary Clair, I pray for Gordon's soul," she said in a soft voice.

"Aye, I'd decided to wed Gordon and remain in Scotland. But God has a way of changing things for us, does he not." Mary Clair wiped her eyes that were red from crying.

"Ye have lost yer sire and now Gordon. Can ye ever forgive me fer his death."

Mary Clair grabbed Deirdre's hands. "Milady, never blame yourself for this. We both know this is Wrothbury's evil." She pulled the coverlet up to Deirdre's shoulders. "Rest, milady. Allow the babe in your womb to settle." She went to throw a log on the fire, stoking it, the fire now sending out warmth.

David entered and looked around at the activity. His eyes met Seonaid's who ushered the rest out of the room. She remained and went to stand next to the fire, warming her hands. David approached the bed. "Deirdre, I'm having graves dug in our cemetery."

His words wrenched renewed sobs from Deirdre.

"Dinna cry, sister. I've had men search the area and cannot find signs of Wrothbury. Once again he has probably remained in his castle whilst sending out others to do his cowardly deeds."

"What of your orders to join our king?" She met her brother's gaze.

"I'll not leave Foxlair until Richard comes back. By now he knows he was tricked. When he returns ye must leave for France. It's the only way to keep ye safe."

Her brows knit into a scowl. "I don't think I'll be safe anywhere. 'Tis most assuredly Wrothbury will keep trying until he succeeds."

"Aye. And with the warrant calling fer yer head, he believes he's within his rights to do so."

Deirdre gave a perceivable nod. She lay looking at her brother, towering over her, resembling Papa so much it was as if he had returned to protect her. David's face was marred with the loss of friends, the skin under his eyes purple and smudged. She owed a great deal to David, her life, Joanna's, and Richard's unborn child. Her brother would give up his life for her. But the lives lost this day, would take a long time to settle into either one of their memories, if ever.

David took a seat on the bed next to her. "Listen to me. Bonnar was the brother I never had. I mourn his loss greatly. But if something was to happen to ye, I could never forgive myself. D'ye understand what I say?"

"D'ye blame me for Bonnar's death?" Miserably, she searched his face for the truth.

"Never that, Deedee. His death was not yer fault. Bonnar finally heard the words of forgiveness from ye. Words that for years, he sought to hear. The day Wrothbury took ye from here ate at him. At first, he talked about it a lot, but as time passed, he became silent. When he learned Richard had helped ye and planned to rescue ye from the cage, he started talking about ye again. He asked me if I thought ye could ever forgive him."

"What did ye say, Davey, what was yer answer to that?"

"I told him he would have to ask ye that question. He was the one seeking forgiveness."

A large knot formed in Deirdre's throat, threatening to cut off her air. She took a deep breath and sought his hand. "Why did I have to be so stubborn? Words are cheaply held, are they not, and yet such simple words of *'I forgive'* spoken months ago could have made such a difference. Now I carry the same burden as Bonnar. I should have told him and didna. My heart has been cut out."

"We will put yer heart back where it belongs, this I promise."

"If only ye can," her voice was fraught with hope.

Seonaid moved to take her hand. "When David makes an oath, ye know he keeps it."

Deirdre contemplated Seonaid's blue eyes, so soothing, and so wise. "Ye are like a sister, Seonaid."

David started to leave. "Seonaid and I'll be in the great hall."

Alone with the exception of Joanna whose soft breathing came from the crib, Deirdre snuggled under the coverlet. Images of recent events whirled in her mind until finally she fell into an uneasy slumber.

Richard unmercifully whipped the lathered horse. The horse whinnied and faltered. Its breathing became labored, its front legs buckled, it pitched onto its side, pinning Richard's left leg.

"Merde," he grunted and pushed against the saddle with his right leg. Nothing moved. When the horse tried to rise, a shift in its weight allowed Richard to scramble free. He got to his feet and eyed the horse who had valiantly carried him throughout the night. Hearing its labored breathing, knowing it was dying, and taking mercy upon it, he unsheathed his dagger and sliced its jugular.

As the horse's blood soaked into the ground, Richard glanced back the way he'd come. There was no sign of anyone who'd started out with him. He'd long ago outdistanced the soldiers that rode with him. He threw off his chest armor, then his cloak.

Knowing Foxlair was just over the rise, he started running. His sword bounced in a bruising tempo against his hip, hammering his body. Unwilling to break his stride, he unbuckled his holster and let it drop. The only weapon he now carried was his short dagger.

Slowly pushing open the trapdoor, Wrothbury peeked inside the chamber. His gaze swept the room until he spotted his sweet wife sleeping. He watched her chest rise and fall with each breath. Hearing mumbling jabbers, he glanced over to see his daughter sitting in her cradle. She stared at him from between the bars. She leaned forward to see him better and grinned. His plans were to kill Deirdre, grab Joanna and be off before anyone was the wiser. But Joanna's grin made him pause. He climbed out of the hole and moving with care laid his chained-mace upon a chest. Being mindful of the rushes and trying to be silent as he dragged his bad foot, he approached the cradle. His daughter had grown in the months since he'd last looked upon her. Soon, she would be a year old.

He put his hands under her armpits and lifted her from the cradle. He held his daughter for the first time ever. She reared her head back to stare at him. His heart thumped. She resembled her mother. Her hair was the same bright color of Deirdre's. The only thing he could find of himself was her eyes, the exact color of his, gray. She whimpered and stretched toward where Deirdre slept. His temper flared, even now, his daughter wanted nothing to do with him. She didn't know who he was.

Deirdre's eyes popped open. Something was wrong. Usually, Joanna's soft mumbling baby talk would awake Deirdre. But Joanna sounded frightened forcing Deirdre to roll over. Her heart missed a beat and bile rose in the back of her throat.

Wrothbury stood next to the gaping black hole of the trapdoor, the hinged cover tilted high. He held Joanna. Stale cold air breezed up out of the hole and into the chamber filling it with a dank musty smell. Travel-stained, his black cloak thrown over one shoulder, he wore chest armor dirty from his journey. His dagger and long sword were scabbarded at his waist. Shriveled, his back more bowed than the last time she'd laid eyes on him, he was still a danger.

Deirdre squelched her fear, was over being surprised by the man who she loathed with heated intensity. In a way expected him. How astute that he remembered to use the trapdoor. She'd forgotten that he knew about it.

Joanna held her arms out. "Mamm...ma...m," she said, and dared a frightened glance at the stranger holding her.

Ignoring the crunching pain in her back, Deirdre got to her feet. She gave Joanna a wide smile.

Wrothbury's eyes flared as they settled upon her rounded stomach. "It appears that once again I surprise you whilst sleeping, good wife. To think, I could have killed you just now, but that would have been cowardly. I want you awake to see my blade enter your body. As your blood flows out and you die, the last thing you see is me walking away with my daughter. Joanna no longer recognizes me and that grieves me deeply. I surmise she thinks the Frenchman's her sire. That is about to change. Everything about your life is about to change." He gloated at her. "Have you nothing to say? To plead for?"

"Oh…but ye are a coward," her words spewed forth. "Hiding behind a child just now. Ye attack defenseless women."

She had no intentions of letting him take Joanna away from her again. This man had shattered her and her family's existence. She was going to be the one to change his life for good. She meant to kill him. As she continued to stare at him the realization came over her that this was no longer about Wrothbury, or her, it was about her father, Bonnar, Gordon, David, her clan and all the people around her. It was about her children's futures, especially Joanna's.

Out of the corner of her eye, she saw that he'd placed his chained mace on top of the large chest.

"Put Joanna down, Wrothbury. Ye'll not be taking her anywhere this day, or ever."

For a brief moment, surprise creased his craggy features. But then his aging skin turned red and a vein bulged across his forehead. "Madame, never give me orders concerning my own flesh and blood. Joanna is mine. She is the rightful heir to my domain and all my holdings. Or have you convinced yourself that she is the Frenchman's?"

"I try to forget how Joanna was conceived."

He chuckled, sounding like something that crawled up from the depths of Hades. "To be sure, that is something I'll never forget. The only pleasurable thing about you resides between your legs." His eyes settled on her thickened waist, his face turned ugly with hate. He snarled, "It looks like there will be two of you that will not live past this day."

Deirdre knew he was fighting for control at the knowledge she carried Richard's child. She started for the door but could see that Wrothbury had thrown the bolt while she slept. God in Heaven. She'd be dead before anyone could break down the heavy door.

Wrothbury, apparently realizing her intent, spoke in a low voice, "'Twill do you no good to call out." He placed Joanna down on the floor and started for Deirdre.

Deirdre, more agile and faster than he ever could be, grabbed the mace off the chest. Feeling braver with a weapon, she held the handle with both hands. The deadly spiked-ball with dried gristle from his last conquest, dangled from the two-foot chain, its great weight making it hard to hold. She menacingly shook it.

Undaunted by her stab at bravery, he sneered a laugh, and slowly unsheathed his sword, the sound of it clearing the scabbard chilling. He lifted it skyward and started advancing.

Joanna stood, and taking a few tottering steps fell into the open trapdoor.

"Joanna!" Deirdre screamed at the sound of Joanna's body slapping down the stone stairs. Her loud shrieks echoed back out of the hole.

When Wrothbury turned to see what had happened, Deirdre swung the mace. She aimed at his head but hit his shoulder with such force that he staggered backwards and had to put his broadsword against the floor to keep from falling. His hand went to his bleeding shoulder.

Deirdre bent on getting to Joanna, shoved past him and went down the opening.

Richard propelled his body through Foxlair's large doors with so much momentum that he had to put his hand down to keep from falling. Hearing loud conversation in the great hall, he dashed inside.

David shot to his feet and started for him.

"Where's Deirdre?" Richard blurted. His chest heaved, hurt. He wiped the sweat coursing down the sides of his face.

"She was attacked. She's now safe in your chambers."

"Was Wrothbury killed?"

"Nay. I searched, dinna see the man."

Richard hurried across the room and grabbed Andrew Brodie's claymore from its mount on the wall. He ran toward the spiral stairwell, taking the stairs two at a time.

David caught up with him, dogging his heels.

"I was tricked—Philippe wasn't wounded." Richard's feet hit the landing, and he started down the hallway. He bellowed, "Deirdre."

"She is well. I left her but a short time ago."

Richard started to open the door but it resisted his attempts. Realizing it was locked from within, started pounding. "Deirdre—open the door—Chéri—I'm back."

Met by silence, realization slammed into their minds at the same time.

"Christ above," David said. "The trapdoor! Does Wrothbury knows of it?"

"Oui."

Led by Joanna's penetrating wails to where she fell mid-way down the stone stairs, Deirdre scooped her up and hurried down the rest of the stairs. Up ahead in the corridor, a flickering torch helped light her way. Wrothbury had planned his escape well, even made sure he could see his way out.

"Dinna cry, sweet bairn. Yer mam's here." Her voice must have soothed somewhat, for Joanna's wailing turned to whimpers as she relaxed against Deirdre and held onto her bodice with a death grip.

Hearing Wrothbury's strange dragging gait coming behind her, Deirdre pounded down the dark musty tunnel. Memory was her map as cobwebs assailed them, stringing gray dirty threads across their bodies. Rodents squeaked and dashed away. The sides of the dirt walls dripped with water. Her feet splashed in puddles.

Hoping that Wrothbury's misshapen leg would keep him well behind, she continued. Joanna began to cry, the sound was like a beacon, telling their position. Deirdre had no way of silencing her and ran doggedly on. The mace bounced in her arms, so did Joanna, their weight pulling on her shoulders, tiring her. At last, she came to the end of the tunnel and the door left ajar. She stepped out into the calm bright day.

Squinting against the sun, Deirdre faced the hillside. She searched for hers and David's trail they had etched into the ground from their many treks up the steep incline. It was there, but grown over. Plunging head-long up the path, she rapidly moved until it became harder for her to do so. Up she went, sometimes crawling. She grasped bushes growing on the path, to help pull her along. Joanna's weight, along with the mace, had her back screaming for relief. Winded, her mouth dry, she couldn't swallow.

The slope was dotted with giant boulders and bushes that wore the red-gold of fall. Pausing to look behind her, she was stunned to see that Wrothbury was near. In desperation she put Joanna down and turned to face him.

Elation came over her when she spotted Richard and David busting through the tunnel door. They paused to get their bearings and search her out.

"Help!" she screamed. Holding the mace, she continued to back up, feeling every stone through her soft-soled shoes.

Wrothbury, out of breath and wheezing, grabbed hold of a boulder to steady himself. Joanna was near enough that he could grab her.

Deirdre began moving up the trail, trying to lure him away from Jo-anna. It was working, he started coming on.

"I hate the ground ye walk on!" she taunted with a false bravado.

"I'm going to kill you and cut the Frenchman's bastard from your womb," he challenged, and quickened his pace, surprisingly agile for his age and bad leg. Rocks rolled from beneath his boots and skittered down the slope.

Deirdre waited. When he was within three arm lengths away, she rounded on him, letting fly with the deadly mace. The spiked ball slammed against the side of his head, the spikes piercing.

He screamed. Blood coursed down his neck, soaking into his tunic shirt. He staggered sideways, shaking his head like a giant bull. He reached up to feel the damage she'd wrought with one blow from his own weapon.

"Damn yer Scottish hide, you think to kill me?" he roared.

Deirdre tried backing up, the hem of her skirt caught under her foot causing her to trip. She fell backwards landing hard against the rocky ground. The pain in her back flared.

Wrothbury leaped onto her. His body pressed hers against the hard rocks beneath her. He gripped her neck in a strangle hold. His thumbs pressed her windpipe, sending a stinging pain to spread inside her throat. She clawed at his fingers, trying to pry them away, but his grip was vise-like. Her heels dug into the earth, loosening the ground beneath them.

Wrothbury had gone beyond rage. With one hand clamped on her throat, his other went to her abdomen clutching the soft flesh.

"I would tear the Frenchman's seed from you," he spat as his finger-nails raked and tore at her flesh.

Hurry Richard—hurry. The unspoken words screamed through her mind, her vision becoming a misty haze.

"Release her!" Suddenly, large hands gripped Wrothbury around the chest and hauled him away from her.

Richard—at last. Clutching her throat and gasping for air, Deirdre lay against the rocky incline.

"Get away, Deirdre," Richard yelled.

She crawled back out of the way. Richard held her father's claymore aloft, ready to bring it down, to protect her.

Wrothbury's shortened leg allowed him to maneuver better on the wicked slope. He picked up his mace and swung it in a blurring circle over his head. Moving closer to Richard, he whirled his weapon. Feeling the breeze of it, Richard jumped back out of the way. It slammed against a boulder sending chips of rocks flying.

Richard swung the claymore. Wrothbury ducked around a large boulder, using it as a shield.

Peering around the rock, Wrothbury taunted, "I had her first. My tarse broke her maidenhead."

"I will have her love forever," Richard countered.

The truth of his words affected Wrothbury who lunged with a snarl.

Deirdre could only watch as the two rolled and skidded against the rough ground, the rocks cutting their skin, breaking the branches from small bushes, destroying whatever was underneath them. Coming out on top, Wrothbury sat on Richard and grabbing up a rock hit him hard on the forehead. Richard yelled a curse, a cut opened up in his hairline. Blood from Wrothbury's wound dripped onto Richard's face. He slugged Wrothbury in the jaw then managed to buck the man off his stomach. Jumping to his feet, Richard's foot caught in a bramble causing him to pitch headfirst onto the ground. He rolled out of the way of the descending mace and picked up the claymore.

Like a crab, Wrothbury sidled over the rocks trying to maintain his balance and kill Richard at the same time. They fought, sword against mace until the mace's chain wrapped around the claymore, and in one quick motion Wrothbury wrest it out of Richard's hand and sent it cartwheeling into the air. Wrothbury triumphantly scrambled onto a wide, flat boulder. He took another swing at Richard's head, but missed.

"Wrothbury," David called out attracting the man's attention, "This is for my father, Andrew Brodie." He released the powerful bowstring sending an arrow slicing through the air and piercing Wrothbury's throat.

Gurgling, the earl dropped the mace and fell to his knees. His face tinged purple. He frantically grabbed at the arrow shaft. He pointed at Deirdre and whatever he would say was lost in a burst of blood from his mouth. He pitched forward off the boulder and came to a rest at Deirdre's feet. The mace clattered from the rock and landed on top of him.

Stunned, Deirdre could only stare at the lump on the ground in front of her. She knelt beside Wrothbury. Alive, he stared at her; his bloodied mouth still wore a perpetual sneer.

She leaned close, and whispered, "Remember when ye killed my father and told me that the life I knew was over? Well your life…is over. I will piss on your grave."

His mouth worked, he struggled to speak. His dying breath whistled out of the wound preventing any words. Then there was silence. A great weight of relief lifted from Deirdre, a relief that a man so deformed by hate was as last dead.

David, carrying his bow, stopped beside her and helped her to her feet. She took the weapon from him, and fingering the taunt string, said, "This day yer aim with this bow has been most true. Ye have saved my life and that of my unborn child many times over. God will never forget this day, David Brodie, nor will I." Her lips quivered a smile as she beheld her brother. "Papa watches and approves as well."

"Aye. That arrow was fer Papa, you, Richard, and all the Scots killed by this man. Joanna is never to know what happened here this day." David went to collect Joanna who had fallen asleep on her rocky perch.

Deirdre eyes were on Richard. Trying to hold back tears, she ran into his embrace.

"Ah…Chéri, I've died a thousand times thinking I wouldn't get to you in time. I couldn't have prayed more if I was the Cardinal himself." He folded her into his sturdy embrace and she gladly snuggled against his chest, listening to his strong heartbeat.

"Richard…ye didna know how much I needed ye this day."

"Oh…I know exactly how much. But you held your own against Wrothbury, oui." A smile cut his dark stubble. Covered with dirt and grim, his face was never more handsome to her. He tipped her chin up and gave her a soft kiss.

David approached carrying Joanna, who with her eyes rounded in fear, held her arms out to Richard. They quickly checked her over for injuries. Her cheek was bruised and dirty, her hands and knees scraped and bleeding, and she had messed her wraps. Finding no broken bones, Richard held her.

"Da," she said, and buried her face against his chest while grabbing a handful of tunic. Richard cupped her head, his fingers stroking burnished curls. She shuddered out a breath and looked at him and Deirdre with trusting eyes that pooled tears.

"Little mademoiselle," he said, "You and your mère are forever safe."

A piece of parchment tumbled in the gentle wind catching their attention. The breeze pushed it across a large rock, and it continued its breezy course until it butted up against Deirdre's ankle.

Richard bent to pick it up. Reading the soiled paper, he blurted out, "Mon Dieu, chéri." He placed the paper in her hand.

Deirdre read it not once, but three times or more. Looking at her brother's puzzled face, she began to read.

"Be it known on this day, September the eighth, the year 1307, that I, Edward II, King of England do rescind said proclamation of one Edward I, releasing Countess Deirdre Brodie Wrothbury from her present imprisonment."

When finished, overwhelmed by strong emotions, she sunk to her knees to pray to her Lord, giving thanks for putting the pardon back into her hands and giving her freedom.

Holding the king's coveted words of freedom in one hand and Richard's hand in the other, Deirdre regarded the man she loved more than anything.

She said, "Always you, Richard, always you."

24 Hope Is Unbroken

Foxlair, March 1309

For the second time in as many hours, Richard leaned over the cradle to study his infant son. He'd been ushered out of the room earlier by Caitrina who he found was just as militant about men being around a birth as she was about pulling arrows out of a body. Before the door closed on his face, he'd barely been able to discern that his son was well formed and had all his appendages.

Casting a wary eye at the tightly swaddled bébé, he wondered how in Hades his son could breath, and set about freeing him. Leaning over the wooden cradle, he slowly removed the wrap that covered his son's sex to make sure he had all his working parts. Now that he had him unwrapped, he decided to explore, and gently turned the baby from front to back. He couldn't help but smile at the no-neck head that held soft wispy black curls at his nape. Turning the little mite back over, the bébé stretched, and tucked his legs tight against his body, like a frog. He squeaked, yawned, and made a sucking motion with his mouth.

Richard glanced over at his wife to make sure she still slept, and then continued to get acquainted with his son. He traced around the fat double chin, tickling as he did so, waking the bébé. Like a bird, he opened his mouth searching for food. Richard wiggled a finger inside the tightly balled up fist and watched as the tiny hand latched onto his finger with a grip that was amazingly strong. He leaned closer and squinted at fingernails so small he could hardly see them.

"Antoine, what a petite thing you are," he whispered, liking how the name sounded. He'd just named his son after his own sire.

With feelings that threatened to overcome him, Richard scooped him up out of the cradle, and nestled him against his chest. He breathed Antoine's milky scent, Deirdre's scent. He kissed the tiny cheek turned to him. He would give up his life for this precious little one.

"He waits for his sire to name him." A smile creased Deirdre's lips from where she lay propped on one elbow and staring at him.

"I just did. The name slipped out as easily as yours and mine. I named him Antoine, after my sire. We shall call him Antoine David."

She beamed at him. "Richard, to name him after yer sire is most generous, and ye honor my brother by calling him David." She patted the bed, beckoning. "Richard would ye hand me his swaddling clothes. Our wee bairn can squirt clear across the room."

Richard laughed. "Oui? I would like to see that."

"Aye, well ye missed it. He has already gotten me in the face when I was checking as ye are now doing."

When his son started to cry, Richard grabbed up the swaddling clothes and sat on the bed. He handed Antoine to Deirdre, but felt inclined to play with a tiny bare foot. She crooned a soft Gaelic song and started to loosen the laces on her nightdress, but Richard stayed her hand.

"Allow me, mon chéri." He unlaced her bodice and parted it, releasing her breasts heavy with milk. The mere sight slammed desire through his loins. "You are most beautiful."

Deirdre pulled her eyes away from Richard long enough to cup her breast and tease the nipple across Antoine's mouth that opened, seeking.

Richard drew in his breath as Antoine's small mouth latched onto her darkened nipple. "I think to be my son right now, for it has been too

long since I've been able to make love to you, Countess de Strasbourg."
He kissed her cheek, then her mouth, and reluctantly stopped. Watching
Deirdre feeding his son was an image that would always stay in his mind.
"By the saints, how I love you, wife." His voice shook with emotion as
his hand reached out to stroke her cheek. Antoine drifted back to sleep,
his sucking stilled.

"I thank you for giving me a son."

"Husband, ye can thank me all ye want, but I couldna have had him
without yer help to begin with." She removed Antoine from her breast,
his mouth releasing the nipple with a loud popping sound.

They laughed. Richard pulled her top together and laced the ribbon
tight. Deirdre wiped Antoine's mouth, and then snuggling him up to her
bosom gave him several gentle pats on the back bringing forth a loud
burp. She placed him on the bed and put a fresh wrap around the baby's
loins before swaddling him with a blanket. Grinning, she handed Antoine back to his sire.

The baby started to cry with a shrill and powerful effort.

The door opened to a bevy of chattering females. They merged
around Deirdre. Caitrina, clucking like a fussy hen, snatched Antoine out
of Richard's arms and put him in the cradle most gently.

"Out ye go, milord." Maude showed Richard the door and closed it
behind him.

Deirdre watched with amusement as Mary Clair held Joanna and
pointed at the baby. "Joanna, ye have a baby brother."

Joanna's eyes were on the interloper in her old cradle. "Nay." She
pouted. But then she said nay to everything.

Seonaid, due within several months, stared at the wee baby, her own
girth kept her from bending too far.

Caitrina, having returned to Foxlair to help with Antoine's birth,
fussed about Deirdre, checking to see how she bled.

Maude sidled up next to Deirdre and took her hand. All she could
think to say was, "Oh...Milady, who would have ever known that your

life would turn out so grand."

"Richard has named him Antoine David," Deirdre said, and stared at all the grins bestowed upon her.

Richard joined the men in the great hall. Philippe, standing next to the table and holding a carafe of wine, motioned at him. "I wondered how long you to last up there. This was just delivered." He reached into his tunic and handed a missive to Richard.

Richard broke the de Laci seal and read aloud to Philippe. *"Richard de Laci, mon frère, I have fretted about your long absence and have received word that you will soon return home and bring your Scottish wife, the Countess of Strasbourg. Imagine a woman with such valor as she. When you return you can meet and give your approval of Sir Julien Quesnel. We both wait patiently for your signature upon our betrothal. I love Julien, but at times, I have such a strange feeling that mayhap Julien is not the man of my heart. I await your guidance and remain faithfully your sister. Lady Pernelle de Laci."*

"Just as I thought, Philippe," Richard said. "Pernelle is confused as most women about the matter of marriage."

Conner Kincaid, sitting next to his Uncle Macadie, asked, "This Pernelle is your older sister?"

"Non, she is the runt, the last of us siblings." Richard started to say more, but Philippe interrupted.

"We have a brother who is younger than Richard and I, but older than Pernelle. His name is Valentin."

"Speakin' of names, have ye named yer son yet? When do we get to see him?" Macadie asked Richard.

"Oui, Macadie. I've named him Antoine David. You will meet him in good time. You wouldn't want to be up there now. Wait until the room clears of females."

Macadie appeared to be thinking about the name. "Antoine? A fine name for a little nub."

Philippe spoke up. "Richard, you've named your son after our sire.

He would approve."

Richard addressed those around the table, but more so his brother. "I think to leave for home when my son is two months of age. Both he and Deirdre will be much stronger by then. What say you, Philippe?"

"That will be the end of May. If you encounter no problems, you should reach home no later than mid-June. Hopefully the crossing will be calm."

Philippe's reference to *you* and not *we* wasn't lost on Richard who was disinclined to voice his suspicions, but did. "Philippe, you talk as if you're not returning home with me." The look on his brother's face confirmed what Richard already knew deep inside.

"I'm not. Richard, Scotland's cause is mine. I cannot abandon this country. I feel like I leave an unfinished war behind, as if I've laid down my weapon on a battlefield and simply walked off to give the enemy a victory that he doesn't deserve." He clasped Richard's arm. "Caitrina has a need to continue helping her father with the healing, trying to do some good in this mindless English aggression. I had meant to tell you alone, certainly before now. But the excitement of your son being born gave me no chance."

Seeing Philippe's determination, Richard sought to agree. Taking the edge of his brother's announcement, he clapped him on the back. "Then you must stay behind and do what you feel is right. I'll miss you greatly."

"I know, but no more than I will miss you, our home, Pernelle and Valentin. The Bruce has offered me Blackadder Castle, and the Earldom that comes with it. I'll be able to watch the western border more closely. Most of the mercenary soldiers we grouped in France have chosen to remain with me. Now that you know, I'd like to give Etienne the choice to stay here or return with you."

Philippe's words made Richard more than aware that his brother sought a life and title of his own. That he no longer needed to depend on Richard's charity and good nature. That as a warrior of Scotland he stood on his own. Yet knowing all this didn't make it any easier for

Richard to accept that he was losing his life-long companion. His own life would be a little less enjoyable, and Château Falaise a little quieter.

They all turned at the sound of someone's heavy footfalls on the stone entryway. David entered with Blake riding on his shoulders. Andrew and Little Dee walked beside him. Andrew and his sister made a beeline for upstairs. David swung Blake to his feet, and the lad hastily followed his siblings.

David went over to the table and filled a goblet with ale. He then went to stand next to the de Laci brothers.

"Is the wee one born yet?" David asked.

"Oui, a few hours ago. I've named him Antoine David," Richard said.

David cast a fond glance at the men around him. "A gude name. With ye as his sire and Philippe as an uncle, he will have much to live up to."

"David, you will give him even more to live up to. I expect that you will be steeped in valor come the next campaign," Richard said and motioned for them to take a seat.

After getting comfortable next to Richard, David started talking. "I still have an arrest warrant against me by the English fer pelting the old King with a rock. I'm listed alongside the Brus as an outlaw against the English." David paused and took a sip from his chalice. "The King of England promises to start an invasion of Scotland this summer. I'm not sure what to believe. In the meantime the English garrisons throughout Scotland are fending fer themselves and most are starving. Robert has warned those that aid and abet the English will lose their homes and castles. I've asked Robert for permission to crenellate Foxlair and he has given it. With four towers and battlements all the way around there will be no getting past the guards I can keep posted. I'm hoping ye can help me draw up the plans, Richard. I'm moving my family in here after ye leave fer France."

"And that sits well with Seonaid?" Macadie teased.

"She has no choice, I've made up my mind," David said and narrowed a scowl, daring them to say otherwise.

"Well, David, perhaps Philippe can help with the fortifying of Fox-lair, as he is remaining here in Scotland. Blackadder is to be his," Richard said and couldn't keep the undertones of sadness and pride out of his voice.

Macadie garnered Richard's attention by clearing his throat, "Coont, I'm thinkin' to go to France with ye. And…and…"

"Oui, and?" Richard coaxed him.

"I would like to take Maudie with me and live with ye at yer domain." His fingers dwarfed the stem on his goblet as he drained the liquid.

"With Maudie?" Richard winked at Philippe and chuckled.

"Aye, that's what I said, with Maudie, me wife."

"Wife is it? Since you haven't married the woman yet, do you plan to tell her that you're taking her to France as your wife?"

"Oh…aye. Today's the day I'll do the askin'."

Richard folded his arms, it wasn't often he bested Macadie and he was relentless. "What if Maude doesn't want to marry you? You can be ornery at times and you cheat at chess."

"Ah…what d'ye know about me cheatin' at chess? Has Maudie been tellin' stories?"

Richard shrugged. "You think to be happy leaving Scotland? We wear breeks over there, not skirts." All the men laughed, but Macadie laughed the loudest.

"That remains to happen about the breeks. Besides, us men wearing a skirt allow the lassies a faster feel." Macadie had the last say.

At that vision they all laughed, but Macadie laughed the loudest.

Richard shook his head at the wily Scot's practicality. But in truth, he was happy to know that Macadie wanted to go. He would fill the void that Philippe's remaining behind would make. Richard's mood lightened some.

But now Macadie was serious, "I can always come back, can I no'? And Conner here wants to go with ye as well."

"Oui, a ship sails both ways. It's settled then." Richard stood and glanced around. "Now who would like to see my son?" And as all the men stood, a wide grin broke Richard's face. "Come then. We will unswaddle him but Deirdre says to be careful as he can piss clear across the room. Imagine what strength his tarse has to do that."

David chuckled, and could only shake his head at Richard's delight in his first born.

They all followed Richard up the stairs and into the chamber filled with women who sat circled around the bed sewing baby clothes and chatting. As their needles darted in and out of the fabric, their eyes suspiciously followed the men who cast sheepish glances their way.

Deirdre stared with amusement as Richard pulled the swaddling clothes from his son as if to prove indeed he'd sired a male child.

"Here is your nephew, Philippe. The next boy will be named after you."

Philippe ran a finger across the tiny cheek. "If the child that Caitrina carries is a boy, he'll be named after you, Richard. To say your name will be like having a small part of you beside me here in Scotland." Philippe clasped Richard's arm.

Macadie took a gander at the child. A smile spread across his face and he hastened a wink over at Maude. He tickled Antoine under the chin, and then squinted at Richard. "Coont, he has yer dark hair. Come to yer Uncle Macadie, little Nub." Macadie bent to pick him up just as the baby's tarse went rigid and pee shot upward like a geyser, soaking a dark spot on Macadie's chest. "Damnation, little Nub," he exclaimed looking down at his soiled tunic.

Maude sniggered as she approached Macadie. Her brown eyes twinkled as she tucked escaping hair back into her headdress. The scar on her temple from Roger's sword was now a pink line. "Macadie Gunn, yer tunic needs a gude scrub. If ye don't mind, I'll do it for ye?"

"Nothin' would please this Scotsman more." Taking Maude's hand, he escorted her from the chamber.

Macadie waited until Maude made her move, a good one that dealt him a loss of another queen and a gleam from her as he admitted defeat. That was all right by him, he was more than happy to give her some joy in winning a board game, because there was even more happiness that he thought to give her.

"Cadie, want," Joanna said from where she stood, flexing her fingers, trying to reach a chess piece.

Not letting this wee bit of a lassie distract him, he put a wooden bishop in her grasping hand.

"Maude Warren if ye didna think it too forward of me, I'd like to hold yer hand." He shot her a canted stare, his bushy eyebrows pulled low, and with bow-strung anticipation, waited for her reply.

"My hand?"

"Aye, leddie, are ye def? Yer hand, I'd like to hold yer hand." He plopped his big rawboned paw on top of hers, dwarfing it.

They sat that way for a while, peering straight ahead. He counted flies flying lazily about the room. She smiled at Joanna who was busy messing up the chess pieces. Maude glanced upward at the tall ceiling and shifted in her chair.

Finally, Maude said, "If ye don't mind me askin', are we to sit here all day with our hands touching or d'ye have something on yer mind?"

"Yer pushy," Macadie blustered, and being a weathered warrior who never had to court a woman, he harrumphed and tried again. "I akin this to fightin' a battle, ye know…how to slay yer opponent and not get yerself gutted."

Maude drew back and stared like she was taking his measure. "Ye akin talking to me is like getting gutted?" Outwardly she was ruffled, inwardly she was totally thrilled and knowing what he was trying to say and unable to, made his efforts all the more enduring.

"Ah…ye know what I mean to say. I like ye, Maude Warren. I'm tired of rolling up at night with nothing but a blanket and hard floor beneath me."

"Macadie Gunn, mayhap ye need to say what ye mean. 'Cause it sounds like ye think talking to me is like planning a battle. And at night ye want a warm bed beneath ye and not the cold floor."

When he started to clarify his meaning, Joanna threw a bishop that smacked him upside the head. "Aye, jest like a lass to get attention, hit the man then smile at him like ye did nothing wrong." He scooped Joanna up and placed her on his lap. He began bouncing her on his knees and singing a jaunty tune. "Giddy-up, giddy-up, giddy-up horse, take the fair maiden to towne."

Joanna squealed with delight, clapping her chubby hands.

"Giddy-up, giddy-up, giddy-up horse, the fair maiden's off to buy a gown. And would Maude Warren marry up with me?" He ended that with an off-key note and slyly continued bouncing Joanna while cutting a sideways glance over at Maude. She returned his stare with a surprised one of her own.

"Did ye no hear me, Maude?"

"I heard ye, Macadie Gunn."

"Leddie, ye are the most horned-toad woman I've been around, and why is that? I'm goin' to France with the Coont, d'ye want to live in France or no'?"

"Milady already asked me to go to France with her. Aye, I want to marry ye."

Macadie's brows hit his hairline and giving Maude a big grin, he put Joanna down and watched her toddle off toward the next table.

"Ye know, that little lass has won me heart. Reminds me of my little Issy that I told ye about. Mayhap ye can give me a son?" He took Maude's hand and while kissing it, did a lift of his eyebrow, wagging it at her. The look wasn't lost on Maude.

"A son is it? First, I'm a battlefield and now I'm a breeding pen. Ye have to know that in all my years married to Thomas I never conceived, so perhaps I can't. Ye need to be thinking on that."

"Then it'll be up to me to try my verra best to see if I can get ye with child." He winked.

"So, I hear ye to say that ye'll have pleasure in the trying?" she said with quick wit.

"It'll be my pleasure." Another flash of the bushy brow, but Maude wasn't done yet.

"Macadie Gunn, what I haven't heard ye to say is that ye love me. A woman likes to hear such." She straightened the chess pieces on the black and white wood.

"Well I do, or I wouldna be askin' ye to marry me." His jaw firmed.

"Ye do what?" She twisted the knife just a little more.

"Ye know."

"Do I? Say it or I take back my yes," she said and smiled ever so sweetly.

"Damnation!" He shot to his feet just as Joanna tottered out the open door and started after her.

Richard, walking in, caught the escaping little maiden and scooped her up to toss her high.

"Père!" Joanna giggled.

From where she still sat, Maude spoke. "Macadie, what were ye about to say?"

"I love ye, Maudie," he mumbled under his breath.

She cupped her ear and leaned towards him. "Did ye say something? I thought ye spoke, but hmm...not verra well."

"Damn it all, leddie, I love ye!" he shouted.

Both Maude and Richard grinned at him. Richard bent to set Joanna on her feet. She immediately went to the game board and with one swipe of her hand scattered the pieces.

"Are we going to have another wedding before we leave for France? If so, then you need to hurry and do the deed," Richard teased.

By now, Macadie was wearing a deep scowl and looking like maybe this wasn't such a good idea after all. "Nay, not until we get to France,"

Macadie said, thinking he had the last word.

"We will marry on the morrow. So, Count Strasbourg, if ye will help make it happen, I'd be most thankful." Maude stood and taking Joanna's hand, pointed a finger at Macadie. "I'll be waiting fer ye in the little chapel, around midday, aye."

Without further ado, she breezed out the door walking Joanna next to her. Joanna's little feet did a fast shuffle to keep up.

25 Her Valor Flourishes

The ship, anchored in the inlet, had been loaded with supplies, and was ready to leave for France. The only thing left was the horses and people.

Deirdre stood in her private chamber having one last look around. Insisting on taking something of her family with her, her father's bed had been dismantled and loaded on the ship. The room's silence echoed of past lives, of her parents, of her son born here, of everyone who had slept, lived and loved here.

She should be glad to leave this country behind with its wars and truces that never hold, but she wasn't. What bothered her the most was the knowledge that she would probably never see David and his family again. The knot in her throat tightened.

"Deirdre?"

Brushing tears away, Deirdre turned to see Seonaid standing there.

"Where is yer sweet bairn?" Deirdre asked and smiled.

"Marlene is with Bess."

"And the others? Maude, Macadie, all those who leave with us and those who don't?"

Seonaid reached out to take Deirdre's hand. "Everyone waits for ye." Her lower lip quivered. "I'll miss ye greatly."

"And I ye, Seonaid. How strange our lives have turned out."

"Yours most assuredly. I canna believe all that ye have lived through. They say legends have already been started about ye. Minstrels sing songs of you. Our children will be taught to think of ye as the caged countess who escaped. I expect yer name to be alongside William Wallace and Robert de Brus."

"Och…Seonaid, ye be teasing me. I'm a mere Scottish woman who has the same hatred for the English as do all Scots who battle against them."

"But I wonder, how many of them have spit in the King of England's face and lived beyond that day. How many have been caged and gave birth whilst being imprisoned? How many have escaped prison and lived to tell the tale? Nay, ye have an inner strength that even men wish to have. David says yer name will be forever whispered by every man who breathes the air of Scotland."

"I've been given a status that isna right. There are many before me who are more deserving. All the men who fight alongside Robert de Brus. So many more—"

Richard stepped into the room interrupting what she would have said. Behind him followed Philippe and Caitrina. The brothers had said their goodbyes in private and Richard, reluctant to return home without Philippe, tried to change Philippe's mind one last time. But Philippe was firm. A truce, shaky at best, had been made between England and Scotland. Philippe took advantage of the lull in fighting and moved into Blackadder Castle and garrisoned it with his army. Caitrina was happy to be staying close to her father and to make him a grandfather in the near future.

Deirdre and Seonaid reached out to take Caitrina within their circle. They hugged one another and all three fought back tears.

When they parted, Richard took both Seonaid's and Caitrina's hands and bent to place a kiss on each one. "Seonaid and Caitrina, we will miss you greatly. And you, Seonaid, I heartily agree with your words about my countess. She is a woman of valor."

Grinning, Philippe moved to stand next to his wife. "We all feel that way." His gaze went to his brother's face.

Seonaid did a small curtsy. "Count Strasbourg, 'tis thanks I give ye for making Foxlair and the land thrive."

"That you will be living here in Foxlair and carrying on what I started is thanks enough. Live well and within God's grace. The same for you Philippe and Caitrina, stay well." Richard linked Deirdre's arm within his. "Madam, it is time to board the ship."

Mounted on her horse and riding beside Richard, Deirdre vowed not to look back and tried to swallow the lump in her throat. They went through the stockade's open gate where Deirdre was surprised to see most of the clan milling around. In front of the clan David stood alongside Seonaid who held their infant Margaret. Blake, Little Dee, and Andrew, clustered around them. Andrew grinned and waved. With them were Conner Kincaid, Macadie and Maude who held Antoine. Mary Clair was in charge of Joanna who clasped her hand tight. Bertrand, Richard's squire, stood close to Mary Clair and was whispering in her ear. She smiled. Philippe and Caitrina were mounted on their horses.

The clan's lookout horn sounded loud and foreboding, sending shivers down Deirdre's back. Alarmed she glanced at Richard who appeared equally puzzled. Six riders crested the knoll and came on in a fast pace, their cloaks flapping behind them like the wings of a giant bird. The men of the clan drew their claymores, waiting, and recognizing Robert the Bruce's heraldry, they became at ease.

One of the riders stopped his lathered horse. Facing Deirdre, he removed his cap and flourished it at her. A fine coating of dust stained his clothing, his gray hair and bushy beard. His blue eyes held a twinkle just for her.

"Milady, I'm James Douglas, friend of King Robert de Brus. King Robert heard of your departure and bids ye a safe voyage. He says that ye are a true woman of valor and wants to honor ye for yer steadfast loyalty to him and Scotland." He removed from his saddle pouch a circlet cast in silver that flashed in the sunlight. "This gift is from our king." He maneuvered his horse next to Deirdre's and stood in his stirrups to place the circlet over the veil covering her chestnut locks. He took her hand within his and raised her arm high, looking at the clan while doing so.

"Her valor flourishes!" he bellowed in a deep voice.

The clan took up the chant. "Her valor flourishes! Her valor flourishes!" Their voices resonated around the inlet.

"Well said, my love." Richard smiled at her.

Deirdre, wiping tears, turned her attention to the gruff warrior beside her who had traveled a long way. "James Douglas, ye must thank King Robert de Brus. And tell him that no matter where I reside, he will always be my king."

James Douglas removed from his pouch several missives and handed one of them to Richard. "For your King of France from Scotland's King Robert." The other he gave to Deirdre. "This is for ye, Countess de Strasbourg."

With a questioning stare, Deirdre accepted the parchment and broke its wax seal. As she read, her mouth creased into a wide grin. "This edict is from Falconshire's new constable, Emerson Crowther. With the King of England's permission, I have been pardoned of all crimes against me." She handed the parchment to Richard. "This is the second time in my life that I agree with the king of England. This edict I will cherish forever." She laughed and bowed her head at James Douglas. "Baron Douglas, ye and yer men must slack your thirst and eat. There is food inside Foxlair. I've something I must attend to. May I have yer permission to leave?"

"Ye dinna need my permission, Countess Strasbourg. Travel with the Lord's blessings."

Words no sooner spoken than Deirdre spurred her horse. "Follow me, Richard." She then paused next to David who jumped on behind her.

Deirdre guided her horse over the knoll and to where the clan's dead was buried. David dismounted and then helped her down. Richard came off his horse and approached. Deirdre walked to her papa's grave and bowed her head. She prayed to herself and asked for God to replace her hatred with forgiveness. To put from her mind all that had happened to her. The future was what mattered. When finished praying, she walked over to Bonnar's and Gordon's graves. She bent to pull a few weeds. Wrothbury's body had been buried somewhere nearby, she knew not where. At first she wanted to burn it and throw his ashes to the wind, but David said for the earl to be buried in Scotland's soil would have the man constantly turning over in his grave with no rest ever. She agreed.

At last, her gaze took in Richard and David, the two most important men in her life.

"I think Papa would be most proud," she said.

David visibly swallowed and agreed. "'Tis true. As am I."

Richard smiled and pulling her close, placed a kiss on her hand.

"Madam, I'm most proud of you and what has happened here this day."

"Hope is unbroken, aye?" she said, and stroked Richard's cheek.

"Oh…aye," he said, jesting in a Scottish brogue.

Both Deirdre's and David's laughter echoed around the inlet.

Epilogue

France, June 1309

The journey from Scotland to France happened without incident. After landing at Calais, Richard moved his people by caravan toward his domain across France and next to the Rhine River that separated his holdings from the Germanic lands beyond.

They'd been traveling on Strasbourg land for a day now and where the forest was thick with tree trunks the size of a castle's turrets. Shafts of sunlight fought to penetrate the forest floor where the canopy of green allowed a mere beam or two. The smell of damp moss assaulted the riders. Squirrels scolded and birds flit from branch to branch.

Conversation was minimal as Richard, ever mindful and alert, led them on a road cut through the forest by centuries of constant travel. It was safe, yet not safe. Harness's jangled, chainmail clanged against armor, wagons carrying people and supplies rattled and banged with each turn of the wheel.

Deirdre, on a roan-colored mare, marveled at the landscape around her, and found it wasn't too different than Scotland's. Her wee children, Antoine and Joanna, were in a colorful painted wagon, and being taken care of by Mary Clair and Maude.

"Richard, milord, are we near yer castle?" Deirdre, dressed in a gown of blue with a matching cloak, reached forth and patted her mare. The circlet given to her by Scotland's king kept her veil in place.

"Soon, chéri, soon. You'll be able to see our home in the distance when we clear the woods." Dressed as the warlord he was, he wore chest armor over his tunic. His breeks were black, and covering all was a brown cloak made from the finest of cloth.

Richard, shifting Saladin's reins from one hand to the other, had long been aware of a hooded figure who had been riding parallel from them for the last hour or so, and who kept a good distance between them. The person garbed in men's dark clothing with a hooded cloak, rode a horse as black as the midnight hour. A long sword dangled from the saddle horn. Choosing this moment to steal another glance at their mysterious guest, Richard was taken aback to see the rider gone.

"Ah, just like a rat, the person has scurried away." He pointed to his left and grinned at both Deirdre and Bertrand.

Deirdre peered past Richard to where the ghost rider normally rode. "Who do ye think the hunter to be? Yer brother Valentin?"

"Non. You will soon see," he answered.

Conner, riding next to his Uncle Macadie, wheeled his horse around and thundered off in the direction the rider had disappeared.

"Conner—wait," Richard called after him to no avail. Conner, with his long blonde hair streaking behind him, was beyond hearing.

The ghost rider had skillfully maneuvered his horse through the trees, finally coming out into a large meadow. The rider glanced over his shoulder to see he was being followed. Slapping the reins against his mount's side, he urged it into a spirited gallop. Conner, not to be deterred, was fast behind. Pulling alongside the cloaked figure, Conner launched himself at the rider and knocked him off his horse. They landed in a bone-jarring crunch against the ground and became a tangle of limbs as they wrestled in the dirt, grunting and rolling.

Conner, who was taller and stronger, came out on top and sat on his foe. Their chests heaved in exertion. The rider's gloved fist shot out and socked Conner in the jaw, snapping his head back.

"Och, ye puny whelp of a man!" Conner, irritated to allow such a blow, wanted this done. He used his knees to pin his opponent's arms against the ground. The person, squirming and fighting, caused the hood to slip down over his face. He tried bucking Conner off, but couldn't budge him. Conner, fuming at this interloper, grabbed him by the chin and held his jaw firm. Resisting the urge to strangle the person, he jerked the hood off only to have a cascade of long black hair tumble out.

Conner stared into snapping green eyes, and the most beautiful face he'd ever seen on a woman. Recognizing the de Laci look of her made his gut clench. He scrambled to his feet and made a clumsy attempt to help her up. She slapped his hand away and got up on her own.

"'Tis sorry I be to have fought with ye," he said.

Her answer was to punch him hard in the gut. "*Vous êtes un homme habillé comme un païen!* You are a heathen dressed as a man." She pulled her dagger and held it out in front of her, menacing it at him. *"Païen!"*

He grinned and held his arms up as if to surrender. "I could say the same for ye. Thought ye a man dressed as ye are. 'Tis gude I dinna know what ye call me, aye?"

Richard's party cleared the forest. Stifling a laugh at Conner being held at knife point by his petite sister, Richard reined in Saladin and held up his arm to stop those behind him.

"Perry—Pernelle de Laci, sheath your weapon, he is a friend. Cease!" Richard yelled. "Pernelle, I command you to stop this childish behavior. This was not a greeting I anticipated."

"Nor I, mon frère, nor I. You can blame this—this barbarian who attacked me." Her lofty gaze slide over Conner's tall frame. She sneered at him as if he were a lowly rat.

Conner returned her gaze with equal hostility. Yet chivalry had him forming a stirrup with his hands and helping Pernelle back on her horse.

He then mounted his own stead.

"I thought ye meant us harm," Conner said.

"Païen, I thought the same of you," Pernelle retorted.

"I have a name, 'tis Conner Kincaid."

"You act like a païen, look like a païen, so I will call you one."

"Perri, cease," Richard ordered. "Monsieur Kincaid is not a heathen, please refrain from calling him such. Speak English in front of our guests. I see you ride Kashmir, even though I told you not to."

Pernelle shrugged. "Mon frère, I can handle this horse with ease. My plans for your homecoming were also ruined by this….by this païen…ah person…Kincaid." Becoming demure, she bowed her head at Richard. "Welcome home."

Richard sought Deirdre's hand. "Countess de Strasbourg, this is my hellion of a sister, Pernelle de Laci. Pernelle, welcome my wife, Deirdre. My son is in yonder wagon of whom you will soon meet."

Pernelle smiled, her eyes twinkled as she spoke. "I welcome my sis-ter-by-marriage. It is good to have you here." She jockeyed her horse next to Deirdre's. "Not only does my brother bring a wife, he brings an infant son as well. Our home can do with the sound of a child."

"Pernelle, what is this?" Richard flared his arm to take in the long line of soldiers in front of his domain.

"A planned welcome—ruined." Pernelle darted a hateful glance at Conner. She stood in her stirrups and signaled.

Two men broke from the line of soldiers and raced toward Richard. Their cloaks flapped in the wind, their horses hooves chewed up the meadow. As they drew near, both were bare-headed allowing Richard to recognize his brother Valentin. The other man he didn't know.

They slowed their horses to a walk, and stopped in front of Richard and Deirdre.

"Richard!" Valentin grinned. "It has been too long, mon frère—too long."

"Oui, it has. Who is this with you?" Richard asked.

Pernelle maneuvered her horse between Valentin and the other man. "Richard, this is my betrothed Julien Quesnel. His parents, Baron and Baroness of Luxembourg will visit later."

Julien nodded slowly. Richly dressed, his tunic and hose were various shades of red, his cloak a dark blue. Sweat curled his short brown hair around his forehead. He tilted his head back, a slight movement, making him appear haughty. His eyes, sky blue, took in the tall warrior who had fought with Pernelle. Instant dislike creased his handsome features into a frown. Yet, in good manners, he directed his attention back to Richard and bowed his head.

"Comte de Strasbourg, we meet at last."

"Pernelle has written to me of you. I trust you have been made welcome in my home." Richard's plans on showing off his imposing domain to Deirdre were sliding into irrelevance. His arm stretched out to bring his countess beside him.

"Deirdre, this is my brother Valentin de Laci. Next to him is Julien Quesnel, Pernelle's betrothed. Everyone, meet my wife, Deirdre Brodie de Laci, Countess de Strasbourg."

Valentin, a younger version of Richard, down to the black hair and emerald eyes, jauntily nodded at Deirdre. His smile was contagious. He bowed and then flared his arm out, swirling his cloak about. "I welcome you to the de Laci family." He nudged his horse next to Deirdre's and took her hand for a kiss. "Enchanté, madame, enchanté."

"Och...ye be most charmin'. Jest like yer brother."

Julien Quesnel took Deirdre's hand and pressed it against his lips. From this man came no warmth. His gaze, cold and aloof, took her in. His actions reminded Deirdre of Wrothbury.

"Mon frère, who are these people that travel with you?" Pernelle asked.

Richard beckoned his friends forward. "This man, Macadie Gunn saved my life many times in Scotland. Macadie, this is my brother Valentin, and my sister Pernelle." He gestured at Conner. "Er...Conner Kincaid whom you already met is Macadie's nephew."

Macadie flashed his grin at the de Laci's. "I'm friend to milord and now to ye as well. My wife Maude is in the wagon with the children."

Julien nudged his horse close to Conner's. "I'm Julien Quesnel. Have you apologized to my betrothed for almost killing her? I could have you whipped for even touching her."

Conner's hand started for his claymore, but he paused and left it sheathed. "Aye," he said, and nothing more.

Pernelle managed a shrug. "Pay the heathen no mind, Julien." She stared at the rugged-looking, yet handsome Scotsman. A smile barely creased her lips while her cat green eyes held secrets.

Valentin tilted his head in a nod. "I've been told that my brother Philippe will soon have a child. He has asked me to join him in Scotland. Perhaps I will."

Richard smirked. "You will find it a country at constant war with England. But if you so choose to go, you will do so with my blessing." Richard kneed his horse, and with Deirdre beside him, started forward. "Milady, that is what I've longed to show you." He pointed across the meadow.

Even at a distance, the castle's might was evident. Falaise stood as though the legs of a mighty God were indeed the cliffs that held it. Deirdre counted eight battle towers that loomed tall, like giant black sentinels with what looked like another castle enclosed inside the outer perimeter walls.

"Richard, what is that structure coming out of the center of the castle?"

"That is the keep, the heart of the castle where we live. Look, it has four towers of its own and is connected by spiral stairs in all four corners. There are six levels with over six chambers of living quarters on each level. The great hall consists of the entire bottom floor. Our home could be defended from the keep if the outer walls were breached," he said, most prideful.

"Gore...I never thought Château Falaise was so big." Yet after all that she had been though, and with Richard by her side showing her how, she would be a good chatelaine over their home. She raised her head high, squared her shoulders, and clicked her tongue, urging her horse on.

As they drew near the castle, the soldiers moved to line the entrance and welcome their lord. Richard acknowledged Raymond Bretel his sergeant-at-arms. Raymond's grin cut through a mass of red beard and mustache. Always dressed for incursions on Strasbourg land, he wore full armor and a cloak of blue. His shield was decorated with Comte de Strasbourg's heraldry. He bowed his burley head.

With Deirdre at Richard's side, they rode under the barbican that had a large antler rack mounted to the high curving archway. The rack held a sword, and on each side of the rack, blue banners with the Strasbourg heraldry whipped about in the wind.

Deirdre glanced up at the display then questioning at Richard.

"My ancestor's sword. It guards all who enter this gate, and is said to drop from its rack to pierce the heart of a traitor or one who would harm the de Laci's."

After dismounting, and helping Deirdre down, Richard signaled for the stable boys to take their reins. Richard and Deirdre went to the wagon, and opening its back door, helped its occupants out. Richard set Joanna on her feet. The little girl ran to clasp her arms around Deirdre's thigh.

"Mam," she squealed. Mary Clair ran after her and Bertrand was quick to Mary Clair's side.

"Allow me, Mistress Gunn." Richard took Antoine from Maude's arms.

Maude shook her skirt out just as Macadie walked up to her.

"Mon dieu—your son at last." Valentin smiled and stared at the child.

Pernelle, standing beside him caressed her nephew's fat cheek with her finger. Her eyes softened for the tiny infant.

"Oui, this is my son, Antoine David de Laci, the future Comte de Strasbourg."

Walking toward the keep and the servants who stood there, Richard took Deirdre's hand and held her arm high for all to see.

"Rencontrez mon épouse, Deirdre Countess de Strasbourg, et votre chatelaine Obéissez-la dans tous ce que ele demande de vous."

The people cheered, and Deirdre grinned as she observed Richard's smiling face.

"They welcome you, their chatelaine, my countess," he said.

Raymond Bretel approached and bowed. "Milord, this arrived at dawn." He handed Richard a message with France's King Philip's seal.

Richard accepted the missive. He slid his finger under the purple-colored wax and broke the seal. He read. His mouth set in a thin line as he folded the parchment and put it into his waist pouch.

He glanced at Deirdre. "We can talk later. King Philip summons me, but is most generous and gives me a few days to settle," Richard said with a smirk. "And now, my love, allow me to escort you inside your new home."

After a long evening of festivities, Richard and Deirdre were in their private chambers. Richard squatted in front of the giant fireplace and threw logs on the fire that snapped and sent sparks up the chimney. The chamber, large and spacious, held Andrew Brodie's bed, which Deirdre sat upon. Tapestries depicting battle scenes covered the walls. Rugs made from animal skins were piled thick on the floor. Huge chests, chairs, and a table holding a wine carafe and goblets helped to make the room homey. Antoine slept in his cradle next to the bed. Joanna was given her own chamber down the hallway, and cared for by Mary Clair.

"You are most tired my love, for I see purple smudges under your eyes. The day has been over long, the evening as well," Richard said.

Deirdre, had just finished nursing Antoine and tried to lace her bod-ice, but her fingers were not her own. She fumbled with the laces.

"Oh—crack it...." Exasperated, she clasped her hands in her lap as tears welled in her eyes.

"Chéri, what is the matter? Are you not happy with our home?" Con-cern creased a furrow between Richard's brows.

"I dinna know what is the matter. Mayhap I feel strange in a strange place. Foxlair was indeed my home and I knew everyone and everything about it. Mayhap I realize how far away I am from David, Seonaid, their wee bairns...Scotland...." Her sniffles intensified.

Richard lifted her chin as he produced a cloth and dabbed at her eyes. "Do you say I must take you back to Foxlair?" He teased.

"Nay, I dinna know why I feel so sad. Imprisonment in the cage did-na incur such tears. I have never felt safer. I canna explain it. Mayhap I realize how great my duties here will be and that frightens me."

"This will pass. Soon you will wonder why you felt this way. Would you like me to summon Mary Clair to help you ready for bed, or should I stand in her stead and help you?"

"Nay, ye can do it, Richard." She managed a weak little smile for him as he removed her shoes. "When d'ye leave for Paris?"

Richard studied her while massaging her foot. "Ah...I believe to have found the cause of your tears. It is because I'm leaving you so soon after bringing you here?"

"Aye. If I could keep ye by my side forever, I would do so."

"And I would be content to do so, but the king commands me." He pulled her to her feet and started unlacing her bodice. "Maude, Mary Clair and Pernelle will be here. Our children will fill your days."

"And all will be good company for me. Joanna is becoming most ad-venturous." She turned reddened eyes up at him while helping him out of his tunic shirt. "Must ye go?"

"France's king is called the Iron King. While on his side and doing his bidding, all will be well. If crossed, his ruthlessness is equal to no other ruler. I am my king's warlord and in order to retain my domain, I must obey him when summoned."

She paused, holding his shirt in her hands. "And a king's summons can be of no gude. What does he want of ye?"

He took his shirt from her and placed it over the chair. "When I was in Scotland, instead of me joining the Bruce and leading my king's army, I put Philippe in charge. He fought in my stead whilst I went to rescue you and Joanna. Now King Philip reminds me of what I did. I'm being sent to Italy—Rome. It concerns the Templars. His majesty deems to annihilate them down to the last man."

"And ye will thrust the sword to do this?"

"I pray not, but I'm foolish to think otherwise."

"I understand," she said.

"Chéri, King Philip knows of your endurance in the cage and says he would like to meet a woman with your valor. He would also like to have your fealty." Using care, he helped her to step out of her gown.

When she shivered, he led her to the fireplace then backed away to sit on the chair and began removing his boots. The fire turned her chemise into gossamer fabric, giving him a peek of the body that he so loved. When she started toward him, he halted her with a raised hand.

"My love, stay as you are for I'm putting to memory the look of your body, teasing me, hinting of delights to come."

She watched him stand, bare-chested and wearing only his tight breeks. "Then does my husband intend to rob me the pleasure of undressing him?"

"Never. But give me a moment to pour some wine and move the rug closer to the fire."

Deirdre glanced down at the bearskin rug. "D'ye mean to ravish me on this rug with that animal's eyes lookin' at me? I dinna know who leers the most, ye or that animal."

"Oui, I mean to ravish you on that rug and my leer is much better than the one that beast wears." He set the wine goblets on the floor, and then helped her out of her chemise.

Her eyes veiled with passion as she unlaced his breeks then sank to her knees and helped him out of them. She smiled as she pulled him down to kneel facing her. Their bodies melded together as the cool firmness of each other's flesh touched off desire.

He laid her back and as the firelight skipped over her body, he kissed all the places that glowed. She framed his face between her hands and lost herself in his eyes that mirrored back the emotions that swirled between them. Love, fear, hope, but most of all, their freedom.

She murmured against his firm lips.

"Always you, Richard…always you."

The Beginning

Acknowledgements

This book, a long time in coming won numerous awards in sponsored Romance Writers of America™ chapter contests. It is the first book in a series that portrays women of valor who in generations fought the battle to even exist and be heard and not treated like cattle. I bow to those women.

There was indeed a real life Countess Isabel Buchan of Fife, who crowned Robert the Bruce on March 26th, 1306. In retribution, Edward 1, the King of England, had her caged. Countess Buchan survived in the cage for 5 years after which she was released and lived in a convent the short remaining years of her life. Imagine the valor of this woman. The cage incident fed me my story line and Countess Buchan's courage gave me fodder to create my own countess and a woman of valor.

The next book in this series, Depth of Deception, due out in the spring of 2017, continues with another strong-willed woman.

I'd like to thank my critique groups, writing clubs, judges, agents, editors, and fellow authors who have been involved with this story.

I need to give special thanks to my husband Ty, for his patience while I write, and to my daughter Whitney Bodine for her encouragement.

I must mention Jodi and Debbie from Jan's Paperbacks in Aloha, Oregon, who are true believers in my stories.

And, dear reader, I'm thanking you most of all.